Little Criminals

Little Criminals

Short Stories

Kurt Rheinheimer

EWU
P·R·E·S·S
Eastern Washington University Press
Spokane, Washington

Printed in the United States of America

Cover design by Jennifer Reid
Book design by Daniel Morris

Acknowledgements

Appalachian Heritage: "Debut"
Cold Mountain Review: "Moon Beach"
Glimmer Train: "Fla"
The Long Story: "The B&W"
Michigan Quarterly Review: "Dogs;" "Baltimore"
The Nebraska Review: "Shoes"
Phoebe: "Hooks"
Quarterly West: "Umpire"
Roanoke Review: "St. Louis"
Shenandoah: "Telling Brenda"
The South Carolina Review:"The Stop"
Southern Magazine: "Homes"

"Grand Strand" is scheduled for publication in *Glimmer Train*

"Homes" was anthologized in *New Stories From The South: The Year's Best, 1989* (Algonquin); "Umpire" was anthologized in *New Stories From The South: The Year's Best, 1986* and in "Bottom of the Ninth: Great Contemporary Baseball Short Stories (2003, Southern Illinois University Press); "Shoes" was anthologized in *New Stories From The South: The Year's Best, 2001*. "Baltimore" was reprinted in *Baltimore City Paper* and anthologized in *Voices in Fiction and Non-Fiction* (LongRidge). "Dogs" won the Lawrence Foundation Prize for fiction.

Library of Congress Cataloging-in-Publication Data

Rheinheimer, Kurt.
Little criminals / Kurt Rheinheimer.
p. cm.
ISBN 0-910055-96-3 (alk. paper)
1. Middle West--Social life and customs--Fiction. I. Title.
PS3618.E565L58 2004
813'.6--dc22

2004013173

For Walter, who has stood by with faith in the stories for dacades, and for Gail, who knows them as well as I do.

Contents

Dogs

West of Grand Island, the southern flat of Nebraska is broken by the nearly parallel lines of Interstate 80, old U.S. Route 30, and the Platte River. Along and a few miles to the north and south of the three lines are small, sun-baked towns which gain more identity and status from the number of grain silos at their western edges than from more traditional measures, such as population or number of retail outlets. In one of the larger of these towns, on a Thursday afternoon in August, Stella Merriman stood on the heat-softened asphalt of what until early winter of the year before had been a grocery store parking lot. She was surrounded by an expanse of perfectly shined hub caps which sent the high unguarded sun darting back up toward her eyes with any movement she made. All across the lot the heat pools sent little wavy lines of pure midwestern hot spell rising up off the pavement. Behind Stella, in the back of the van—the only shade they had—Hubber Johnson flipped slowly through the pages of a car-customizing magazine, the sweat dripping off his chin onto his bare, dark-haired chest, over his belly, and on down to form a v-shaped patch of wetness at the crotch of his khaki pants. He had been talking about the possibility of yellow velour seat covers, to set off the blue interior.

Really, there was no reason to be there because anyone who was going to do any buying had done it in the morning. Any fool knew there was no sense in being out at this time of day, and nearly half the pickups and vans had already packed up and left for the day. Those that were still around would stay through the evening, trying to catch the after-supper trade, which was nothing at all what it once was—because of people getting burned out on flea markets, Hubber said. And most of those who had stuck it out had gotten a good spot up along the front of the empty store, where there would be shade by about seven or seven-thirty.

Stella and Hub did mostly household goods. The best thing they had now was a kerosene heater that was perfect except that the wick was missing. Hub said they ought to get at least twenty for it, and Stella told him no one in his right mind would hand over twenty dollars for a heater when the temperature was up over a hundred for the third day in a row. They also had two quilts, a stack of ceramic bowls, three little tables that almost matched, a toaster, five or six screwdrivers, and the box of little junk that was always in the back of the van. It held bobby pins, hair curlers, baseball cards, chapsticks, tire gauges, toy whistles, and ball point pens. Hub had had the ball points for years. They were the fat kind that wrote in your choice of three colors, and each one had "Say No to Drugs" on it, in big black letters. Hub had found the whole bunch one day in a dumpster in the back of the K-Mart in Omaha.

And of course they had the caps. Hub never went anywhere that he didn't have at least a few hub caps with him. In fact, the flea market was more of a sideline for him. His main money, if you could call it that, came from the fact that he was a supplier for three cap and cover stores in Buffalo and Phelps counties. That was how he got his name, or course, when it was really Donald Leon Johnson. Nobody called him Donald except his mother, and anybody who even tried to call him Leon got a cold stare and no answer. He told Stella once that if God had meant for him to be called Leon, He would have stamped it on his forehead. Stella knew that he loved a shiny wheel cover at least as much as he loved her. Some nights when he had just come across a nearly mint Caddy cover, say, he'd take the whole evening working out the little rust starts, and then stay up half the night Simonizing the hell out of it.

Stella didn't mind the heat on the lot so much as that Hub wouldn't move up by the grocery store building once some of the people had left. "Hell," he would say, "they have their damn Furniture Row up there, and they don't think we're good enough anyway, so hell with them." Stella couldn't understand that because Hub usually marched right up to people and told them just what he thought, but for some reason he was a little scared of the furniture people. She watched them now, sitting under their umbrellas with their coolers out. Every once in a while she saw a beer can flashing in the sun even though the police had not allowed drinking for two summers, since the night there was a big fire and a fight the same night.

"We ought to get the hell out of here," Hub said while he was still working on being angry at the furniture people. He puffed up his face a little and stuck out his chest and walked around in a few little circles, and then it was over. That hoppy walk, along with his old-time, too-long flattop was a lot of how Stella knew she loved him.

"You could be right," she said, but as she spoke a little foreign car drove onto the lot, its tires making a ticking noise like snow studs because of the sticky pavement. The car would hold them up a few minutes. Out of a habit she had learned from Hub, Stella looked first at the wheels, even though she knew he didn't have any caps for Toyotas, or whatever it was. And sure enough, the front driver's was gone. The car drove past them and back toward Furniture Row. Usually the whole lot picked up a little when a foreign car with a young couple drove on, because they were the ones with the money. But in the heat everybody was slowed down some. The couple got out up near the furniture. They were both tall, too tall for the little car—and they looked all around the lot before they moved, the man pulling lightly at his beard and the woman holding her hand up to shield her eyes even when she wasn't looking in the direction of the sun.

"A rocker," Hub said as he and Stella watched the couple. "And maybe a few tools. And then they'll be by to ask about that cover, if they think of it." He looked away from them, in a gesture of disgust that was as mild as his strut. "Maybe we should ride out to Anson's."

"That's a long ways," Stella said. Anson was Hub's brother, who lived up in McPherson county, in the middle of nowhere, where you never knew what you'd see. Sometimes at night you'd hear wolves or something "And you know the van hasn't been doing too good in this heat."

"I do know where Anson lives and I do know how the van is doing," he said, looking down and sideways at the same time. He was testy about the van because he knew it needed work. He had just spent forty-some dollars putting in deep-pile sky-blue carpeting up overhead, even when he knew there was something wrong with the carburetor, and the radiator needed a good flushing or a new thermostat, he wasn't sure which. "If we left right now we'd be there by seven."

"I guess so," she said. Visiting his brother was not her favorite thing to do, because Hub always ended up drinking too much and telling Anson all the ways that he and Stella did it—all while Stella was sitting right there blushing.

"Good day for a drive and there sure isn't anything doing here," Hub said. He was talking himself into it.

"What about gas?" Stella said, knowing it was no use.

"We got gas," he said, twisting his face at her. "There's more than half a tank." He hated talking about gas. He made most of his cap and cover money by driving all over—to all the wreckers and garages and parts wholesalers—and it took him ten or fifteen miles to calm down after a fill up. Stella hated to see him mad, and hated to see him spend his money just to get down so many miles of road.

"Maybe we ought to see if Cassie wants to go," Hub said while they were watching the young couple look at some old picture frames leaned up against the back of a pickup truck. "Haven't seen her in a while."

"Could be," Stella said, and wiped some sweat from around her neck. Cassie was her half sister, divorced now for eight months and still no real boyfriend. Stella was more or less neutral on Cassie going, because Cassie was only twenty-eight and had nice teeth and a big firm chest, and long blond hair that was only slightly dyed. Stella herself was thirty-seven, but even back at twenty-eight she had already lost the tooth, and had already been too big in the waist and hips. Basically Cassie was a lot better looking than Stella, and had some of the same blood in her, and so Stella was always a little uneasy when Hub was around her, especially when there was drinking going on, which always got Hub back to one thing.

The tall man was squinting down at the shiny caps now, pulling lightly at his beard. The woman stood behind him, using him as a shield from the brightness and heat. She did a quick little dance on her tennis shoes and then looked away while the man said hi to Hub. Hub said hi back and then stopped, allowing the man to go ahead and ask his question. "I lost the front left there," he said. "I guess if I don't see it you don't have it, huh?"

"That's just about the exact size of it," Hub said. "Mostly Ford, Buick, Pontiac and Olds covers out today, et cetera. You never can tell about tomorrow though." Hub always said that stuff about tomorrow even though he knew good and well he wasn't about to touch any foreign covers.

"Okay then, thanks," the man said, and turned back toward the woman, who was doing another stupid little dance routine.

"Right-o," Hub said as the couple started back up the lot toward Furniture Row. When they were halfway up there Hub turned to Stella. "Christ, what does he think, I keep some hidden in the glove compartment? Let's go Stel. This place is getting to me." He kneeled down and started to stack the caps. Stella climbed into the back of the van and started stacking those into the wooden racks that Hub had built in behind the seats. Then she went back to get his stacks. They had done it a thousand times together, like an Indy 500 team. Sometimes Stella thought that all the things they did best together happened right there in the van.

When they were looking around to see if they had forgotten anything, Hub poked Stella's arm and pointed up toward Furniture Row. The tall man and woman were trying to figure out a way to get a rocking chair into the little car. Hub folded his arms over his chest to watch. "What did I tell you," he said. The rocker didn't have a chance to fit in the trunk. "Damn toy car with toy hub caps and now they're trying to squeeze a damn toy chair into it." He did a quick little rooster circle. "Could be toy people for all I know." He unfolded his arms, spat a quick, precise stream, and then bounced up into the driver's seat. Stella walked around to her side and then Hub aimed them off the lot, the caps clinking into place behind them. The breeze into the side window was the best thing that had happened to Stella all day, both because of the wind and the fact that she loved to have people see her riding way up high in Hub's tall blue van. She liked the van even better now that Hub had done some baby blue highlighting under the windows and just above the body chrome. The trim paint was almost the exact color of the overhead carpeting and made a nice contrast with the dark blue body paint.

They were all the way into town before Stella convinced herself that Hub was really going to Cassie's. She lived on the north side of town, right at the edge where it turned black, and every time they went up there Stella got depressed all over again about the time Cassie went with a black man for almost three months before they both went back to their senses and their own kind. Cassie lived in a big house that had been separated into apartments, and the whole building was a mess. People left garbage out on the landings, and the police came by once in a while to pick up one man for public drunkenness or wife beating, whichever they hadn't done the last time. Stella used to worry about Cassie living there, but after a while she gave up because Cassie was all live-and-let-live herself. She had her own life. She went to work—at the HoJo restaurant down at the Interstate—and came home and left the rest of the building alone. Stella thought it was her basic who-cares attitude that made Hub like her so much. That and all the marijuana she smoked. Hub and Stella both knew that she smoked it almost every night after she got off work. One night a long time ago, when Hub and Stella had stopped by for a visit, they found Cassie in front of the TV—nothing on but bra and panties—eating cold green beans out of the can, picking them out with her fingers and sticking them in her mouth like french fries. And she looked up at them with her slow-blink eyes and held out the can. "These here are mighty good," she said with a big smile. "They must be genuine Green Giant, these little boogers." And she laughed a long laugh. Then she stuck another two or three into her mouth, letting a little bit of juice run down her chin and on down into the split between her breasts. Later on Hub told Stella that Cassie had been Grade A stoned. Stella had tried marijuana a few times, but to her it was basically just a lot of coughing and then getting sleepy. She said a bad cold did that for her just fine.

"Don't need any," Cassie called out when they knocked on the door. Then there was some laughing. It sounded like two women instead of a man and a woman.

"We don't have none to give away, neither," Hub shouted at the door and laughed his little puffed-up laugh as he looked at Stella.

"Good God, it's Big Sis and her full-time," Cassie said as she came to the door.

In the kitchen was Cassie's friend Carolyn, from work. There were two opened Falstaff big boys on the kitchen table, and two more leaned-over crunched-up ones at one edge. There was nothing else on the table except the big blue and orange HoJo ashtray with two lit cigarettes and a pile of short butts in it.

"Me and Carolyn are winding down from a hard day," Cassie said as she sat back down. Hubber pulled up the last chair, and Stella settled for the on-end Coke crate that served as Cassie's fourth chair. "How about a brew?" Cassie said, and Hub said sure, and Stella said maybe a Coke. At the refrigerator Cassie bent to look around, and her yellow halter top fell open just enough to give Hub a clean shot at her big left breast, and then she came back up, asking if some diet Dr Pepper would do for Stella, and Stella said sure. "So," Cassie went on as she brought the beer and a half-empty Dr Pepper, "what brings you two love birds by at the time of day? Everybody got their caps on straight?" Cassie and Carolyn laughed, and Stella wondered if they had already been smoking marijuana.

"Business wasn't for diddly squat," Hub said. "And we were getting fried to hell."

"Really," Carolyn said. "Hot as baby puke out there." She wore a halter top too. Blue, and not cut in so close as Cassie's. Carolyn was about halfway between Stella and Cassie in height, but her chest was somewhere about the size of Stella's and Cassie's added up. Both Cassie and Carolyn were dressed in blue cut-offs that just barely covered the line where your leg turns into hip.

"Sounds like us," Cassie said. "They had the thermostat up to what?—ninety, Carolyn? And business is way down. Damn I-80 is practically empty. Or at least not as many people are stopping in to see Howard."

"We were thinking of going out to Anson's," Hub said.

"Oh yeah?" Cassie said. "Sounds good." Once when she had gone out with them, she and Anson had decided to shoot a rabbit for them all to eat, and she ended up shooting a big piece of her right shoe off—where the big toe would have been if the shoe hadn't been too big. It just barely cut the side of her foot. "Hell yes," Cassie said. "How about you, C?" she said to Carolyn.

"Where now?"

"Hubbie's brother. Out past North Platte or some damn place."

"I'm off till tomorrow night, same as you."

Cassie went to the refrigerator and got a new six pack and two more tall boys, and they all headed for the van. Hub rearranged the caps and flipped up the back seat for Cassie and Carolyn, and they were on their way. They went four blocks and then went back to raid Cassie's refrigerator for ice to keep the beer cold.

Hub didn't have a CB or a car phone in the van, but his favorite thing in the world for years and years, next to hub caps, was to pretend he was using a CB, especially out on I-80. He did all the static in between just like the comedians on TV used to. As soon as they were on the big highway he started in with his hey-good-buddy-gotcher-ears-on routine, talking into his fist like it was a CB mike. "This here is Hubber with the Rubber out of Noplace, N.E.B." Then he did his throat noise. "Ten-four, Hubber, this here is the Desert Rat out of West Omaha on the big white stripe out to the Mile High. I be on the hundred and four yard line and where be you?" Throat noise. And on and on. Stella wondered how he could talk so fast and so funny when he had only made it to the fifth grade before they kicked him out for being too big for elementary school. But he kept it going for miles, with everything half-rhyming and going by too fast for Stella to keep up with. It was almost like Hub got smarter when he was up on the seat driving the van.

They had done only about twenty miles when Cassie called for the first pit stop. Hub stepped it up to almost seventy to hurry on to the next exit, but the van wasn't running too smooth. They took advantage of the stop to stock in some more tall boys and two big bags of Cheetos—all on top of the twenty-eight dollars it cost just to put the van up to almost three quarters. Cassie and Carolyn put in two dollars each for the whole thing. "We're ready to roll now," Hub said, and Stella pursed her lips and fought the urge to say something about all that money just to drink and drive.

The Platte is an odd, broken-up little river as it flows across Nebraska. In some places it is almost as wide as the Interstate, and at others it looks like a dying little stream. But what it has done is to create a whole series of sandy pits and swampy areas, and even a few lakes, all along itself, as if to prove that if it can't be a full fledged river with boats moving up and down, at least it can make a few changes on the dry flat land that spreads out for miles on either side of it. When the van began to sputter and miss even worse than it had been—a little less than halfway out the Interstate—they decided to get off at the next exit and take the van back along the sand road that runs beside the river until they could find a good spot to stop while Hub straightened out whatever the problem was. He told them it was nothing much. Stella knew they should go ahead and try to make it to Anson's, if not turn back, both because Hub's nothing-muches lots of times turned into big problems, and because there looked like the possibility of storms out to the west. But again she didn't say anything, because she knew it was no use.

"We'll have a regular picnic," Cassie said. "Beer and Cheetos."

"Right you are," Hub said. "And maybe a dip."

Stella wasn't too keen on the dip idea either, because with all the beer there was a strong possibility of a skinny dip, which she didn't care for at all. Hub spending a whole day with two halter tops was one thing, but buck naked was another thing altogether.

They got off the interstate at a little county road with the towns a long ways in either direction from the exit. They were already in the real empty part of Nebraska. Sometimes it amazed Stella that in the very same state you could get stuck for an hour going one block if you made the mistake of hitting the football traffic in Lincoln, and then could out here where you could go for hours and never see anything except short grass. At the end of the off-ramp all the businesses were shut down. The gas station had been a BP, and from the price signs they decided it must have been closed for a long time. And there had been a little quick store, but it was boarded up across the front and the plywood was already bleached out from the sun and wind.

"Christ," Cassie said. "And we're getting low on the brew."

The whole place looked strange to Stella. All the signs had a sun-faded look, as if everything had been shut down for a long time—as if the interstate just didn't come there anymore. There was a little low-slung restaurant building too, closed up tight. Not a car on any of the lots except an old Plymouth parked beside the gas station. It had four flat tires and a torn Cornhuskers pennant on the antenna. The pennant moved lightly in the wind that had begun to come up. Hub slowed the van, gunning the engine to keep it from stalling as they looked around.

"Talk about ghost towns," Cassie said.

"Really," Carolyn said.

Stella did not like the feeling she got, just off the interstate as they were. Usually when you got off, you went a little way and there was everything. Gas, food, motels, gift stores. But here there wasn't anything. You could look up and down the thin white county highway in either direction and there wasn't a thing to see, as if the highway's only reason for being there was to separate two sides of rolling prairie that looked exactly the same. A few pieces of dried-up grass blew across the sand-colored road, and the hot breeze made a whistling noise in the side vent as Hub coaxed the van along.

"Nope, not too much doing today, is there?" he said as they looked for the river road. Once they were past the ghost corner and the tires were clicking over the tar lines across the highway, Stella though the van might be running a little better, and said maybe they should get back on the interstate and try for Anson's. She didn't like where she was.

"Nah," Cassie said. "I'm up for the dip now."

Hub went past the little road, and then did a big U-turn, spilling a little bit of Cassie's and Carolyn's beer. The van bounced over the sandy, rutted road, and off to the left you could see the Platte—narrow and almost gone in spots, with a big reach of sand on either side of the water.

"Can't swim in that puddle," Cassie said.

"Too small for gnats," Hub said. "Much less Big Stel." They all laughed, except for Stella. She spun in her seat to glare at Hub, but then made herself smile. She knew if she got angry they would start in on her and not let up for the rest of the trip. "Nobody said I was swimming anyhow," she said after a few seconds, and then looked out her side of the window to the side of the road where the river wasn't. It was just plain Nebraska out there—just small hills and short grass, like the back of a camel or something. There were no fences or other roads that she could see, and she wondered if the land ran like that all the way down to Kansas. "I bet you get to Kansas and you can't even tell the difference," she heard herself say.

"Kansas?" Hub said. "Who the hell said anything about Kansas? We're going to Anson's soon as I get the carb cleaned out."

"I was just saying," Stella said. Sometimes she liked to think about the shapes of the states. She could still name all forty-eight plus Alaska and Hawaii, but she wasn't quite sure of the fit of some of the states up above New York. Most of the time she didn't care that she hadn't realized school was important while she was in it, but at other times she wished she could be in a big classroom with sunshine coming in the whole big wall of windows and shining right down onto a big pull-down map with a handsome geography teacher standing in front of it. Sometimes when she was worried or scared—about money or what Hub would say to somebody—she could think about going back to school for geography, and feel better.

"Over there, Hubbie," Cassie shouted into Stella's thoughts. "There's a little like pool or something. See?"

They all turned to look, and Hub slowed the van. It nearly stalled, and he revved the engine to keep it running. Then he let it slow down until it stopped rolling. "Welp, here goes nothing," he said, and turned off the motor.

"You should've pulled over," Stella told him. They were in the middle of the road.

"What for?" he said. "Nobody here but us chickens."

"Really," Carolyn said.

Stella looked at Hub to make a face, but she didn't do it because she knew he was showing off for the women. He got out of the van and started for the river. "Hey," Stella said, "what about the carburetor?"

"I'll get it. Let me look at the damn river a minute, okay? It's slightly hotter than hell out here, or didn't you notice?"

Cassie and Carolyn got out on Hub's side of the van and walked toward the river, carrying their cans and swaying a little on the hills and high spots. Stella guessed they must have had two or three big boys each, plus some from the six pack. The heat seemed worse than it had back in town. Stella wondered if anybody else noticed the clouds building up, or that the wind had picked up just a little more.

"Whoa," she heard Hub shout, and turned to see him grabbing onto a bush next to the river. He had sunk in up to his knees, and had had to drop his beer to reach back at the bush. "It's like goddamn soup," he said when he got back out. "And I wasn't even all the way to the edge."

"Maybe over here," Carolyn said. She had walked out close to the water at a different place, onto a little sandy spot. But after a few steps she started to sink too, and turned back in a hurry.

"Great," Hub said. "All the way down here and nothing to do."

"Oh, there is one thing to do, and don't you peek, either, Hub," Cassie said as she went behind a cluster of the stubby weeds. "Got to shake that dew off the lily once in a while, you know."

"I guess it's time for me to get to work," Hub said, and then turned to call out to Cassie, "much as I would like to watch."

After a few minutes everybody had a spot along the shady side of the van, facing the river, while Hub was up front, where he was half in and half out of the sun. He poked around, and then hit something a few times, and then came and sat down with them. He said he would have to wait until things cooled down a little. "Like to burn the piss off my finger," he said. Cassie and Carolyn were about to drain the last of the beer, and Stella wasn't sorry.

When they had all been quiet for a while Stella asked Hub how far it was out to Anson's from where they were, and Hub said it was two more exits out the interstate and then about forty more miles, and then everybody was quiet. You could feel the heat coming through the van from the hot sun, and if you listened real hard, way off in the distance you could hear the faint sound of a car on the interstate. The wind had died a little, but the clouds were still building.

"Weird out here, isn't it?" Hub said after a while.

"Dead is more like it," Carolyn said.

"I heard this stuff once," Cassie said as they all looked around, "about those giant electric wires all through here making all the cows and other animals all crazy and wild, for like a hundred miles in every direction."

Everybody looked up for wires. "What wires?" Carolyn said.

"You don't have to be able to *see* them," Cassie said. "They could be way over on the other side of the Interstate. It's like invisible radiation or something. I saw it on the news once."

"What, those big ones?" Hub said.

"Yeah," Cassie said. "With those big stands that look like France."

"France?" Stella said.

"You know, that big tower. Or like in monster movies."

"It's not that," Carolyn said. "It's the nuclear plants."

"What is?" Hub said.

"You know. Freaking the animals and all. Making it so weird out here."

"Bull," Hub said. "It has to get out first."

"What does?" Cassie said.

"Like in Russia that time," Hub said. "It leaks out of those fat-assed towers and into the river. And then you mix in some of that volcano ash from that St. Helen's mountain and you can kiss one river goodbye."

"The volcano moved all the rain up into damn Canada," Cassie said.

Hub looked at Cassie with his eyes opened wide. "Christ, Cass, what the hell have you been smoking? When was the last time you checked out Canada?"

"Geez, a nice fat J would go good about now, wouldn't it," Cassie said.

"Really," Carolyn said, "and I don't have a seed to my name."

"Me neither," Cassie said. "What about you, Hub? Got a spare in the glove compartment?"

"Just fired it up last week," Hub said. "Had it in there for a spare for a couple months." Stella knew he was lying, and that he was showing off because of the beer. She didn't say anything.

"What about you, Big Stel?" Cassie said, and everybody laughed. "Christ," Cassie went on, "can you see Big Stel stoned?" They laughed some more. "I'm talking really stoned now, not just some little red-eyed nod out." And they all laughed again until Hub finally got up to see if the engine had cooled off.

"She'd be telling us she was in another state or some damn thing," he said as he got to the front of the van. "Kansas or some shit." After they all laughed some more everybody got quiet while Hub worked. You could hear him clicking around. It sounded to Stella as if he didn't know what he was doing. She listened a while and then she told everybody she thought they were crazy to be talking about electric wires and nuclear stuff and volcanoes and marijuana, because what they really needed was for Hub to get the van running again.

"Really," Carolyn said. "I can't wait to get out to Anson's for a brew and a J." She got up to go use the bush.

"How goes it, Hub?" Cassie said when Carolyn was back. "Looks like rain out there. Time to get this mother rolling."

"Christ," Hub said. "I don't think they put this thing back together right the last time it was in the garage." Stella knew that was a lie too. He said that when he didn't know what was wrong.

"Right, Hub," Cassie said. "Right. Tell us all about it."

Stella looked back over her shoulder at the clouds. They had filled up most of the sky now, with a dark gray color that looked like ink. "Geez," she said, "those things are going to open up."

"You'd think somebody'd be by here once in a while," Cassie said.

"No lie," Carolyn said. "But then who needs quicksand?"

They laughed a little at that, and the girls edged up closer toward the front of the van. If you looked toward the back, you got specks of stuff in your eyes, from the wind.

"It's going to pour," Cassie said.

"Get inside already," Hub said.

The girls got into the van, which was still hot, even with the wind and windows down. Cassie took the driver's seat and Carolyn the front passenger seat. Stella got in the back, straining up to try to see out the front and watch what Hub was doing. She could only see the top of his head, and his tufty flattop was blowing in the wind. Every once in a while the van moved with a gust.

"At least it's not a damn tornado," Cassie said.

"How do you know?" Stella said. She was a little more worried now, out in the middle of nowhere with the van not running and a storm blowing up. She knew Hub had a tendency to pretend bad things were not really happening. Once they had been stuck in a snow drift up near Anson's for seven hours, and Hub didn't really do anything about it except try to talk Stella into a better way to keep each other warm. And when he got over being turned down he started to talk about new wood finish for the dash.

"Because it's blowing like hell," Cassie said. "It's all still when there's a tornado. Christ, Stel, where have you been?"

Stella didn't say anything, and then they heard Hub close the hood. He came around the side of the van, holding his hand up to his face, and motioned for Cassie to get out of his seat. He hopped up into the van, and had to use two hands to pull the door shut. "In twenty seconds you won't be able to see twenty feet," he said.

They all sat still and watched out the windows while the wind picked up little sticks and parts of bushes and weeds. Stella was scared. She didn't like the feeling in her stomach. It reminded her of the time she and Hub had been shot at out in Custer county—when some men thought Hub was stealing a wheel cover that was already rightfully his. That time, and this time too, she had a feeling that things might turn real bad all of a sudden. When there was a big clap of thunder she jumped in her seat, and noise came up out of her throat.

"Take it easy, Stella," Cassie said. She sounded irritated. "Haven't you ever seen rain before?" Stella could tell from Cassie's voice that she was scared too. Her face was a little whitish.

"I sure as hell don't see any now," Hub said.

"Over there," Carolyn said, and pointed out the side window—across the rolling field.

Stella looked out. Far across the field she could see rain—a big white area where it looked like it was pouring. "You can smell it," she said. It was the smell that made it hard for her to breathe, where the heat in the weeds and dirt got mixed in with the cool wetness of the rain.

"Roll 'em up," Hub said.

Stella climbed over the back seat to look out the back of the van, where there was a broken place in the sky. The sun wasn't coming through it, but it was a real break in the clouds. And the darkest clouds must have been right over the van, because she couldn't see them out the back any more. "How come it doesn't rain?" she said, and there was another big clap of thunder before anyone could answer.

"Same reason you get a dry tit on a cow once in a while," Hub said. "No reason."

"But it's everywhere," Cassie said. "It's just missing us."

"Really," Carolyn said.

Then the wind started to calm a little, and out the side window the rain sheet had moved farther along, in the direction the van was facing, moving across the plains toward Omaha, the way all the storms did.

"It's not going to rain a drop here," Cassie said. "It's blowing right the hell over."

"Look over there," Hub said, pointing across the river. "It's pouring over there, too."

For another ten minutes they searched all around for rain, or for a full break in the weather. The wind had slowed more, and for a time the clouds seemed to drift back over the van, as if the rain were backing up to catch them. Then there was a bigger break in the sky out to the west. The sun did not come back, but the heat did. It was even worse than it had been before the wind, as if the air had filled up with moisture to match the heat. As the wind died they rolled down the windows, and Stella realized she was sweating all over. She looked at the others, and they were all wet too. The rain-heat smell came in stronger, and they all sat still, as if beaten down by the weather. It was hard to breathe in the van.

The dusk was beginning to creep in, but Stella could not make herself tell Hub to get back outside and work on the van. For some reason she wanted him to stay inside.

"Listen," Hub said all of a sudden, and held his hands up to make them stay quiet.

Stella held her breath and strained to hear. She couldn't hear anything—not even the faint sound of the cars on the Interstate—and then she did hear it—a deep growling sound from far away. She tried to believe she didn't really hear it.

"Wolves!" Hub said in a shouting whisper.

"Wolves?" Carolyn whispered back.

"There's no wolves out here," Cassie said, almost in her regular voice.

"Well, listen for yourself," Hub said as he came back next to Stella to look out the back window of the van. He cracked the back open just a tiny bit and as he did the barking came all at once, in a burst of noise that was louder and much more frightening than the thunder had been. Hub pulled the door shut. "God," he said. "There's six or seven of them."

"What?" Stella said. She wanted to cry.

"Dogs," Hub said, "Look out there." He had his nose pressed up against the glass. Stella knelt in front of the other window and looked down at the dogs. They were slick and wet-looking—they had been in the rain. They were all terribly skinny, and their tongues hung out too far. "They're wild," Hub said. "And hungry as hell."

"Jesus," Stella said as a horrible smell hit her. The dogs carried the rain-heat smell, with something else mixed in. Dog crap and wet hair, she guessed. They were the skinniest dogs she had ever seen. She had to push Cassie off her back when she had to turn around to vomit from the smell, but she forced it back down. Most of the dogs looked like German shepherds, but there was one that looked like a boxer, and another that was a retriever, and one more that looked like just any dog you'd see in somebody's yard, except too skinny. You could see the ribs on all of them, and their hair was missing in spots, along their sides. The barking was so loud that nobody tried to talk for a while. They all just pressed against the back of the van to watch. Then another big dose of the smell came up at Stella and she turned around and threw up into one of the hub caps. She heard Cassie groan behind her. "God damn, Stel," Hub said, and looked at the cap.

"We're in trouble," Cassie said, almost shouting. "They're starved. They'd eat us alive if they got the chance to get at us."

"No lie," Carolyn said.

"They're wild," Hub said. "I heard about some dogs like that the last time I was up at Anson's. People just stop feeding them, and so they form into packs and roam all over the place to look for food. Anson said there was a pack up near the South Dakota line that ate a little girl."

"Hub, stop," Stella said, and put her face in her hands to cover the crying.

"It's true," he said. "All over this end of the damn state. Packs of them."

"So what are we going to do?" Stella said.

"We've got to get the hell out," Hub said, and moved back up toward the driver's seat. "Dump that puke out the window," he said, and then said "no, on second thought don't." He sat down at the wheel and reached for the key, just as if the van were running fine. He turned the key and the engine groaned a little and then quit. The dogs separated, as if reacting to the noise. They were all around the van now. They were breathing fast when they weren't barking, and scratching at Hub's fancy paint job. Their claws made a screeching noise that blended in with the breathing and barking, and made the whole thing sound like a horror movie. Hub kept turning the key again and again until the ignition sound was down to just a little groan that could barely be heard with all the dog noises. It was easy to tell that there was no way in the world that the van would start. Stella reached up and put her hands on Hub's shoulders, to keep herself from crying more, and to help Hub think better about what was going on.

"It's not going to start, Hub," she said.

He shrugged her hands off his shoulders. "It's okay," he said. "It's okay." He started to say that over and over again, as if it went with turning the key. Stella wondered if he might be losing his mind—doing and saying the same things again and again, but she forced herself not to think of that, because she was afraid she might lose hers too if she did.

She knew it wasn't okay though. It was getting darker by the moment, and the dogs weren't about to give up. There was nothing else around to pull them away. She had to use the bathroom so bad that she started to wet herself twice in a row, and was a second late in catching it the second time. The heat inside the van was getting worse, with all of them sweating, and the dog and vomit smells mixed in made it seem even hotter. Carolyn was kneeling in front of the back seat with her hands over her ears as her forehead rested on the back of the front seat. Cassie was sitting in a back corner, rocking slowly from side to side, without any expression on her face. On some of the windows now there was dog spit, full of little bubbles that had blue paint specks in them.

Stella looked at everybody else and listened to Hub saying it would be okay, and then she told herself that she was going to have to stop crying and calm down. At first she could not do it, but then she closed her eyes and tried to think of something completely different. Something a million miles away from the van and the dogs and the sweat. What she started to think about was school. And after a while she made herself see the whole map of the United States in her mind. She could see all the square midwestern states stacked around Nebraska, and then she pictured the van right in the middle of the whole country. And in the middle of the road. Then she thought about the fact that all over the rest of the country, people were washing up the supper dishes or getting ready to watch a comedy show on TV. And when she thought about the nice neat map and about all the funny, friendly people on TV, she could think that things really were okay—that the whole country was fine, except for the four of them. It was that picture in her mind—of the map and the people—that made her think that somebody would get up from watching TV and come to help them out of the problem they were in. After all, they were just off the Interstate, next to the Platte River, out on the flat of Nebraska, in the very middle of the map of the whole country.

HOMES

"Let me put it to you this way," Tommy says to the husband, reaching up to put a hand on the man's big soft shoulder. "I'd never in this life put you in anything I wouldn't live in myself." Tommy glances at the wife when he says in this life, making sure she sees his spiritual side. "My family's lived in a home almost identical to this one for over two years," Tommy goes on, taking his hand from the shoulder and looking the husband in the eye, "and we haven't had any call to move. Come to think of it, I'd love for you folks to come by and visit us sometime. Just look over the home and get a sense of the real pleasures of mobile home living. We've got the room, the comfort, the furnishings, the safety we need. I know when your family comes along, safety will be an even greater consideration than it is now," he says, and steers them around to the side of the trailer. "See these?" He points at the side of the unit. Then he looks up into the hot, clouded sky, as if searching for rain. "These are steel bands—made of the same metal that goes into skyscrapers and jet aircraft. And each Greenpath home is steelbanded to its foundation in four separate locations." He gestures upward over the top of the unit, guiding their eyes over the first of the bands and then allowing them to glance along at the others.

With safety taken care of and the wife kind of patting the husband's arm—he is brushing her away subtly while he pretends to inspect the trailer's construction—Tommy knows he's close. "Listen," he says suddenly and just a little too loudly, projecting an air of importance and consequence, "this is not the kind of thing you jump right into." He smiles and makes eye contact with each of them. Then he speaks quietly. "It's not quite like deciding between a Quarter Pounder and a Big Mac, is it?" He smiles broadly, forcing them to do the same. "So let's go back to the office, have a Dr Pepper, and sit down and talk about it." He watches them as he mentions the Dr Pepper. Older couples you use coffee. Younger ones that look like they have a little money, you use something light like Seven-Up. These couples—he works in construction and she works in a laundromat and says she does some ironing—you go with Dr Pepper. He leads them back around the side of the unit and across the rock lot of Greenpath Homes. Out front the big banner is almost still in the air. YOUR GREENPATH HOME: $249 A MONTH AND NO MONEY DOWN, it says in huge green letters on a white background. Tommy hesitates as he starts to ask the husband if they maybe didn't know each other in high school. His fear is that the man never made it that far. He starts more cautiously. "Don't I know you from someplace, Bob?" he says when they are halfway to the office. "Softball maybe, or church, or maybe Monroe High?" The husband, who has said nothing since giving his name and talking about his job, looks fully at Tommy for the first time.

"High school maybe," he says. "When'd you get out?"

"Been out five years," Tommy says, holding up his right hand to show off the ring.

"I was two years ahead of you," Bob says, "but maybe I do remember you. You ever have Fisher for English?"

Tommy sees his opening. "Twice," he says, with no recollection of anyone named Fisher. "Flunked my butt hard the first time and I just barely made it through the second."

Bob laughs out loud, looking at his wife for verification of this evidence of his intelligence. She returns his smile, apparently glad he is perking up a little. "He was tough," Bob says, "but I got out of there in one go-round."

Inside the office—a lux double-wide with Astro-turf steps and deep carpet everywhere except in the kitchen—Tommy guides them toward the soft drink machine. "Mountain Dew, Pepsi, Grape, Orange, Seven-Up, Dr Pepper," Tommy announces as they reach the machine, as if he is about to treat them to a gourmet meal. They both ask for Dr Pepper and Tommy pops hers open first. Bob makes a half-move toward his pocket and Tommy waves him off grandly. "Are you kidding?" he says with great mock offense. "These here are Greenpath quarters." He grips Bob's elbow briefly as he hands him the can. Then Tommy pops open his own, takes a long swig, and leads them down the hall to his office. Once they've got the safety worry out of the way and a Dr Pepper in their hands, and Tommy can see that the wife wants it, there's no way he can lose. Candy from a baby, he tells Ellis and Tucker and the others when they ask him how he keeps turning them over. Instinct, he tells them. Then he feels like he's bragging and won't say anything. But Tommy Conners sold his first Greenpath home before he was out of high school. He looked at his hometown of Blueston, saw eight thousand people, a bottling plant, four bars, a rubber belt factory, a dead foundry, and the Greenpath dealership, and decided the only thing he'd touch was Greenpath.

In the office, he sits Bob and Shirley down, looks them in the eye and asks them point-blank what they have in the bank. No problem at all, he tells them when they answer. No problem at all. He gets out his calculator, asking what they might be able to get from their parents. They look at each other and come up with a total of two hundred dollars. Great, Tommy tells them. Fantastic. He plays at the calculator, multiplying thirty-five times thirty-five—he has been trying to memorize all the squares he can—and looks up at them triumphantly. "Three-fifty," he says. "I can put you in that beauty with the rust appliances—this year's model—for three-fifty down and two-forty-nine a month."

"But the no money down?" Bob says immediately.

Tommy didn't expect that. He already went over the banner with them. He tells everybody that right away—that it's only on one or two used units and there are even better deals on new units.

"You're right, Bob," Tommy says. "You're absolutely right. And there are two of those units out there we can put you in without you giving me so much as a dime. That blue one we looked at first, and a one-bedroomer back at the edge of the lot there." He stands, as if he'll run them out there right now to show them. "No no," Shirley says. "We understand." She turns to her husband. "We'd be dumb to get a little one when all it takes is three-fifty to get a big new one." She says this in a semi-whisper, as if Tommy's not supposed to hear it.

Bob shrugs in apparent agreement.

"Smart girl you married there, Bob," Tommy says, and gets out the paperwork. They're nailed. His second sale of the day and the seventh of the week. The quarterly sales prize for the region—a week in the Bahamas—is long-since in the bag. No way anyone can catch him. No way anyone east of the Mississippi can catch him.

The main reason Tommy likes church picnics is that Paula is the best-looking girl by far, and the only one who dresses like you're supposed to for a church function. Today, on a coolish day for summer, she has on a baby-blue cotton dress with a row of little yellow daisies across the top, which runs across her chest about halfway between the top of her breasts and her throat. The dress has a sort of starched look to it—it is firm and pure to Tommy's eye—and over it she is wearing a little white jacket that has the same look. The jacket is cut short—not even to her waist—and in combination with the dress, it makes Paula look strong and innocent and good, which is what Tommy wants to see in her. She looks like Easter to him as she moves easily among people, talking about the weather and her children, who are with her mother. Paula is so pretty and perfect in the sun that Tommy feels a real ache of some kind. It is not quite a sexual feeling, or even quite love—it is more a vision of wifely perfection and Paula's fulfillment of it. Tommy moves through the crowd with almost equal ease as he watches her. He talks about baseball with men who are nearly all at least fifteen years older than he is.

At the picnic there is lots of chicken and potato salad and baked beans. In the glen near the little creek that runs through the church property, there are twelve or fifteen picnic tables scattered out and all covered with white paper tablecloths that stand out brilliantly on the new green grass that the grounds committee put in spring before last. At these picnics, sometimes Tommy and Paula sit together and sometimes they don't, preferring to spread themselves out and let themselves be seen and talked to by more people. They are, because of their youth and good looks and poise, the darlings of the older church people as they stand with big bellies and broadening hips and talk about how young and lucky the Connerses are.

Today, midway through the picnic, as Tommy is talking about all the power-hitting shortstops in the major leagues, there is a sudden shower. The water falls in fat drops onto the white tablecloths and into the tubs of potato salad, and washes some of the barbecue sauce off the chicken. The women stand from the tables almost in unison at the first drops, gathering bowls and trays and running in a waddly, bent-over mass toward the main building, making noises that sound almost like clucks as they worry over their food, their shoes and their hair. The men, with no food to protect, are more leisurely—a few standing to look at the clouds and others continuing conversations as they walk in. By the time the women have gotten everything inside and the men are approaching the building, the rain stops as suddenly as it began, leaving behind a brief rainbow, a truncated picnic and greatly increased humidity.

People will now wander between tables inside and outside, going one place for food and another for conversation.

Paula is among the first women to come back outside. As if by magic, or perhaps youth, she is much less affected by the weather than the older women. Her hair, arranged in soft dark curls around her face, has not been mussed, and her dress and jacket have somehow repelled the drops, or perhaps absorbed them without evidence. She steps outside into the renewed sunshine and looks directly at Tommy, who is talking to his junior high school baseball coach, Buddy Hansen. Tommy is trying, for at least the tenth time, to talk the Coach out of buying a mobile home. The Coach, who is perhaps Tommy's best friend, has been talking for months about selling his house and moving into a trailer. As Paula comes near them, Tommy can almost feel her will and power to separate the two men—can nearly smell her wish that Tommy not have anything to do with the Coach. And the Coach himself, who wanted Tommy to go on from high school and play college or pro baseball instead of marrying Paula, seems to feel it too, and begins to edge away from Tommy. He says he ought to find his own wife, and see how upset she is with him for eating too much.

"You look gorgeous, Paula," the Coach says when she is still fifteen feet away and he is already leaving. "Just gorgeous." It is as if he is twenty-three and she is nearly fifty instead of the other way around, so boyish and proper is his retreat.

"Well, thank you, Buddy," Paula says, stepping over a muddy spot.

"Catch you on the flip side," Tommy says to the Coach.

"Right," the Coach says.

Paula slides her pale bare arm in under the tan linen sleeve of Tommy's jacket. She leads him out toward the end of the new grass, out toward the little creek that runs in toward town. They played along the brook as children. And though they did so separately, their families like to tell stories about them playing together and getting to know each other, and being perfect for each other even at that age. The creek is narrow and meandering, set down into a four-foot wide miniature gorge where the water moves gently over small rocks.

"I was talking to your daddy inside," Paula says as they walk. Tommy is immediately irritated for two reasons. One is that since she is walking him away from the picnic, he knows she wants to talk about something. Moving out of the apartment maybe. Or his job. Ever since the Bahamas trip she has been asking about moving. She's been telling him they should have cashed in the trip money and bought a house. This threatens Tommy in a way he's not sure he understands. He wants to know what she thinks about things, but he does not like it when she disagrees with what he has already decided is best for the family. She wants a house with flat ground and a big yard, so Annie can learn to walk—so they can have a real life, and can't they afford it with all the money he's making now? Tommy yelled at her when she said that, telling her she'd be the first to know when they could afford the kind of house they wanted. Second to know, she corrected, and Tommy stopped talking to her. The second thing that bothers Tommy about the walk and talk is that he did not know his parents were at the picnic. They had said they were going to stay home and work in the garden. But Tommy does not say anything about either of those things. He allows his arm to be held and his pace to be dictated by his pretty wife.

"And he agrees with me, Tommy, on how you're getting shorted, on how you're shorting yourself. I didn't say a word to him and he just started telling me how he thought you are so much better than just selling mobile homes. He said real homes. Or maybe even commercial real estate. Commercial real estate, Tommy. In town."

Tommy can feel heat at his neck and under his arms. He almost never yells at Paula, but has gone as long as two days without saying anything to her except what needs to be said to be sure the children get taken care of. "I think that may happen sometime," he says softly. "But I have a few things left to learn from Porterfield and some of the others."

"And he said he didn't see any reason you couldn't run your own business too, Tommy," Paula says, as if he hadn't spoken. "With as good as you are with the paperwork and all, you'd be a natural. Plus closing a deal."

"Those are things that everybody at Greenpath does."

"How come they didn't go to the Bahamas then?" she says, with a hint of a whine in her voice. "I think he's right, Tommy. You're just a little too scared to quit. We have money in the bank and you'd find something fast—I bet they'd come looking for you once the word got out."

Tommy decides not to say anymore. He has been working since he was fifteen and has never left a job without having the next one to go to. When he has thought about quitting, it has been to go to school, to take a few business courses. But Paula never mentions school because she is afraid he'll listen to the Coach and go somewhere to play college baseball. Once the Coach said to Tommy that if Paula had to choose between Tommy having either a woman on the side or a chance at pro baseball, she'd take the woman on the side.

"Well, I can see there's no getting anywhere with you right now," Paula says into his thoughts, and pulls at his arm to turn them back.

They walk in silence for a distance and then she lets go of his arm. "I don't mean to push," she says. "It's just that you don't know how good you are. You should hear people talk about you."

Tommy has heard people talk about him since the seventh grade, when he could go get a grounder in the hole at short and fire it across to first as well as any high school shortstop in the state, or so they told him. He has never understood how it has ever helped him to have people talk about him, and so he has listened less and less over the years. "You certainly do look pretty today," he says to Paula as she walks in front of him to go into the church. She smiles quickly back over her shoulder but doesn't say anything else to him.

At the apartment on a Tuesday afternoon, Tommy and the Coach are carrying a big, blond-wood-framed mirror up the steps to go into the dining room. The mirror is as wide as the table, and like so many of the other pieces of furniture in the apartment, it just sort of came to be Tommy's. His mother bought it to go in her dining room and when it didn't match the wood in her table closely enough, she gave it to Tommy instead of going through the trouble of taking it back. "Who needs a mirror to watch themselves eat anyway?" she asked Tommy. He thinks it will work well in his dining room, which is really a little dinette off the kitchen. People have told Tommy that for somebody twenty-five years old—especially a guy—he has a great sense of furniture and how it fits in a room. The Coach shakes his head over Tommy and furniture, saying that if he didn't know better he'd think Tommy had some fag blood in him.

Paula is away on a bus trip with a group to see the amazing frescoes in two little churches in North Carolina. She read about them in the newspaper—they're supposed to be as pretty as Michelangelo's and are drawing hundreds of thousands of people to a place that's only a hundred and seventy-five miles from Blueston, and so she wanted to see them. Tommy told her if they turned out to be as pretty as she thought, they could drive down with the kids and make a Sunday trip out of it.

The Coach is now a guidance counselor at the junior high—now they call it a middle school—where Tommy was the best baseball player in the twenty-seven years history of the school. The Coach used to get Tommy out of classes, buy him beer, even set him up with easy high school girls, starting when Tommy was in eighth grade. The Coach said Tommy was going to be all-state in high school, but two things happened. One Tommy could have told him—he stopped growing at just under five-seven, two inches taller than his father. And the other was that Tommy met Paula—actually sort of discovered Paula—when he was in the tenth grade and she was in the ninth. He decided he needed to work, and didn't have all the time it took for baseball. The Coach did nothing short of blow up over that, asking Tommy who in the hell he thought he was to pour all that baseball talent down the toilet for pussy that barely had hair on it yet. After maybe a month he calmed down most of the way, and has kept up with Tommy ever since. He still tells Tommy two or three times a year that they ought to get in touch with one of the teams that already knew his name back in junior high. Tommy laughs, and the Coach tells him he has the best arm he's ever seen in his life—that Tommy wouldn't have to hit even .240 to be an all-star.

"What are you going to do with this mother?" the Coach says when they are most of the way up the metal stairway between the two sets of apartment buildings.

"You mean the mirror?" Tommy says.

"You know what the hell I mean," the Coach says. Tommy has been trying to get the Coach to cut down on his language—as a way to get Paula to like him a little better.

"Mom was going to put it in her dining room so I thought about that," Tommy says as they flatten the big mirror over the turn in the stairwell up to the third floor.

"Doris wouldn't even think about where to put a mirror," the Coach says. "I bought one right after we got married to go in the bedroom and she freaked. Literally." He laughs. "It's been in the garage for at least fifteen years. I think the damn dog peeing on it once in a while is the only use it gets. Another reason I need to sell the damn house. We live in two rooms, keep all the junk in the basement and the attic and never even look at it. It's a waste of space with no kids anymore." The Coach's daughters both got married right out of high school and moved to big cities. Tommy decides not to say anything to the Coach about buying a mobile home. Tommy has told him a dozen times it's a bad idea, but the

Coach sticks with it, as if it's because that's what Tommy sells. Tommy puts his end of the mirror down so he can open 306. He hates the apartment as much as Paula does. The door is metal—a thin, hollow-sounding metal just like the stairs, except the stairs are sort of corrugated, and the door is painted white so it looks like wood. The whole apartment sounds tinny and hollow to Tommy, sort of like a trailer, and he wouldn't live in one of those if they paid him. What Paula hates is being up on the third floor with the kids, especially with Annie just learning to walk.

"In here," Tommy says to the Coach, walking backwards into the dinette. The apartment smells like plastic, and Tommy has never been able to figure out why.

"When are you going to buy a house, Tommy?" the Coach says, as if he is thinking about the smell too. "Or at least a trailer?"

"Next time I win the sales contest," Tommy says, just realizing it as he says it. "Next time I win I'm bagging the trip and taking the money to look for a house over in Cauthen."

"Cauthen?" The Coach is sitting at the dining room table now. It is just big enough for Tommy and the family, and when somebody comes to dinner, they have to bring in the coffee table and let the kids eat off that.

"Yeah," Tommy says. He is tapping at the wall to find a stud. "Paula likes it over that way."

"Paula Shmaula," the Coach says with a long breath. His jealousy of her seems to get stronger as his own marriage gets worse and he doesn't have kids to coach anymore. It's as if he got stalled out with Tommy, as if Tommy was his big hope for somebody he had coached to go on to be a real star in high school, and maybe in college or the pros. But when Tommy met Paula and stopped growing, the Coach stopped growing too. Within two years after Tommy left junior high, the Coach moved into an office and started getting fat. Right now he is signed out from school for an appointment with a consulting psychologist.

"She has a sister over that way," Tommy says. He has always been real calm and even with the Coach over Paula. There's no real reason to be angry with him about it—it's just a little frustrating that he doesn't have any more to do than to hang around with Tommy Conners now that Tommy doesn't need girls or beer or anything the Coach can tell him about baseball.

"So what's with the mirror in here?" the Coach says, as if to change the subject. "You going to watch yourself eat?" Tommy laughs and says that's just what his mother said.

"Smart woman, your mom," the Coach says. "If I'd've been two or three years older, you never know." The coach says that about Tommy's mother every time she comes up in a conversation. She is a softly overweight woman of fifty-four. She is still attractive, maybe especially to men like the Coach.

"Does this sound like a stud to you?" Tommy says as he taps the wall with the back end of a screwdriver.

"Not till your voice gets a little deeper it don't," the Coach says, and laughs.

Tommy goes into the kitchen and gets a big nail out of his tool drawer. "I should use one of those toggle bolt things," he says when he comes back in, "but I don't have any."

"You got any beer, Tommy?"

"Coach, it's two o'clock in the afternoon. Aren't you working?"

"Hell yes, I'm working," the Coach says in mock offense as he spreads his beefy arms over the table. "I'm counseling one of my old students on how to hang a mongo mirror in his dining room so his kids can see what great manners the old man has. Twice." He laughs.

Tommy starts driving the nail while the coach is still talking. It feels good and strong going in—he's hit the stud dead square, he decides. He tilts the mirror away from the table and looks at the wire that runs across the back. It is hooked to either side with a little eye screw. Tommy gives them a pull to make sure they're tight. Then he stands by his end of the mirror with a hand on his hip, as if he's asking if the Coach is going to help or not.

"What about you, Hot Shit," the Coach says as he stands up. "Aren't *you* working?"

"Coach, the people I work with don't leave for the day at three fifteen. That's about when they start to show up."

They hang the mirror but then take it back down because Tommy left too much of the nail sticking out and so the angle away from the wall is too severe. Tommy hits it four or five times and they hang it again and then sit down at the table to admire it.

"You going to give me a beer or not?" the Coach says.

"You forget where the refrigerator is?" Tommy says in the same mock-irritated tone the Coach used and that they have used with each other most of the time since Tommy was an eighth-grade hotshot who would range out into the outfield and take fly balls away from the outfielders.

The Coach pulls the tab on his beer and says, "Bussscchhh," the way he always does, no matter the brand. Just as he is about to finish the word, the mirror crashes off the wall and onto the floor next to them. It doesn't break immediately when it hits the floor—it falls straight down—but after it does hit, it falls into the back of the chair on that side of the table and big pieces of glass fall—almost in slow motion—to the dinette floor. The Coach reached for the mirror about the same time it hit the chair. He and Tommy stand up—Tommy was across the table from where the mirror hit—and then the Coach says, "Shit, Tommy, if you'd've been over here you'd've caught the damn thing. No way those hands would have missed it."

Tommy doesn't say anything. He glances at the nail—he drove it in too far, he decides—and goes to get the broom and trash can. They pick up the pieces, and Tommy wants to blame it on the Coach, but knows he can't. By the time they've finished cleaning up, the Coach is ready for another beer. He goes and gets it and sits back down at the table. Tommy says he's going back to work.

At the door, Tommy pauses to say something else to the Coach about getting back to work, but decides not to. The Coach tells him to keep selling those hillbillies all those trailers they can't afford. Tommy doesn't say anything to that, and looks past the Coach to the empty mirror frame. The Coach looks back over his shoulder, following Tommy's line of sight, and then tells Tommy if they'd hung it in the bedroom where it belongs then it never would have broken. He laughs and takes a sip of beer.

A few days later Tommy is standing with Van Ellis at the Coke machine in the office. Everybody else is at lunch. Tommy is there because he just closed a sale—a brand new double-wide to a middle-aged couple he never thought would buy—and because his car is in the shop for a tune-up and oil change; and Ellis because he likes to sit in the office next to Tommy's and listen to how Tommy does it—how Tommy tells people the walls in the trailers are soundproof, for instance. "You know," Tommy always tells them, "the kids don't need to hear quite everything, do they?" Then the couple laughs and Tommy laughs and he has another sale. Tommy has known for a long time that Ellis listens to him, and lives in mild dread that one day Ellis will pick that time to sneeze or cough and send the sound right through. Right now, though, Ellis is congratulating him.

"It's balls," he's saying. "Everybody around here thinks of you as Mr. Churchpew himself, but what it really is looking like a damn altar boy and then pulling off the shit you do." Ellis looks down at Tommy with what appears to be a combination of admiration and jealousy. Ellis is in his early forties, tall, and his gut seems to get a little bigger by the week. He has been a steady, unspectacular mobile home salesman since he left high school, and for most of that time with Greenpath. He is one of the reasons Tommy thinks about leaving—he doesn't like to picture himself as someone forty-five, fat and selling mobile homes.

"You know, I could just whisper over here and blow your sale," Ellis is saying. "And you know they could check into the construction bullshit you sling. And you know you could hit Porterfield after a bad night with one of those wild-ass financing deals you pull. But no, you're Tommy Conners and you just grab it by the balls, smile that little choirboy smile and pull it the hell off every time." Ellis hits Tommy, just a little too hard, on the shoulder.

Tommy smiles and puts coins into the machine. "What'll it be, Van my man," he says. "Drinks are on me."

"Shit," Ellis says. "I'm going to lunch." He turns, pushes the door hard enough that it bumps against the side of the trailer, and heads out to his car. Tommy goes back to his office and figures his commission on his calculator. It comes out exactly the same as it did in his head. This will be the fourth sale he hasn't told Paula about. Of the last ten, he's mentioned six. This seems to have had the dual effect of making her talk less about getting a new job—maybe because six sales over that long is a bit of a slump for Tommy—and allowing Tommy to put some money in reserve, maybe against the day when he does go in and talk to Porterfield. He tells himself that the thing that has put him even close to thinking about leaving is not Paula at all, or even the message from his father, which never was delivered directly to Tommy. Instead, it is what happened to a seventh-grade classmate named Aaron Hutchins.

Aaron Hutchins was the biggest nerd ever to hit seventh grade, and never changed a bit all the way through high school. The only thing that changed was that his acne got worse for a while, then a little better, and then he went away to college. Now he's been back from college for just over three years and is making a giant fortune in telephone services and equipment. It irritates Tommy that he doesn't even exactly understand what Aaron does to make all that money. Just that the big company got broken up and then optical cable came along and then cellular phones and the internet, and Aaron Hutchins got up from his computer and his acne medication long enough to step into the right place at the right time. Tommy looks out his office door into Porterfield's office, where there is a computer terminal on the desk. Tommy has never seen Porterfield use it, but Tommy has heard that all the inventory's in it—you just punch up the right key and a description of every trailer in the region comes up on the screen. Then you push another button and the whole thing comes out on a piece of paper. As Ellis' car rolls off the lot, Tommy goes into the office to look at the computer more closely. He has a feeling that if he knew how to use it, he could make more money out on the lot, and that if somebody as goofy as Aaron Hutchens can make money with one, then Tommy ought to be able to make a lot more. Porterfield has been talking about getting terminals for all of them, but then he's also talked about company cars, matching jackets and a retirement plan, too. The machine just sits there—like it belongs in a hospital or someplace—but Tommy has the feeling that it is somehow keeping an eye on him. He goes back to his office to call the two couples who are close and whose financing he has already arranged.

He reaches the husband of the first couple, who says he has decided to stay in the apartment a while longer. "Hooee," Tommy says into the phone. "An apartment is money down the tubes. *Straight* down the tubes." Tommy knows as he says this that he is reacting too strongly. Any other day he would compliment the guy on his thought and decision-making abilities, and then feel his way toward the edge of the money-down-the-toilet number. "What the hell," the man tells Tommy. "It's my money the last time I checked." And he hangs up the phone. Tommy holds the receiver and looks at it for a moment before he hangs it up. He starts to dial the man's number again and then stops, asking himself silently why he was tempted to call again when it didn't have a chance to do anything but make the guy angrier.

While he is dialing the wife of the other couple, he hears a car roll onto the lot. He puts the phone down, thankful for a face-to-face customer. But it's Porterfield. Tommy watches him from the front window of the trailer. He gets out of his car—a new black Chevrolet—and adjusts himself at the crotch as he starts for the trailer. He just turned fifty and has been selling trailers since he was nineteen. He owns stock in Greenpath, and like the ministers who ask for money on TV, he genuinely believes he is helping a lot of people by putting them into Greenpath homes. And so Tommy has come to admire him, and to learn from him. Things like how to be sincere as all get out with your customers and still make money for yourself.

"Yo Tommy," Porterfield calls as he comes in.

"Yo," Tommy calls back.

"You got the fort, huh?" They have not had a secretary for almost a month, since the last one walked out.

"I guess," Tommy says. "No big raids going on right now, though." Tommy is sitting at his desk looking at his hands. He is thinking, for a reason he doesn't know, that maybe if he'd had bigger hands, he might have given baseball a try.

"Come on down here," Porterfield calls out to him.

Tommy goes down the hall to the office with the computer. Porterfield tells him to sit down. Then he rubs his hands together a moment and looks up at Tommy.

"You know what this business needs, Tommy?"

Tommy says no, he doesn't.

"More like you," Porterfield says immediately. "Two more like you and we'd blow the roof off headquarters, Tommy. You realize we have the second smallest territory—for population I mean—in the company? And the third-highest sales? That's fifty-eight territories in eleven states, Tommy." Tommy has heard all of this many times. "Where can I get more like you, Tommy, do you know?"

Tommy shrugs, smiling off to one side.

"I mean it. Even one more like you. I send these guys down to damn Houston for all that training and they come back hung-over and gung-ho for three days and that's it." He takes a little cigar—a

Garcia y Vega that Tommy likes the smell of—out of his pocket and looks at it a few seconds. He looks over at Tommy and then back at the cigar. "And what if you left, kid?" He looks hard at Tommy, as if trying to gauge his reaction. "Where would I be then?"

Tommy shrugs again, wanting the conversation to go away. "Nobody's irreplaceable," he says. "New people break the records whether it's Babe Ruth or Greenpath Homes."

Porterfield smiles as he lights his cigar. "And you know what else?" he says. "It's not just every record getting broken, it's every man having a price." He smiles at Tommy again. "So I'm prepared to do two things for you, Mr. Conners. To put you in charge of the rest of those bozos, for another grand a year, and to add a full percentage point to your commission. Make that three things. You tell me today and I'll make it effective today."

Tommy moves his hand back over his hair and makes a little whistly noise as he blows out some air. "That's heavy stuff," he says. "And real flattering." He stands up. "I get to think about it till five?"

"Till eleven fifty-nine," Porterfield says, "if you want it to show up in your next check."

Tommy starts out of the office. Once he is back at his own desk, he hears cars on the lot. He goes to the window and sees that one is Van Ellis back already and the other is the Coach, here again, Tommy assumes, to try to get Tommy to sell him a home. Tommy thinks for one second about a two-year-old dented double-wide at the back edge of the lot and how pleased the Coach would be with it—for maybe a month. Then he opens his desk drawer. He takes out his calculator and a half-eaten pack of cinnamon Life Savers. He takes the little glass-framed family portrait off the top of his desk and sticks it in the inside pocket of his jacket, and then goes out to meet the Coach. The heat has built up on the lot, as it will when you have that much shiny tin in one place. The Coach waves at Tommy from across the lot and Tommy waves back, genuinely pleased to see the Coach. Tommy meets him mid-lot and puts his arm up over the pudgy shoulders of the first person who ever told him he was a star. The shoulders are thick and maneuverable under Tommy's arm, and seem to carry within them the soft, mushy feel of the Coach's current life. At the car, Tommy deposits the Coach on the passenger side, and as he goes around to get in and drive them off the lot, he is thinking about how long it will take him to get both their lives back on the track where they're supposed to be, how it's either Tommy or nobody to make the moves that need to be made.

UMPIRE

The town of Blueston sits on a little flat piece of flood plain confined by the river at one edge and by the abrupt start of Cullhat Mountain at the other. It is a foundry town that had its best days in the forties and fifties, when the hot waste water ran freely down into the river, and gawky steel forms rolled away on big flatcars headed north. The weeds around the foundry offices are as tall as the men who once worked in the thick wooden chairs inside, and reach up as if to look into the high, wavy-glassed windows, each of which has a trim arc of on-end brick above it. On a summer day in Blueston the heat builds along the river in the midday hours and then rises to collect—late in the afternoon—in a little low spot between the flat and the first quick rise of the mountain. It is on this little scoop of land, amid a few small and poorly kept houses and a thin line of rock road that runs up the mountain, that Callis Field is located. It sits with its back to the town, and in 1937, when the diamond was laid out, either nobody had the power to hit the ball more than 284 feet into the thick air to right, or someone just stuck the plate down somewhere and forgot to think about the fact that the start of the mountain was going to dictate that the right field line would be unnaturally short.

Reid hates the field because of the heat. The whole league is hot, but this field seems to draw it and hold it, so densely that the dust doesn't rise right on a slide. The outfield—in deep left-center—is damp even in dry spells, and downright mushy in the spring. As Reid brushes the plate in preparation for the start of the game he watches the red-orange dust as it hangs low to the ground, clinging to his shoes more thoroughly than dry dust would. He comes up from the plate, kicking the heels of his shoes against his shin guards, and allows himself a furtive glance up into the stands, just behind the plate. There is no sign of Ellen, as he knew there wouldn't be—it is too early—and there are no more than twenty-five people on the long rows of two-plank, deep blue benches that make up the "box seats" behind the plate. Above those seats, in a home-made-looking booth, are the two guys from WBLS, already barking out information to their vast audience. Reid likes to see them up there because they are a consolation to him. They broadcast rookie league baseball—Class D, it used to be called—to a town of 16,000 people over an AM station way down at one end of the dial. And all this while anyone who is really interested in the game can come out to Callis Field, pay hardly anything, and see the game in person. The WBLS guys are seven million miles from the big league broadcast booth they dream about at night, especially with all the ex-players bouncing in front of men like these, who probably decided at age ten they were going to be broadcasters. The two men up behind Reid are farther from their hope than Reid is from a big league plate with an inside chest protector and real meal money.

Kammler, a big square man of German descent who is thirty-three years old, will work the bases. He comes slowly in toward Reid as they wait for the Blueston Braves to hit the field. "Anything in those shadows out there deep, cover me," he says to Reid, as if Reid doesn't know to do it. "Right," Reid says. "Foul pops by the screen, you watch the runners," he tells Kammler. "Right," Kammler barks back. "No lip and keep it quick." He turns his big body then, claps his hands together twice, and jogs out toward first. Reid doesn't like Kammler because he is too old to be working for $57 a game—$3,700 for the whole summer, for Christ's sake—in a hot-town rookie league. Reid has already told himself that this is it for him. This is his third year in the Southern Mountains League—made up of a bunch of little towns you never heard of in Tennessee, Virginia, North Carolina and West Virginia—and he will turn twenty-five in the winter. A year of umpire school and three years at the bottom is more than enough. Either he gets an offer to move up after this season, or he goes back to Fremont, Nebraska, to play softball and drive into Omaha every day to work full time for his brother, who is a lawyer.

Kammler is clapping his hands again, trying to get the Braves onto the field. He has told Reid that in his eleven years of umpiring, the teams have gotten slower and slower to come out, as if they want to make you stand there so everybody gets a good look at you—to let the crowd warm up its collective hatred of umpires. At last the Blueston first baseman breaks out of the dugout. "Number fourteen," the radio/PA team barks into Reid's neck, "the first baseman, Cary Banders." He stretches out the end of the name. "Banderrrzzz," it comes out, as if to cover for the small applause generated by the crowd. The other players follow by position, each with an elephantine syllable at the end of his name.

The Blueston catcher is a short, squat kid named Lucas. They signed him out of a junior college after they'd already run through three other catchers with broken fingers and pulled hamstrings. You can take one look at Pat Lucas and know he is going no place whatsoever. He reminds Reid of catchers in Little League. The fat kid, basically, who is dumb enough to sit back there and scream and holler and sweat his brains out. Lucas is that red-faced kid grown up a little, and he is so surprised, so damned amazed to be in professional baseball that he has lost all perspective on the fact that he really is still that red-faced fat kid. As Reid settles in behind the plate, Lucas is already shouting out orders to his infielders, who are casually picking up grounders and ignoring the catcher completely.

"Gonna call them strikes when they're strikes, balls when they're balls," Reid tells the pudgy red neck beneath him. "Anything you don't like has already been called and won't be called again. Stay down there to give me a good look and everything will be fine." Reid used to give this little soft-voiced talk to all the catchers, but has let it go as the summers have worn on and his reputation has begun to precede him. But Pat Lucas needs it. And as Reid speaks, the neck gets redder. Reid sighs deeply, motioning the leadoff man for Prestonburg into the box. Another night of listening to gripes on everything up to a half foot off the plate.

Ellen Childress is Reid's entire version of the collective girl-in-every-town dream of the Southern Mountains League. There are two or three players in the league—tall, statuesque young men out of colleges—who will have you believe they've long since accomplished the feat. Reid weighs the factors of girls' love for baseball players against the size and conservatism of the towns, and he doubts it. If anybody has done it, he suspects it might be some runty little infielder with a whole lot to prove. It is Reid's opinion that the farther up into these hills you get, the ropier the women are. Or else fat. No middle ground between the lean, hard-armed girls with freckles and straight, no-color hair, and the ones who grew up round. Ellen, he tells himself, is almost an exception. Her hair is dark brown, and she fills out the back of a pair of Levis the way a girl is supposed to. Smooth and full, but not too full. Ellen has a daughter who is ten and a son who is nine, and they come to the games on some nights, and stay at their grandmother's on others, when Ellen comes by herself. Henry Childress, Reid learned one soft summer night, left the county when the children were six and five, with a woman who has since made the local paper on two separate occasions for flimflam schemes on the Amtrak train that comes through Blueston at three in the morning without stopping. So Ellen has raised the kids by herself and taught fourth grade at Blueston Elementary and, as she tells it, had no inclination at all to have anything to do with another man from her home town. Reid tells himself that before he came along she was well on her way into the process of shriveling up into a dried vine and turning in her femininity in return for martyrized motherhood. If she brings the kids she's there by eight, and if not a little later, staying to talk with her mother before heading to the park.

"Like hell," the beef-necked catcher squawks. "It wasn't even on the black."

Reid easily resists the temptation to agree—the pitch was indeed four inches *off* the black—as the Prestonburg leadoff man trots down to first with a walk. Reid feels heat at his own neck. Already there are voices behind him. "Yeah, get them off to a good start, ump," says one. "Just keep it on your shoulder," comes another, ostensibly talking to the second hitter. "He'll send you on down to first too." Reid thinks often about levels of intimidation in different leagues. He has decided that it is worst in these little one-show towns where people have nothing to do with their anger except spit it out at an umpire on a baseball field. So they sit, ten or twelve feet away, and rip him to pieces. In the major league cities, Reid's logic goes on, there are a few major league hecklers, to be sure, but at least they are farther away, and held there by something more substantial than the thin, undulating chicken wire that separates Reid from the locals in this town. They will gain strength as their numbers increase through the innings. And as their volume increases so too does their daring, as they prod each other on to greater insults, in the manner of children trying to get each other into trouble in a classroom.

The second Prestonburg hitter, mercifully, pops out on a 3-1 pitch that was a ball, and Reid is spared the crowd's momentum being built more rapidly than it needs to be. But as the Blueston team comes to bat in its half of the first, he is aware that the town's biggest voice—a man Reid has shouted at through the chicken wire—has arrived. He is a middle-aged, roly-poly man with hair worn in a flat-top. There is no drinking in Callis Field, and so the flat-top and his buddies have to step outside the park every inning or so for a nip—a situation which gives Reid a small break, but which also tends to build the level of comment and to destroy their notion of the flow of the game just enough to allow them to make mistakes of judgment—condensing batting orders, confusing hitters and situations just enough to be able to berate Reid for something that is not quite related to the actual progress of the game.

The level of pitching in the Southern Mountains League has gone up a notch or two this season. The consensus among the umpires is that these things go in cycles, while the hitters of course attribute it to a corps of umpires which favors pitching over hitting. On this night Reid is particularly impressed. The Prestonburg team is using a small left-hander who nibbles at the corners and fields like a cat when they try to bunt on him. He is a college graduate, and about twelve steps ahead of the league in guile and craft. Reid is sure he will move up fast—perhaps before the season is over. And Blueston is using a tall right-hander who is just out of high school—of the type who will walk the bases full and strike out the side in the same inning. By the end of the fourth inning each team has no runs and one hit, and Reid feels the game settling into a pitcher's duel—so long as neither team has a fielding lapse and the tall right-hander doesn't lose the plate.

After the fifth Reid brushes off the plate even though it is clean, and stares openly up into the stands to look for Ellen, having conquered the temptation at the end of each of the last two innings. "Don't look up here for help," the flat-top screams immediately. "There ain't no eye doctor up here." Reid feels his face warm. He has left his mask on to cover his eyes, but a good umpire baiter does not let any opportunity slip by. Reid waits, expecting—dreading—the first comment on why he is really looking up there. Somehow, through dumb luck or perhaps respect for a school teacher in a small town, or maybe just plain stupidity, his big talkers have never mentioned her. And again, as he settles in to start the sixth, they have let him look and made no mention. They are staying with the eyesight theme, their favorite. "You realize he does see well enough to find the plate to dust it off, anyway," someone yells, to general laughter. Reid misses Ellen behind him. In her silence through the jeers she helps him absorb, allows him to remain stoic when he would rather not. Her absence annoys him to a degree that he knows it should not. He has no claim on her. One of her kids could be sick. Or her mother maybe. Or maybe a PTA meeting. No, not in summer. Reid has traveled through six ratty little mountain towns to have Ellen sit behind him for these three games, and now he is finally here and she is not.

In the top of the sixth the big right-hander walks the first two batters. The pitches are all high, and there is not much static from behind. The Blueston manager, a no-hit shortstop who made it to the big leagues for a cup of coffee years ago, trots to the mound and tilts his head back to talk to his pitcher. The kid nods, hands on hips, and the manager trots back. No delay. No casual shot at Reid. No nothing. Reid goes back to his crouch and calls a ball high. "Wait till it gets there," comes a voice from behind. The next two pitches are also high, and down along the right field line people are moving around in the Blueston bullpen. As Reid calls a strike on the next pitch, with some protest from the Prestonburg bench, he feels a strap snap on his left shin guard. It is one of the criss-crossing straps which hold the shin guard in place, and the feeling of looseness annoys Reid immediately and deeply. He has always associated umpiring with tight control. And especially when you are as little as he is, you need a feeling of total firmness and containedness—a secure possession of the game. And the sloppiness at the inside of his left knee—the shin guard will not fall, but will slip slightly until the arch of his foot stops it—is just enough to compromise Reid's feel of control. If things do not feel right you can't do the job right—you don't have the same confidence, and if you don't have the confidence you don't have conviction, and if you don't have conviction people are all over you. Especially if you are small. Reid begins immediately to try to discount the annoyance, to equate it with a lingering drizzle. It is there, and must be dealt with, but it cannot become your whole focus. He cannot stop and fix the strap because it has torn away on the sewn side, and even if he could repair it he would have to endure the complete attention of the crowd while he stopped to work on it. So he has no choice but to deal with the irritation. He reminds himself of other umpiring problems. Guys working with diarrhea. Broken toes. Alone, for God's sake, with a hostile crowd. He glances out at Kammler who is bent, hands on knees, just behind the mound, and is glad he is there.

The hitter walks, loading the bases and putting the potential go-ahead run at third. The Prestonburg catcher—David Harkness—is the batter. He is a tall, strong kid who almost never complains about a call. He is perhaps Reid's favorite player in the league, with a good chance to move up, though Reid has never seen anyone run more slowly on a baseball field. His stride to the plate brings increased chatter from the Prestonburg bench. The first pitch to him is on the corner and Reid shoots up his right arm. "Christ, I didn't know there was called strikes on visiting teams in this town, did you?" comes a voice from behind Reid. "That's the first one tonight, isn't it?" David Harkness steps out briefly—as strong a registering of disagreement as he is likely to make. The next two pitches are high. There are a few shouts from the crowd to take the pitcher out. Reid expects the manager to do just that. But he does not, and the kid comes in with a good pitch that Harkness taps weakly toward short. The drawn-in shortstop, in his eagerness to come home and cut off the run with a force, bobbles the ball momentarily. Pat Lucas is screaming "Home! Home! Home!" as loudly as he can. The shortstop guns the ball in, and Pat Lucas, in his eagerness to get the ball to first for the double play, pulls his foot off the plate far too soon. He has taken a full step before he catches the ball, and Reid has no choice but to call the runner safe at the plate. As Kammler calls Harkness out at first, Pat Lucas is throwing his mask at Reid's shins and jumping up and down. The little manager comes out in a hurry, and the chicken wire behind Reid is suddenly a maze of voices and faces. "We had him by a goddamn week," Pat Lucas is screaming again and again as he shoves at his manager's chest to try to get through him to Reid. "You're so goddamn short you can't see to make the call." The manager is pushing at Pat Lucas, trying to keep him from getting kicked out of the game. He doesn't have another catcher. In the infield all is quiet. No one has come in to join the protest because they all know Reid made the call. But at the fence there is pandemonium. "It's a force out, you blind asshole." "You never read the rule book? You don't need a tag on that play." "Can you believe this? Guy throws just the pitch he wants, and then a bush ump goes and blows it for him. Could be the difference for that kid on the mound out there." The voices are blended and irrational—too close to Reid. The manager still has not said a word to him, to Reid's relief. The call was so clear as to be indisputable, and the silence confirms that the manager knows it too. But the crowd and Pat Lucas are of one blind mentality. By now they are talking about where Reid stays in Blueston—a line of taunt that frightens him slightly. He hopes against knowledge that Ellen is back there, hearing all of this—but he knows she is not. She would be able to tell him if the threats are real or just the idle blather of half-drunk, small town fans from where she grew up.

At last Pat Lucas is calmed and the game resumes. Reid expects an under-the-breath barrage as the catcher settles in, but instead there is total silence. No infield directions, no hum-babe-shoot-it to the pitcher, and not a word to Reid. Maybe the boy has realized that he was wrong. Or, more likely, he has decided to pout because no one took up for him except the crazy fans. Reid hitches the shin guard and settles back to the game. Behind him now the taunts are no longer as consistent. He has come to realize, in his three years, that there is an optimum pace to umpire baiting, and it takes the right kind of game, the right levels of alcohol, and the right kind of weather to have it go just right. There is a certain pace and momentum to be built. When there is one huge explosion, it often kills the momentum for the rest of the game. Reid hopes it will go that way, instead of this being just a lull before another roar.

"He could've went to a Japanese ump school," comes the first distinct voice when things are calm, and after Reid has called strike two on the next Prestonburg hitter. "I'm not too sure they have force outs over in Yagashaki." There is general laughter, and the hitter pops meekly to second.

The Prestonburg right fielder steps in, twitching his neck and back muscles. "Nah, I doubt it was Japan where he learned," comes another voice. "He didn't meet the height requirements over there." Louder laughter. The batter fouls the next pitch high and toward the screen. Reid jumps out of the way of the catcher and comes back to watch the attempt. The ball falls just on the crowd side of the chicken wire screen, scattering his baiters momentarily. Reid steals a futile glance for Ellen.

"Get up there where you belong," comes a voice.

And when Reid is back in position behind the catcher, "I think he started out in the Three-I League." A pause, while the first pitch comes in. Then the same voice, with the punch line. "You think he would have made it out of there with at least one eye left." Explosive laughter. They use that one game after game. The hitter swings at the next pitch and lines the ball hard toward left field. The Blueston left fielder gets a good jump on the ball and dives for the short hop. But Kammler, running out from behind the pitcher's mound, throws up his thumb immediately and forcefully. Reid looks down, and adjusts the shin guard. The Prestonburg manager, once a pitcher for the old Washington Senators, takes off for Kammler from his third base coaching box. The two Prestonburg baserunners are right behind him, swarming all over the square umpire. Reid could have predicted it. One big rhubarb generally means one more big rhubarb. Kammler walks away from his accusers—out toward center field as the Blueston Braves trot in, some with open grins on their faces. "You just plain totally blew it," Reid can hear the Prestonburg manager shouting. "He trapped it and you took it away from us. Get help. Go ask. You blew it—maybe he saw it." Kammler walks away as Reid thinks of a time in Clairsburg when a rookie ump named Pelouge, of all things, reversed a call of tagging up too soon, that Reid had made. Reid was so mad he couldn't see, and Pelouge made enough similar calls to be out of baseball within two months after that one.

The manager and the runners have moved Kammler out into the short right field corner now, and he has turned to head in toward the plate—along the first base line. He is leading them to me, Reid cannot help but think, but halfway down the line Kammler turns back across the infield. Reid is grateful, and knows that he should start out to break it up, even though Kammler did not help him with the call at the plate. But before Reid starts out, the manager gives up on Kammler and comes in toward Reid, his arms in the air even as he takes his first step. "You gonna let that crap stand?" he says to Reid when he is still forty feet away. "Are you the home plate umpire? Are you?" He is building momentum as he comes in. Reid spreads his legs slightly and folds his arms across his chest, feeling the pounding of his heart. He is, of course, trapped. He can go talk to Kammler, tell him he saw the play differently, back the older man down, and then face the Blueston team and fans, as well as having to establish where the baserunners should be. And risk the wrath of Kammler. Or, he can stonewall for Kammler, and face the loss of some respect from the old pitcher, who knows full well that Reid is a good umpire, and that he cannot desert another ump. Reid has always known that umpiring is the ultimate no-win situation—you call them right and nobody notices—or some drunken fool convinces the crowd that you haven't called them right—and you make one mistake and it hangs there forever. No praise for doing it right and all kinds of hell for one mistake. But this situation is even worse. Reid not only cannot win, he cannot escape with full self-respect intact. If you second-guess another ump you quickly become an outcast among your peers, who are as patient as the devil himself in waiting for their opportunity to hang you out to dry. And if you allow one bad call to stand, a manager will never let you live it down, even though he knows you had no choice but to do what you did.

"Leaving shit like that lay around on the field doesn't get you any closer to the majors, son," the old pitcher is saying to Reid now, calm and almost polite as he stands in front of Reid and goes for the jugular. Reid tells him the call has been made and the inning is over. "There's no real purpose served," the manager goes on, as if Reid had not spoken. "It leaves a big brown ugly spot on the outfield and in your record. You don't think somebody from the league's not up there? You have a chance, son, and the guys that make the majors don't pass those chances up."

Reid turns away, hating the line the manager is taking with him, because it is the perfect blend of fatherliness and con. He starts up the first base line, seeing his own instant replay of the short-hop catch in left. Kammler, still out behind second, does not move. He is smoothing the infield dirt with the toe of his shoe. "One call like that sticks with the guy," the manager is saying now. "You eat one here and you'll be eating them the rest of your short umpiring life." Reid knows he is right. And that Kammler is not worth protecting. It is only Kammler's connection with the other umpires in the league that holds Reid back. "Nestor Chylak had a call almost exactly like that one time," the manager all but coos into Reid's ear. "It's tough, I know." Reid realizes that he has changed his own course, and is headed out toward Kammler. He tells himself that it is only a coincidence, but the drumming of his heart at his neck tells him otherwise. He thinks of the fact that he is doing this godforsaken, impossible job for $3700 a summer—that he is out here in the sticky dust and tobacco juice night after night for practically nothing. There is no justice in having to handle two full teams of highly unreasonable men for $57 a night. He wonders what federal mediators make, sitting in air-conditioned offices with people who do not curse them. He straightens, looks at Kammler, pushing the murmuring of the manager's voice out of his head.

"You okay?" he says to Kammler.

Kammler looks up, feigning surprise. "I hit that little dip there, behind short, as he went for it. Could've bounced my head a little." He looks down again, at his infield dirt.

Jesus Christ, Reid thinks above the renewed protests of the Prestonburg manager, he's caving in like a mud dam. Why the hell didn't he do something himself? Why stand out there like some kind of Kraut statue and hope it will all go away, or that the other guy will handle it? Reid fights the intense heat in his face—made of both pity and anger for Kammler—and asks him if he saw the play as a trap.

"Could've been," Kammler says, this time not even raising his head. And all at once Reid is ready. His hatred for Kammler becomes complete, as does his realization that the game is totally his to handle. All of this mingles with his need to see justice prevail. There is simply no call to be an umpire if you aren't after justice, in every sense of the word. Reid remembers that from umpiring school. And he hears his own words to others as he explains why he is a bush league umpire—the courts may get prostituted by plea-bargaining and the inequalities of social station, but on a baseball field, and maybe nowhere else in the world except on a baseball field, there is only one answer. You are either safe or out. There is no second degree safe or involuntary out or any of that crap. Reid starts to go to Kammler, to at least put on the appearance of having conferred and reached a mutual decision. But in his distaste for the older man he turns away and starts toward the plate. He motions for the Blueston manager, who is already running toward him, having read Reid's body as it moves resolutely toward change. "Oh no," he is screaming. "Oh no you don't. Oh no, oh no, oh no. This isn't the Pony League, you little runt, where the daddies talk you into the calls. This is goddamn professional baseball. There is money on the line here, you little runt. This isn't fucking Sunday afternoon slow pitch." Reid tells him to shut up, which has no effect whatsoever, and so Reid begins his explanation in a soft voice, into the rantings.

"The infield umpire and I have conferred," he begins, "and have agreed that the ball was trapped, as we all saw. Therefore, the batter will be at first, the runner at third will come home, and the runner at second will advance to third. There are two outs. Blueston will take the field." He turns to walk away, hoisting his chest protector into place and pulling his mask down over his face.

"Like hell we will," the Blueston manager is screaming. "Like hell. I won't play another goddamn second with you out there making it up as you go along. What's the goddamn sense?"

Reid sets himself behind the plate, as if it might be a haven from the chaos around him. Behind him, at last, the baiters have caught on to what is happening, and are warming to the task. "Look at God out there in the ump uniform," somebody—a female—is screaming. "He runs the world. Reverses history. Walks on water." And then, with the license and encouragement provided by the female voice, the men begin to curse Reid unmercifully. He is a runty motherfucker and they'll run him out of the league and the state. He couldn't umpire with binoculars strapped to his face. Where did he leave his guts? There is a place in Russia for him and other traitors and yellow bellies. Why didn't his mother ever teach him not to make up stories? How much is Prestonburg paying him to screw over the home team? How long have he and the Prestonburg manager been queering around together? His ass is grass. They could find better umpires at the state hospital. And on and on.

Reid stands unmoving, suddenly lifted above it all with a vision of a headline in a newspaper about an umpire being beaten to death in some obscure southern town on a hot summer night. With a "60 Minutes" crew doing a follow-up investigation. Reid can see the reporter standing in left field, pointing down to the spot where the short-hop catch was made. Reid turns toward the

Blueston dugout. "If Blueston is not on the field in thirty seconds," he says just loudly enough to be heard, "then we will have a forfeit. It makes no difference to me. This is my game to call and I will call it correctly." He aims his comments toward the old shortstop, who is the only person on the field who is his own height. "You saw him short-hop it, same as I did."

"Go to hell," the manager says. "Don't tell me what I saw. You don't go around undoing a baseball game. You want to go back to the second when you blew that 2-2 pitch to my cleanup hitter? Maybe we should go back to the first when you called two strikes in a row on pitches that were down at the shoe tops. Huh, what do you think?"

Reid says nothing, refusing to give the manager anything to use for fuel. Reid can see that he is calming slightly, can see that the manager knows the umpire is right, and is now doing no more than going through the obligatory motions of winding down, so that his team does not lose respect. "Look, if you're going to change one, you have to do it right away," he is saying now, almost as if giving Reid advice. "You don't walk around the field for twenty damn minutes getting your nerve up." He is shooting both arms up in the air as he talks. But his words are now much softer than his gestures. "These are kids out here. They have to know what to expect. You can't be surprising them all goddamn night." He is heading for the dugout. "Baseball isn't supposed to have trick endings," he says over his shoulder, and then looks ahead to the dugout. "Get the hell out there," he screams at his bench, and the softened din behind Reid erupts again. Someone is hitting one of the support poles with something—a bat perhaps—and the noise is deep, hollow and awful. Reid can feel it go through his head. For the first time he wonders if there is a cop in the place. Or anyone who has some sense, some perspective. "Give them twelve outs this inning, ump. What the hell's the difference?" the tirade begins, and deteriorates from there.

At last, when some order is restored and the baserunners are in position, and Pat Lucas has greeted Reid by going through an extended imitation of someone throwing up, the PA man behind Reid asks the crowd for its attention. "The Blueston Braves are playing this game under protest." Reid starts to spin around, knowing that the announcer has made it up. But he checks himself, repeats his order to play ball, and hitches the shin guard, all at once aware that through the whole hellish sequence he forgot it, and survived with the looseness. He allows the pitcher six warm-ups and they are ready to go. The Prestonburg hitter settles in and Reid tells himself to block out the crowd and get back to the game. The big Blueston pitcher goes into his windup and throws. And just as Reid starts to move his right arm up to call the pitch a strike, he suddenly realizes that Pat Lucas is not going to catch the ball. The fat red neck is falling off to one side of the plate, as if in collapse. Reid realizes that the ball will hit him at the precise moment that it does indeed hit him—high on his upper left thigh. He buckles as the pain registers, immediately grateful for the cup and the fact that the slight break of the ball at the end and his own beginnings of an attempt to jump have spared his genitals. He is aware of cheers from behind the plate as his face hits the soft red dirt of Callis Field. He raises himself back to one knee almost immediately, to watch the field. He is trying to decide if the ball is dead or in play. It has rolled up the first base line, as though he has bunted it with his thigh. Of course it is a live ball. And the runner from third has broken for the plate. The Blueston first baseman scoops the ball with his glove and in the same motion flips it to Pat Lucas, who has raised himself to one knee also, bumping Reid as he does. Lucas takes the throw, whirls and waits for the runner, who realizes he will be out, and therefore barrels into Pat Lucas as hard as he can. Pat Lucas tumbles back through the batter's box but holds onto the ball, and while Reid gives the out call from his kneeling position, Lucas goes after the runner with his mask. Both benches empty immediately, and for one brief moment, when he realizes he cannot yet stand, Reid imagines himself being crushed to death by two groups of sweaty young men fighting over a chunk of rubber set down into the ground at the far edge of some little no-name, no-count town. He has had dreams like that—when there are nine pitchers instead of one, and he has to call all the pitches at one time. As he tries to stand, Reid sees Kammler arriving at the plate. He does not come to Reid, but goes to the fight, which is already being broken up by both managers and some of the players. The crowd is at the screen, and as the fight subsides Reid wonders what has kept them from breaking onto the field. Finally, as players begin to straggle back to dugouts, the Blueston manager comes to check on Reid. "Leave him down there," comes from the crowd, several times. Reid accepts the manager's hand and pulls himself to a tentative standing position. As he tries to put weight on the leg, Reid hears the manager saying that the fat catcher will never play again for the Blueston Braves. Reid has to fight off the urge to tell the manager that it is Reid's decision on who gets kicked out of a game, and then nods and moves to dust off the plate. "Aw, the little blind guy hurt hisself," comes from behind him. Reid straightens, turns—now not caring what they say—and searches openly for Ellen.

As if to frame the events of the inning—as if to put them into glaring focus—the rest of the game ebbs away peacefully. In their half of the eighth the home team goes in order. In the top of the ninth Prestonburg gets a runner to second with one out but strands him. In the bottom of the ninth, with the crowd thinning and the throbbing in Reid's leg building, the Blueston leadoff man hits a long drive to left that just clears the fence, making the score 2-1, Prestonburg. "Hey ump," comes from a remaining baiter, "you realize the score is now one-nothing us? Do you, you blind cripple?" Another Blueston runner reaches with one out, but the last two hitters strike out against the little left-hander, and the game ends.

As the teams and the umpires head across the field to the clubhouse beyond the outfield fence, Reid walks alone, trying to minimize the limp, while Kammler talks to the Prestonburg pitching coach, and others walk in little clumps of three or four—motioning, pointing, gesturing—recapping the game. For all but Reid, perhaps, it is no more than one game in the Southern Mountains League schedule, now ready to be tucked away into the records. Another little pile of statistics that will find their way into *The Sporting News* and little newspapers here and there around the country. Reid watches Pat Lucas, perhaps the only other person walking alone on the field, and allows himself one brief moment of feeling sorry for the red-necked fat kid, whose baseball career will consist of these few games in a rookie league. Back in his hometown—Reid pictures him being from a dying coal town in Pennsylvania—he will brag about the time he took an umpire out with a fastball and got the runner at the plate on the same play. Reid has been a part of the forming of one boy's legend and claim to fame. Reid envisions Pat Lucas as a drunk, semi-toothless man of forty, going to the same bar every day to see if there might be someone who has not heard the story of the catcher and the ump and the play at the plate.

Reid decides that Ellen has met someone new since the last time he was in town, and she has decided that the easiest way to let him down is to just not come back. Reid views this speculation with a calculated calm, as if the events of the evening need a cap—to be sure that he can maintain in the face of total adversity. Near the gate in the deepest part of center field he catches sight of someone running along the fence. He glances up and sees the flat-top baiter moving at bouncing-gut top speed toward the opened gate. He is carrying a bat, and Reid understands immediately what is happening. Ahead of him, the players have not seen the man, and Reid does not call out to them. He brings his chest protector up into his left hand, and prepares to protect himself once again.

"You lousy motherfucking asshole," the man screams as he comes through the gate, and the screams alert those in front of Reid. "You got no reason to pick on Blueston. This is a championship town and you are screwing it all up. And you aren't going to do it anymore."

As the man nears Reid three or four players move in and tackle him easily, and as he lies on the ground Reid sees tears in his eyes. Reid sees the face as if it is being presented to him in a slowed-down pace—almost as if he can see what will happen a fraction of a second before it does. In the eyes Reid sees a boy who grew up in the town and who has perhaps never been out of it, a man who probably held one of the jobs that aren't there any more. As the players rise and move the man back outside of the field, a policeman arrives from out of nowhere, so far as Reid can tell, and the drunken fan, now crying freely, is led passively away. Reid waves toward the players as they look back at him just before re-forming their clusters.

In the umpire's showers—they have separate stalls in only two of the Southern Mountains League towns—Kammler is off-hand, nearly jovial. "Good goddamn thing we don't get one of those every night," he says over the opaque divider. Reid is not sure whether he means the blown call or the game as a whole. He does not ask. "How's the leg?" Kammler goes on.

"It's all right," Reid says. Actually, it is a deep, red-purple color, and is raised in the shape of a large male breast. He has tried to touch it to gauge the depth of the injury, but has not been able to. Toward the bottom half of the circle are stitch imprints, almost as perfectly distinct as on a baseball. Reid moves the leg constantly in the shower, trying to keep the swelling and tightening from becoming too severe.

"At least I get the plate tomorrow night," Kammler is saying. "Save you some bending."

"Right," Reid says. He is not sure he will be able to walk, much less run into the outfield to cover fly balls. For one brief moment he considers walking out. He could get in his car and start for Fremont, as soon as he is dry and dressed. He could be there in twenty hours, and walk into Dr. Branch's office and have him look at the leg. He wonders what keeps him here—what real reason there is to stay. With sabotaging catchers and no-show women, he can think of none. But he pushes the thought aside as quickly as it occurred to him, amid new visions of a league commendation as a result of his handling of the game. But of course there was no one from the league in the stands, and so his only hope is that something will come from one of the managers, who don't tend to think past the next day's pitcher, a cold beer, and payday, so far as Reid can tell.

He touches his upper thigh as lightly as he can with a towel, while Kammler is still in the shower, singing Garth Brooks songs in a voice that is as bad as his umpiring. Kammler, who teaches junior high school history in the off-season, once told Reid over four or five beers that he still thought he could be a pretty fair MOR country singer if he put his mind to it. Reid almost laughs aloud as he remembers this through the pain in his leg. He pulls a yellow pullover down onto his chest, then steps to the mirror to look at the bruise again. It is bright and large and alive, more riveting than the clump of his sex next to it. He knows he should go to the hospital. The only real benefit that the league offers is that if you are injured in a game they take care of it. Reid doubts he will go, and decides to admire his thinness in the mirror, the hang of the yellow shirt at his waist, the sturdy look of his legs. He grimaces as he bends his left leg to pull up his underwear, and then repeats the pain with dark blue slacks. He slips his sockless feet into Cordovan penny loafers, throws his baseball clothing into the laundry cart, and puts his soap and shampoo into his bag. He combs his hair back so that it will dry light and full as it falls back forward, and tells Kammler he'll see him back at the hotel or something.

"You want to wait?" Kammler says, sounding almost offended. Reid is not sure why Kammler wants him to wait. They have not spent an evening together since their first three or four games together. Reid wonders if the older man is offering protection from the bat wielder. Or is just lonely himself, or if he perhaps is looking for a way to apologize for the blown play.

"I think I'll go ahead," Reid says. Outside he decides to be wary, but sees nothing. There are only four or five cars on the forlorn rock lot just outside of Callis Field, and the moon-tinted expanse of space away from the cars appears to be empty, without threat. Reid walks even more slowly now, allowing himself the knowledge that the leg may really need attention. He doesn't know a doctor in Blueston, but is sure that there is one associated with the Braves. He pictures the doctor refusing to treat him, berating him for bad calls, and telling him to see an eye specialist. He is all the way to his car before he realizes that the front tires are flat. He throws his bag against the hood of the car—a six-year-old Toyota he inherited from his father—and then winces as he tries to stoop to see if the tires have been cut or just deflated. He holds his bad leg out straight behind him as he bends to look. Halfway down he comes up again and spins around, fists formed.

"No," she cries, as if already hit. "It's me."

"Jesus," he says, "don't sneak up…"

"I'm sorry." She is moon-lit, damp-looking. A plain, thin white blouse allows her tan to show through, even at night. The blouse is tucked into newish blue jeans. Several fingers of one hand are stuck down to the second knuckle in a tight front pocket as she narrows her shoulders as a part of an apology. "I guess I really did want to surprise you though. I saw you and Fred Southmire…"

"Who?"

"The guy with the bat. I'm sorry I'm so late, Lenny, but Michael has a fever and kept crying, and I really get worried over a fever in summer. I kept trying to leave and Mom kept telling me to. What happened to your leg?"

"I got hit," Reid says, "with a fastball. And now my damn tires are flat. How come I didn't see you when you saw this Fred guy?"

"I was on my way in from out here, and then I stopped and decided to let you go ahead and shower. I thought it might embarrass you to have the girl show up right after this guy tries to club you. I have my car, Len." She motions toward her car, an old red Impala that Reid, in his pain and anger, failed to recognize. "I'll get Triple A to come out for you." She touches his arm lightly now, as if sensing that he needs to be approached tentatively.

"Let me just look at the tires," he says.

She pulls more strongly at his arm. "It's okay, Lenny, it's okay. They'll fix it. And we'll get Southmire to pay for it. He's always sorry the next day, and he's one of the few still on at the foundry, so he can handle it. And he will." She guides him away from the Toyota, taking his bag. She moves her arm around his waist, as if to help support the bad leg. Reid conquers a momentary urge to limp more severely, to lean into her. As they move toward her car the first breeze of the night hits the back of his neck.

His body moves in sympathetic motions with hers as she moves him toward the driver's side of her car. He has always driven when they are in a car, and the injured leg will not keep him from doing it now, especially since the car is an automatic. At the wheel, as he turns and looks back over his right shoulder to back the car out, she slides herself in beneath his arm, and brings her own arm across his stomach as she pushes her head to his chest in a soft, quick hug of sympathy and apology.

On the empty little road toward town Reid glances back at Callis Field. The mountain behind it is silhouetted by the moonlight, and the angles of the gates and walls around the field are softened by the light and the huge dark mountain behind them. On down the road, the town is still distant enough to be unspecific—to be made of a spread of lights that are yet so small as to be mistaken for reflections of the stars. The tall foundry buildings at the western end of town reach up into the night as if in competition with the mountains for the light of the moon. As Reid drives with Ellen next to him, the town is somehow transformed. Covered with night, it takes on the little-town virtues she talks about so often, and which excited Reid when he first got out a map to see where his new Southern Mountains League job would take him. With her little shoulders beneath his arm, he is able to allow her to embody the feel and spirit of the sweet southern town he had expected to find. It is the feel of the shoulders that overtakes him as he aims the car along the last ridge before the road turns to pass the flat-roofed restaurants and bars that signal the beginning of downtown. The dull throb of his leg is all at once no more than evidence that he has done his work for the day and done it well, and has earned this drive into the night. He is poised just then—still high above the harshness of the town, and at the first soft edge of love for the woman.

DEBUT

Talley has to walk the mile and a half to Becky's house because her brother borrowed the Buick in the morning to go into town for a piece of copper pipe and didn't return the car. By now it is late in the afternoon, and though the day has cooled, the air is still tight with the thin whine of insects and a high haze made of road dust and pollen. Talley doesn't mind the walk on the dirt road or the heat, or the fact that Batey used the Buick and never brought it back when his own truck was sitting in the front yard with no more wrong with it than that he hadn't gotten around to bleeding the brakes. What Talley does mind is being dressed in a lime green shirt with darker green trim around the collar, and dark green slacks. And black shoes with heels. He is dressed in the silly green clothes because Becky wants him to look that way when they go to the Hilltop. Every few steps Talley sniffs at the air, the way a cat does when it is put out into the evening. The sun glints through tall, skinny beeches to play at his eyes as he walks. Talley is thirty-four, and as thin and long-limbed as the trees.

He has walked the road—County 642 on the map—hundreds of times during his life. It used to run across U.S. 11 and then on to Blueston, but when the interstate came through it cut off the road and the plans to pave it in the middle of noplace. Talley still uses 642 to get over to 11, where he runs what Becky calls an oversized fruit stand. Talley sells pottery and rugs and legal fireworks and gadgets and cigarettes and a lot of other things in addition to the fruit. For a long time he offered all the cider you wanted for a dime, until it got too expensive. Becky does not like his business one bit. He bought it when she was twenty-one and he was twenty-five. They had been going together for almost three years at the time and Becky agreed with Henry Settles, who owned the store before Talley, in the opinion that Talley was a fool to buy it. The interstate had long since sucked away all of the out-of-state traffic, and they were the only people with money to buy anything. Settles said he had waited for years for the traffic to return, and only wanted nine hundred and fifty dollars for the whole thing. Then Settles, who was leaving to live in Florida, threw in the Buick Talley still drives, and Talley couldn't say no.

Talley and Becky are going to a tavern out on Route 11. Before it was the Hilltop it was Tommy's and before that the Starview Lounge. Now there is a little stage for a band, and the waitresses all dress alike in skirts that look like tablecloths to Talley. The place used to be just a bar, no matter what the name was, and you could go in and have a beer in peace. Now it is fancy, and some nights there is a charge at the door. The last time Talley was in, there were a lot of players from the Blueston baseball team in there. They were big and hard-armed and loud. They seemed like invaders to Talley as they nodded their heads to the music and drank their pitchers of beer. All of it made Talley angry for some reason that he did not understand. Maybe it was just seeing a business along Route 11 doing okay. Maybe it was the fancy bar or the baseball players or the band or the cover charge. So he left.

Talley's own business used to stand between an East Coast station with twelve pumps and a motel called the Shimmering Willows. When Tally was a boy, the Shimmering Willows had individual cabins that sat back off the highway in a grove of trees that were not willows. While Henry Settles still owned the stand, the East Coast station cut down to four pumps and they quit painting the Shimmering Willows every spring. Talley sat out in front of his store over the next few years and watched the motel go out of business. The cabins no longer have any windows in them. Sometimes at twilight they remind Talley of skeletons. The East Coast station changed to Gulf for a while and then went out of business, leaving Talley's as the only business on that side of the road for nearly a mile in either direction. Across from Talley's is an unpaved turnaround that has not changed for as long as Talley can remember the highway.

For six months back about five years ago, when Becky and Talley were going to get married, Talley let her brother run the store. Becky told Talley she would leave him forever if he didn't get a real job and save some money for them. He went to work at the foundry in Blueston when there were still a few jobs there, and saved nine hundred dollars. Then he and Becky had a big fight over the date of the wedding and Talley quit the foundry and went back to the store full-time. They did not get married then, and have not since. People don't expect Talley and Becky to get married anymore. People ask each other why they don't at least live together, and people who know Talley and Becky well can measure the seasons of the year by the fights Becky and Talley have, usually over Talley's backing away from a date for the marriage. Becky won't see him for a week or so, and then it will turn summer, or whatever season is due.

Becky is going to sing in the Hilltop. People have been telling her that she could sing since long before she met Talley. She used to sing solos in church, and once sang at a wedding of some people she barely knew. When she first told Talley about the audition at the Hilltop, he told her she couldn't do it, and they had a big fight out of season. It took him two days to calm down enough for her to go, and he knew that part of the reason he gave in was that she would have gone anyway. He told her there was no way he'd come see her if she got the job. After the audition she showed up at the store—for the first time in months—to tell him about it right away. Talley was out front talking to a man about how his genuine Indian blankets were better than regular Sears blankets, for example, because of the Mohican weave. And Becky just butted in with her news. Talley said, "Excuse me, Miss," and went back to his customer.

As Talley walks, he envisions Becky getting ready, with the new dress. He has known Becky Arrington for almost fifteen years, and so he can almost know what she is thinking without even being there. He can see her now in her bedroom, standing in front of her mirror playing with the loose frills of the dress—making them fall over the tops of her breasts in different ways. She is too proud of her breasts to Talley's mind. She bought the dress in the Belk store over in Cauthen and paid about as much for it as you'd pay for two new radial tires. She held it up in front of herself when she first got it home and yelled until Talley looked at it.

In less than an hour they'll be in the Hilltop with her in the dress. She plans to start out with "Silver Threads and Golden Needles," because she says you need to start an audience with a relatively up-tempo song. Then she will start in with the slow, aching ballads she has learned from Patsy Cline and Tammy Wynette records. She never listens to anything new.

Talley sees her finish with the dress and then move to the top of her dresser to mess with her earrings and maybe rearrange the pictures she has in little wallet-size frames she got from Wal-Mart. She moves the pictures every time she is angry or nervous. Once her brother Batey told Talley that every time she has a fight with Talley, the two pictures of him go all the way down to the right-hand end of the dresser. One of the pictures of Talley is when he got home from the army and still had his uniform on. He told Becky they would get married soon, and she told him in that case they could just as easily wait until then to get fully reacquainted, if he knew what she meant. He can remember the feel of the lower part of her back as they kissed. He can see Becky leave the dresser now, pushing at her hair and then sitting down on the bed to practice the beginnings of her songs. She will be waiting for him when he gets there, glancing at her watch.

At the house, Talley sees Batey Arrington's shoe bottoms before he sees anything else. Batey is under the truck and his father is inside. They are bleeding the brakes.

"Woo, look at Long Tall Talley here this evening," Ralph Arrington says over the steering wheel.

"Pump it," Batey says from under the truck.

"Talley is all greened up just the way Becky said he would be," Ralph says. He grins at Talley as he reports this to his son. "Brand new shirt with dust all over his shoes."

Talley walks by the truck without looking at Ralph. "Keys in the car?" he says.

"In on the kitchen table," Batey calls up.

Talley goes into the house and sits down at the kitchen table. He twirls the keys in his fingers and looks above the refrigerator at the clock. There is a piece of food near the nine. It has been there for as long as he can remember, but he has not thought about it for a long time.

"Talley?" Her voice is high and excited.

"I'm here."

"Are we going in the Buick?"

"They're still bleeding the brakes in the truck," Talley says, as if this is an answer. He rubs at his shoes with a paper napkin that was on the table. Becky comes into the kitchen and Talley looks up, immediately aware that she is trying to make an entrance. He goes back to his shoes.

"Aren't you going to say anything?"

"I think they're still bleeding the brakes," Talley says.

"You know what I mean," she says.

In the yard Batey and Ralph are still in their positions at the truck. Ralph says Talley and Becky look like the Greendust Twins. Becky asks them how they can still be working on the truck when she is due on stage in less than an hour.

"You two go ahead," Batey says, speaking to a wheel. "We'll get cleaned up and be right along."

Becky walks to the truck and kisses her father. She kicks one of Batey's shoes and tells him if he really does go to the ballgame instead of coming to see her that she'll never speak to him again. He tells her to take it easy, that there isn't even a game tonight, and then Talley and Becky get into the car. She places herself carefully on the seat and smooths the dress. Talley backs the car onto the road without a word. He doesn't say anything while they drive along 642, going too fast and leaving a high trail of dust behind in the twilight. When they are near Route 11, the car begins to sway beneath them, and Talley stops. He gets out and walks around the car and announces a flat tire.

"It can't be," Becky says in a high whine. "How can we have a flat now?"

"I guess a nail or a piece of glass," Talley says. He sits down on the front bumper of the car. There has not been a spare in the car since he got it from Henry Settles. When something goes wrong with a tire he stops at the station in toward Blueston and buys a used tire for a few dollars.

"We can't just sit here, Talley," Becky says. "I'll be on in less than an hour."

"I'll be on in less than an hour," Talley says in a boyish, high-pitched imitation of a female voice.

"One of us will have to go back and get Dad and Batey," she says.

"They'll be here before either one of us could get there," Talley says.

Becky gets out of the car and walks up toward the front to look at the tire.

"Well I can't just sit here," she says. "I'll go crazy. I'm going back to get them." "Suit yourself," Talley says. He slides off his perch on the bumper and sits on the road, his back against the car. The sun has already sunk below the ridge on the far side of Route 11. Talley pulls at a thread on his pantleg and listens to the cars out on there on the highway. Every car is a potential customer for the store, shut down before dusk for the first time in a long time. He judges the traffic to be heavy. After a few minutes he calls out Becky's name. There is no answer. Then he thinks more about the noise of the traffic. He has been watching traffic on 11 since he was born. It used to be as sure and regular as his own pulse. Trucks used to roll up and down all night long when he was a boy, doing the commerce of the Eastern Seaboard, before the interstate took over.

After a few minutes he stands up and looks at the tire again. He kicks at the wheel and then gets in the car. He lets his forehead rest against the bumps on the steering wheel and reads dead gauges on the dashboard. He knows Becky can sing. He doesn't need to hear her to know. She used to sing for him over records played low. It made him ache for her when she forgot he was there and started concentrating on her voice. The tendons in her neck got tight all the way down to her collarbones. Talley can hardly stand the thought of other people seeing that. And Becky getting paid for it. He pushes the clutch and starts the Buick. He lets the engine run a while, as if he listening for a ping or something. Then he starts slowly along the road. The bad tire thumps softly and the car sways easily. At Route 11 he makes the turn away from Blueston and the Hilltop. He drives along the shoulder toward Talley's Store. Cars zing past him. It is less than half a mile to the store.

He rolls the Buick onto his rock lot, letting it coast in, as if this will help save the tire and rim. He looks briefly at the tire when he gets out. He unlocks the wire gate that encloses the front of the store, and then goes back for the lights. He got brand new lights after a man from Richmond who did lighting for a living told Talley he could increase his after-dark business fifty percent if he got fluorescent lighting to replace the overhanging lights that had been there forever. Talley didn't particularly believe the man, but after he thought about it a while he did put in some horizontal blue tubes across the front. He's not sure if business has changed any or not. But the bright blue tubes do seem to make the store stick out a little farther toward the road. Talley goes back to the cooler and takes out a sixteen-ounce Pepsi and sits down in his chair. The upholstery sticks out in gray tufts at the arms and the edge of the seat. In the chair Talley feels at peace for the first time all day. He does not have to think about Becky and the Hilltop. He can think about traffic. On the highway it is nearly dark now, and the cars are fast and sure. He doesn't care if they stop or not—just that they are there. His father used to tell him about the days before the interstate, and before that about the railroads. His father said that just as the interstate took the traffic away from 11, so too had 11 taken it away from the railroads. Talley's father worked thirty-four years for the Norfolk & Western, and saw Route 11 as helping to take away his livelihood. Talley wonders what the railroads killed. Wagon trails maybe.

When he has made himself angry enough about the traffic getting drained away from Route 11, Talley stands up and throws the Pepsi bottle across the highway to the turnaround. It lands without breaking and Talley goes back to his chair. He curses the flat tire and Becky singing at the Hilltop in front of all those baseball players. A car pulls onto the lot next to the Buick. Local plates. A man Talley doesn't know gets out of the car. "Cold beer?" he says to Talley. "Nope," Talley says. "No beer here." He has said that a thousand times if he's said it once, thinking each and every time that he'll try to get back the ABC license that Settles had and gave up when Talley bought the store.

Talley sits in his chair and watches cars pass. He bites at a spot on his lower lip until it hurts. When he has waited long enough he goes back and turns off the blue tubes and puts the wire gate back in place. He gets in the Buick and backs it straight across the highway into the turnaround, as if he's going to take off fast. Then he starts his slow, bumping drive down the shoulder toward Blueston. Someone in a speeding car yells something at Talley that he does not understand. At 642 he looks back up the road for the truck. He sees nothing but darkness. He keeps the speedometer between ten and fifteen, letting himself rock with the car. He drives for four miles, shouting randomly at things he sees, hears and thinks about. Mostly about Becky.

When Barnes' 66 comes into view—it doesn't have that kind of gas anymore, but the sign is still there—Talley pushes down a little harder on the gas, as if to make it appear that the tire just then went flat on him. He pulls up past the pumps and aims the Buick toward the closed-up service bays. Eddie Johnson rocks off a chair by the oil display and walks over to Talley.

"Ate that one up pretty good, didn't you Talley," he says, and flicks ashes.

"Good enough," Talley says. "You got a rim around this hellhole?"

"Oh lots, Talley. Plenty of rims. Any particular size?" Eddie Johnson laughs a quick laugh through his nose. "And did you want a tire to go with it?" He laughs again.

Talley doesn't say anything. Eddie Johnson pulls open one of the service doors and goes into the bay that is filled with tires and batteries and generators, thrown at all angles. He comes back with a worn tire on a rim.

"My size?" Talley says.

"G-seventy-eight fourteen," Eddie Johnson says. "A Vernon Talley Special." He puts the tire on the ground and rolls it toward the car. The tire bounces off Talley's front bumper while Eddie Johnson goes back in for the roll jack.

"Seen Becky and Batey and their dad go by here like ninety," Eddie Johnson calls out as he knocks some tires off the jack. "All ready for the family debut, I guess."

Talley feels blood in his face, knowing Eddie Johnson isn't worth the trouble.

"Had two cars stop by here to ask where the Hilltop was," Eddie Johnson says with a quick laugh. "Four, five guys in each one. Ballplayers, I'd guess."

Talley decides it is a lie, but feels his face get warmer. It is possible that the team that's supposed to start a series tomorrow night is already in town, helping to turn Becky into a piece of sought-out public property.

"You see the ad in the Cauthen papers?" Eddie Johnson is rolling the jack under Talley's car. "'The Hilltop presents Rebecca Arrington—New Country Singer'?"

"Put the tire on the car," Talley says.

When the tire is on, Talley gives Eddie Johnson a twenty dollar bill without asking how much the job costs. Then he gets in the car and heads out onto 11, the headlights flashing up against the trees as he hits the dip at the edge of the lot. On the straightaway where he learned to drive, Talley takes the Buick up past eighty before it starts shimmying, and then slows for his approach to the Hilltop. The lot is full of cars and pickups parked all over the place. Talley stops his car on the opposite side of the road and walks across the highway. He can hear a band but no voice. In the lot, several men are standing behind a truck, drinking beer and laughing. They are big enough to be baseball players, Talley thinks. As he steps into the Hilltop, Talley relaxes slightly. He suddenly remembers the green shirt with green rimming and the dark green slacks. He pays the cover and starts in.

"Yo Talley." It is Batey calling him. He and Ralph are at a table back against the wall, waving.

"Oh, Talley, you got her this time," Batey says when Talley is three tables away. "I mean she is *fit*. Where you been?"

"Check the store," Talley says. "Forgot to lock up."

"That's good, Talley," Batey says. "She won't buy that if you paint it gold."

"Shut up, Batey," Talley says softly. "Where is she?"

"Back in the office," Batey says. "Waiting for the band to get warmed up so they can announce her."

Talley tells Batey to shut up again and then he walks away from the table and past the bar to the hallway where the office and the restrooms are. He pushes open the office door. Becky is talking across the desk to the man who hired her. She looks up quickly at Talley and then turns with some ceremony back to the man at the desk. "I'll just keep singing, Burt," she says. "No way crowd noise is going to bother me. I've waited too long for this." She smooths her dress with an affected flourish that cuts to Talley's heart.

"What can we do for you?" Burt says to Talley.

Talley takes a step forward. "You can just give me a minute with the singer here," he says softly. "I need to apologize for being late." Talley has to force an exaggerated smile to cover the sweetness of what he has said. Becky looks up at him and then moves her eyes away when he looks at her.

"She's on in just a minute here, son," Burt says, standing. He moves past Talley and out the door.

"Don't say a thing," Talley says to Becky before Burt is even all the way out the door. "I came in here to tell you we'll get married tomorrow." Becky's face falls momentarily limp and whitish. Talley thinks about that he didn't know he would say that until he did. Becky looks away from Talley for a second and takes a breath. "Well, Talley, with the blood test and all—"

Talley winces at her technicalities and waves his arm. "Whenever," he says. He stands still as Becky looks him up and down in his green uniform. He can tell she's trying to see if he's telling the truth, and he wonders again himself. It just all came out when he saw the split of her breasts peeking out of her dress across the desk to Burt.

Becky stands to kiss Talley, just as Burt comes back into the room to tell her she's on. She leans and kisses Talley on the cheek, not disturbing her frills, and follows Burt out the door, waving a little-girl wave back at Talley. Talley winces again and then gets up and goes out into the hallway. He goes down past the restrooms and the stacks of Miller kegs and goes out the back door, into the warmest night yet of the new summer. Maybe he will marry Becky Arrington. Maybe he will. But there is no way he'll go out into the bar and take a chance on her announcing it right there on stage before she starts in with "Silver Threads and Golden Needles." No way in hell.

TELLING BRENDA

It's been a whole series of things the last few weeks, but the major one right now is Brenda all of a sudden deciding to come home for a visit after three and a half years. She called last week to say she'd be here yesterday or today. When I told Elaine, who's been my neighbor and best friend since Brenda was about two, Elaine started right in on the room situation.

"Whatever the problem with the room," I told Elaine right off, "she's brought it on herself. Nobody put in any kind of special request for her to stay away for years at a time."

To which Elaine couldn't say all that much, especially considering that some of the airplanes Brenda struts around in land less than three hundred miles from here. But that's the way Brenda's done it, like maybe this town, this house, this family—what's left of it—aren't good enough for her anymore. When she first got the airline job, she did come back now and again—especially when her daddy was alive—but once she moved to Hawaii to live with two girls who went to *college*—in an apartment so high up she says she looks down on the volcanoes—she just decided she didn't have any need to come home and see her mom anymore. She moved out about three months after Vince died, and has stayed away from here as if she thinks maybe she'll get back and not be able to leave again—which is exactly what she used to tell Vince and me, starting back when she was about ten. "If I ever get out of this town, I'll never be back," she would say in some way or another, and two years out of high school—after working about half that time in a snooty restaurant in town—she got the airline job and started working on proving it. Since then she's scaled back the home visits until it's gotten down to just about zero.

Elaine keeps wanting to make it like a celebration. Like I should just take the three years and forget it and welcome Brenda with open arms. Elaine, who in real life has worked for the meat department for the Kroger Company for thirty-some years, lives the rest of her life in this kind of fairy tale where for one thing she thinks she should have been Patsy Cline. And she will tell you any day of the week that somebody or other is looking at three or four of her songs down in Nashville even as she speaks, and that she knows she'll hit it big as a songwriter before she's fifty-five. She's been adding five years to that ever since her twenties. She specializes in those songs with trick titles, trying to figure out how to write one like "Drink Canada Dry" or "The Old School." Right now she's working on one where the singer tires of her honey, so she's getting new tires on her car before she retires from the relationship. "It's got the road and everything it in," she told me yesterday. But that's about as far as she gets toward real finished product. She tried for years to get Brenda to sing—the one good thing Elaine ever did with her—but it never worked. It was like the more she tried, the more Brenda resisted.

Not that has anything to do with the changes in Brenda's room. Actually, I had started displaying some of the collections—records, books, posters, some of the larger things—far before she left, some of it before she was even born. Before she came along, I had all the 45s Elvis ever made up to that time. And I have all of them since, too, by the way. She knew about the collections from the day she could know about anything. And so did Vince for that matter. The first time I ever saw Vince was at a hop when I was fourteen and he was seventeen. He had already heard about me from somebody as a matter of fact, because the first time we danced—it was the

Everlys' "Bird Dog"—he said to me, hey, aren't you the one who knows all the words to all of Elvis's songs—even the other sides? And of course I was and of course that never changed over the three years before we got married or the twenty-nine years we were married after that. Vince's mother told him one time before we got married that if Elvis came along and so much as asked me to shine his shoes, that I'd have been gone so fast you wouldn't have seen a shadow. And I was just hot enough over that to tell her it was probably true. To her face. So no grief about Vince, please. He knew from the start. He even helped me put up the first shelves for the collections—out there in the front room. And that was way before Brenda said anything about leaving. Vince knew from the start. Elaine used to tell him it was no real problem, and that may have helped. The only problem was that for several years there she was working on a song called something like "I Married Your Daddy Cause Elvis Wasn't At The Chapel," but she never found a decent rhyme for "chapel" and finally gave up on it.

Vince's mother, on the other hand, still finds ways to get to me—through her friends who know my friends—little hinty things about

Vince's heart and her heart and Brenda's heart. Melodramatic, if you ask me. Once, not too long after Vince died, she told some of the girls at the hospital—I've been a nurse's aide with the newborns for more years than I'll admit—that what happened was that Vince just got totally squeezed out of his own house by Elvis garbage—that's the way she put it—which is ridiculous when you consider that there are still three big saws and a bunch of car magazines and two rifles down in the basement. Plus nobody ever messed with Vince's TV chair and magazine corner no matter what. And I never said I didn't love Vince, because I did. He was a good provider, and the railroad kept him away just enough to make it good when he was home. Plus Vince understood, really, that he had to have his interests and I had to have mine. It wasn't like I was really *after* Elvis, or anything, and about half the times I went to Graceland while Vince was alive, he went along. Just like I went with him a bunch of times to the car races in Charlotte and Martinsville and you name it. I think Vince resented never having a son, or even any more kids after Brenda—people on pediatrics always joke that you can't have kids when you're around that many being born, and I'm not so sure there isn't something to that. Elaine wrote a song back in the '70s on that—I think the first line was something like "I'm with him in bed at nighttime, with the babies all day, but one of my own, Lord, there's just no way"—and maybe he conveyed that in some way to his mother. And when you get right down to it, in addition to Vince knowing full well about where he fit in my life, way before we got married, he also carried sort of a rock'n'roll torch himself—for Brenda Lee of all people, which I'm not so sure didn't have something to do with the push he gave when it came to a name for the now long-awaited airline stew, who happens to hate it so much that she spells it *Brendah* sometimes, which I think is worse. She would hate it even more if she knew it probably came from Brenda Lee. Which is part of why I keep telling Elaine to give me a break with the whole thing. "How Brenda takes the news about her room is a whole lot more up to Brenda than it is to me," I've told Elaine over and over again. "The place is straight and neat, and there's plenty of room," I told her, "so just back off in her behalf." Then Elaine took it upon herself to remind me of this one newspaper guy when he came in and took one look at the Teddy Bear collection and a few statuettes that I have in the den and then wrote that I barely had enough room to move around for all the Elvisana, as he called it in the paper.

Which reminds me of one of the other things that's been bothering me lately. I used to let the papers in any time they wanted to do a story. Show them the rooms, let them take shots of anything they wanted. But a few years ago a couple of things mysteriously disappeared, including a set of autographed posters, and so I put an end to it. And I'm not sure the papers didn't have something to do—indirectly at least—with the problem I have to face next week right after Brenda's visit, assuming she lasts a week—because she has the choice of either staying in the room with me, on the rollaway in the basement or—and this is if she can choose to be careful—in her old room, on the bed that has been made up to look just like the one in Tupelo that Elvis slept in as a boy. Anyway, whether she lasts a week or not, a week from tomorrow is when I have my hearing with the zoning commission over the yard. You may have seen this in the papers no matter where you live, because even though both of the biggest stories were done here by the local paper, they were both picked up by the AP, I think it was, and sent out all over the place. One was about two years after Elvis died, and the second one was on the last anniversary of his death. Elaine's brother out in Ohio saw the second one in his paper. What has happened since, though—and maybe it was building before the story because several people down at the end of the block had been complaining about property values ever since I started to build out there—is that the city is making me come in to talk about how some of the buildings in the Graceland model are too close to the street. I thought it was a crank call at first, and I thought it was a crank letter the first time, but I guess what they're trying to tell me is that the Chapel building—it's no bigger than a small doghouse—is less than fifteen feet from the street, which they say is in violation of the building codes or the street codes or some damn thing. Meanwhile, up and down the streets in this neighborhood you have doghouses and tool sheds and yards full of flamingos and bird feeders and broken-down cars, and Elaine even has two of those little black guys—painted over, of course—holding their hands out, and it's me they decide to go after. Over in the southwest section of the city they have homes tours and mansions and bed & breakfasts that people come to look at, and they like it because it builds up the neighborhood—makes for civic pride and the like. Over here, except for the mini-Graceland, you got zip. One or two yards with nice Christmas lights, but that's what, two or three weeks out of the year? I'll appeal through city council and all the away to the Supreme Court if I need to. They're talking about the largest scale model of Elvis's home in the state of Virginia, and probably the largest outside of Tennessee and Mississippi in case they don't realize it, and I know it's to scale because I spent over two years—and both Vince and Elaine helped me with this—getting the exact dimensions of the place. It took so many letters I lost count, but they finally got it through their heads that I wasn't trying to blow the place up or break in—just that I wanted my model right.

I think, looking back on that time now, that Vince and Elaine both were probably humoring me along, like I'd never really get out there with the wood and the nails and paint and start the thing. But even before Elvis died, I had the wall built and the driveway in, and the little shrubs, which by the way are rapidly getting out of proportion again. Vince refused to mow that end of the yard toward the end—said it was too cluttered to get through. Anyway, once he died—a massive heart attack—I started on it strong. And Elaine seemed to take over as the new major doubter. "Are you sure you want all this in your yard?" she kept asking.

By the end of the summer after Vince died, I had over half of the real work done. Since that time it's been mostly cosmetic things. It took two months to find somebody to build the little gates. I'd go into these fence places, and they'd have these miniature fencing displays to show you how your fence will look, and I'd think surely *these* guys can do it. Two of them said they would and never did. We're talking about two little pieces of gate like two feet high and a foot wide, for God's sake.

Hold on, there's the phone. I have a call in to Graceland for some information on the next birthday celebration down there. I'm working on putting together the biggest bus tour ever to go down there out of this region. So I imagine it's them.

It wasn't them. Have you ever had a grave salesmen call you? Creepy as hell. This is the second one that's called in the last two months. They must have some kind of computerized deal where they have everybody in there and once you hit fifty-five, they start calling you every other week to see where you want to get buried. The last time one called I told Elaine about it and she started giving me this whole history on how her whole family was already all set for Emerson Heights Cemetery, as if I didn't know.

"You know," I said to her, just thinking of it then, "I think I may have them go ahead and put me in the ground right out there somewhere in the Graceland model."

We were drinking coffee in her kitchen and Elaine got up and went over to the sink to mess with the dishes, like women do when they get upset. "In your *yard*?" she said in kind of a high voice while she looked out into her own back yard. "You want to be buried in your own yard? You think the city would allow that? You think anybody would ever buy the property?"

"It's just an idea, Elaine," I said. "Take it easy."

"And with Vince over in Highview?"

"Hey," I said, maybe as much to get her goat as anything, "we could always move Vince, you know?"

She didn't get over it for weeks. And I'm still thinking about it. Anyway, as I was going to say, the other thing that torques me is that I know Brenda will at least pretend to hate it, and ask me how a grown woman—a responsible grown woman with a job in a hospital, she'll say—can have all this Elvis crap around. But even with all that, Brenda has never really taken the time to inspect the whole model out there, and I'd kind of like her to see what the old lady put together, from concept to carpentry. And I'd like that to happen without her having the satisfaction of knowing that the city is out to have the whole thing taken down, or at least put in the back yard.

Okay, so Brenda's due, Elaine's always carping, the city's on my back, and then there's the newsletter. My own newsletter. I'll admit that for years it just got circulated among some friends here in town, and before that never got beyond Vince and me and Elaine, but I have it on pretty good authority that *Elvis Notes* is the second-oldest continuously in-print newsletter on him ever. I've done four a year since back in the sixties, and before that I kept scrap books and wrote stuff up from them at least that often. While he was alive, Elvis got a copy of every single one, and I still send them to Priscilla and Lisa Marie when I know where they are. My mailing list is up near a hundred now, which is a hit in the pocket book when you consider postage these days, and the cost of running them off. But that's not the thing that bothers me. What gripes me is that I've never gotten a dime's worth of help from anywhere. Not from the Elvis himself—who never acknowledged what I sent him over all those years—not from Colonel Tom, not from Elvis Inc., or any of the fan clubs or conventions or anybody. Like *my* newsletter isn't good enough. Maybe because it comes out of Virginia instead of Tennessee—I can't figure it. But I can tell you here and now there isn't anybody around who knows more about Elvis to put in a newsletter than I do. Sometimes Elaine reads it and shakes her head and asks me how I know all that stuff. And sometimes when she talks like that I just go off—give her my own question-and-answer quiz show. I have a set of three by five cards with millions of Elvis facts on them. I can hand the whole box to Elaine and have her ask me any one she picks, and it's about ninety-nine percent I'll get it right. Questions are on the front, answers on the back. Here, let me grab the first three questions I see. *Which twin was born first, Elvis or his brother?* The other boy came first, at four a.m. on January 8, 1935. Elvis was half an hour late, as usual. *Where did the family live when they first moved from Tupelo to Memphis?* Apartment 328 in the Lauderdale Courts. Elvis was fourteen. *Where did he first hear the music that would change the world once he digested it?* WDIA in Memphis, after it almost went bust and then went to a black music format in 1948—like they knew Elvis was out there to listen and learn.

I could go on and on, but if you want more, then try the newsletter. And I know you can't know for sure that I didn't turn any cards over, but I swear on a stack I don't need to. Elaine can vouch. It's the kind of stuff that's stayed with me, the way stuff about your own kids does. But still, the newsletter has been a burden. Once, right after Elvis died, some people took a whole lot of my stuff—out of my memorial issue from right after he died—and ran it in two other newsletters like they'd made it up themselves. That's happened a lot over the years. People are like that. They see something they want and they just take it, without much of any thought about what it might mean to somebody else. Take the hospital for instance. I've been on that ward long enough to see a whole generation grow up and come back to have its own babies. I must have seen a hundred nurses come and go—maybe more.

Wait a second, there's the door. If it's not Elaine then it must be Brenda, sauntering home after all these years, and the first thing she'll have to say is either how I've ruined the yard or how could I have gained all this weight. Or maybe what the hell happened to her room.

It wasn't either one of them. I think the Mormons must be attracted to the model or something because it seems like every other week they're around here in their Wal-Mart suits with their newsletters. Vince used to say they spelled their name wrong—that the second "m" wasn't supposed to be there, but I guess that's a little unkind for people who are doing their best. But have you ever seen those newsletters? Circulation's way up in the millions, they claim. I don't believe it for a second, unless you count all the ones they leave at people's doors because people would rather fork over some small change and get the boys off the front porch and get back to the dishes or whatever. I don't mean to sound sacrilegious or anything, but it does gripe me to see their stuff going all over the world while the *Elvis Notes* goes noplace. Plus who ever heard of selling religion door-to-door anyway?

As I was saying before the disciples of Joe Smith came by—what a name for a founder—you need to be careful about trusting even the people you've known the longest. Listen to this. In the entire time I've been on pediatrics—beyond a quarter century as they say—in all that time there have been, to my knowledge, five babies to go out of there with the King's name. And nobody—again that I know about—with both names. Elvis Aron. And you think about that there are about eighty-five babies born there a month. Elaine is way better at percentages than I am, and she couldn't even figure out what that is—but it is five out of about twenty-two thousand. Fairly low, I'm venturing. Lower than the general population, I'd bet. Especially here in the South. I figure there must be thousands—I mean did the Presley family *invent* the damn name? Hell no. It existed way before Gladys and Vernon gave it to their boy, and it will exist a whole hell of a lot longer than some of the names that kids leave the ward with these days. We must have had ten little girls named Taylor in the last year or so. And all of a sudden Zachary is all over the place. Last week there was a boy went out of here named Racine of all things. Not to mention all the names I've never even heard of, even on a Wisconsin map. But what I'm getting to is all the garbage I'm getting all of a sudden. It's not like I'm the only one with a pet name for the babies. You hear a lot of Poopsie, Dumpling, Lambikins, Sweetie, Tiger, Honeybunch, Punkinnose—you name it and I bet I've heard a nurse use it. But one particular staffer calling the boy babies Little El nearly cost that one veteran her job a couple of weeks ago when Betty Henderson—a hotshot night supervisor who must have been here all of three years—took it upon her skinny little self to go to Hayward and tell him she felt it was incumbent on her—he said that was the word she used—to let him know there was somebody on his staff who was trying to influence parents on what name they used for their kids. Here she is barely out of puberty, plus treating kids like they come out of computers instead of mothers, and remaining without doubt one of the quickest around here to panic when one of them is short of breath or won't stop crying—you can guess who they come to—and *she* is trying to convince Hayward that I'm not doing my job right.

And Hayward—he's been in charge of this floor for ten years—has the gall to be influenced by this tightass—pardon the French—to the extent that he actually calls me in to talk about it. Sure, he was off-hand and said it was no big deal, but the pure idea of that kind of crap. I told Elaine that that girl doesn't know the real Elvis from the guy who empties the trash cans in the canteen downstairs. And Elaine agreed for a change. Because when you get right down to it, most of that girl's generation has got this attitude about the King—that he was a fake from the start. Now I'm first to admit that he let his talent go to hell as bad as most any major star ever has, but for those years and years there, there was simply nobody that could touch him for talent or charisma. You ask any of the big stars—Jagger, Springsteen, Dylan, any of them—and they'd tell you it all started with one person at one place at one time. And that's Elvis in Memphis in 1956. They all know it. And even Brenda, if she ever gets her hifalutin Hawaiian heinie here, she knows it too. And maybe will be ready to admit it when she sees her mother's finished product out in the yard. Maybe she'll come in and say Christ, Mom, what a job out there. Fat chance. Actually, it's a snowball's chance in hell. And you know, there's a lesson in there she could learn from him if she never learned another thing, and one there's no way she could deny—and come to think of it maybe this is also the thought that could finally get Elaine's songwriting career out of the basement: There was just nobody in this world better to his momma than Elvis.

MINORS

Stanley

"The thing about this guy warming up is that he's the first big leaguer ever—in the whole history of baseball—ever sent all the way back to rookie ball from the big leagues," Stanley is telling the man who just sat down next to them in the stands. "Can you imagine pitching for the St. Louis Cardinals one year and all the way back to the Appalachian League the next?"

The man turns to his wife to relate—with glee—what he's just learned from the boy next to him. Then he turns back to Stanley and looks down at him with a smile.

It surprises Porcia that grown people who must be baseball fans could walk into this little ball park on this night and have to learn about who's pitching from an eleven year-old boy. That Rick Ankiel is all the way down to a league where the towns have five thousand people and names you never heard of. Like Pulaski, Virginia, or Johnson City, Tennessee, which happen to be the two teams playing on this night that Porcia and Stanley and Dorrie have come to watch him pitch. It is a two-hour drive and there is a forty percent chance of rain, but Stanley loves Rick Ankiel more than any other player ever. Plus there wouldn't have been a question about going anyway. It is a Friday night, and neither Porcia nor Dorrie had to even trade a shift.

By the top of the fourth, there's a little bit of a sprinkle starting.

"I told you," Dorrie says easily. Dorrie is Porcia's younger sister—by two years—and got the baseball bug only about six years ago, the same time Stanley did, when he was five and Dorrie was twenty-three. That was also the year after Dorrie got her divorce. Porcia, Dorrie and Stanley have been going to games all over the western side of Virginia and down into the Carolinas every summer since, and Porcia has told Dorrie enough times that the deal with the rain is the same as with the game itself. Just as you never step on the third base line when you're a pitcher heading into the dugout after a good inning, you don't take an umbrella or a rain coat to watch a game, or it'll rain for sure. It's the only disagreement Porcia and her sister ever had about going to the games, and Dorrie relented that first summer, after they drove the sixty miles to see a Class A game and got drilled. Simply because Dorrie took an umbrella.

This is the best game they've been to all year. Rick started slowly, only getting one strikeout in the first, but then he stepped it up and struck out the side in the second and got two more in the third. Plus he is basically cute, and also batting third. By the time he got the three strikeouts in the second, the man next to them decided he wanted to keep score, and Stanley showed him how. The man—maybe fifty—kept turning to his wife with an expression that said *do you believe this kid?*

The rain seems innocent at first—you can see blue all around the one light-gray cloud—but then it opens up as if from nowhere.

"Rick won't pitch no more," Stanley says as they stand up to move out of the rain. "You can stick a fork in him for tonight."

"How do you know?" the man next to them says. He and his wife are walking along with Porcia and Dorrie and Stanley.

"That left arm's just too valuable," Stanley tells him. They are walking with the couple toward the covered part of the stands.

"Boy sure knows his ball," the man says to Porcia.

"Yes, he does," Porcia says, and musses Stanley's hair.

"It's from my dad," Stanley says. "He was on his way up the ladder, but got killed in a car wreck before I was even born, and so he never had a chance at the Show." Porcia told Stanley that when he was five, the first time he asked about his father. He has never asked again and never sought any other details.

"Oh, my," the man's wife says.

"No biggie anymore," Stanley says, smiling up at her. He tells the man to keep his scorecard dry, because it might be worth something someday.

Porcia is both proud and almost frightened when it comes to her son and baseball. Once he finished one year of tee-ball, he refused to play anymore, but he knows more about players and rules and farm systems and card values than Porcia and Dorrie put together. Porcia and her mother used to argue about why Stanley doesn't play. This while her mother—who is built fire-hydrant style just exactly the same as the other three of them—knows good and well why he doesn't play. Stanley at eleven weighs exactly the same that Porcia did the last year she felt like she had a body that would give her a chance with a man—as if she wanted one—a hundred and seventy-four pounds.

"Rick pitched good," Stanley says to Dorrie, "and that means if you can get me down there, I can get him to sign some of the cards." Dorrie has a girlfriend from work who goes with the brother of one of the players on the Johnson City Cardinals.

"Let's see if it's *really* going to rain first, Stan," Dorrie says, and bats at the back of his head, "before you start sending me down into the dugout."

Stanley slaps the side of her leg and uses that hand to direct her glance out onto the field, where the ground crew is sliding around on their sneakers while they push the rolled-up tarp out over the field so they can roll it back and open it up. You can see little bullets of wet red clay shooting up off the infield, the rain is hitting so hard. "I'm telling you," he says, "Rick is toast."

"Not that you never been down in the dugout before, rain or no rain," Porcia says to Dorrie over Stanley's head, just as Dorrie is turning to look out on the field. Porcia says it with a little teasing, sisterly grin and Dorrie crosses her eyes and raises up one side of her upper lip at Porcia.

"No more than you wanted to but didn't have the balls," Dorrie says.

Porcia likes to pretend that she's just as hot for ballplayers as her sister is, and is glad that the couple they were with got up, apparently to leave, just before Dorrie said that.

"You keeping them cards good and dry, Mom?" Stanley says, as if to move the conversation somewhere else. They are five rows up in the covered section along the third base line, behind the visitors' dugout. You can look across the field as the ground crew finally starts to pull out the tarp, and see the home team's players sitting in their dugout in a neat row, watching the rain. Porcia uses that image as sort of a mirror to know what's going on with the Johnson City players.

"Rick's already in the damn shower," Stanley says, as if he knew what she was thinking.

The under-cover seats are just long slabs of concrete that are harder than sidewalks. Porcia finds a spot to stand along the aisle where she feels like she's not blocking anyone too much and stops to look at the field. "He might be right," she says to Dorrie. "That left arm's too precious to let cool down this long and then send back out there the way the temperature changes with a thunder shower. He could wreck a rotator or something—and *never* get back to the bigs."

"All right already," Dorrie says. They all look at the top of the visitors' dugout, as if expecting that one of the players will look over the top and tell Stanley to come on down himself and get Rick to sign the cards. But it is raining so hard—and now even at a little bit of an angle back into the dugout—that Porcia knows it's not going to happen.

"I'd say this delay is going to be long enough to keep the box score out of the paper in the morning," Stanley says.

"We'll be here till midnight and after two getting home," Porcia says.

"So then what's my big damn hurry to get down there?" Dorrie says.

Porcia and Stanley look at her at the same time and with the same roll-eyed, roll-headed expression. It's as if Dorrie wants to pretend she doesn't know what her job is here. Porcia does all the driving and the tickets, Stanley handles the cards and other collectibles and the game details, and Dorrie uses her smile and charm and clear skin to get them into places they otherwise might not get. Plus with a ready-made contact like her nearly best friend being only one step away from having her hand in a second-round draftee's jockstrap, there's not really a challenge at all to get Stanley down there.

"Hell with this," Dorrie says all of a sudden, and strides out from under the cover—away from her sister and nephew, but in the opposite direction of the dugout.

"Clubhouse!" Porcia and Stanley say to each other and at the same time, and slap two high fives in a row. You get to a player in there, it's a thousand times easier to get things signed than at the end of a dugout in the rain, because nobody's watching and so they don't have to look cool and turn you down if you ask for maybe ten cards to get signed. You get a ballplayer on a stool in a clubhouse—just showered or getting ready to—and he's more at ease. Most of these players aren't even twenty years old yet, and Porcia has seen enough of them to know that Dorrie's perfect blend of motherliness and flirting—just enough to make them homesick for both—is unstoppable. It's like her size is not even a factor. And truth be told—Porcia will tell anybody this—there is no one in the world who carries two hundred pounds any prettier—any softer and better spread around—than Dorrie Cregger, who took her maiden name back as fast as lightning once she could—maybe as much to get rid of Rankin as to get Cregger back.

Right now it's just a matter of Porcia and Dorrie watching out for Dorrie to pop back around the corner of the clubhouse ramp with the high sign for Stanley to head down and hand his pen to Rick Ankiel, the big leaguer back in rookie ball headed who knows where from here. And with probably less idea than Stanley what those signed cards might be worth some day.

Dorrie

This was a time when Stanley was on a school field trip all the way to Richmond for three days toward the end of the school year. He didn't want to go, of course, because even in the second grade he was already eat up with baseball, which is why they didn't tell him where they were going while he was going to be away. Porcia had been trying to convince Dorrie to try a baseball game as a way to get away from her troubles, and so Porcia had the two of them plan their days off around it to drive all the way to Myrtle Beach for three Class A games in a row. Partly it was their mother's idea. She told Porcia she couldn't think of a better way to get Dorrie's mind off the divorce than to get her to go with Porcia to one of her dumb minor league games—to numb her out a little, was the way their mother put it. The divorce happened after Dorrie lived for three years with what both her sister and mother had told her in no uncertain terms on the very first day he first showed up was just plain trailer trash with an extra-crappy attitude about the world as a whole, which he was going to unload right the hell onto Doreen Jeanne Cregger the second he got the legal chance.

Which is exactly what happened, in what Porcia and her mother knew to be *the* classic case for Dorrie of once-he-marries-me-he'll-change-his-ways. But of course when the eyes are as sick with it as Dorrie's were at the start, there's nothing you can do but sit by like a stump and watch. And Dorrie held out as long as she could—for pride and hope and the embarrassment of it all—while the asshole didn't change so much as his underwear, and took all his self-hate directly out on Dorrie, sometimes not even waiting till he was drinking to start in. The first time Porcia knew for absolutely sure there was no chance was after they'd been married about three weeks, and Ronnie had gotten all these your-momma's-so-fat jokes from someplace and he was telling her them—"your momma's so fat her belly button don't have lint, it has a *sweater*"—and asking Dorrie if that one was going to apply to her if she ever had kids. The unexplained bruises on her and the days-at-a-time disappearances for him were not far behind. But Dorrie went straight ahead into it for a year and a half—playing the total Queen of Denial—and then it took her exactly another year and a half to get herself back out, get him restrained and even be able to talk about doing something with her big sister.

So the trip to Myrtle Beach was her first getaway after that chapter from hell. It didn't occur to Porcia till afterward that maybe taking her wrecked-up sister to a sinbin coastal town might not have been the best first outing as she worked on re-adapting to the part of the world that doesn't kick the shit out of you and get plastered every night. They got off work at five in the afternoon and drove down, rolling in just before midnight, checking into the condo—just across the street from the oceanfront—and went to sleep.

The next day they did the regular beach things—down toward the water, then the boardwalk, then a buffet and through some shops—to get to the part of the day where it was finally time to head out to the ballpark. Porcia got them great seats, right behind the visitors' dugout. The three-game series was against Frederick, from up in Maryland, and Porcia wasn't sure who to tell Dorrie to root for because neither team was from Virginia, and if the scorecards were up to date, there was only one Virginia player on each roster, so she told Dorrie they should just watch awhile and decide who they liked better.

Dorrie complained a little about the heat—"if I'm going to sit out here and sweat like a pig, I'd at least like to be able to jump in the ocean"—but pretty soon she started talking about how to decide which team to root for.

"Let's see," she said. "The uniforms? How many wear their socks up and how many down? If anybody winks at us?"

"You need to watch a few innings and see who you like," Porcia said.

"Or maybe just butts," Dorrie said, and laughed. "These seats you got us put us in pretty good position to get a good look at these boys walking up to the plate. For complete butt inspection and ratings, I'm talking about. There goes a nine-point-five right now." She pushed at Porcia's arm and directed her toward the Frederick hitter, whose pants were as tight as a football player's. Dorrie was suddenly in the best mood Porcia had seen her in for years.

From there, after Dorrie sipped along on two cups of beer, it went downhill pretty fast, and she ended up crying by the seventh inning. Porcia wasn't at all sure Dorrie was going to want to come back the next night, but the next day Dorrie said hell yes, of course they were going, and did they have the same seats for this game as the last one. Porcia told her they did—for all three games—and Dorrie said she had decided she was basically going to root for *everybody.* "They are all soooo cute," she cooed, and pinched Porcia on the face. "Just babies out there. Big strong babies, but really just babies overall."

Porcia looked sort of cockeyed at her sister. "We're here to watch baseball, Dor', not find you a new problem."

Dorrie smiled at that as if she understood, but by the third inning of that game she had picked up on how to rag an ump and shout out to players from the stands, and already had a few people around her cracking up and waiting for her next line.

"Sweetie, you don't have to hit the ball at all," she called out to big blond twenty-year-old outfielder who had just struck out on three pitches, "you can just stand there and look pretty for me." He looked up at her, trying not to grin.

And once she'd gotten over her certainty that the home plate umpire's emphatic called-third strike gyrations were not necessarily done to embarrass the young man who'd just gone down, she came at him with this: "Mr. Ump, you can be just a little less atomic-bomb about that strike three call, buddy." Then she paused a second and finished: "Especially when the pitch missed by a foot, you know." The umpire turned, puffed up his face a little as if he'd just been challenged by a player, and then shook his head and went back to work.

There was an inning when the Frederick second baseman—a short, scrawny kid actually from Maryland—dove in the dirt to cut off a ground ball up the middle. Then on the next play he went out into short right for a pop up that he dove for but couldn't quite get to, and then—the third play in a row that he was in the middle of—took the throw from the shortstop and got knocked over completely as he turned to throw to first to complete the double play. As he trotted in toward the dugout after that play ended the inning—dusty and sweaty and breathing hard—Dorrie clapped as hard as she could for him as everyone else in the stands watched her. When he got almost to the dugout steps, she called out to him. "You got a lot to prove out there, don't you, honey?" Everybody around her, including Porcia, cracked up.

What Dorrie did, it was clear to Porcia, was see them as boys instead of ballplayers, and the natural separation of their being on the field and she in the stands gave her all the license she needed to talk to them as if she were out with the girls and they had happened upon a group of muscle-bound pretty boys who were ready to flirt and ready to be ogled. And she was just innocent enough—staying on that edge between cruel and caring—that it worked for everybody. It broke up the stands, it charmed the players and it kept the umps on their toes. And it was all safe for Dorrie. She understood the game and its nuances so fast that Porcia had to ask her if she'd been sneaking somewhere to learn it.

"You never told me I could sit right down here and see who they are," Dorrie said.

During the third game of the series, several players looked right at her as they came in from the field, as if waiting. After the right fielder ran into the wall trying to make an over-the-shoulder catch, he loped in sheepishly, almost as if asking Dorrie to go easy on him.

"That's the *warning* track out there, darlin'," she said immediately, as if she'd read his thoughts. "They named it that for a *reason*, you know. It's *warning* you that if you don't slow down, you're going to smack your head into something *very very* hard."

That game got out of hand—the score was 12-3 for the visitors by the seventh inning—and at the end of those last two innings, Dorrie went down to the corner of the dugout, stuck her head around the corner and talked to someone in there for a few seconds before the game resumed. Porcia asked her when she came back to the seats who the hell she was talking to, and Dorrie told her never you mind. And then, in the ninth, she said she was going down by the clubhouse to wait on the third base coach—who at least was in his twenties—to maybe have a beer or something.

"Like you need another beer?" Porcia said, her head all pulled back on her shoulders in amazement.

"You can come too," Dorrie said.

Porcia put her head back into its incredulous, big-eyed, pulled-back position and told her little sister to give that plan some serious consideration. "Think about what you just now finally got yourself out of, Dorrie," Porcia told her, and Dorrie said she didn't care about that and this was a whole new chapter of her life.

"Isn't that what you and Mom told me like a billion times—a new chapter? And am I supposed to turn down nothing more than a beer with a guy just because I happened to have the problem I did?"

She seemed determined to Porcia, but not completely. Porcia took a look around the little stadium to think about what to do. She turned in her seat to face Dorrie fully. She said her sister's whole name—the one she was born with—and put her hands on Dorrie's cheeks to make her look right into Porcia's eyes.

"I'm going to ask you the last favor I'll ever ask you," Porcia said to Dorrie, and gave a little speech about coming on back to the room with her right after the game, just making popcorn or something and checking the TV—just this one night. Dorrie didn't resist Porcia's hands on her face, and she didn't resist what Porcia asked for. She reached out and hugged Porcia, and when they came apart, they smiled at each other. Then Dorrie said she was definitely going to hold Porcia to that last-favor-ever part, especially the next time she got asked out by a ballplayer. They drove home the next morning, and Dorrie was from that day on just as big a fan as Porcia and Stanley.

Porcia

This is why Porcia held her sister's face that night in Myrtle, why she has never told her mother about it when she tells her mother everything else in the world, why she named Stanley Stanley. This is the night the two worst things that ever happened to her happened. This is the night, back when she had just turned twenty, that she went to the baseball game with her father and three of his friends who played softball with him, because she had finally gotten her license and she knew they drank too much and she had decided she was going to rescue her father from himself. She'd heard her mother on the phone with the big man from the dealership, talking about one more time and Harvey would lose his job, and if he didn't he would just piss it away on his own by not being there when customers were, or else he'd die at a too-young age because of his weight and very bad habits. Porcia heard all this because of her mother's habit of going all incredulous. Of saying, "piss it away?" Or, "one more time?" back into the phone so you would know it had just been said. Or, "well, he's always been heavy, it's just who he is." Porcia knew how her mother talked and knew what her father did, partly because she had worked part-time at the dealership since four months after she graduated from high school, and while she was in the office, he was out in the showroom or the lot pretending to try to sell cars.

The car was a big Lincoln that Trailer Ford Lincoln Mercury had let Harvey have five or six years back. Instead of a new one every other year the way they used to. The softball game was on a field along the James River, where the heat and mosquitoes collected in the summer as if they were funneled in directly from hell. What Harvey and his buddies did was get off work early—take lunch at four o'clock—and hit the bar to get ready for their game. It was easier for his buddies to rearrange work than for Harvey because they worked at the foundry, where you could flex your hours a little, and where customers didn't start showing up in the afternoon about the time Harvey was checking out for the day. In a way they hated it when they had the 6:15 game because it cut down on their before-game drinking time. But on this night they were okay with it because they were going out to the minor league park to knock down a few more after the softball. They were ball freaks all of them, and for the first ten or twelve years after they'd gotten out of high school had been part of one of the best slowpitch teams in the western half of Virginia.

So Porcia took them to their softball game from the bar, and stayed for the game, where they got beat by a bunch of younger, smaller, quicker guys—guys who couldn't knock it over the fence the way the forty-somethings still could, but could run the bases and hit the cutoff man and hit the ball where it was pitched to near perfection. Then she loaded them into her father's car—as foul-smelling a bunch of people as she'd ever been around—and headed toward the stadium. There was a cooler in the back seat and they broke out cold ones for everybody. One of the men in the back leaned up to Harvey in the front seat and said, "Hey, a cold one for the young chauffeur too?" And Harvey said sure, what the hell, she's twenty, so ask her.

Porcia said no three or four times, and then, when they were only a few blocks from the stadium, went ahead and took a beer, as much to shut them up as anything else.

"You're all right, Porsh," the beer offerer said. "Good driver, good drinker, and pretty good lookin' too." The men all laughed in agreement and Porcia turned to give them all a polite smile. They smelled like the combination of old sweat, old beer, old clothes, old breath and new-beer bullshit that they were.

Porcia did have one other little reason to drive them to the game. Two of the pitchers from the team—fairly high draft choices with a chance to make it someday—had come down to the dealership to do a TV spot for the great trade-ins and interest rates you could get at Trailer FLM. Three other players came down with them, and Porcia, as the youngest in the office, was put in charge of making sure they had sodas and snacks while they hung around waiting for the ad agency and the production people to decide where the sun was and who needed to look in what direction and whether or not people would get the message with "this is one pitch we know is a strike every time." Porcia got the player-care job even though the older ladies didn't do a thing but gawk and talk the whole time the players were there.

Which actually wasn't all bad as far as Porcia was concerned. She ended up with tickets for the rest of the series and a pretty-much ask-out from the backup catcher, who was built just about the same as she was.

Things didn't begin to turn bad until the seventh inning of the game. Her seat was right behind the home-team dugout on the first base side, and her father's and his buddies' seats were back up a ways behind the third-base dugout. Freddy, the backup catcher, had stuck his head out of the corner of the dugout maybe four times through the game, first to say hi, then to tell her stuff about what was going on in the game.

"That bunt was just to get the guy over to second to try to get that run in," he looked up to tell her in the fourth.

"Hey, I know what a sacrifice is, bench-boy," she said back in mock offense.

She'd kept an eye on her father's group all through the game, and it was in the bottom of the seventh—with the home team up by the run that had come around after the sac bunt—that she missed them. She bolted out of her seat and headed to the parking lot. The spot where she'd parked the car was empty. Her first reaction was hating it that she'd let them slip away when she'd vowed to herself that she'd drop them off anywhere they wanted except a bar after the game. The second thing she thought was that her father had left her without an immediate way home. Not that there weren't phones in the stadium and both a mother and an aunt at home and glad to run the fifteen-block errand to come get her. It was more that her father never said anything, or left notes, or explained how things would happen. He left it for you to figure out, if he thought of how it would affect you at all. The next thing she thought was to start walking toward home and call from a phone if she saw one. Then she had a new set of thoughts: *What the hell*, was basically what it was, *he's been getting himself home drunk for all the years I've been alive, so why should I worry about one more?*

So she went back into the stadium and as she headed down to her seat, Freddy Perlous was looking up at her, right in the middle of the inning. When she got back down close, he turned and asked her where the hell she'd been. He seemed to still be teasing, and after she told him she had to check something with the car, he told her he was going in to catch the top of the ninth. He stuck his right arm up in the air. "They don't try to steal when Freddy P's behind the plate," he said, and ducked back into the dugout.

After the players exchanged high-fives over the win, Freddy came over to Porcia and told her a bunch of the players were going out to the Bee Run Inn after they showered, and he hoped she'd wait for him and go along. She'd never been inside the Bee Run, but had been by it on drives with her mother out to the old-school fabric store way out in the county. It looked rough and sort of exciting to her, sitting all by itself along a stretch of twisty two-lane road. She told Freddy she didn't think so. He put on a frown, told her he'd look for her in no more than ten minutes out by Gate B, and disappeared into the dugout.

Porcia walked slowly back up the steps toward the exit. She wondered if her father ever went to the Bee Run. Then she thought about calling her mother. Then she thought about waiting for Freddy and asking if he'd drop her off at home on his way out. At the top of the lower stands, along the promenade between the good seats and the bleachers, she walked along slowly, and then turned and looked back at the field. Part of the lights were already turned off, giving the field a look of deeper colors—dark green in the outfield and rich brown in the infield—as the ground crew started with their rakes and carts and little tarps—to put the field to bed for the night. She wondered if anyone had ever told her or if she knew it on her own: A well-kept baseball field under the lights just after a game was one of the prettiest things in the world.

There were two other players with Freddy—a tall, Latin-American pitcher and a little red-headed infielder. The car was an old Buick, and Porcia sat in the back with Freddy. The infielder drove and the pitcher rode shotgun. They teased Freddy about his first date all season. After two blocks, Porcia heard the *phwoosh* of a can opening in the front seat. Before they got to the Bee Run, the players had all had two and Porcia one. She could feel herself edging away from fear and hesitation toward just relaxing and seeing what happened. After all, how many of the girls she had gone to school with—especially the ones who had gone off to *college*—had ever hung with pro ballplayers?

It was that relaxation, along with no one knowing her or even checking her ID at the Bee Run Inn, that helped put Porcia where she ended up that night, which was a mile farther out the road from the Bee Run, in the back seat of the car with Freddy while the other two took a little walk with their beers down along the stream. Porcia was not quite afraid and not quite excited. She had had a few beers in the Bee Run, and had continued with the same attitude and approach she'd carried as she'd been walking toward Gate B: *I'll just go along here a ways and see how it goes, see what happens.* Freddy was so quick and smooth with her she was almost not sure it was really happening. At least till he was all the way inside her. The summer after eleventh grade, Jeremy Clarence took her out four times, and the last time got it sort of in, but then he seemed to melt away before much of anything ever happened, leaving her to wonder both if she were still a virgin and why he never called her again. Freddy was big and strong and hard and sure, and loud-whispered *ooh-baby ooh-baby* over and over again into the side of her face as if it were the chorus of a song, until he was finished. Then he pulled up off her and let out a loud whoop like he'd just hit a home run or something. And then, before Porcia could even get her shorts pulled back up, the other two players were right there at the car windows on either side, grinning in at her while Freddy was telling them about what fine, prime, fresh meat this was, as if Porcia were no longer there. She told herself she still wasn't going to be scared, but after both back doors opened at once, she felt everything going sort of dreamy and not completely real, as if she'd be able to go back later and see that none of this was actually happening, or perhaps change things around if she wanted to.

Afterwards, they laughed gently and tried to put their arms around her when she told them she would find her own way home. She wasn't exactly angry or even exactly hurt, but had a strong feeling of wanting to be by herself. She had a sense that something terrible had happened to her, but that she wasn't quite sure what it was. Then she reminded herself of what she had done, but for some reason, just then, she could not make it seem completely horrible.

"It's three in the morning, honey," Freddy cooed into the same side of her face he'd used earlier. "And we're out in the middle of nowhere. You can't walk. It's miles back to town."

"I know where I am," Porcia said softly.

"But your momma will worry," he said. The other two players were in the car, looking ready to go. "Nobody's going to hurt you. We just want to get you home."

Porcia thought about her mother and aunt, who would have both gone to bed by ten-thirty without a worry that Porcia wasn't in yet, and that they wouldn't know a thing unless Porcia wasn't there when they got up around seven-thirty.

In the end Porcia compromised. The three players all lived in a house near the ballpark, and she agreed to ride back just to there, and then walk home. She told them over and over again that she just felt like a walk and it was really only a few blocks and it was a safe neighborhood. Freddy was the only one who would really talk to her, as if he didn't know to be ashamed while the other two did.

She liked the walk. She hurt up between her legs, but the walking felt like a way of making it go away, of putting what had happened behind her. She felt herself start to cry—involuntarily, like when you vomit—three times during her walk, and each time she held it back. She was still two blocks from the house when she saw enough extra light to consider that it might be *her* house the lights were coming from. As she came around the last corner and saw that it really was her house, her heart raced for the first time that night. All the lights were on downstairs and the front door was open. Neither of the cars was out front. She was trembling by the time she was inside to look for a note or something else that could tell her what was going on. She found nothing, and as she stepped back outside to look for clues there, she heard Mr. Kelly's car start in the driveway next door. Then he was next to her, not looking directly at her, but telling her to get in the car.

The massive heart attack that had killed her father that night became, over a short time, a strong, tall, bullet-proof barrier to the other thing that happened to her over the same hours that he was dying. Once she convinced herself there was nothing she could have done to change the explosion of his heart into his chest, she learned to hold his death up before her and allow it to define that day in her life. Even when she knew for certain that she was pregnant, it was her vision of her father dying way too young that she held onto. It was only her certainty of what he would have wanted that made her decide, full of tears, that she wouldn't have an abortion. And it was only after her mother begged her not to jinx another person with the name *Harvey* that she gave any consideration to any name but her father's.

Though she would not go back to the home ballpark until the season and a half that it took for Freddy and the other two to move on—the pitcher was promoted up a level and the other two were cut loose by the organization—Porcia turned back toward baseball both for comfort and for a name for her son. Once she gave up on Harvey, she decided immediately on the name of the first big-league player she'd ever heard about from her father. Harvey had always described him with words he never used anywhere else—words she didn't know he knew: "a smallish, elegant, modest man from up in a little no-count town in Pennsylvania." A man who'd always smiled and turned away praise even though he'd won seven National League batting titles. The boy who would carry that name came into the world with the same skin tone she had, the same squarish face and thick hands—all twelve and a half pounds of him—as if God had seen to it that his father's genes were muted way down in favor of Porcia's. She looked down on him when her mother handed him to her for the first time, and she knew three things all at once as she learned his face. First, that he was a miracle. Second, that he would grow up to be able to brag to his friends that his mother never touched even a beer. And third, that he was never going to have brother or a sister, because Porcia's life from that point was going to be dedicated one hundred percent to Stanley Musial Cregger and whatever it was he wanted from the world.

THE B&W

The two men could be brothers. Both stand under five-nine and carry less than one hundred and fifty pounds on small frames, with a minor cluster of the weight gathering just above their belts. Their hair is wispy and dirty-blond, reaching down onto white shirt collars that fit them loosely on this morning as they prepare to enter U.S. District Court in Roanoke, Virginia for the beginning of a trial in which both will be convicted, with their sentencings to be held later. Their sport coats, black or dark blue and shiny, are ill-fitting and new-looking, bought for the occasion. The men are awkward in the morning sun, escorted into the courtroom as people with cameras walk beside them, recording for the midday and evening news the look of the jackets and the shirts, the quickness of glances, the faint goatees kept despite counsel advice to remove them for this series of days.

The men—Michael David Pitts and Samuel Gene Kidd—are both from just outside the little town of Norton, in far southwest Virginia, where their fathers worked in the coal mines in their early and mid adult years. Pitts' father died of lung disease at age thirty-nine, when his only son was fourteen. Pitts' mother lives near Cincinnati, married to a man who runs a shop that sells reconditioned vacuum cleaners. Michael Pitts has not seen his mother for an amount of time he could not guess, though he'd say some time more than five years. She does not know about the charges against him, so far as he knows, and will not be present for the trial. Michael Pitts's two sisters live near where they grew up. One runs a cash register in the Kroger in town and the other stays home and raises children. Both are married, and for many years took turns inviting Michael to holiday dinners until his tendencies to not show up or to arrive in some state of agitation or inebriation caused both of them to give up. Sometimes Michael brought women with him, women the sisters characterized later to each other as the very worst kind of white, mountain-hollow trash.

Samuel Kidd's father, retired with a modest coal pension to a life built around the big black reception dish in his yard and a refrigerator full of Budweiser beer, still lives in the house where his son grew up. He has been married to Samuel Kidd's mother for something more than forty years, though they sleep in different rooms in a small house built by the coal company in the 1930s, and do nothing together except go to Gatlinburg once a year, to shop and to stay for six days in a motel that looks up onto the Smoky Mountains. When Sam goes to his parents' house to visit, he marvels out loud each time that his father seems skinnier—"except for that beer gut"—and his mother seems heavier. "I'm working on it, Darlin'," she says to him, smiling.

Neither Michael Pitts nor Samuel Kidd finished high school, and they became friends after they'd left school and were trying to get jobs at the automobile parts plant that was to locate in the county where they lived. They filled out applications at the same table, turned them in at the same time and got up to walk out into the sunshine to wait for the plant to actually arrive in the big square shell building the county had put up two or three years earlier for the purpose of attracting a big company. Michael needed a ride. Sam offered one, and they began to discover that they'd been within two years of each other in school, with Michael the older. They traded recollections of teachers, of the specifics of their departures from school, and then shared the good fat joint that

Sam had saved as a reward for himself for going down and filling out the job application. Three days later they took a stereo with CD player out of an unlocked car parked downtown at just after midnight, just for the fun of it. Neither had ever done anything like that before. But Michael knew where they might be able turn the stereo into forty-five dollars, and Sam knew where they could turn part of the money into another good fat joint. That was twelve years before they get out of the car to head into court. They have remained friends for all of that time, except for a period of about a year while they fought over a woman who'd told each of them she loved him and wanted to move to California.

One thread of the reason the two men are walking into court begins with a man named Kenny Rogers, who lives in the little town of Vinton, next to Roanoke, where Virginia starts to flatten out toward the east and become more populated. He is not *the* Kenny Rogers, and has long since tired of people asking him if he knows when to hold 'em and when to fold 'em. Kenny Rogers is forty-eight and big—six-three and over two hundred and twenty pounds. His hair is graying, and for a time he wore a close-cropped beard that looked like the other Kenny Rogers'. He's been remarried for eight years, and one of the passions he shares with his wife is motorcycles. He carries the smallest doubt somewhere inside him about if she loves bikes as much as he does, but every time he asks her about it she is adamant. "Why would I tell you I like something if I don't?" she says. "Where else have you seen that from me?" Or, "Don't you think we've been together long enough that any fake stuff would have worn off by now?" Then she pushes at his chest like she is going to knock him down. That—the pushing at him to make him smile in spite of himself—is his favorite thing that happens with her, though he would not tell her that.

What he does with the bike to help overcome his doubts about her real love for riding around with the wind hitting her and the hard asphalt just one moment of non-concentration below, is to make the bike as comfortable as it can be. She says she loves the new seat and the big mirrors. What he carries home on the day that he and Gina will first cross paths with the two men from Norton is the best thing he has ever gotten for the bike. He walks into the kitchen of the little white bungalow where they live by themselves because all of their children are grown up and moved out. He wants to be careful not to appear too excited.

"Just a little spin," he says. "Not Wyoming or anything, you understand, just a little tool-around to keep the spark plugs sparking. The tacos will hold till we get back."

"Burritos," she corrects, smiling at him and moving toward the door.

"Right," he says.

Outside on the seat of the bike, he has the helmets pre-perched, facing each other like the football helmets that smash into each other at the beginning of one of the networks' pro football games. Tilted back just right. A perfect pair of sleek black head protectors staring into each other's faces.

"Ooh, new helmets," she says, just as he knew she would. He knew it because he positioned the little mikes to be on the other side from where she would come out of the house, so she'd have no chance to see them right away.

He picks hers up just as she gets to the bike and sets it softly down over her hair. "We'll whisper sweet nothings right through the wind," he says to her. As he was carrying the helmets out of the store earlier, this is what he wanted to say, but he didn't think, when it came time, that he would.

"What a great idea," she says when she discovers the mikes. She is sincere, he can see.

When he has his helmet on and they are both on the bike, he says "let's go," in just above a whisper.

"Just as soon as you're ready," she says in full voice. He jumps a little, involuntarily, and she says she is sorry for being too loud. "They're so good," she says.

He heads north of town—the direction they usually take to go around the city and out west of the metropolitan area.

"Not all the way to Wyoming, but maybe most of the way, right?" she says to him, and squeezes at his midsection.

The two women who will also walk into the courtroom met each other in the outer office of a two-man law firm before they had anything to do with the trial. Lee Allender was twenty-six, and had been encouraged by a coworker to at least inquire about getting legal help in reference to what had started out as a small traffic accident in a grocery store parking lot.

"I'm really just looking for advice," Lee said to the woman in front of her, sitting at a pretty desk that seemed to have too many papers on it to be a receptionist's desk. "And I saw in the yellow pages that the initial consultation is free here, so I thought I'd try. I don't really have money for a lawyer and the whole thing is ridiculous anyway."

"What is it?" the woman said. Her name, Lee would soon learn, was Ellis Strawb, and she was a sort of paralegal for the two lawyers who worked behind the big dark wooden doors behind the cluttered desk.

"Just a fender bender really," Lee said. "But the guy who hit me is denying it's his fault."

Ellis and Lee talked about the accident for half an hour. Ellis took notes, and Lee wondered if this was going to count as the free initial consultation. At some point in the conversation, Ellis interrupted things long enough to say that it wasn't. Lee thanked her. When they finished talking, Ellis made an appointment for Lee with one of the lawyers and told Lee she'd walk her out since she was on her way to lunch. Their friendship, if not born at the cluttered desk, came brightly into being as they shared lunch that day. Ellis was thirty-one, unhappy in her second marriage. The first one, she hastened to mention, was not unhappy, but had ended anyway. Lee, the owner of two masters degrees—music and English—had never been married and said she wasn't really sure if she'd ever be. She worked for a magazine publishing company, processing advertising materials. Ellis was slightly thinner than the also-thin Lee, and wore her black hair long and loose, with her pale skin lending her a vaguely ghostly appearance. Lee was darker skinned, slightly shorter, and kept her brown hair cut close to her head.

Their friendship grew through Sunday afternoon hikes in the mountains of Virginia. When they first met, Lee was the owner of new and hardly worn boots, and when she made mention of them to Ellis in a disparaging comment about herself and the foolish, hopeful purchase of the boots, Ellis said she had a pair she hadn't used in the two and a half years since she'd been married again. By the time winter came and they had a dozen day hikes behind them, they were already planning for the next spring, when both had decided to leave their jobs to do something more interesting in the summer. At that moment of mutual confession about leaving good jobs and good employers, neither had a precise idea just what it would be she'd do, but within moments they decided to hike the full length of the Virginia section of the Appalachian Trail together, more than five hundred miles. Their decision was to go north to south, so that they'd at least be in the higher mountains as the weather warmed.

Months later, they were on schedule at the halfway point of their hike when the focus of their walk shifted from their boots to themselves. Their childhoods, their schooling, their families, their hopes for the fall, and last, their uncertainties about men.

"If this summer doesn't do one other thing for me," Ellis told Lee near McAfee's Knob, "it has definitely given me the courage to leave Gene. All these steps give me a lot of time to plan the steps I need to take when I get back."

"Are you sure?" Lee said. Her reaction was automatic to such situations—to give it every last try.

"Absolutely," Ellis said. "If it's wrong you have to get out of it. I just wish I were as wise as you—to not get involved until you know it's right."

"That's the kind view," Lee said. "The other side of that coin is that if you never even try, you never know what's right and you never get to find it."

Ellis shrugged. "It's so much easier with a woman," she said. "I mean with you it is anyway. I say whatever I want, whatever I think, and it's not judged, not stored away to be held against me." She looked at Lee. "You've been a lifesaver for me these last few months."

Lee smiled and told Ellis thanks. She reached and squeezed Ellis's hand quickly as they broke into an open spot on the trail. The sun was warm. It occurred to Lee that Ellis was the best friend she'd ever had.

What Gina and Kenny talk about on the bike with their new microphones is their day at work. Gina is surprised, because he asks first, about her day.

"I don't know if it was the scanner or the product number or what," she says, "but I kept getting $3.97 on these sale sandals, and $9.97 on the big box of freezie pops when everyone who brought them to the register knew good and well they were half price. So the head cashier—it's a new lady, real nice, but she doesn't wash her hair—is not sure why it's happening either, and she's getting real frustrated like maybe it's my fault or something. And so we have to keep getting out the void sheet for all this stuff, and of course the new registers won't let you ring up manually any more, and so you know there's going to be a drawer audit at the end of the shift, and..." She stops talking because she decides she is going on too much on one thing, wasting the new microphone batteries or however they work on all this detail.

"How do you guys do half of $9.97?" he says. His voice is soft and clear in her ear. "Up or down?" He is a carpet and remnant salesman at Floor City and asks her a retail question every now and then, she thinks, because he thinks Havens—where she works—is a marketing genius. Which they sort of are, Gina feels, because they compete head on with Kmart and Wal Mart when all they have is thirty-four stores in the mid-South.

"Up, silly," she says, because she knows he knows.

"We've been using that penny as a sales tool," he says. They are heading out of the dense part of town, to where the roads open up and he will tease that Wyoming really isn't all that far. "'Fifty percent off a $499.99 carpet,' we tell them. What we're doing now is saying hey, let's knock it down to $249 and then knock off another five bucks. And they go crazy. They think they got a great deal, we make it all up in delivery and installation and the other side dishes, and in the meantime we've got a customer for life for a crummy six bucks."

"Where are we going, Kenny?" she sticks in.

"Just keeping the spark plugs sparking," he says. He pauses, perhaps thinking about if he should say it. "You know, Wyoming really isn't all that far once you get out here." They both laugh for the first time into the microphones and then they are quiet for a mile or so before she goes back to her day.

"We had some creeps in there today."

"Oh yeah?" Kenny says.

"Two ratty looking guys buying camp stoves and tents and stuff. Little beady-eyed guys in their forties or so. With those spindly little goatees you see that look like they grew in at sixteen and never filled out any further. Creeps."

"You paid some pretty damn close attention, didn't you?" Kenny says. He's a little loud.

"Security was all over them," she says. They are west of town now, out on old U.S. 311, toward Wyoming.

Back when Kenny was still living with Annette, he and Gina used to ride out this way, sometimes to do a little sparking of their own in the woods. Kenny was shy with her—all but reluctant—telling her she'd get poison ivy in places she never saw. She had to practically drag him. But they were new, and he knew what was at the end of the hike, and so he'd do it. He even talks about it now sometimes, but in an ancient-history kind of way, as if they were kids then, and middle-aged people now.

"So?" Kenny says into the mike.

"So?" she asks, and then realizes what he's talking about. "They have these profiles now at the stores—like the FBI—where when certain people walk in you hear the security codes right away. It's really not fair. You walk in young or scruffy or black and they start scoping you, you know?"

"How many?"

"How many what?"

"Guys."

"Two. Just the two."

"They steal anything?" They are sloping up the mountain now, and Kenny is pulling hard, cleaning those plugs.

"I don't think so. They brought everything up to the registers and paid for it pretty as you please."

"Weird," he says.

They are near the spot where they used to stop and hike. Gina asks him if he remembers their hikes, and squeezes at his waist.

"I remember," he says. "I was just thinking, as a matter of fact, how nice it is we have a bed now."

"True," Gina says, picturing their bed, which has a little light hooked on the headboard and then a million car and bike magazines all over the dresser and the floor, making it appear the room should slant down that way. "But it was fun out in the B and W, huh?"

"B and W?" he says.

"The bushes and the weeds, Kenny," she says with mock impatience. That was their code for their woods adventures back when. He forgets word stuff immediately, but remembers the bore size on an engine forever.

"Yeah," he says, "it was fun. A little sticky-bushy sometimes, but it was fun."

"We could try again," she says, and lets her hand fall down in front of him a little.

He turns his head to one side and then the other, as if someone will see them or hear them.

"Really," Gina says. "Nice afternoon like this and all—no worries, no commitments aside from the Mexican. Why not?"

"Ah," he says. They are down in the valley now, riding along a pretty creek with barns and silos beside it.

"Maybe on the way back," she says.

"Maybe on the way back," he says, as if relieved not to have to deal with it right now.

"I bet they're lezbos," Michael says. He hands Sam the little binoculars they came across at the first shelter they stopped in after they started their try at life in the woods, close to a month back.

"You never know about chicks these days," Sam says. "More and more of them go both ways."

"Or can't figure out which way to go except right after some poor guy's money."

They laugh, and exchange the binoculars again. They have come to live in the woods for two reasons. Or one reason each. Sam got married a year earlier, to a woman even Michael told him was the last person in the world on the qualified-to-marry list. The only thing that changed after the marriage was where she lived. All of her old boyfriends still came to see her, with at least most of them trying to come by when Sam wasn't home, and after three months, Sam started carrying around a gun to try to protect his matrimonial property. There were two or three fights, and then the girl's father got a restraining order to keep Sam out of his own house because, the father said, Sam was abusing his daughter. Sam went to the father's house and showed the gun, after which the police were called, and Sam left to find Michael to see if maybe Michael wanted to get out of town for awhile too.

Michael wanted to get out of town, it turned out, but not to a bigger, better town, the way Sam had seen it happening. Michael had gotten a check as a part of his father's black lung disability benefits—a check for a little over seven hundred dollars—and had decided he wanted to get away from city life and go live in the woods for awhile. Take a bow and a good rod, and live off the land. Nothing but a sleeping bag and a good knife, was what he said.

"A tent?" Sam said.

"Hell no," Michael said. "There's shelters and buildings out there in the national forest all over the damn place. Tents are for pussies."

They both liked the woods, but after a stretch of days they went into town just north of Roanoke for some supplies. "Not the damn comforts of home," Michael said when Sam razzed him some for breaking down. "Just some basic camp shit." They were lucky hitchhiking, and were back in the woods in four hours.

Sam takes the binoculars one more time. "Skinny-ass things, huh?"

"There's no in-between," Michael says. "Either too skinny or too fat is the way they are all over these mountains."

"You sure tried enough to know," Sam says. "Not that you ever got your actual hands on much."

Michael laughs. "You either." He looks through the woods, putting his hands up to make fake binoculars. "Think they'd like some visitors?"

Sam snorts. "Yeah, about like they'd like a bear to stop by."

"Why?" Michael says. "Out here in the woods all alone for who the hell knows how long, eating berries and camping out with the mice and muskrats—they're probably dying for some human male companionship." He puts up his fake binoculars again and makes his own snorting noise.

"Yeah, like you've had any luck with pussy the last five years," Sam says.

Michael slaps Sam on the shoulder. "Sometimes, my man," he says, "you have to work on making your own luck."

"They'll get the wrong idea and scream like banshees and get out the pepper spray and all," Sam says. He is moving with Michael in the general direction of the women.

"Just a visit," Michael says. He is doing his best cat-movement imitation—a little hunched down and real quiet and smooth. "It's the setting sun this time of day that gets a forest creature moving," he says softly to Sam as they walk. "You just got to get up and stretch and go see what you find in the woods."

The way Gina talks Kenny into stopping on the way back is to tell him she needs a pit stop, which is the truth. At the turn-around point of their ride, they stopped at the little fake country store—it's a standard convenience store with wood across the front—where she had a Corona and he had a three-color kiddie bomb pop.

"It's just to *pee*," she assures him, but lets her hand fall into his lap as they pull into the lot where the trail crosses the road. She tells him again what really good mikes he's gotten. He reaches back and pats the side of her leg as he stops the bike. There are six cars on the little lot.

"Which way you walking?" Kenny says. "North or south?"

"We used to go north," she says. "Up along that ridge."

He gestures in that direction, ready to follow. She's surprised he has agreed. He doesn't like to leave the bike, even with all the security on it, and he never leaves the helmets.

"We just carrying the helmets?" she says.

"Good idea. It's not like we're hiking for miles or anything, right?"

"Right," she says, "just like we were only going to ride around the block."

He smiles and takes Gina's hand for the little way that the path is wide enough as they start along the Appalachian Trail—a spot they haven't been for years. Gina takes care of her need as soon as they are two hundred yards or so from the road and there is no sign of any other hikers. After that, Kenny doesn't turn them back, and Gina doesn't protest. It's cool among the trees, and as they climb, they quickly get up onto a ridge where the view is back to the west. Gina wonders if he is walking them far enough in that he might agree to find a soft spot.

Once they are well along the first ridge, it's clear to Gina that it's going to work. He does a little grabby-grab at her backside and asks what she's going to do with the leafprints she's going to end up with back there. They pause where the trail turns off the ridge, to consider going down the hill. Gina says this is the exact spot where they used to turn down, and Kenny says he thinks it was a ways back.

"I don't know," Gina says. " I think we tried it once and there was almost like a cave down there, remember?"

"That was along here?"

"I think," she says. "I mean this is the only place we came."

"What if I head down and do some preliminary scouting?" he says, like he's imitating a boy scout. "Make sure we get a sweet spot." He leans over and kisses Gina lightly.

"If you and I are there, there'll be a sweet spot," Gina tells him. She finds a rock and sets her helmet down next to it.

"Get ready," he says as he starts down the brushy hillside.

"Don't look too far," she says. She knows he will look until he feels absolutely safe, because that is the only way it will work for him. Gina looks both ways along the trail. There is nobody in either direction. She thinks about the underwear she has on. She pulls at the waistband of her pants to look. Big plain white ones. He won't care. Then she thinks about her big stomach sticking out like it does when she is sitting. He's never said a word to her about it.

After she's waited the amount of time she has to discount because she is basically impatient, she stands to stretch and look up and down the trail again. She can feel the first edges of dusk, and she's anxious to be back with Kenny. She reaches toward her ankles to stretch and hears a little noise at her helmet, like there's a bird or a chipmunk whisping around in there. She's reluctant to investigate, but reminds herself that the longer you wait with things like that, the harder it gets. She makes herself reach down for the helmet. She picks it up fast and in one motion turns it over to look inside.

"Can you hear me or not?" It's Kenny talking in an urgent whisper. *"Gina!?"*

"I'm here," she says, not thinking to whisper.

There's a scraping, shuffling noise as if he has rubbed against the little sponge cover on the mike. It occurs to her that there is some reason for her to whisper too. *"I'm here,"* she tells him, this time in a whisper. He doesn't say anything. She decides he's still got the mike covered. Deer, it occurs to her. Or maybe a bear or something else dangerous. *"Kenny?"* she tries again. She starts toward the edge of the ridge holding the helmet up to her ear. Then she puts it on and hears her name again.

"I'm here," she whispers. *"What is it, Kenny?"*

"Don't talk," he says. *"Even in a whisper. Just listen."*

"Okay," she says, and then realizes she wasn't supposed to.

"Just listen," he says again. *"Just listen. There's something bad going on down here I think. I got down near where the cave is and ended up below it, and there are two men with two women back up at the mouth of the cave. They have a knife on the women, Gina. It looks bad."* He pauses. Gina steps back from the edge of the ridge, afraid they might see or hear her. *"I don't really think I can move,"* Kenny says. *"They're between where you are and I am. And I think*

if I move and they see me, there's no telling what they'll do to me or to them. To the women."

Gina uses the smallest whisper she can imagine. *"Can I even talk like this?"*

"What?"

She asks again, at the same level.

"I guess so," he says. *"Do you have your helmet on now?"*

She tells him she does and asks him if the women look scared.

"Shitless," he says. *"They don't seem to know quite what they want to do, but it's definitely not a cooperative deal. The women look like they might be thru-hikers—all skinny and stringy haired. The men look more like city guys. Just cheap clothes and old tennis shoes."*

"What are they doing now?" She can feel her own fear building. She realizes she must have stopped breathing to listen to Kenny, and now her heart is drubbing at her neck. She feels heat behind her ears.

"It's almost like they're kids," he says. *"They sort of talk with each other and then to the women, almost toying with them, but I'm not close enough to hear what they're saying. One of them has that knife he keeps waving around."*

"How far away are you?" She looks up and down the trail again, and then again. She wonders why nobody has come from the parking lot or nobody is heading back to it before darkness arrives.

"I don't know. Maybe 30 or 40 feet. It's only their concentrating on the women that has made them miss me—oh Christ, the other one has a gun. I guess it's—yeah, it is—like a little pistol. He's just sort of showing it off and grinning."

"Are you behind a tree or anything?"

"Sort of. There are lot of trees between me and them, but they're not all that big. I think if they turned and looked hard, they'd see me."

"How in the world did you get past them on the way down?" she

asks. The heat has spread down her neck and onto her upper arms.

"I don't know. I thought of that when I first saw them. Maybe they were just concentrating on the women too much. What if I just ran right at them and started yelling and ..."

"No!" she interrupts, and then goes back to making sure she controls her whisper. *"If there's a gun and they're as nuts as they sound, they could just panic and shoot everybody."*

"I can't just stand here forever," he says. *"Jesus, the knife guy is getting right in on one of them. God, he just flicked a button off her blouse and cut her bra in half right in the middle. She's bleeding. Wait, now he's pulling away, like he's apologizing, reaching for her face. She's got her hands at her chest and he's trying to get her to stop crying. He cut her chest."*

"Like he's sorry?" She can't picture a guy cutting a woman's bra off, cutting her chest and then being sorry.

"Sort of. Like he was just playing. I need to do something."

"No, Kenny," she says. *"It's going to get dark soon. Then maybe there'll be more options."* She is concentrating on staying calm and trying to help Kenny do the same.

"Like what?"

"I don't know," she says.

"Maybe you should go get help—go flag somebody at the road to call the police."

Gina doesn't feel good about leaving him stuck down there at the cave, and can't imagine things staying the way they are now long enough for her to get all the way back to the road, find a car, send for the police and then come back into the woods. That seems like half an hour, and so she tells him she thinks it will take too long.

"What's the alternative?" he says. She thinks she hears impatience in his whisper.

She decides not to question him about it. *"What are they doing now? Is she bleeding bad?"*

"I don't think so. Nothing really different."

"Just standing..."

"Wait, the other guy is getting close to the other woman, leaning in like he's maybe going to kiss her. It's the one with the gun. This is awful, Gina. These guys are major creeps."

She decides she needs to talk to him, just to keep him calm, especially if something awful really is about to happen. *"What do they look like?"* she asks.

"I told you," he says. *"Creeps. Thirties or forties maybe. Ratty looking punk guys."*

"My God, it's them," Gina says. *"It's them."*

"Who?" Kenny says.

"The guys in the store today."

"Yeah, right," Kenny says. *"Wait, he's pulling away. He's taking the gun back away from her neck."*

"It was on her neck?"

"Almost. He just sort of carried it there as he was leaning in."

"What do we do?"

"God. Time's going by and we're paralyzed."

"You've got to protect yourself first, Kenny," she tells him. Kenny's son told her once that when he—the son—was about seven, his father dove in front of a car that was backing out of a driveway to push his son and his bike out of the way. It was a football-like play as the son described it. Kenny just dove into the street, nailed the bike and boy with his face and shoulder and sort of blocked them out of the way. Then he hit the pavement hard and rolled as the car driver finally looked behind and realized there were people there. Father and son were both safe, but Kenny's legs and the side of his face were cut and scraped. It worries Gina that Kenny will get impatient down there and answer to the same call. She tells him again he needs to think of himself first. *"You just don't know what crazy guys'll do, especially when there's a gun."* The heat is all over her now—in her crotch and onto the tops of her legs.

"But if I could somehow catch the women's eyes before the rest of the light goes away," he says. *"If they knew I was here and we could coordinate movements or something, assuming they can still see me at all. It's really starting to get dark down here in the trees."*

She wants to tell him that things like that work only in the movies, and to try to figure out if it really is the same men who were in the store. Instead she asks him what's happening now.

"It's like they don't know what to do," he says. *"They sort of go toward the women and then back off. They laugh and then they turn back—oh, God . . ."* The sounds from the mike are suddenly muffled, as if he's covered it again.

"Kenny?" she says. *"Kenny?"* She reaches up and presses the sides of the helmet, as if it will bring the sound closer. *"Kenny?"* There are more muffled sounds and then a thumping noise as if his helmet hit the ground, or maybe a tree. She decides she shouldn't talk anymore, though she wants to. And then she does hear: "Behind those trees," she hears first. And then, "Cut him off over there." She realizes she is hearing through her ears instead of through the helmet. The men are shouting at each other. "He saw the whole thing," comes what she takes to be the first voice again. "Forget him," comes the other. "The women will get away."

Then the voices are quickly farther away. She decides that once Kenny was seen, he ran on down the ridge rather than risk leading them toward her. And she's standing still. Should she go down there and try to help the women, or does she make a run for the road and help, and hope that Kenny will find his way back to the road once he gets to the bottom of the ridge? It's almost dark. She can't hear the voices now. She takes off her helmet and starts running toward the road as fast as she can, feeling that there are people moving all around her in the quickly falling darkness. When she is coming down the last slope to the road, she is stopped short by the sound of a gunshot. She does not realize she has dropped her helmet until she sees it bouncing off the rocks away from her. Her hands, out from her body, come back to her mouth in an involuntary movement to try to make sure she doesn't scream. Her breathing is as heavy as it has ever been. She searches all around her body, looking for signs of blood from herself.

"You're just way braver than I am, I guess," Lee says to Ellis. They are in Lee's car, nearing the courthouse. "I mean you're actually looking forward to it."

"I don't know as I'd go that far," Ellis says, "but people do need to be held accountable for what they do, and these guys did bad things."

"And they could do more bad things, is my point," Lee says. "They serve a year or two or something and then come looking for you and me. I know I'm a chicken at heart, but still."

"So we should just let them walk now?"

Lee and Ellis haven't been hiking together since the summer evening when they were trapped for more than two hours by Michael Pitts and Samuel Kidd just a little more than a quarter mile from a fairly busy highway. This after they had spent most of their summer to that point at least a day's hike and often more from even a small paved road. It was that irony—the realization that danger was everywhere and help wasn't necessarily anywhere—that caused them to abandon not only the rest of their hike to the far southwest corner of Virginia, but also the practice they had developed before then of hiking together as often as they could. For nearly a month before that day, they spent every waking moment together, and now they do not talk for weeks at a time. In the time after they spent several days with police and other investigators, Ellis pulled away from her certainty about leaving her husband, at least for a time, and as Lee found a new friend—they ride bicycles together—Ellis found herself wondering if Lee might be gay, and then struggled with what in the world the relevance of that might be anyway.

There was never anything even close to an open conflict, except this: Some six weeks after all the statements were taken, and three weeks after the two men were at last caught—after they had avoided search parties and dominated the front page of the Roanoke newspaper for twenty-two days—Ellis called Lee to invite her to go with her to visit the Rogerses.

"Just stop by and say hi and thanks and how sorry we are," Ellis said when Lee did no more than clear her throat in response to the question.

"I don't know," Lee said. "I never thought of that. I mean we told them that plenty back at the questioning and all."

"Most people wouldn't think to visit now particularly, I don't think," Ellis told her. "I think we all tend to want to stay as far from anything and everything that reminds us of it. But aren't we all people, and didn't we all live that day together?"

"We did," Lee said, "but I don't know. I mean the reunions you hear about are for things like graduations and sports championships and other happy stuff. You don't hear much about people getting together to relive bad things."

"It's not a reunion, Lee," Ellis said, feeling the slightest edge of heat when she did not want to. "It's a matter of paying a courtesy visit to the people who may have saved our lives in one way or another."

"What do we really have in common with them except for those hours?" Lee said. "What would we talk about but that? Or that we haven't already talked about?"

"Maybe you're right," Ellis said, working her hardest to sound calm, but wondering if underneath it she was being ironic. "They're older, they're interested in different things, they live out in Vinton. What would they have to say to us?"

"Right," Lee said weakly, as if uncertain too about Ellis's tone.

"Okay then," Ellis said. "You doing all right?"

"Pretty good," Lee said. "Pretty good overall."

"Well good."

"And you?"

"Oh, you know, Gene and I are never going to be quite the ideal couple, but he's home more, and we're trying to do a movie and dinner at least every other week. And he's talked about trying meditation together, so you know." She stopped herself, not wanting to let things flow with Lee as she had on the trail, when the two of them had seemed closer than sisters. Lee, perhaps thinking the same thing and feeling regretful, prodded Ellis on, and so she talked more—about how hard Gene tried sometimes, how long and hard he had to work to get the little bit of sales he got since he had the worst territory in the company—and stopped herself three more times before she finally felt sure that she needed to release Lee from what felt like the edges of discomfort over too much hubby talk.

"If you do go," Lee said just before they hung up, "would you give them my best?"

"Oh sure," Ellis said brightly and immediately, but after she'd set down the phone she turned and spoke to it again. "You *can't*, but I'm supposed to *for* you?"

Ellis never went to see the Rogerses at home. She and Lee had both visited Kenny in the hospital when he was recovering from the single gunshot that had entered his body on his right side just below the waist, where it had torn through the flesh of his hip and then been stalled by his spine. He was a gracious, almost apologetic man on the first visit, telling them he wished he had been able to do more, had been able to move sooner and spare them the torture of not knowing what would happen to them. He was propped in bed, and no one said anything about his legs. His wife was at work. Kenny told them his wife was absolutely sure that she had seen the two men earlier in the day, at the Havens store where she worked. Ellis and Lee looked at each other, as if wondering to each other what that meant.

On the second visit, a day before he was to be sent home in his new wheelchair, he spoke of the same kind of thing, but he went further, in a different tone.

"They shot me in the back is the main thing I think about," he said after they'd talked a few minutes. His wife, in a chair back at the window while the two women visited up close at the bed, jumped up and came to him as if he'd pushed a button for emergency help. She brushed Ellis as she arrived.

"No, Kenny, no," his wife said softly, and put her hand on his chest.

"These are people who were there," Kenny told his wife. "It's only as personal as I make it, and these are people who were in those woods."

"Please, Kenny," she said.

He folded his big arms over her hand and then looked at Lee. "The part that's hardest for me is that they shot me in the back," he said.

His wife put her head down on top of his arms and then allowed her legs to sort of fold under her so that her head pulled off his chest and she was kneeling by the bed with her head beside his waist, her face on the tight white sheeting. "Please don't, Kenny," she said again. Ellis couldn't tell if her voice was muffled by the mattress or by crying.

"Maybe we should go," Lee said.

"No," Kenny said. "Well, certainly you may, but let me say what I've wanted to, because even though Gina doesn't think so, I think it may help me over time." He put one of his hands on his wife's head. "I should have been running to you, not away from you," he said. "I stood there for way too long, not doing anything."

"You were protecting us by not moving," Ellis said.

"Certainly you were," Lee said.

"I was just plain not sure what to do," he said. "And if they hadn't seen me, I'd probably still be standing there wondering."

"Stop, Kenny," his wife said, now clearly crying. "Please. If we agree not to blame me then we have to not blame you either."

Ellis looked at Lee and then at Kenny. "You're so wrong," she said to Kenny. "You saved our lives and we got away with little more than two hours of drama. One little cut." Her hand went, involuntarily, to the small scar at the center of her chest. She wanted to tell him that the only cowards were the two men lurking in the woods that day. But she didn't want to use the word, and could not think of another before Gina Rogers stood up to thank the two younger women for coming by to visit, and to tell them if she didn't see them before, she would see them when the court date came around. She all but ushered them out of the room.

Now Lee pulls the car onto the lot directly across the street from the courthouse.

"Isn't this the phone company lot?" Ellis says. It strikes her as an odd place to park. She looks at the tall federal building in front of her, and then along the street in front of it, in both directions. *What if we are in the wrong place at the wrong time again?* she thinks. *What if parking here assures that something happens that wouldn't have happened if we'd parked where I thought we would?*

"I think it was at some point, but I don't know now. I don't know where else to park, do you?"

"No," Ellis says. "Sorry. I mean you did drive for us after all."

They get out of the car into the cold clear day. The wind cuts down the street, carrying nothing in it but dry cold. As they cross the lot, angling into the wind as they walk next to each other, Ellis sees the Rogerses coming down the small hill to the left of the courthouse as they face it. Gina is behind the chair, holding it back slightly as it comes down the hill to make the turn to go up to the courthouse.

"There they are," Lee says. "Kenny and Gina."

"That means that Pitts and Kidd will be right down there, to the right," Ellis says. "They'll come at us from that side since Kenny and Gina are over there. We're all in our same positions again."

Lee takes hold of Ellis's right arm with both hands, the way a woman might take a man's arm when she is walking into the cold and seeking comfort, or to give it. "They're not there, Ellie," she says. "The defendants don't come in the front door. They're probably already inside, plotting with their slimeball lawyers about how to get off." She squeezes Ellis's arm. As they walk, the Rogerses make the turn toward the building. There's a ramp that parallels the steps up to the little courtyard around the front door. When they reach the ramp, Gina lets go of the chair and starts walking up the stairs, which are closer to Ellis and Lee than the ramp that Kenny starts up. Kenny's arms pump at the wheels. His face turns toward his wife, and he smiles as he pushes his chair.

"Look," Lee says. "I think he's racing her up the stairs. He's smiling because he knows he's going to win."

Ellis looks up the street again for the two men. There are no cars at all, and far up the street is an old woman, walking away from the courthouse. Ellis looks at Kenny and Gina again as Kenny reaches the top of the ramp and then looks back at Gina as he speeds on toward the big doors.

"Or maybe he's running toward them this time," Ellis says. "Running right the hell at them."

FLA

The only reason Stella agreed to even think about going was that Hubber had already bought a book that probably cost more money than he had spent on books in his whole total life, if he'd ever bought one at all. What he bought was a gigantic Rand McNally roadmap book for all fifty states. Hub spending money for a book did two things to Stella. One was to let her know he was serious about going, and the other was to allow her to get to look at a book with a map of each state in it. For many years, in the times when she thought about how bad she felt for only getting into the ninth grade, the thing she thought about to feel better was geography—about being in a nice new classroom with the sunshine coming in the windows and lighting up a big pull-down map of the United States, with a handsome geography teacher standing in front of it talking about all the big square midwestern states being stacked up there nice and neat in the middle. She loved to picture herself in that classroom, and then to think about a picture of herself and Hubber and where they were on the map—in almost the exact center of Nebraska in almost the exact center of the country.

Actually there were two more reasons she decided to go. One was that she believed what he said when he said, "Hell, Stella, you don't want to go, you don't have to go. It's no particular skin off my ass." He was sick of Nebraska, and had never been out of the state in his life, and only a few times out of the four or five counties—out west of Grand Island along the Platte River—where he bought and sold hubcaps to earn the little money he had. He set up at the flea markets on the weekends, and sold some to shops in the area, but he had been doing it for more than twenty years and had never been able to afford a van that was less than four or five years old when he bought it.

"I'm tired as hell of baking all summer and freezing all winter," he told her. "Tired of this flat-as-hell desert-ass land and people going crazy over the damn Cornhuskers like they were God or some damn thing." He had never mentioned football before in all the years—eighteen now—they had been together, as if he hadn't even been aware it was there. It may have been that as much as anything that made her sit up and think that he meant it. He was going to pack up his hubcaps and leave whether she went or not, or at least that was his bluff.

The other thing was that she actually had two hundred and twenty dollars he didn't know about. Not that she was trying to hide it—when she started squirreling away little bits, she thought about surprising him with new seatcovers for the van—but now that she had it up to that amount and this was about to happen, she figured she'd keep it in reserve in case they had an emergency or something weird happened and she had to come on back by herself.

Plus Cassie, her half-sister, kept telling her to go for it. "First off, Stel," she said, "first off there's no way in hell he'd go without you. He could bluff it a ways, maybe ten big bad miles all by himself, and then he'd be right back asking you what the hell is taking you so long to get ready, like it was him who had forgotten and left you behind. Hey, he couldn't even *do* it by himself. And second off, what the hell have you got to lose? Like maybe your great job waiting great tables in that great restaurant? Like maybe sitting out in the freakin' oven every Saturday and Sunday to try to sell ten dollars worth of hubcaps so Hubber can get smashed with his brother that night? Or maybe buy himself another broken-down van?" She made a snorting noise. "Or maybe it's me," Cassie went on in a loud voice and then smiled too big. "Maybe it's you're so close to fat old Cassie that you just can't bear to take off from this hellhole and try something new."

"You're not fat," Stella said.

Cassie made a loud farting noise with her mouth and moved her hands back and forth between herself and Stella. "Not too many ways people can tell we're related, Stel, but add us up and divide by two and you still have a number that starts with a two."

Stella thought for a second that Cassie was calling *her* fat, but she decided Cassie was really doing her best to get the best for her, so she didn't say anything.

"Plus the wild hair up his butt is *Florida*?" Cassie said. "I mean it's not quite California, but hell Stel, when was the last time you were out of the Cornshucker State? In like a previous life?"

"I've been in seven states," Stella said, almost in a pout, because Cassie knew it.

"Hoowee," Cassie said. "You take off for Florida and you might be in that many in one day. That is if the van doesn't go blooie between here and Omaha."

The way Hubber—his real name was Donald Leon Johnson, but there probably wasn't anyone left in the world except Stella who knew that—the way he got the Florida bug was the way he got every single bug in his whole life, which was from a drive up to his brother's in Phelps County. Stella hated those trips because the visits always ended up with three things. Way too much beer, at least some marijuana, and a whole lot of talk about sex and the women Hubber's brother had been with since the last time they were up there. Or at least *said* he'd been with.

On this particular visit, the main topic for the evening, after too much beer and a joint or two for the boys—Stella had tried it a time or two years ago, but all it did was make her sleepy and cold and slightly afraid of things she wasn't usually afraid of—the big topic was how in the hell Anson all of a sudden out of nowhere had all these channels on his TV. He had one of those little dishes outside, but he hadn't paid the bill, he said, and even when he had he never got all the stuff he had that night. Plus he said it wasn't even hooked up anymore.

"It's just sitting out there to impress the neighbors," he said, and he and Hub cracked up. There were no neighbors for miles in any direction.

Anson got up from his ratty old burned-arm chair, walked up to the TV and grabbed hold of the old rabbit ears antenna that sat there. He picked it up a few inches. "It's *this* mother," he announced, holding in out for them to look at. "This is the same damn antenna I used to watch Twilight Zone on, and Rod Serling put some seriously good shit in it back then, and now it's bringing in mongo channels from everydamn where. Mars, for all we know."

Hubber and Anson cracked up over that and then Hub said it might have to do with the ozone hole letting in more signals from the satellites.

"The ozone hole?" Anson said to Stella. "Where does he get this shit, the Science Channel?" Anson and Hubber went nuts another five minutes over that, like the words "Science Channel" were funny.

Anyway, this one channel they found was full of travel programs, and both Anson and Hubber—it usually took Anson being wacko on something too to get Hubber fully insane over it—got totaled over the stuff on Florida. Stella knew it was mostly the beer and the dope that was doing it to them, because on a regular day, if either one of them, sitting in a chair by himself, had come across a travel channel, he'd have flipped through it faster than those channels where they sell painted plates and fake coins all the time. But no, here they were with their mouths open over this guy talking about part of Florida.

"As you make your drive back up from the Keys," the guy said "—and be sure to plan at least two nights in Key West and then two more on your way back up Highway 1—then start to plan your next exploration." This is where Hub went over the edge, because he had already said he needed to get up off his ass and get down there to the Keys at least to see those little tiny deer and the fish that glow in the dark. The guy went on to say that when you get back up from the Keys, you basically hang a left there by Miami and you are in the Everglades. "Alligators will be as close as you are to your television right now," the guy said. "And this is not a zoo or even a wildlife preserve. No, this is the place these beautiful creatures have lived for thousands upon thousands of years, in the remnants of what amounted to a river fifty miles wide and several inches deep that flowed south from Lake Okeechobee to the Florida Bay." Hub and Anson were laughing at the name of the lake when the show moved away from the pictures of the alligators and showed these birds with necks as long as a garden hose, and more of the blue and purple and yellow fish. Hub leaned way in toward the TV and said that's it, I'm vapor. I'm going to fucking Florida, you watch me.

"Shee-it," Anson said, and Stella thought some version of the same thing to herself. One visit to Anson's not too long before, Hubber and Anson had decided they were going to go to Alaska and work on a fishing boat. But as usual, in the morning they didn't mention it to each other, as if no one remembered, as if no one had said it.

But the day after the travel channel, Hubber was talking about it non-stop. "There's a reason all those weird-ass channels came in on Anson's tube," he said. "To tell us something. But you know what? Anson won't go. And neither will Cassie for that matter."

Stella thought about that and hoped it was true. She knew Hubber had a little bit of a thing for Cassie even though he never quite said it. She was nine years younger than Stella, maybe not quite as heavy, and with all her teeth still there. Stella had one on the side that needed to be replaced. "No, you're right," she said. "Anson's too dedicated to sitting there farting in his chair all night and Cassie thinks Dickie is going to ask her to marry him." Dickie was the manager of the motel along I-80 where Cassie did some front desk work, some maid work and even the grounds when they needed her to.

"Looks like you and me, Babe," Hubber said, and came over to hug her. Stella sort of half pulled away, both because she knew he'd still smell like beer and also to show that she was a little unsure about the whole thing.

"Or else it could be just me myself and I," was Hubber's response to that. He took them to the library—another first in the time she had known him, and the first time she had any idea he knew where it was—and asked if they had a map of Florida he could look at. The library lady at the desk said yes, they had quite a number of atlases right over there at the atlas stand. She said it sort of prissy, like they were already supposed to know that. Hubber did a little squinty prancy imitation of her talking as he walked over there. None of the maps in the atlases seemed to have any roads on them—just mountains and rivers and big blue ocean parts—and so he couldn't quite show Stella what he wanted her to see.

"It's like you have eight jillion cars driving up out of the Keys here, and another eight jillion—well, maybe six—driving out of the Everglades, and they all meet up right there at Florida City." He pointed to it on the green and yellow map they were looking at. "And that's not even to mention Miami over there"—he pointed again— "and all the traffic that has to come out of there. It's got to be like hubcap heaven. And real cars instead of all the dead-ass sun-baked old shit that drives around this cornbin."

Stella looked around quickly and told him to watch his language in the library.

"Oh yes," he said in the imitation voice, "especially over here by the quite a number of useless-as-hell atlases over here at the atlas stand." He laughed out loud, as if he hoped the library ladies would hear.

"How come it just says *Fla* all through here?" was what Stella asked when they were finally on the road. They had left four different times on three different days and come back because one day it was already dark and the other times because they had forgotten stuff. Now was the first time she had a chance to get the road book out and start to study it the way she had wanted to since Hub first bought it.

"What the hell are you talking about, Stel?" Hub said. You could tell he was nervous about the whole thing. About leaving his apartment and his spot at the flea market and his brother and his hubcap suppliers and who knows what all else. "What do you mean '*fla*'?"

"It doesn't say Florida half the time in here, it just says *Fla*," she explained.

"Why don't I do this, Stel?" Hub said. "Why don't I just give you some coins, see, and I'll stop the van and you can get out and find a phone and call somebody who gives a rat's ass. Plus maybe if you'd gotten out of damn elementary school you'd realize there was such of a thing as abbreviations." He said the last word real drawn-out, like he wanted to show her he knew a big word. It gave Stella a sinking feeling in her chest and stomach, and so she shut the book and shut up herself. Hubber, who never had told her how far he made it in school, of course didn't say a word, even though he knew good and well he had hurt her feelings, and so they spent the first hour and a half—maybe eighty miles over toward Omaha—without saying anything to each other. Stella would have said something if he had gone the wrong way, but he didn't—who could get lost on I-80 to Lincoln and Omaha? For awhile she tried to think about what he might be thinking about. She figured he was worrying some more over leaving. He had given up his apartment and flea-marketed everything in it to get the money to go, but he acted like the apartment—ratty and small and hot as it was—was still his. She figured he thought about that for awhile and then switched to maybe worrying about the van and how it would do going halfway across the country. It was a Ford van, and people in the hubcap business always made fun of it. And her own father had always told her that Ford stood for Fix Or Repair Daily. Or maybe Hub was worrying if he had brought the right quantity of hubcaps with them. He had left maybe half his inventory with Anson, and had packed the rest in the back of the van where they always were. That left hardly any room for suitcases and stuff for the two of them. One thing for sure, she figured, was that he was not worrying about her.

The first thing he did say was, "What's the deal with worrying about Fla now anyway, Stel? We need to concentrate on the states we have to get through to get there. Got any like Miss or Ark in that book?" He didn't look at her, but you could see at the side of his face that he was pleased to make that joke with her.

She smiled in spite of herself. It was hard to stay mad at Hubber very long because he was basically okay under what Cassie called all that banty rooster bullshit he always put on. "We're already in the Miss—at least the Missouri Miss, but I think they call that Mo to keep it separate from Mississippi—but I don't know if we're doing any Ark. This big map in the front of the book shows the whole country and makes it look like we should head into Illinois, then a little piece of Kentucky and then Tennessee and …"

"God," Hubber interrupted. "Tennessee must be like nearly there, right?

"Not hardly," she said, and smiled over at him even though he still wasn't looking her way. She got a little shiver all of a sudden as she looked at the map. She had the whole country right there in her hands in front of her and she would be able to explain to Hubber every little bit of where they were going. "Tennessee seems like a Southern state," she said, "the way Florida is, but you know what, Hub? Parts of Tennessee are actually farther out toward Nebraska than Chicago is."

"Woowoowee," Hub said, "listen to little Miss Geography Pants showing off for the whole class."

Stella wanted to get quiet again but she decided not to. Half the time he didn't know he was being cruel. "Somebody's got to tell us the way there," she said.

"Oh, like I couldn't?" Hub said. He pulled the van off the interstate onto the shoulder and slowed it down in a hurry. "Here," he said before the van was even fully stopped, "hand it over."

Stella let go of the map book and folded her hands in her lap and looked ahead. Once he went that far, it was best to just let him go ahead and finish. The trucks were going by in a hurry and giving the van a little nudge of wind every time one went by. Hub looked at the map in the front, then paged through to find different states, finding them so slowly that you could have thought he wasn't entirely sure about the order of the alphabet. As she did many times, Stella felt slightly angry and slightly sorry at the same time. Lots of times when words were long, he would tell her he really was getting to where he needed glasses and could she help him read it. And for all she could remember—eighteen years worth—he had never even tried to use a roadmap.

"Big damn country," he said after a few minutes of looking.

"It is," Stella said, careful not to say anymore.

"No way this piece of shit will make it all the way there," he said, pulling at the steering wheel. A huge truck sped by and pushed hard.

"Sure it will," Stella said, and reached over for his arm for a second. "You and Anson have this thing running like a charm."

Hubber made an air noise out the side of his mouth, sounding a lot like Cassie when she did that. He put his blinker on, looked in the mirror for awhile, and pulled them back onto the highway.

The next afternoon, right after they actually entered Tennessee, the front left tire blew. Hub held control real well as he slowed the van down, but with that much speed to start with, the tire was completely chewed. When they stopped, you could look back and see pieces of tire like the trucks leave along the interstate.

While Hub was jacking up the wheel, he started talking about Florida. "You realize that the Everglades used to be sort of one big river, Stel?" he said at one point. He was squatting there at the tire, with one leg cocked out and sweat running down his face. The sun was right on him, and she could see how thin his hair was, and how he was starting to show age in his face. He was fifty-one years old. He looks like a real man beside the road fixing a tire, Stella thought. She wished the air conditioning worked in the van so that he could get in and cool off after working on the tire. "It was fifty miles wide and a few inches deep," he went on.

"No," she said, acting surprised. She remembered that from the travel show at Anson's, but it was a surprise to her that Hub had it right there in his mind to tell her. He never remembered anything except tire and hubcap sizes and what a good price was for any hubcap you could think of.

"'No'?" he said. "What do you mean, 'no'?"

"You know," she said, like 'no lie'."

"Why the hell would I lie?"

"Well you wouldn't. It was just a surprise to hear it."

"No shit," he said. "How often you find a river fifty miles wide, even if it is only a few inches deep."

"Well the Platte's got the few inches part," she said, thinking about home, and the times they'd been out along the river with Cassie and her friend Carolyn, drinking beer and sitting in the sand.

"You're right there," Hub said.

The van had a thump in it when they started back up. "Shit," Hub said, and slapped at the steering wheel. "I knew that spare wasn't worth diddly." They drove slowly and got off at the next exit.

The only gas station was an old no-brand. There was one service bay, but it looked like it hadn't been used in years. The guy who took the money for the gas said he really didn't know too much about tires and that there wasn't really much around this area. "I'd say just stay here on 112 instead of getting back on the interstate," he said, "and then limp her on in toward Nashville where there's more stuff—more tires stores and Wal-Marts and such."

"'Limp her on in'?" Hub said when they were back in the car. "He needs to limp on *this* awhile." He grabbed at his crotch. But he stayed on 112 and drove not faster than about 40 until they found a place that could look at the tire. What they said there was that the tire—the spare—was shot, and that there was also a rupture in the CV boot.

Hub threw his head back and to one side when the man said that. "Like hell," he said.

"Hey," the man said immediately, "you can hop in the fucker and drive right on out of here if you like, asshole."

Which is what Hubber did.

They spent a hundred and eighty-six dollars at a place right near Nashville to get the van running right again. Hub's view of that development was that they needed to get on down to Florida as fast as they could to start earning money.

"You going to sleep through Florida?" was the first thing Hub said to Stella two mornings later. He was standing beside the bed with all his clothes on.

"What time is it?" she said.

"Late," he said. "Almost seven."

"Late?" Stella said. She sat up in bed. The curtains were closed, so you couldn't tell at all if it was just before dawn or two o'clock in the afternoon. She was astounded all over again that they were in a motel. The other nights on the trip, they had slept in the van—Stella stretched out on the floor just behind the front seats and Hub in the passenger seat tilted back as far as it would go. But last night late, after they'd driven all over the place trying to figure out if this really was the same Florida City they were aiming at, Hub pulled them into a motel that had buildings going back as far as you could see. Big rectangular buildings that looked sort of like a military base. All the motels had had price signs out, and all of them had seemed cheap. This one was the cheapest, Hub had announced. Stella hadn't paid all that much attention because she'd had no idea there was any chance they'd stay in a motel. "Plus it's hot as hell outside," Hub said as they pulled in, "and tomorrow we start making money."

Stella got up and pulled back the curtain. The sun was so bright she felt pushed backwards as it blasted in on her. You couldn't tell if it was mid-morning or mid-afternoon. And with the air conditioning, you couldn't tell about the temperature either.

"It must be a hundred already," Hub said, as if he knew what she was thinking. "I was out there for fourteen seconds, which is all you need to tell." Stella got up to take a shower, trying to see if Hub's hair was wet. He was weird with showers. Sometimes he'd take one three days in a row and then go on strike or something. His hair looked dry to her, but then who knew if he was telling the truth about how long he'd been up.

Outside it was already hotter than what she'd thought from what Hub said—already hotter than she'd thought it would be all day. Out in front of the motel there was roadwork she hadn't noticed the night before. And lots of cars going too slow, it seemed to her. When they got to the edge of the motel lot, Hub started hitting the steering wheel with the heels of his hands after they'd waited maybe half a minute to get out onto the road.

"How come nobody looks over here to let us in?" he said. "We could sit here and try all day." He wasn't hitting the steering wheel hard, but it was that kind of noise that was deep and almost had an echo, and sort of reverberated inside you. The air conditioning was no better than it had been anytime on the trip, only now you could notice it even more. Hub ran all the tricks that used to make it work sometimes. Off and on, with air kept on or blown out. Fan all the way up and then off. Heat on and then off. None of it did anything except blow warm or hot air on them.

"At least we don't have to get to work on time or something," Stella said right after he'd passed on an opening in the traffic that might have been big enough.

"Like hell," he said, and Stella thought about what Hub was going to do about selling the hub caps. "Like hell."

In the full daylight, the strip of road looked crowded and new. It was shiny black asphalt, as if it had been built last week. All the buildings looked new too. There was a Long John Silver's and a Taco Bell and a big Texaco same as anywhere they'd been. Sometimes while they had made their drive halfway across the country, Stella would squint her eyes and block out some of where they actually were and then try to see stuff—through her squinted up eyes—that would tell her where they were on the map. Back in Mississippi she had done that with the river and then once more when she saw some of those hangy gray weeds on the trees. She was happy to be able to tell where she was. Now she couldn't tell at all. There was no beach or palm trees or big old-time buildings or jungle or anything that looked like the things on the travel channel back in Nebraska. There were little wavy heat things coming up off the road just like back there.

"This sucks bigtime," Hub said when they were finally moving. "It's all cars from right around here, it looks like. Plus all the same stores and stuff. The same cars and traffic as anyplace."

"What did you think would be different?" Stella said.

Hub whipped his head around toward her and touched the brake like he was going to pull off. "What's with you?" he said. "Where the hell were you when we said all that stuff about Florida? About *Fla.*" He looked ahead a second. He was right on a big old Cadillac's bumper. "Who the hell was that talking all that crap about the map and the Everglades and all—Hillary Clinton?" He laughed.

She reached to touch his arm, which of course he pulled away. "Let's go see the Everglades," she said, "and see if they're any different."

Hub moved his head down a little and looked all around out of all the windows in an exaggerated way. "Duh," he said. "I *think* that's where all these signs have been saying we're headed."

"Oh," she said, "we're on the road to it now?"

"Since we made that left off the road nobody can get on, Miss Queer For Maps, or didn't you notice?"

Stella looked out the side window to keep from getting mad and to look at the land. It didn't look anything like the Everglades. She reached down into her bag and pulled out the doughnuts she wrapped up from the continental breakfast in the building where you pay at the motel. She had been afraid continental breakfast might be a lot of tea and little crusty biscuits or something. Hub wouldn't even go down there and look. What it turned out to be was all doughnuts and sticky buns. Hub wouldn't go in, but when she brought him a spangle-covered, you could tell he was pleased. He told her that made it even a greater deal that he got them on the room. Now she was all ready to surprise him again. "More continental?" she said.

He reached right over and took a chocolate-covered. "Hell, Stel," he said, "I guess you might be good for something after all." He used to say that to her lots of times, mostly in bed, but this was the first time she had heard it in a long time.

"How far are they?" she said when it looked like the chocolate covered was calming him down.

"What?"

"The Everglades."

His mouth was full and he gestured toward her map with the hand that was holding the rest of the doughnut.

"I know," she said, "but the coloring makes it look like it's right down the road here—just a little ways."

"Looks like all tomatoes and beans and all to me," he said.

"It looks like back at home."

"Just hotter here," he said.

The road went on like that for miles. In most of the fields there were people picking the crops. Short, darkish people all bent over into the shiny green plants. Big trucks were parked at the edges of the fields or all the way into them, and in the few fields where there were no people, there were giant sprinklers spraying water all over the plants. It reminded Stella of a big outdoor factory, but she didn't say it. You could see things sort of like that back in Nebraska with the corn or soy beans, but this seemed different. Greener and bigger and with more people. Hub didn't say anything either for a few miles and then he asked her if she remembered the big freeze they'd had down here to make all the vegetable prices go nuts.

"You mean last winter?"

"No, last summer," Hub said, and let out a mouth noise.

"Sort of," she said. "How do you remember that?"

"You," he said. "You said the restaurant was going to raise prices and that would cut down on customers and they would probably fire you."

"They never did."

"No shit, Sherlock."

"I mean raise the prices," she said. "I think they got a new vegetable supplier or something. Got them from Mexico or New Mexico, I think."

Once they had passed the signs that said you were actually in the Everglades, hardly anything changed except that the big flat land no longer had vegetable fields all across it. There were no jungles or alligators or anything else except signs to tell you you were there. Every few miles there was a turnoff of the main road. Hub turned off on the first one and when he saw that all it led to was a little board walkway out over the same field, he turned around and drove back out without stopping. He told Stella to get a message to him when the attack of the alligators started. It sounded sort of like he was going to take a nap or something, even though he never did and he never let Stella drive.

Maybe five of six turnoffs later, they saw a lot of the cars in front of them turning off on one road. Hub followed them.

"Maybe this one has a shortcut back the hell out of here," he said. They followed the cars in a slow line down to a parking lot. Some of the cars went in there, but the lot was full. A little farther down was another parking lot. There were lots of people with cameras walking around. Japanese and Chinese people, lots of them, with cameras, and Americans too. Cars were moving slowly, looking for parking places. You could see kids running around all excited, telling their parents they wanted to go back.

"This is where they have the alligators," Stella said. Then she saw two signs telling about alligators and not to feed them.

"Well guess what," Hub said, "unless they come out here and eat some of these cars, we're not going to stop and see them."

She looked over at Hub. She could tell he was not going to wait for a parking place. There was sweat on the side of his face and you could see round sweat circles down onto his shirt. She wanted to tell him that they had driven a long way to get this close to the alligators and then have him just turn around and drive back out. She didn't say anything, but concentrated as hard as she could on finding a place to park.

Back at the road, Hub turned right—back toward where they'd come from. Stella thought to herself that they had plenty of time, and that maybe on certain days it wouldn't be as crowded. She wondered to herself if this was the weekend. She couldn't remember for sure. The days had run all together on the road. Hub stuck his arm out the open window and let the wind blow it around a little—just his hand sitting there in the speed breeze waving all around like he wasn't paying attention all the way. Sometimes when the wind came in like that, the hubcaps clinked against each other in the back. Stella didn't like the combination of noises. The wind was making pressure on her ears and the caps were clinking and she couldn't be sure if Hub was making a little humming noise too. He was driving too fast, and from what she could remember of what she saw on the way in, they seemed to be getting back faster than they'd gone in.

When they passed the buildings at the beginning of the Everglades, Hub rolled up the window and said they ought to sue the damn travel channel for making shit up.

"They just show you the part they want you to see," Stella said.

"I wonder if they ever do one on Nebraska," he said. "What would you show there?"

"The Cornhuskers," Stella said. "And maybe that market in Omaha."

"Who asked you?" Hub said, and wiped at his face.

"Besides you?" she said.

Hub looked at her. "What should we do now, go down to the Keys and check that disaster out?" They were back at the biggest, busiest fields.

"Maybe get some lunch first," she said. Up ahead one of the trucks was driving out of the field to get up onto the road. When Hub saw it, he started to speed up, maybe so it wouldn't beat them to the road.

"It'll stop," Stella said.

"Like hell," Hub said, "it'll get in front of us and go ten miles an hour and it'll take us a week to get back out of here."

The truck was moving toward the road as if the driver wasn't even looking down the road to see if anyone was coming. Stella wondered if there was some kind of law that you had to yield to a vegetable truck when it was full. "Slow down, Hub," she said. "I don't think they see you."

Hub kept his speed up as long as he could, as if he was playing sideways chicken, and then hit the brakes just when the truck saw them and slowed down too. There was a loud popping noise when he hit the brakes—not like a tire exactly, but something sounding like a big thick balloon bursting—and then her side of the front of the van seemed to go down lower than the rest of the van. Then the engine made a high loud whirring noise as if Hub had gunned it, but the van was stopping. The truck was trying to pull onto the road just ahead of them. Hub's face was all red and pinched up tight as he looked at the dashboard and pulled at the steering wheel. As the truck came almost to the road, the driver took both his hands off the steering wheel in order to push both his middle fingers out the window toward Hub. The truck swerved them and came back toward the feild. It went straight for a short distance further and then rolled off the edge of the road and into the ditch, at the same time that Hub steered the van onto the edge of the field. Stella looked back and saw the truck had tipped over, spilling the buckets and baskets of beans that had been stacked onto it. The van stopped when they were all the way into the field, crushing a few bean plants. Hub didn't say anything. He turned the key off, jammed the shifter up into park and pushed the door open. He slammed it so loud that Stella jumped even though she knew it was coming. Hub kicked the door after he was outside, and then walked around the van and opened the back.

"Right here," he screamed, and grabbed a stack of caps and threw them onto the dirt at the edge of the field. Stella was surprised. There were times when he got a nice cap—for a Cadillac or a Chrysler—and would spend hours polishing every little rust start out of it. Now he had just thrown a whole stack into the dirt. "Right here is as good as anywhere to set up in this hellhole." He threw another stack down, sending a loud crashing noise out into the hot day. Some of the caps slid back under the bean plants, and others spread out on the dirt. The sun was so bright off of some of them that you had to turn your eyes away. Out in the field beside the van, all the workers were standing up now, looking over toward the van and Hub and the shiny hubcaps. All those workers standing up across the field reminded Stella of squirrels when they are eating a nut, and a noise comes along and they stretch up real tall and curious to see what the hell's going on.

BALTIMORE

About a generation after the Beltway was finished and the land around it no longer appeared scraped and awkward next to the new highway, a new stretch was cut down through the marshy points and necks east of the city. The new highway rode tall and concrete-white above the salvage yards and filling stations and sheet metal shops that had evolved over the previous forty or fifty years to help serve the workers from the steel mills and the aircraft plants and the harbor itself. The new highway was an extension of the Beltway—a new outer loop—and connected the eastern part of the county with Interstate 95, the aorta of the East Coast interstates. So the new piece of highway tied the flat, forgotten east-county bogs and peninsulas with the whole country—to the big midwestern manufacturing cities that had built the implements which now formed the big piles of rusting metal you saw every mile or so when you looked down from the new highway. It was as if the factories in Detroit and Gary and Akron had sent their finished goods eastward toward the sea, and along the way the machines had picked up more and more rust and disrepair until they had stalled completely in the junk yards all over the damp, short-treed lands along the upper reaches of the bay.

And on all of those peninsulas, the housing had grown up as patterned as the businesses. Whether you drove the twisting old blacktopped two-lanes built in the thirties or one of the new boulevard-size white roads that were slowly replacing them, you'd see the same evolution of houses. First built were the flat-roofed shanties put up between the wars and right down next to the water. Next, back a ways from the water, were rows and rows of small, cookie-cutter houses built during and just after World War II to accommodate the men who came up from the South to work in the factories and to start families. And last, spread along the boulevards, were fast-rise apartment buildings built in the sixties and seventies. They took on the dingy look of most of east county almost before they were completed, even before their lots started to fill with old GM and Ford cars.

Walker doesn't drive the new white interstate stretch. Hardly ever, anyway. He tells people he doesn't like looking down on the land where he grew up, and doesn't often go anywhere the new high bridge down over the harbor can take him anyway. He sticks to the roads he knew as a boy, as they snake their way through the lowlands to lead to all the diners and stores and low-slung bars where he takes his big gray Eastern Systems truck every day, where he earns his money on every Eastern Systems dumpster that goes up over the cab and empties into the big bin that rides behind him.

He's on the road early these days. He used to have trouble getting in on time, but now that Candy does aerobics every morning before she goes to work, he is up early and wanting to get going. She gets up before it's light, and spends close to an hour doing things to her hair before she goes to exercise. When she first started—almost four months ago—Walker got angry because he thought it must be something else that got her up so early in the morning. Who in her right mind would want to get up over an hour early to go jump around and sweat for forty-five minutes? She told him three other girls at the bank had been doing it for almost a year and had lost weight and even added an inch or so to their chest measurements, and didn't he want her to look good for him? She invited him to go too, and after about a month, he tried it once. He got up at ten till six and put on some cut-offs and tennis shoes, and took along his work clothes in a plastic grocery bag. She took him into the club—all smiles like it was her favorite place to be in the world, and introduced him to people left and right. What it was was almost non-stop jumping. Some of the music was okay—the Beatles and other old rock, and even a country song here and there (when they played the first one Candy grinned at him as wide as she could through her jumping and sweating, as if to say, see, this *is* great, because they play your favorite music)—but Walker got tired quickly. He felt awkward and gawky trying to follow the commands and movements through the loud music. He was tall—almost six-two—and kind of broad-shouldered. Most of the other men seemed to be small and flexible, like little gymnasts. Walker's stomach muscles wouldn't hold up for the abdominal exercises, and his arms got quivery real fast when he tried the bowling pins some of them used while they jumped around and ran in place.

But worse than all of that was the way the women looked. There were thirty-five or forty in the class, he guessed, and maybe half that many men. Most of the men were dressed in gym shorts and t-shirts—just like you'd see on guys playing pick-up basketball. But the women wore little one-piece things that looked like bathing suits with a pair of colored panty-hose underneath, or just a leotard, or little shorts-and-tops sets. And when they bent in all the different ways they bent, you would watch the men watching them. In just that one morning, Walker saw four women's panties under their little shorts. Later he told Candy that with all that twisting and pushing they did, he wasn't so sure the whole class wasn't just for singles to get warmed up for what they were going to do after work. Candy laughed and said there was no concept of sex—no concept of gender, she said, as if correcting herself—in the class, and Walker looked at her wondering where she was getting a word like that to use. No, she told him, nobody had ever made a pass at her the whole time she had been there. Didn't she have on her wedding band? And didn't she always go with at least two other girls—also married—from the bank? Geez, Frankie, she said, get out of the dark ages. She made him feel embarrassed in a boyish way.

He never went back, but since that day he has gotten up early with Candy while she gets her stuff ready—packing up just the right make-up colors she wants to go with the clothes she's picked out. She has a new purple gym bag with a thousand compartments in it. The purple color and the compartments make Walker uneasy, as if she is hiding little pieces of her life in there. Some mornings she says she feels like he's watching her, like she's a kid or something. And Walker thinks, yeah, maybe I am watching you. But he's not sure why. He knows he loves Candy more than he ever has. They've been married just over four years, and dated for more than two years before that, but there is something different now, something he feels he needs to watch, without quite knowing what it is.

He likes his Friday run. In fact, though he's been telling people for two years that he needs to do something more challenging, he likes the job. His mother tells him that driving a truck around all day is not making the best of his abilities, and Walker tells her she might be right, but in a way he's using his love of geography—that he likes driving all over the roads that show on the Geographical Survey Quadrangle maps he's been collecting since eighth grade. He agrees with his mother and Candy that he ought to go back to school—he went to college for a year and a half before he started driving one summer and never went back, and now he puts if off from fall to fall. The Friday run takes him a little north up into the part of the county where things haven't gotten so congested. It keeps him away from the Beltway for the most part, and from most of the big malls, where the bins are always getting blocked by parked cars. It is also the day that takes him by his old elementary school, and goes closest to Candy's bank.

There is something wrong with the hydraulics on the left side of Walker's lift, and so he goes into the day—into every day—dreading a real heavy load. There was one on Wednesday, at Carroll's Plumbing Supply, that the lift wouldn't handle. That's not just the pick-up money he loses, but there's the potential of a call to dispatch and then a reprimand to him for leaving a full bin full. They'll get on you for hitting bins too soon and for low daily totals, but the thing they hate worst is not emptying a full bin. Even if you have reported the hydraulics defect over and over again and nobody has fixed it. The bin at Walker's old school is light, though, and rides up over the cab and sets in smoothly and dumps clean, Walker can feel. It's a feeling he likes, knowing what the bin is doing. He used to tell Candy about how he could tell what was in them—how you could tell after you'd turned over ten thousand dumpsters what kind of stuff was in there, and how much it weighed. For a while she liked hearing that, and he liked lying in bed with her explaining how he had maneuvered the truck that day and how he'd been the top driver for the week—six hundred and eighteen bins in a week was his record, and only the drivers who worked downtown, where there was a dump every ten feet, had beaten it. And they'd talk in the dark about when he was going to get off the road and into a supervisory job. But once Candy got on with the bank—before that she had been daytime co-manager of the 7-Eleven just down from the apartment—and got to work on a computer, she was less interested. Walker wondered, somewhere deep inside him, if she had a feeling that his job wasn't as good as hers, even though he made twice as much money.

From the school he runs a string of three bars, a convenience store, a gas station, another convenience store, a restaurant, and then heads toward the Eastern Diner, where he stops for Friday coffee. The Eastern sits right on Route 40—up north and east of the city. The highway is Walker's favorite in the world because it is frozen in time, and the Eastern is a favorite for much the same reason, along with its feel of friendliness. There is a clipping from a magazine on the wall behind the cash register in the Eastern—showing a big, full-color picture of the outside of the restaurant, along with photographs of other highway diners that look like oversized house trailers with a lot of extra chrome on them. Candy told Walker that the magazine was mostly making fun of the way the diners look and that the people who ran the Eastern didn't even realize it. Walker told her maybe, but that the article also talked about them as forms of post-war highway art, so he wasn't sure.

Inside now, he hooks his cap over one of the posts on the coat tree just inside the door, and takes a seat at the counter. He knows most of the faces around him. Route drivers tend to end up at the same place at the same time every week, and so after a while you know who gets into what truck and what kind of doughnut he likes and whether he's divorced and what he thinks of the mayor. Walker takes a counter stool next to Dave Meyers, who has the Charles' Chips route for this end of the county. The last time Walker talked to Dave Meyers, he was talking about leaving the chip route and going on with Coke, but he worried about the weight he'd have to handle, and the possible strain on his back. "Not to mention my front," he said, loud enough for the waitresses to hear, and they'd all laughed.

"Still doing the light stuff, huh?" Walker says as he sits down.

"Yeah, what the hell," Meyers says with a smile. He doesn't say anything else about it and Walker says something about the Orioles getting rained out two days in a row. Meyers is the only person Walker knows who cares as much about baseball as he does.

"At least they're not losing," Meyers says. He tears two sugars open at the same time and dumps them into a new cup of coffee. "Face it, Frank, it's just not the same with them anymore." He taps his spoon against the side of his cup. "It started when Weaver left, got worse when he came back, and things haven't been right since."

"It might go back farther than that," Walker says. "Like back to when National Beer sold them. They were meant to be with National—a nice little regional beer running a nice little team the same way they ran the brewery—and so they built champions."

Meyers looks at Walker and smiles. "You've got a pretty bad case of them, don't you, Frank?" he says, and Walker smiles back. Meyers asks about the hydraulics on the truck.

"About the same," Walker says. "They won't replace anything until it's totally shot."

"I know the feeling," Meyers says.

They don't say anything while Walker orders coffee and whole wheat toast. He used to eat three or four doughnuts in here, but Candy has convinced him that he's getting to the age where he needs to be thinking about his metabolism. "Metabolism?" he said to her when she told him that, and she said damn right—metabolism. One day it's *gender*, the next day it's *metabolism*. She told him one day soon his body wasn't going to burn stuff up as fast as it used to and wham, he was going to weigh two hundred pounds before he knew it. Not to mention the strain he was putting on his heart with all that lousy food he ate all the time.

"How's Jane Fonda?" Meyers says, as if he's reading Walker's thoughts.

"About the same too," Walker says. "Every morning at the club, half the morning with exercise tapes at home on Saturday and Sunday. Your basic fanatic."

Meyers tears off two more sugars and dumps them into new coffee. He shakes his head. "Better than my weekend, anyway," he says.

Walker doesn't say anything.

"At least you had somebody around to watch," Meyers says.

Walker still doesn't say anything. If a guy is getting ready to talk about his wife or his girl, you let him pick the pace. You don't go asking a lot of questions until he shows you it's okay.

"I mean it's pretty damn empty at my place right now," Meyers says.

"No kidding," Walker says. He can't remember Meyers' girl's name right now, but knows Meyers has been with her ever since Walker met him.

"Nope, no kidding," Meyers says. "Last weekend. Saturday night. I'm thinking we should go rent a movie or something and I hear her back in the bedroom scraping around—I thought she was rearranging the furniture—and pretty soon she's standing there in the hallway with two suitcases and is telling me she'll be back for the rest of her stuff." He pauses, takes a sip of coffee. Walker shakes his head, hoping Meyers will notice.

"And I'm standing there with no idea what in hell is going on," Meyers says. " It's better to do it clean, Dave,' she says to me." He blows air through his teeth. "She's dressed to kill—like she's on her way out the door and straight to Acapulco or someplace—and she's telling me it's better to do it clean. And you know what? I never even asked. I didn't want to know his name. I didn't want to think about her taking off for some new place with some jerk so he could rub his hands all over her pussy hair—I just didn't want to know." He takes another sip of coffee, looking around as if to make sure the waitresses didn't hear the last part.

"Damn," Walker says softly. He tries to picture the clothes, and when he does—a fancy, light purple dress that is low-cut and has a slit part-way up one leg—he envisions Candy in it, standing out in front of the apartment next to her Paseo telling Walker it's cleaner this way. He picks up his coffee to help get rid of the picture.

"Damn is right," Meyers says. "Two and a half years. Two point five years of my life I gave to her because I thought she asked for it. You know where I met her? At a track meet. Can you believe that? I took my son from my first marriage to this meet for like all ages at the Armory track and here is this gorgeous woman in these matching yellow sweats—I mean the sweetest pair of sweats you ever saw. Lemon-colored, like. She won the 440 in those things for her age group—like she knew better than to take them off even for the race." Meyers stops talking and looks at his coffee. "What the hell," he says, and slaps Walker lightly on the shoulder. "You don't need this crap, Frankie," he says, "and neither do I." He looks up from the counter at the waitresses and asks one of them why his doughnuts always have the biggest holes. They all laugh with him even though it's as standard a line as there is along the counter in the Eastern. Meyers talks a little about the new mall up in northwest county and then says it's time he got back on the route.

"It takes more hustle than it used to, doesn't it, Frank?" he says to Walker as he slides off the stool, and Walker agrees and tells Meyers he'll see him next Friday.

Back in the truck, Walker listens to the morning disc jockey joke with the news girl about her date last night, right before she starts reading the international news. The more Walker thinks back over what Dave Meyers said, the more he considers the possibility of dropping by to take his wife to lunch—anywhere she wants. The last time he did that—maybe five or six Fridays back—she got a little edgy about that big dirty truck parked right there in the bank lot, and once Walker got almost all the way over being angry about that, he told her okay, he'd park the truck somewhere dirty and walk to her pristine bank to take her to lunch. Then she congratulated him on using the word *pristine*, even though he didn't mean it, and Walker turned around and walked out and went to lunch by himself. When they made up she told him she really did feel bad about the truck thing, and knew how much he liked it, and that was just fine with her. She said she had no right to judge what he liked, just that management really did like to keep the front of the lot kind of clean-looking. Walker said he understood. And as he was going to sleep that night—after they'd made love better than they had for a long time—he had this sort of half-dream/half-vision of himself rolling up to one of those little branch banks—it wasn't Candy's exact bank—and scooping it up with the forks and dumping all the money and the cranky tellers and the little rack of information flyers into the bin, and then setting the bank back down on the lot with a bunch of cracks in the walls and the sign all mashed. He never told her about that.

In fact, there's a lot he doesn't tell her anymore. He has been thinking of maybe going out west later in the summer—when the Orioles travel out there—maybe taking in a game or two in Seattle and then driving up into Canada for a few days. Actually, for all his love of geography, he hates to travel, and has turned Candy down on every trip she's ever proposed for them except the one to her uncle's cabin in Maine right after they got married. Since then they've been to Ocean City each summer, but nowhere else. Maybe the reason Walker doesn't tell Candy about his travel plans is that he knows he really doesn't want to do it—knows that if he went, he'd be going as much to spite her as for his own pleasure. She knows he likes geography and he has been looking for ways to prove it to her and learn more for himself. He watches the flyers from the community colleges and continuing education programs, but they never have anything. You can take Polynesian cooking or Lotus computers or advanced fashion theory, for God's sake, but not geography. Candy takes a class almost every fall and spring now, usually in banking stuff or computers, although last spring she took one in photography that she ended up not finishing. For a while Walker thought it might be a warm-up to having a baby, because she talked about taking pictures of kids, but when they talked about it she said she needed to get off the counter full-time first—maybe make assistant manager or something—because then they have more invested in you and you have a better chance of coming back where you want to.

Walker takes care of his next four stops with no problems—no cars blocking things and no big weights. On the radio they are well into the dead part of the day—the soft oldies for housewives—and Walker slides in a Bob Seger tape. Bob Seger sings about being older now but still running against the wind, and Walker thinks about how people—from his younger brother to his in-laws—have been giving him grief over Bob Seger for years, telling him to broaden his horizons a little. But to Walker's mind, nothing better has come along. He tells people that the secret to a good song is a nice piano line, a persistent backbeat and a plaintive voice spread just right over the melody line. And who can do that better than Bob Seger, he asks people.

He is aware, as he dumps the Turkey Neck Inn, that he really is going to the bank. It's a little early, but that will give her time to change any plans she might have made. He'll park the truck three or four blocks away, walk in and surprise her, and tell her to aim the Paseo toward the healthiest lunch she can think of, because he's ready. In his head he rearranges his route to take in a machine shop and two restaurants on the way to the bank, and then decides once the Seger tape is finished, he'll play one of the tapes Candy has been trying for months to get him to listen to. It's New Age music, she says, and it's really relaxing. She plays the tapes in the kitchen sometimes when she's paying her part of the bills. The music's okay with him—some nice tunes and guitar and piano lines—but there are two things he doesn't like all that much about it. One is he wonders if it might not just be elevator music moved up a notch or two—you know, where the music doesn't say anything but doesn't get in the way much either. And two, it is pretty much like everything else Candy likes these days—kind of too classy and stylish for her own good or her own taste. Like she's really not quite picking it out for herself. He never did get around to doing it, but one day when he was out on his route and was thinking about her at the bank smiling like crazy at everybody because she wanted a better job, he decided to make a list of all the things she used to like and the things she likes now. The first thing he thought of was beer. She used to like beer the same as he did—good beers like Heineken and Molson—but now she'll hardly touch one. She went to wine coolers first, and lately has pretty much changed over completely to white wine. Same with

TV. Not even the good ten o'clock dramas anymore. Now it's books and magazines for her. Not that he has anything against them—just that he's never quite sure what he can suggest for the two of them to do together anymore.

At his last dump before the bank—a little sub shop called George's that sits kind of by itself along a road that has had the traffic drained away by the new interstate—Walker makes the dump and then slides down off the seat to use George's restroom, comb his hair and get a Coke before he hits the bank. George is not quite as friendly as he used to be when all twelve stools and all six booths were jammed every day from 11:15 until two o'clock, but he knows he still makes the best cheese steak on this side of town. Walker eats there at least once a week, and when he goes in now he tells George how he's taking his wife to lunch—this as a way of apologizing for not sitting down with a cheese steak. George gestures with a wave of his hand, and gives Walker the Coke on the house.

Near the bank, Walker parks the truck at the edge of Hale's Point Shopping Center. It is an old, decrepit strip center—the first one built in this part of the county, and in the time since it was put up—soon after the war—maybe six other malls have gone up in the area, making Hale's Point more and more obsolete-looking as its sidewalks crack and its buildings never get repainted. On the Hale's Point lot the truck does not look so big and dirty, he tells himself. It kind of fits in with the old laundromat and the IGA grocery store that are the closest things the center has to anchor stores. Candy's bank is two blocks away, set right on the corner next to a brand-new, long-armed traffic signal. Walker used to put air in his bicycle tires in the old Gulf station that sat, all through his boyhood, on the lot where the bank is now.

He goes in smiling, though he does not know any of the people at this branch very well. He doesn't see Candy at the counter, and scans the two desks over to the right, where you open new accounts. He pauses, and then decides to go ahead and ask. At the only teller slot without a customer, Bernice Walsh tells him Candy just left for lunch. She looks at her watch. "Couldn't've been more than three minutes ago," she says. "I think they were going downtown to eat. There's that training seminar this afternoon, and so I think they were going on down and staying." She smiles too nicely at Walker, who is embarrassed. But because he does not want to give up on his plan, he asks her if she knows where they planned to eat.

"Well," she says blandly. She is too old to be a bank teller, it occurs to Walker. Ladies with bluish hair are supposed to work the desks, or maybe the downtown counters. "Frances," Mrs. Walsh calls across the floor to one of the little desks, "you know where Candace and them went to lunch?"

Walker feels more warmth in his face, not just at her yelling out, but also because she said *Candace*. It's such a hotsy-totsy name—like Candice Bergen—and makes Walker uneasy. Candy got these little return address stickers in the mail and they say "Frank and Candace Walker" on the first line, instead of "Mr. and Mrs. Frank Walker," like on the old ones. Frances calls back that she knows it was down at the harbor someplace, but she's not sure exactly where.

Back in the truck, Walker decides he is far enough ahead for the day to push on and try downtown, as much as he hates the traffic lights as you drive down there. They are bad enough out in the county, but the closer you get to town, the thicker and more poorly timed they are. Plus the whole feel of the inner harbor makes him uncomfortable. As he takes the truck off the Hale's Point lot he decides to work on not being angry, on thinking about still maybe being able to surprise her for lunch. She used to surprise him in lots of ways like that. Some mornings he'd get in the truck and find candy or baseball cards or something silly on the seat. He never knew how she got them there, but they made him feel good. Which is the way he started thinking about this lunch. He has given her a hard time about her self-improvement stuff, when it really is all good, and he wants her to know that. Now though, on his way into the city, he is beginning to worry—beginning to feel self-conscious about walking into a restaurant while she is sitting there with a bunch of people from the bank. The New Age tape is still in the player, and Walker recognizes a version of "Greensleeves." It sounds good to him, but it takes him back to the list of things about Candy that he never quite wrote down. He left off with books. Lately she's been reading this one where the main guy is separated from his wife, and takes his dirty clothes into the shower with him so he can stomp them clean while he takes a shower, and get two things done at one time. Candy tells him the author is from right there in Baltimore, and that at least the guy had a system for things. There are times when Walker wonders if she is trying to tell him something—maybe wants him to get ready to be left behind or something. That one day she'll come home with really strange stuff—maybe a Beethoven album and some soft smelly cheese wrapped in a little triangle and a big loaf of dark rye bread, and Walker just won't know her anymore—she'll be a whole new person. Sometimes he feels that way about the city itself. People talk about the new restaurants and the shops down by the harbor, and the new stadium and new pride and sense of itself that the city has, and Walker can't understand it all the way. He's been downtown with Candy to eat, and even to see a play. He's been down there with her on festival days to get the "feel" of it she talks about so much. But to him it is all sort of flimsy and unreal. The things he remembers best from downtown have to do with sports. He and his friends used to go to the Civic Center back before the basketball team moved to Washington. They'd go see Earl Monroe and Wes Unseld, and people would cheer like crazy, and then spill out into the street on a cold winter night and still be screaming. It felt exciting and dangerous to be there. Now it feels sort of sterilized to Walker. Or the Colts. He is too young to remember the late fifties and early sixties, but there were great teams even into the seventies, with Johnny Unitas leading the way.

You read about Johnny Unitas, before he died, in *Baltimore Magazine,* and he talked about investments and good neighborhoods and getting shafted by the Colts. Even the Orioles are all corporate these days. The city, he decides as he gets close to downtown, just doesn't feel as strong to him, as masculine, as it used to. It gets written up in magazines for the new retail and culture coming in, and people still talk about the amazing rebirth, but he doesn't quite trust it. Much as he fears the heavy dumps because of the hydraulic problem, he thinks the overall tonnage of stuff he's dumped over the years has gone steadily down, as if all the big manufacturing plants—the steel and industrial parts—have been replaced by little cute stuff that people put on their mantels for a few weeks and then trash, or send to each other in the mail and then trash. He hates it that so many maps show Washington and Philadelphia, but not Baltimore. And that so many people now talk about the Washington-Baltimore area. In that order. He lives in fear that one day they'll take the Orioles away too, leaving a once-major Eastern Seaboard city with nothing but a transplanted football team and a little toy indoor soccer team for pro sports.

Near the harbor area, the traffic is not as bad as he thought it would be. They've gotten things all one-wayed to the extent that traffic flows pretty well. Walker makes a swoop down near the water and then drives up into the streets a few blocks away, where all the glitter and shininess hasn't been put in, and it still looks pretty much like harbor-area slums—the way it all used to. He finds a place to leave the truck—in a head-in parking area where he takes up a space and a half—and starts walking down toward the harbor. All around him the black kids on skateboards are fast and athletic, jumping curbs and rising suddenly into the air as if they had a ramp or had suddenly turned off the force of gravity for a few seconds. It occurs to Walker that they have changed too—maybe in reaction to the harbor—as if they have built their skills in order to better show off for the tourists.

Walker decides to try the White Gull Restaurant first. It's the one Candy talks about most. You go in and build your own lunch—all kinds of fresh vegetables and sprouts and cheeses and meats and every kind of bread you can think of. Six or eight kinds of mustard alone. Walker makes his way through the crowd, not remembering exactly where the restaurant is. He thinks it is down near where *The Pride of Baltimore* used to dock before it blew away in a storm. Candy got all bothered when that happened, and when Walker teased her that it was just a cheap re-creation of the real ship, and didn't have any business out on the high seas, they had a big fight that lasted most of two days. Walker cannot find the White Gull, and begins to look in every restaurant he comes to. He does not look carefully, but steps inside and glances around until someone starts up to ask if it will be just one for lunch, and then turns to leave. He is hoping that Candy will see him before he sees her—that she'll call out to him to come over and sit down. He goes into six or seven restaurants that way, trying to let his height work to his advantage. With each one he becomes more discouraged. Two million people in the metropolitan area and he thinks he is going to drive down here at lunch on a Friday and find one of them? When he's not even totally sure she's here, and even if she is, that she really wants to see him anyway? As Walker cranes his neck in The Cutting Board, he wonders if she thinks of him kind of like she does the truck—a little too big and scruffy to go with the bank, or maybe even to fit in her life. He shaved his beard a year or so ago for that very reason, but still likes his hair a little long at the neck, and with his bushy eyebrows and dark complexion, he feels he looks a little unkempt anyway.

Each time he comes out of a restaurant he tells himself he will look in one more and then quit. He does this five times before he really does turn away from the harbor and start back toward the truck. He is hungry and angry, and needs something to do with the energy that creates. As he gets past the tourists in their bright clothes and back into skateboard territory, he wishes he knew how to use a skateboard—that he could zoom downtown into the business district, take an elevator up to the main conference room at Candy's bank, and then do a few spinning, airborne moves in the middle of the conference table while they tried to talk about customer service. He starts to jog toward the truck once he is all the way out of the crowd. By the time he reaches it, sweat is dripping into his eyes. Inside the truck he takes out the wimpy tape and reaches back into the glove compartment for some good basic rock and roll. George Thoroughgood and the Delaware Destroyers. He revs the engine a few times to make sure he's cleared the skateboarders from behind him, and backs the truck out to aim it straight down toward the harbor. As he starts down the street, his eye catches the worn-silver ends of the truck's big forks as they stick up into the air—forks that have lifted ten thousand big metal bins of every kind of Baltimore garbage you can think of, not to mention the body of a woman in a murder case two years back that Walker helped solve when he thought one night about what a great place a dumpster would be to hide a body. All that lifting and dumping has worn and sharpened the ends of the forks, as if someone had sat up nights honing and polishing weapons until they were just the right tone and temper for battle. Walker likes having them there as the truck heads for the harbor. At the first traffic light he hits red, he brings them down a little from their straight-up position to run out from the sides of the truck, as if they are pointed swords to clear a path. That way, if he does decide to take out a restaurant on the edge of the water, then the forks will catch the sunlight just before they crash through the cute-curtained windows and send all those little chunks of cheese and meat and olive and carrot down to float their way on out into the cold gray water of the harbor.

St. Louis

Calley sat in the rising heat of a summer morning and looked out the window as though it might have been her job. She rubbed idly with her thumb at a sore spot on her chin as she looked. Her eyes were intent on a landscape changed only by the movement of her head to transfer the misfocus of the old glass from one object to another. All the way down the hill to the river, the trees and buildings had a liquid look about them because of the waves in the window. The river itself sent tiny sparkles of sunlight back up the hill, and the distance and the bad glass made the willow tree look like a big green balloon. She sat in the warm room looking outside because it was her day off from the hospital and she had not yet decided what she might do. She had not yet decided if this might be the day. Her laundry and errands were done for the week and so she could think about maybe going down to the train station to see if they had some new schedules. She collected train schedules even though they were hard for her to understand. She brought them home and studied them, feeling proud that they had been given to her by a railroad official. Her favorite name on the schedules was St. Louis. It sounded clean and faraway and different. On days when she did not go to the train station she ran errands for Mrs. Haskins, or walked down to the river, or just sat at the window to think about her mother, who had died when Calley was sixteen.

Even though she liked to have the day off, Calley missed the hospital when she was not there. She liked moving her silver cart around the halls, seeing doctors and nurses and other important-looking people. She felt proud when Mr. Langler told her she did a good job. Remembering that made her miss the hospital, and made her feel afraid that somehow when she got back after her day off, the hospital would no longer be there—that her job and her cart and Mr. Langler would all be gone. She did not like to think about that and so she reminded herself to think about if this might be the day that she would leave the hospital and never go back to it. It would be left behind with the room she rented and everything else in the city.

The girl who had the room next to Calley's was finished in the bathroom, and Calley got up from her chair by the window and went in. She washed her face and brushed her teeth and then went back into her room to put on her blue slacks and light blue blouse. She put on those clothes on almost all the days she had off, because they helped her to know if it might be the day. They made her feel older and smarter. After she had her clothes on she brushed her hair and put on her knee-hose and black shoes, and then sat down by the window again to think about her mother. There were still many days when Calley could not believe that she was gone, even though it had been almost eight years. When her mother died, Calley had been going to Marshall School. She told her mother she wanted to be a nurse, and her mother looked at her in a queer soft way and told her that the first thing to worry about was getting through Marshall School. After Calley's mother and a man were killed in a car wreck, Calley did not go to school any more. At first she decided to take a few days off until the funeral. Then Mr. Roberts from the school came to see her. He did not try too hard to get her to go back to school. He said that some people were just as well off going ahead and getting a job. She told him that she could not stand to live where she had lived with her mother, and he helped her find a new place. And he talked to

Mr. Langler about a job for Calley. The day after she got the job with the hospital, she moved in with Mrs. Haskins.

Mr. Roberts had also helped Calley open a bank account back at that time. She had almost $1,300 in the bank. Sometimes she had a little more, and sometimes less, but for several years she had never let her account go below eight hundred. She liked knowing that the money was there. It made her know that when the day did come she would be able to walk into the bank and get her money and take it to the railroad station and buy a ticket for anywhere she wanted to go. She could see herself in her blue slacks and light blue blouse, carrying her mother's old brown suitcase and her own blue one. Calley wished that her mother were still alive so that they could get dressed up together and get on the train and ride away somewhere. Maybe St. Louis. Calley had three schedules with St. Louis on them. She loved that name.

Calley had gotten up too late for breakfast. Mrs. Haskins served breakfast at seven o'clock every day, and Calley had not gotten up until almost nine. Sitting by the window, she felt hungry. She did not have any food in her room. Mrs. Haskins did not allow cooking except on the first floor, and so Calley sometimes kept cupcakes or doughnuts, but she did not have any now. She stood up and stretched, looking at her light blue blouse in the mirror. She liked the soft way it pressed against the swell of her chest as she stretched.

She picked up her purse, getting ready to go outside. In the hallway it was hotter than it had been in her room. When she got to the bottom of the stairs she saw Mrs. Haskins' door open.

"Hello, Calley," she said. "You know that I have to charge you for breakfast even though you didn't get down to eat. I have to cook for everybody and if you don't eat, that doesn't mean I don't have to cook for you."

"Oh, I know, Mrs. Haskins," Calley said in a serious way. Mrs. Haskins explained that to Calley every time she missed breakfast, as though she thought Calley would forget it every time.

"It's the same with all the girls, you know," Mrs. Haskins said. "The gas and electric and all's got to be paid whether you eat or not. And it's the same for all the girls."

Mrs. Haskins smiled at Calley in an odd way and then she went back into her room. Calley went outside. It was late in the morning and the air was very hot. She wanted some lemonade and maybe a doughnut. Inside the Pic-Quik it would be cool and quiet. There was a breeze, but it seemed even hotter than the still air. Calley saw some men repairing the street. She could smell the hot asphalt and see the heat rising from it as they dumped it into the holes in the street. She could not understand how the men could work in the hot asphalt on such a hot day.

"Good morning, little Miss," one of the men said to her, and smiled in an ugly way.

"Hello," Calley said, and walked a little faster. The man reminded her of Eddie Ferris at the hospital. Once, when Mr. Langler had not been there, and two other people had called in sick, Eddie Ferris had told her he had something important to show her down in the eighth floor supply room. Calley left her cart and went down there to see. When they got to the supply room she saw a strange slow look in Eddie Ferris' eyes, and then he put his hands on the pants of Calley's uniform and would not let go until she screamed. She wondered if this might be the hottest day of the year. She turned down Eleventh Street toward the Pic-Quik. She walked past her bank, thinking about her money being kept in there somewhere—about the walls that surrounded her money and kept it safe until she needed it. She liked to see the bank.

Inside the store Calley looked at the magazine rack. She picked up a Rand-McNally travel book that had pretty pictures of lakes on the outside. She flipped the pages slowly, looking at pictures of mountains and lakes and blue skies and people wearing swimming suits. It looked cool to her. She wondered if there were lakes like that around St. Louis. She looked at the price on the front of the book. Nine dollars and ninety-five cents, it said. Calley thought that was a lot to pay, even for pictures of beautiful lakes. She put the book back in its place and walked to the back wall of the store. The whole wall was covered with tall glass doors, and behind the doors were shelves and shelves of all kinds of things to drink. She looked at the soft drinks and the beer and the milk and the juice, and then opened one of the glass doors and reached in for a carton of lemonade. At the counter she looked through the glass at the doughnuts and rolls and told the man she wanted two of the honey dips. She paid the man and went outside and sat on the edge of the sidewalk to eat the doughnuts and drink the lemonade.

When the food was gone she dropped the trash into the big barrel beside the store. She was not ready to go back to her room and so she decided to take a walk down toward the river. Sometimes it was cooler down there, especially by the willow tree. She walked down Eleventh Street past the lumber yard and the trucking company. Two old men were sitting outside the Used Appliances store on small wooden chairs. On the bridge, Calley stopped and looked down at the water below her, watching the line of shadow that the bridge sent down onto it. Under the shadow, the water was a dark, thick green, like motor oil, and seemed to be very deep. With the sun on it, the water was completely different. It looked runny, the way water really was, and the bright sun made it the color of a lime popsicle. Calley felt the little tremors in the bridge when cars passed behind her. When a fly started to bother her she went on across the bridge.

The railroad tracks ran along the river on the other side of the bridge, and between the tracks and the river was a steep slope and then a broad flat space that ran alongside the river as though there had once been another river running right next to this one. The flat land never seemed to change. Always there were the brown, broken weeds on it, all leaning the same way the river flowed. And bottles and cans and pieces of wood and bits of faded paper and cardboard. It was the same way every time Calley went there. She walked through the weeds and wiped her face with the back of her hand. She stopped at the willow tree. It grew out of the bank of the river, with some of its roots in the water. The tree leaned out over the river as though it might fall in if you pushed on it very hard. The willow made a big shady spot on the bank and over a part of the river. Some of the roots seemed to trap a little pool of water near the bank. Calley stood in the shade and looked at the water. A few tips of willow branches hung down around the roots and the little trapped water spot carried the branch ends around and around in little slow circles. Farther out from the tree the river moved along quickly, and Calley wondered where all the water came from. She wondered how, day and night, there was enough water to keep flowing past the tree. The river never stopped. But under the willow tree in the shade there was that one spot of water that looked as if it would never move down the river. It seemed to be there just to wash the ends of the willow branches that hung into it. She watched the little circle of dark green water and waved her hand at the yellow jackets that had already found her.

Calley heard a train up on the hill behind her, and felt the unsteadiness in the earth. She looked up the hill through the telephone wires at a big noisy freight train. She did not like freight trains. They were slow and loud, and not at all like the fast, narrow passenger trains she saw running on the tracks near the hospital. The train and the river seemed to be moving at the same speed. And maybe the breeze too. It felt to Calley that everything around her was being moved—as though there were something somewhere sucking the wind and the river and the train in the same direction. Only Calley and the little circle of water did not move. The yellow jackets were getting worse and she decided that she should get away from there.

Back on the bridge she did not stop to look at the water in the shadow under the bridge. She walked quickly, looking ahead of her toward the Pic-Quik and the Eleventh Street hill. She felt strong in the hot sun, even with the sweat running down her neck and arms. She walked as though she might have been on some important errand for Mrs. Haskins. At the Used Appliances store the two men were sitting in the same places, as if the heat had melted some part of them and they were stuck to the chairs.

Near the Pic-Quik Calley thought about buying herself another carton of lemonade, but decided she did not want it. Without going into the store and without even looking at it, she could see the magazine rack in her head. She could see the pictures in the Rand-McNally travel book just as though she were standing there holding it in her hands. When she was past the store she looked at her bank again, and thought again about her money inside. She thought about a robbery or a fire on such a hot day. She knew that she would get her money back if anything happened, but she did not like to think about that because then it would not be the same money—it would not be the same soft, important-looking green money that she handed under the window to the bank ladies. It would not be the same money that she worried about so much when she carried it on the bus from the hospital every Thursday.

When she was in front of the bank Calley suddenly made a sharp turn and pushed open the door. She walked right up to one of the ladies and asked for a savings withdrawal slip. She took it over to the little counter where they showed you the date and took her savings book out of her purse and then copied down the account number from the book. She put the pen down and looked at the slip. It had her account number on it, and now this wasn't just any withdrawal slip—it was her own. She picked up the pen again and signed her name and stopped again to look at the piece of paper. She felt very important standing in the cool bank by the little counter. She put the non-writing end of the pen up to her mouth, tasting the cool metal balls of the chain that attached it to the counter. Calantha Sarette: 027-006-42, the slip read. As plain as day. Then she wrote a four and two zeros in the right hand column, the same way she did when she was putting money in the bank. She put the pen back in the little hole and thought about the important piece of paper she had there in her hand. Calantha

Sarette: 027-006-42: Four hundred dollars. That was important.

Back outside in the heat with all that money stuffed in her purse, Calley was a little afraid. The money had been safe in the bank, and now it would be right out in the air if it weren't for the thin leather of her purse. It made her feel that the purse looked different now, with all that money in it. She had been carrying her purse all morning and had not thought about it. Now it felt new and strange, as if she might have been carrying a big blue box of sanitary napkins without a bag.

Calley started up the steep part of the Eleventh Street hill. The inside of the bank had not cooled her off for long, and the sweat ran down her forehead and into her eyes, making them sting. She rubbed at them with her fingers. Near the top of the hill she saw the men still dumping the hot asphalt into the street. They should be finished by now, she thought. They must have known I was coming back this way. Before she got too close to them she crossed the street so that the men would not say anything to her. When she was still half a block away she saw the man who had spoken to her on the way down the hill. He stood straight up and rested his hands on the end of his shovel. He wiped his forehead with a dirty rag that he took out of his back pocket. Calley tried not to look at him. He was sweaty and ugly, with the white band of his underwear up higher on his waist than the top of his pants. Calley walked faster and looked down at the sidewalk.

"Well now," she heard the man say in a loud voice. "The little lady decides our side of the street's not good enough for her."

Calley didn't say anything and kept looking at the sidewalk.

"I think she might be the reason for the heat wave," the man said. "I think she brought it in for all of us." He laughed.

Calley tried to walk even faster. She felt that if she looked at the man again she might get sick right there in the middle of the block with all that money in her purse. She wondered how the man could think that she had brought the heat. When she got to the house she stopped in the hall outside Mrs. Haskins' door to catch her breath. She pressed the purse against her stomach and breathed in big gulps of hot air. When she got to her room she put her purse on her bed and looked at it. Sitting there on the bed it seemed to be her plain brown purse again. She walked over to her closet and opened it, to look at the clothing. Calley liked to see her clothes, cleaned and ironed, hanging in the closet. The best part of doing the laundry was to have all the ironing done and being able to grab all the hooks of the hangers in one hand and then hang them up in the closet—putting a little space between each one so that they didn't get wrinkled and so the closet looked completely full of clean pressed clothing. She kept her white uniforms at one end of the closet. Calley stood staring into the closet as though there might be some message in the clean soft cloth of the things she wore.

Above the clothing on a shelf, one on top of the other, were her blue suitcase and her mother's old brown one. Calley pulled them both down at the same time, thinking that she would make sure nothing had been left in them by mistake. She put the suitcases on the bed and opened them with loud clicks. Both were empty except for a hairpin she found in one of the side pockets of her mother's. Calley left the lids open and stepped away from the bed, with the suitcases sitting there like two big open mouths needing something to eat. She rubbed at her face with her thumbnail as she watched the suitcases.

Even when the closet was empty and she had put most of the things from her dresser into the suitcases too, Calley did not want to think just yet about what she was doing. She knew now that all of her clothes would fit into the two suitcases. She snapped them shut. The sound was dull and thick. There was something important in the sound of full suitcases being snapped shut. She set the two suitcases upright on the floor and sat down on the bed to look at them. Then she got up quickly and went into the bathroom to get her toothbrush and toothpaste and comb. She put them in her purse. Something in Calley wanted to sit on the bed or by the window and think about the suitcases, but something else in the room—the heat maybe, or remembering the sound of the suitcases—made her need to keep moving. She closed the curtain and the bathroom door. She picked up her purse and stood by the suitcases and looked back at her room. It seemed small and dark to her, as though it were a place she did not know very well.

When Calley was outside the building and Mrs. Haskins had not opened her door to talk to her, Calley had to stop and put her suitcases down to slow her heartbeat and to catch her breath. Then she picked up the suitcases and started up the street—away from where the men were working. She walked to the corner where she caught the Number 6 Downtown bus. As she walked, Calley had a feeling that a lot was happening to her today. It reminded her of the day Mr. Roberts told her she had a job. On that day, and on this one too, she wanted to be able to talk to her mother—to be able to sit down at a kitchen table and tell her mother some good news and have them both laugh and be proud. She hadn't been able to tell her mother about the job, and now she couldn't tell her about this day either.

At the corner Calley put the suitcases down and sat on hers, with her purse between her hands. She watched the heat rising from the black street as she looked up the hill for the bus. She could see the watery-looking spots on the street that were always there on a hot day, when you were far away, but that went away when you tried to walk up to them. She was so hot that parts of her light blue blouse were turning darker with sweat. When she saw the front of a green city bus come over the hill she stood up and picked up the suitcases. When the door of the bus opened she had a feeling of wanting to think about if this might be the day.

The bus was not air conditioned, and only a few of the windows were opened. Calley draped her arm over the suitcases in the seat next to her and looked out the dirty window. The Number 6 was the bus she took to work and back every day, and outside she saw the same things she saw every day. There were children on the vacant lot where the gas station used to be, and they were laughing and throwing chunks of dirt at each other. Outside the grocery store there were two grocery boys helping people get their groceries into their cars. Calley had seen these places many times, but now they seemed both far away and just outside the bus, at the same time. It reminded her of the watery spots. You could see them and knew they were there, but then they weren't. She sometimes had dreams when things were real and not real—when everything shifted back and forth between being too close and too far away. She tried hard not to think about if this might be the day.

When she got off the bus she was directly in front of the railroad station. She carried her suitcases right in and walked up to the Amtrak sign and told the railroad official that she wanted a ticket to St. Louis.

"Round-trip or one-way?" the railroad official said. He wore a tall blue hat the way all the railroad officials did. He looked important to Calley. She took in a deep breath as if to help make up her mind and told the railroad official one-way would be fine.

"Coach or first class?" The railroad official was paging through a book as he talked.

"First class," Calley said. She felt good standing there. It was more important to be in the railroad station than anywhere else, even the bank.

"St. Louis, St. Louis, let me see," the railroad official said, turning some more pages. "That is through Chicago and will be one-eighty-two forty.

Calley counted out five twenty dollar bills and slid them under the little black bars to the railroad official. Then she counted out five more and slid them under. She felt proud to have had all that money ready for him when he told her the price of a ticket. He gave her the change and then slid a ticket under the bars to her. Calley felt a little shiver down her back as she put her hand on the ticket.

"That train leaves at 6:40 this evening, into Chicago at 2:16 tomorrow afternoon and St. Louis at 9:20 tomorrow evening," he said.

"Oh, yes, 6:40 this evening," Calley said, holding her ticket envelope very tightly. "I'll just have a seat until it's time."

"Fine," the railroad official said, and nodded his head.

Calley looked around the station for several moments after she had made her arrangements with the railroad official. She looked over all the rows of empty chairs in the building, as though she wanted to find a special one to sit in. Then she carried her suitcases across the shiny stone floor and sat down. She looked up at all the schedules on the walls. They looked very much like her schedules, but were in big white letters, almost like the hymn numbers in church. She took the ticket out of the envelope and read the name St. Louis on it again and again, and then put it back into the envelope and looked up at the high ceiling and over at the railroad official. She listened to trains outside and smiled at the people who walked by. She sat in the chair for a long time, doing these things over and over again. She knew she could manage herself in a train station as well as anyone.

Then Calley looked closely at her ticket again and opened her purse. Inside the purse was a little zippered compartment that had some other tickets in it. Calley did not look at those tickets. She knew all the names on them by heart. Tuscaloosa. Greensboro. New Orleans. Austin. All in official railroad printing and inside their little envelopes. St. Louis sounded better than any of the other names in her purse. When the St. Louis ticket was inside the compartment she zipped it closed and then closed up her purse. She stood up and picked up her suitcases and looked all around the train station again, as if she wanted to memorize it, and then walked outside to catch the Number 6 Eastwind bus that would be by at about ten after five.

THE STOP

They are walking slowly through rain falling so hard that the brown water of the stream has come up to almost cover the part of the rest stop where the big trucks park. It is Pettis's pace they are walking, back toward the car parking. Out on the interstate itself, there are not many cars, but each one goes by with a loud hiss of rain and tires. There are only two eighteen-wheelers on the truck lot—both up toward the exit ramp—and their wheels are half-covered in water. Finally Pettis speaks for the first time since he caught up with them in the lot, and what he says is this: "And don't think just because that mattress and box springs we had is gone that we can't find another one just as new and just as hard." He doesn't look away from what's in front of him as he speaks, and nobody looks at him or says anything back. He is quiet a few more steps into the rain and then he speaks again. "So we'll have the whole damn situation straightened out, right Lardie?"

Her name is Ardele, and she'd never been called anything but Ardie until a year or so after she met Pettis, and maybe she *had* put on ten or fifteen pounds, and he put the L in front of it and kept it there.

"Fuck you," she says quietly into the rain in her face, after there has been enough silence that it sounds like somebody needs to say something else. She is sorry right away, not only because Kit doesn't need to hear any more cussing than she already does, but also because she knows exactly what he will say back to that.

And he does. "That's the general idea. Back to the sack for you and me, Lardie. Now that we'll have a mattress to *your* satisfaction." He sort of sneers over the last two words. He is not a big man, Pettis, and though he is almost forty, he has not put on any weight or lost any hair or aged in any way she can see over the seven years she's been with him. He is built like a boy, with a boy's approach to life and a boy's temper. He is angry enough with life to take most everything she says literally and then go and act on it. Like getting the mattress set before he started out to find her after she told him that another reason she was leaving him was having to sleep on a ratty, sunk-down mattress with springs underneath that sounded like sick cats every time you moved. Or the time she told him, when they had been together maybe two years and things were still new and hopeful, that what she really wanted was just one lousy week of peace and quiet without him screaming at somebody. He didn't talk to her or to Kitten or to anyone else so far as she knew, for one complete week.

He is started talking now, she knows, and he will talk again in a few moments. Then pause again, but for a shorter time, then shorter again, until he has worked himself into talking constantly if he keeps them walking in the rain. "You didn't think I'd know where to track your ass down?" he says with some glee, even though he has already said this to her twice since he drove up next to her not far from her mother's house. "And know right the hell where you'd be at what time? Even right to where your ratass car would break down?" He looks at her, walking next to her in the drilling rain. She doesn't look back at him, but feels his rough smile on her. "You need to get more *creative* with how you run away to Mommy next time, Lardsie." He slaps playfully at the outside of her leg. She does not react.

"Right, Kit?" he says too loud, through Ardie. Kitten Johnson, Ardie's daughter from when she was married, is twelve. She is walking next to Ardie, as they head back to Pettis's truck, which is stuck in the water with Pettis's brother still in it, still sitting next to the passenger door waiting for Pettis to tell him what to do next. He goes for weeks at a time without talking. Not out of spite like Pettis, but because he has a hair lip, and so most of what he says comes out his nose, like he is talking through a towel stuffed into his face. Pettis makes fun of him all the time whether he speaks or not, but no one else is allowed to mock Jimmy Pettis.

"Fuck you," Kitten says softly.

"Stop that, Kit," Ardie says without turning her head or raising her voice. "Stop that right now."

"Yes," Pettis says. "It's not good manners to tell adults to fuck themselves." He laughs.

As soon as he stops laughing, Pettis puts his hand out to the side to stop them walking. "Let's figure this shit," he says. "Lardie's car is broke down back near momsy's, the truck got backed into the damn flood because Lardie was still on the damn lam, and so we are basically up this muddy-ass creek in the wrong state without a paddle. It's like a hundred miles home and nobody in their right mind is going to give four totally soaked people a ride if we hitch." He is looking up toward the main part of the stop, where Ardele and Kitten hid in the restroom as long as they could while Pettis waited them out, like he always does. Ahead of them now outside the restroom is the white car of the lady who came into the restroom and talked to Ardie and Kit, and a green truck nearly as old as the one that Pettis backed into the flood so fast that the mattress pieces fell out and floated away. Ardie is afraid of what Pettis will do next. He is not a bad man, but once he gets an idea in his head—not so much really an idea as what he wants to happen next—he doesn't sort out very well what's a good way and what might not be a good way to get it to happen. In the hard rain, she can feel the other three of them waiting for him to make the next thing happen. Ardie can feel the danger rising with the water.

Just over an hour earlier, Clennie Cobb was riding in the old green truck parked in front of the restroom. As she pulled in, she was thinking about the stop. To her, it was a plain interstate rest stop the same as all of them: an off-ramp, some slant-in parking, the little walkway over to big-fixture restrooms and vending machines with old-looking snacks and candy. Brown-painted trash cans, grassy areas for pets and kids, and a big truck lot out away from the cars. A creek running along the back edge where the land turns into the fields it used to be before the interstate was cut through.

She never would have thought at all about it if not for the man who drove the truck. To Virgil Harris, the interstate stop was a mecca. He went most afternoons and evenings after work, as if it were his second job. He knew the names of the people who emptied the trash cans and cleaned the johns and kept the lot picked up. The first time he and Clennie were on their way out here, two years ago, the first thing he said was: "Look, the stop is like a little version of all of America. You see cars from every state, people of all shapes and sizes, every car and truck that's ever been made." He sounded defensive before she'd said a word about it. Clennie didn't mind going that first time, because she didn't know—for a few minutes anyway—that it was an ongoing thing. They spent an hour sitting in the car, just looking. Then Virgil reached into the glove box of the truck and got out a worn little spiral notebook the size of a fat old paperback, and started to write things down. Clennie didn't ask him that day what it was he was writing, but the next visit he showed it to her.

There were five sections in his notebook, which was his fifth one so far. In section one he kept license plate counts by state. He had at least three from all fifty states, and kept running counts on all the states except Virginia, which he said he did in the first two books, but they filled up too fast. In section two he had a separate list of certain license numbers, paired with descriptions of people who got out of the cars and looked suspicious to him, in case something came up and the police needed the information, he told her.

Section three was weather conditions. Clennie soon learned that Virgil was a little nuts about precipitation, and had taken time off from work—he was a custodian in the municipal building for the city—to go out to the stop when heavy snow was called for. Section four was cars, which, as Clennie mentioned to him, probably should be up with the license plates. He wrote down every car that came in that was more than ten years old, by model. "Cars are antiques in twenty-five years," he loved to point out. Section five was what he labeled "Notes on The Stop," complete with the quotation marks. Things like—and he gave Clennie these examples—when two eighteen-wheelers got into a game of chicken in the eighteen-wheeler lot, or when there was a double murder involving one car from West Virginia and one from Ohio.

Clennie knew he was a strange man, but he was also the nicest and most dependable she'd ever known—not that she'd known that many—and that counted for a lot with her. He'd never had a girlfriend though he was thirty-three, and the way Clennie came into his life was that her job was to deliver biscuits at breakfast and sandwiches at lunch for Cobb's Biscuit World in downtown. And Virgil saw her come into the municipal building a few times—she delivered on a bike—with her hair all wet and her clothes matted down, and she noticed him looking at her. Not because her bra was showing through her wet white blouse, which was the reason a lot of men looked when she was wet, but because his reaction was to be interested in somebody who'd go out in the rain the same way he did.

Virgil drove an old Ford truck that his uncle gave him. He told Clennie once at the stop that when he was sixteen and had just scraped the side of a car, his parents told him that he could never get his license. They were disappointed in him overall, Virgil told her another day, because he had never played baseball when they had named him after a pitcher from a long time ago on the Detroit

Tigers. Not just his first name, but his middle name too. Virgil Trucks Harris, was his name. Virgil said the uncle—his mother's brother—had snuck Virgil out in those years until he learned to drive and finally got the license. Virgil fit the truck. They were both sort of old-seeming and blocky and greenish. Virgil was not really quite green, but he nearly always wore that color clothes and maybe his veins were close to the skin or something. He was sort of an oily man, even though his skin was pale and his hair was sandy colored. He had an odd, almost shapeless shape, like an old truck.

It was pouring rain as they got there. Four cars in the lot, all parked right up close to the walkway to the restroom. One was from Pennsylvania, one from West Virginia and the other two from Virginia. Then across the lot, on the side closer to the highway, there was a pickup as old as Virgil's with West Virginia plates. It had a mattress and box springs in the back, standing up on end and at odd angles, getting soaked. At both windows were men with an arm hanging out in the rain, with cigarette smoke coming out the windows. Virgil pulled in next to the set of cars, positioned his mirror to look back at the pickup, and got out his book to write up the truck right then and there. Clennie wondered if he should get a job as a security guard.

"What did they do?" she asked him.

"If they're moving, why the heck are they way over here in Virginia?"

"Maybe they're moving to Virginia."

"With just a mattress set? In the rain, getting all wet?"

"It's the last trip," she said. There had never been a time when he told her yeah, you're probably right. He stuck with his suspicions once he had them, right through the write-up.

"It's new," he said. "They stole it and now they don't know what to do to keep it from getting wet."

As Randall pulled them into the rest stop for a restroom break, Marla Jennings was wondering if there really was a problem they needed to confront. She knew that even if she decided there was, she wasn't ready to talk to him about it yet. But she worried: On a forty-five minute drive back to town after an early dinner, they shouldn't have to stop to pee, and she shouldn't have to think about his driving every mile of the way. What's a carafe of wine between two people with dinner, was what she told herself to put off talking about it. And the driving was made worse, of course, because of the wind and the rain. Anybody could get blown to the shoulder for a moment. You got up near sixty years old and your bladder wasn't what it used to be, she told herself too. Or: If you had to pee, you had to pee, period. And: After a certain age, had you not earned the right to enjoy dinner fully? Didn't some couples dine out *every* night, with wine?

She reached to the floor behind his seat for the umbrella. By the time he had the car stopped, she had it poised to pop open. She opened her door, ran to the front of the car and met him there under it, and they started a little trot through the downpour to the restrooms building. "I'd race you but then I'd be out from the umbrella and get all wet," he teased. He was a good man, Randall, staying with her happily through all the years when almost every man she knew of his age had made a change at some point. They parted at the entryway to the building, she heading right, he left, as if at an altar. Back through the opening between the restrooms, she saw a wide stream of brown water, up on the grass. She tried to remember seeing the stream before, as a way to gauge how much it must have risen in the all-day rain. She could not picture it in the past, but now the water was wide and fast looking—a soupy, coffee-and-milk syrup moving by fast, full of little sticks and leaves not far from the restroom.

She set the umbrella down on its point and went in. Just inside the door, as if they had been waiting for her, were a woman and a girl, standing against the concrete. They were wet and cold-looking. "Well, hello," Marla said, almost involuntarily.

"Hey," the woman said. She was short and slightly plump, her dark hair matted around her face and neck with wetness. She was dressed in a thin orange blouse, pressed to her chest and stomach because it was wet too. The girl, standing with exactly the same posture, Marla guessed to be ten or eleven. She leaned against the wall like her mother, her shoulders drawn in with the cold, her hair wet and pulled. "You just now stop?" the woman said to Marla.

"You mean just drive in from the highway?"

"Yeah. You see a truck out there?"

Marla tried to remember what she saw in the lot and could picture nothing. "What kind of truck?"

"A pickup. West Virginia plates, with like a mattress and all in the back."

"I'm sorry, sweetheart, I didn't notice," Marla said. "It's raining like crazy out there and I just didn't look." She moved toward the stall, feeling urgency.

"You sure?" the girl said.

"Yes, she's sure," the woman said to the girl. "Elsewise she would have told us."

Marla looked around quickly just before she pulled the stall door closed. There was no one else in the restroom that she could see. As she sat down she thought of Randall. He'd be finished and waiting as usual. Ready to go home and settle in with her to watch TV or read.

"You think you could do me a big favor?" came the woman's voice.

Marla was surprised to be spoken to through the stall door by a stranger. She worked to not be offended. "Well, honey, I'm a little indisposed right now," she said. She felt a light spray of water at her neck, and turned to look. Behind and above her, as big as one cinder block, was a little screened hole. The wind and the rain were blowing through it. It was like a hurricane outside.

"I mean when you get out," the woman called out. "It would only take a second."

"Hold on," Marla said.

What the woman wanted Marla to do was look out onto the lot and see if the truck she talked about was still out there, and if it was, to try to help her figure out a way to not have to go out to it. She said all this in a hurry, as if she were afraid.

"Somebody after you?" Marla said. She turned to go look outside.

The woman grabbed her arm and told her not to go out. "If they see you they'll know we're in here."

"So they're after you?" Marla said.

"It's her boyfriend but she left him," the girl said.

Marla looked at the woman and the girl, and wondered what she could look for if she were a social worker trying to find signs of physical abuse. "Does he hurt you?" she said.

"What?" the woman said. Her face was twisted with irritation maybe, or incredulousness. Or maybe just a lie.

"Never mind," Marla said. "Listen, I'd love to help, but my husband is waiting for me and I really need to get going."

"Wait," the woman said, reaching again for Marla's arm. "I want to stay away from him for awhile, you know? And there's no way out of here but that door. And he's just waiting for us to come out, I guess, if he hasn't left, so I really need to know if I can go out there, but if he sees you come out and then come back in, then he'll know."

"Were you in the truck with him?" Marla said.

"Yeah, we were," the woman said, "but only because he got lucky and drove by us when my car broke down almost all the way to my mom's house. He just drove right up, like we'd called him on the phone to tell him where to come get us."

"Then he already knows you're in here, right?"

"He'll just wait forever," the girl said, as if in disgust.

The woman batted lightly at the girl. "Yeah, he knows," she

said. "He's like playing one of his little games, where he waits as long as he needs to, because we don't have any choice but to come out sooner or later, and he doesn't have anything better to do than sit and wait, so later he can tell you he just sat and waited till you gave up."

"Just like he can stare down anybody in the world," the girl said.

"But you want to stay away from him?" Marla said to the woman.

"Kind of, she does," the girl said.

"Well," Marla said, "I really do need to get back to my husband. You want to walk out with me to see if that throws him off or something?"

The woman made a noise through her teeth. "Yeah, right," she said. "Throw him off?"

"What the hell, Mom?" the girl said. "What's the difference in that and sitting in here in the craphole all day waiting for that stream to come up and drown us in here?"

Before Virgil got out of the truck to go check on the stream, he wrote up the older couple that came in the new white Buick. "They run in to the restroom like that, a little weavy and all, and I guarantee you'll find open bottles or cans between the seats," he told Clennie as he pushed open the door. "I'm taking the book with me in case there's more." He stuck it in his back pocket, worrying it might get wet. As he started out to go look at the water, Virgil looked hard at the West Virginia pickup. The two men were still facing out toward the interstate, each with a hand out into the rain onto the side mirrors. They were moving them to look back at different things. Virgil went back to the truck to tell Clennie he thought it was a good idea for the West Virginia boys to see him out and about, so they didn't get tempted to run over and mess with the old people when they come back out to the Buick.

Then Virgil started toward the stream and nearly jumped out of his clothes. "Why didn't you tell me?" he came back, screaming at Clennie. "This is serious trouble. The cans, the restrooms, the grounds, they're all in danger." He told her he'd be back as soon as he could.

"Wait," she said. "You're telling me you're afraid those guys in the truck will go after the old people, and yet you're going out there in the hardest rain ever for no real reason and leave me here?"

Virgil felt his eyes open wide with surprise. That happened to him lots of times with her, where he was absolutely sure of something, and then she said something that could change it completely if he let it. Then he looked down, trying to decide what to do. He knew he needed to get out there and check on the stream, check on the rain and the wind and what they were doing to the stop. And put down good notes on all of it.

"How about you don't stay too long, and you look back up here every little while?" Clennie said while he was thinking.

"Okay," he said, and went back into the drilling rain. He ran through the restroom opening and down toward the stream. As soon as he got there, he turned and looked at her. He put his arms out to the side to show her how amazing it was, how fast the water was coming up. Then he ran back up to tell her how fast the water was coming up, and also to show her that he was not leaving her alone or forgetting about her and the men in the West Virginia truck. He went down to the water and came back twice, both times telling her that the water was a foot higher than the last time. The second time he came back through the restroom opening, he almost ran into the man from the Buick coming out of his restroom. He wasn't sure whether he smelled alcohol or not, what with all the rain.

Virgil wanted more than anything to stay by the stream. But he knew he had to keep looking up at Clennie, to keep her feeling safe. The rain was coming even harder than it had been. When Virgil looked up the next time, he saw the man moving over toward the women's room as if he was going to go in. Then Virgil saw several things happen almost at the same time. The woman came out of the restroom. But there were two other people with her: a younger woman—maybe as old as Clennie—and a girl. The Buick man started toward them and then Virgil saw the West Virginia truck start to back out of its parking place and past Virgil's truck toward the restrooms. It was going too fast for reverse. As it headed toward the edge of the lot by the restroom, it was going out of Virgil's line of sight. He ran upstream to where he could see past the restroom building. The truck bounced right up over the curb and crashed through some of the bushes—still going backwards. The lighter part of the mattress fell out off to one side and wrecked some more bushes. Then the driver seemed to put on the brakes, but it was too late. The truck slid down the slope off to the side of the restroom building, for a moment coming almost right toward Virgil. It skidded across the grass until its back wheels were all the way into the flooding stream. The water covered the rear wheels. As Virgil moved back down behind the building, the metal part of the mattress tilted slowly toward the end of the truck and then, in what looked like slow motion to him, fell over and into the water. The water started it moving right away. At the same time, the driver of the truck opened his door. He went around the front end of the truck and ran through the rain and toward the restrooms. Virgil moved up toward the lot a little ways. He looked at Clennie. She seemed to be watching the man go toward the restrooms. Then the young woman and the girl took off running—heading out toward the eighteen-wheeler lot at the far end of the stop. The Buick man and woman stood there a second, and then ran back through the rain to their car.

Virgil watched the three people running—the woman and the girl and the man chasing them—and then looked back at the water. It was still coming up as fast as ever, as if he had missed a foot rise while he was watching the truck slide and the people run. The brown water was coming up onto the big-truck lot too, out beyond where they were running. The man was gaining on the woman and the girl. Virgil looked at the water and then at the people. The vending machines were going to be gone soon. Then, as if maybe someone called timeout, the three people stopped running in the middle of the far lot. He knew he had a lot to write down, but he also needed to keep watching for now. All this rain and wind and rising water was completely new to the stop. There had never been anything like it, Virgil was sure, in the twenty-four years that the stop had been there. The creek was rising so fast that you could stand there at the edge, and before you knew it, the water was running right over the toes of your shoes. The trash cans out by the picnic tables had long since been sucked into the water. At first they just sort of got pulled out sideways, their chains holding them to their posts. Then the water got deeper and pulled harder and ripped the chains right off, allowing the can to take on the speed of the river immediately.

When Clennie finally couldn't hold herself back any longer and she ran down to Virgil standing there frozen by the flood, he pointed to the river and told her it was totally out of control. "It's getting higher by the second," he said. "By the second."

"What about them?" she screamed. She pointed over toward the truck lot. Virgil looked at the woman and the girl and the man, but didn't say anything. All three of them were walking slowly back toward the main lot, like they were all friends. They were not in a big hurry, even in the rain. The older people were back in their car, and were starting to pull out to leave.

"What about them?" Clennie screamed again, pointing at the three people. Virgil seemed not to know what to say. It was as if he understood that people getting chased across the lot was important, but he couldn't seem to pull himself away from the river.

"This could be it for the whole stop, Clennie," he said.

She screamed at him again. "What?" she said. She wondered why he wasn't paying attention to the right things. Through the rain, his face was twisted looking, the way a man's face looks when he is about to cry. Or already is crying. But she could not tell for sure with all the rain. "What?" she called out again.

"All of this," he said again. "The tables, the trash cans, the vending machines, all of it could wash away. It could be serious."

She wanted to tell him that it was already way beyond serious, that something was going wrong with the three people, even though they were still walking. She decided she needed to go back to the truck, and told him that was what she was going to do.

He looked at the fast brown water. "Why?" he said.

"Those men, Virgil, have you forgotten them? You were so absolutely sure they were up to no good when they came in, and now you don't even care. You're like stuck at the water."

"It's serious," he told her again.

"They'll steal the truck, Virgil."

He seemed to hear her say that. He took a step and looked like he was going to say something. But then he looked back at the water. He seemed unable to leave it as it poured into the restroom building. The man walking with the woman and the girl was waving his arm through the rain at the man still in the pickup stuck in the water. Waving at him to come on.

"Do you have the keys?" Clennie said to Virgil.

"The keys?" he said.

"To the truck," she said.

"No," he told her. "Unless you brought them, they're still in there."

"They're going to steal it," she screamed into the rain.

"They won't take it," he told her, "because they know there are eyewitnesses here to the theft."

"They don't care," she called out at him. "They don't care."

She looked up at the stuck truck. The other man in it was finally getting out. He had to stand in water up to his waist as he stepped out. Then he started toward the three people walking from the other direction, all of them heading toward Virgil's truck.

"They're going to take it, Virgil," she screamed as loud as she could. "They're going to take your truck." Then she started to run up toward them.

It was the blood out of the mouth of the woman that helped Ardie make her decision in a hurry. Pettis had waited for the woman as she'd run to the truck just after all four of them had gotten in. He rolled down his window, as if maybe he was going to talk to her when she got there. And then, with perfect timing, he threw the door open at her just as she reached the side of the truck. Ardie was packed in next to Pettis with Kit next to her and Jimmy at the far door, and she could hear the air come out of the woman as the door hit her in the chest and her head snapped forward. Her mouth hit squarely where the window was still up an inch or two. Ardie saw the blood and at least one tooth fly even before the woman got a hand to her mouth. Ardie felt her body go stiff then. Whatever else Pettis had done to her, he had never made her bleed or given her a bruise. A man gives you a bruise, you cruise, her mother told her when she was maybe sixteen, and Ardie never forgot.

The woman fell back from the truck door in the rain. The man who was with her—the man who had been running back and forth to the water like crazy nearly the whole time since Ardie came out of the restroom—was coming toward the truck now, but not very fast. Pettis backed the truck out of the parking place and stepped on the gas, headed out over the truck lot toward the interstate. Two things were ahead of him, though. One was the white car with the lady from the restroom and her husband. They were just sitting there, as if they had stalled along the exit ramp. The other was the brown water, which had come all the way over the truck lot and was now across the exit ramp. It didn't look deep enough to stop a car yet.

As soon as Pettis started moving, the white car moved on, as if they had been watching. When the car moved, Ardie turned to look back at the woman. She was slumped over and on her knees in the rain at the edge of the water. The crazy man was just reaching her. The car moving away ahead and the woman down in the water behind strengthened the decision for Ardie. She moved both her hands fast. One reached below the steering wheel, between Pettis's legs. She grabbed strongly onto things that she had never touched any way but softly and clenched her hand as hard as she could. Her other hand grabbed the steering wheel and turned the truck into the water on the truck lot. Pettis's legs seemed to shoot out in front of him with the pain, and the truck made a squealing noise from the engine as it sped into the brown water of the truck lot. Pettis put both his hands at the hand she held him with, screaming at her to let him go.

"Open that door, Jimmy," Ardie screamed as Pettis grabbed at her hand. "Open that door and get out and get Kitten out before you drown." It was not until she said that that she remembered that Pettis couldn't swim. Jimmy she didn't know about. But the water was not that deep anyway. Kitten was a good swimmer.

"You're dead, Lardie, you're dead," Pettis was screaming.

Ardie had to call out to Jimmy one more time before he opened the door, and by the time he did, it opened slowly because the water was right there waiting to come into the truck. By now Ardie had let go of the steering wheel and all four of her and Pettis's hands were down at his crotch. The water was cold at her feet and shins. She could feel how Pettis's teeth glared big and white as he cussed her, the spit flying from his mouth onto the side of her face. The truck was not moving from the engine any longer, but it was still moving. Jimmy rolled out into the water next to the truck. Pettis broke one hand free and grabbed Ardie by the hair. His other hand was against his pants now, protecting himself as Ardie continued to paw at him. She screamed to Kitten to get out of the truck. She wanted to see Kitten's face, but Pettis had her head pulled so that his mouth and teeth were right next to hers. The water was coming up toward her waist now, taking away what breath she had left. Pettis's voice was low and full of hissing, and she did not understand much of what he said to her. Maybe there were no words—only low, dirty noise. She had never tried to overpower him before, and she was surprised that he had not pinned her down right away.

"You hurt that woman," she heard herself say.

"Bullshit," Pettis hissed. "Bullshit." The water was moving up toward her chest.

"You better let me go or we're going to be all the way in the river," she screamed. She tried again to turn to see what Kitten was doing.

"We'll go down together," Pettis said. He tightened his grip on her hair.

On his way home from the storm and the ruckus at the rest stop twenty miles from town, Randall Jennings was pulled over along the interstate just before he would have exited to drive along a wide boulevard toward the hillside neighborhood where he lived. The officer asked him if there was a reason he was driving so fast and erratically. Randall Jennings asked the state trooper if he was being charged with an offense. The officer said he just wanted to check to make sure everything was okay, and asked Mr. Jennings if he'd mind putting his hands on his head and walking a short distance in the headlights of his car. Randall Jennings asked again if he was being charged with a violation and then declined to walk any distance at all in the pouring rain. The officer then told him he'd been running a little more than twelve miles over the limit, and to be careful on his way home. Back in the car, Randall told his wife that the officer may well have recognized him on some level, and couldn't quite pull the trigger.

"You'd have passed anything anyway," she said. "Two or three glasses of wine two or three hours ago," she scoffed.

"Four or five glasses an hour and a half ago," he corrected.

Two days later there was a call to the law firm where he was a partner, from a man Randall had known since high school. Danny Foucher had handled the firm's insurance in its early years, before it had gotten big, and Randall and Danny had remained occasional friends, through golf and a fondness for minor league hockey. Danny's call was on behalf of his uncle, who relatively late in life and nearly thirty years ago had fathered a daughter. The daughter, with whom Frank Foucher had not had contact for several years, had spent the recent years of her life with what Danny described to Randall as "the very worst kind of West Virginia trash."

Randall listened, and took sketchy notes for perhaps three minutes before he understood that what was being described to him was a drowning in a stolen truck out on the interstate on the night he and Marla were out in the remnants of a hurricane as it blew through western Virginia and seemed to cause all kinds of havoc for all kinds of people. He listened as long as Danny talked, hearing every detail. And when Danny paused, Randall asked him a question here and there, as if gathering the facts.

"Danny, from what you've told me, I don't think there's much doubt at all that there's no way she'll be charged in the death, and that her actions pretty much preclude any charge as an accessory to the theft," Randall told Danny. "In fact, I don't think any of it will even make it to court. But I tell you, Danny, the firm has gotten to the point where there's really no one here any more who is really up to snuff on that particular aspect. It's to our loss, but we've really gotten away from criminal over the recent years. I tell you what I'm going to do though, and that's put you in touch with someone over at Hedrick and Ames. Give me a day to make a call or two and I guarantee there'll be nothing at all for your uncle or his daughter to worry about."

And so Randall Jennings made the calls needed to find Danny Foucher's uncle a lawyer from another firm, and then dove into his own work, which revolved primarily around corporate tax situations. As he handled his work over the next few days, as he took notes on the phone or sat in conference with corporate clients, he caught himself on two occasions making sketches of the rest stop—with careful detail as to the width of the parking lot, the distance from the flooded stream to the front edge of the parking lot, the placement of people within the perimeters of the stop at some moment that he had not considered before he found himself drawing.

He thought too, more than he wanted to, about the women he now knew from reading newspaper accounts, to be Ardele Johnson—Danny's relative—and Clennie Cobb, of the same family that ran Cobb's Biscuit World downtown. The business rented space in a building owned by one of the firm's best clients. Clennie Cobb had lost two teeth and taken eighty stitches in the truck door/face collision that Randall saw sketchily in his rearview mirror through the rain. Ardele Johnson, the paper said, had stood in water up to her neck with her daughter and the drowned man's brother as the truck had been pulled into the grossly swollen stream. The tone of the accounts indicated that it was as likely as not that no charges would be filed.

Randall and Marla had convinced themselves, that early evening in the rain when she asked him why he had stayed so long on the entrance ramp back onto the interstate and then driven so fast that he'd been pulled over, that they hadn't really needed to go back and become a part of what looked to be a bit of mountain-hollow feuding spilling into the interstate stop. They had no idea, just then, who owned what truck and who was headed where. And as Danny Foucher had described things to Randall, it occurred to him that he would not really be of much use to prosecution or defense, simply because there was at least the possibility that either side could learn of his near-arrest, and cast doubt on whatever testimony he gave. The case, it seemed to him now, was clear enough anyway. Paul Pettis had stolen a truck, committed assault on one woman and then another. All just before he'd drowned in the stolen truck, even though the driver's side window had been open beside him and the truck apparently never quite completely disappeared under the water. Justice, Randall was reasonably sure, had already been served.

He took pains to confirm with Marla the next evening as they put their books down for the night exactly what would be his own penance for mutely, mentally recusing himself from any association with a case that would likely come to nothing anyway: Simply, they would be more responsible. They would never find themselves in that same situation ever again, with a fear based on alcohol consumption. They both admitted to slight ill-ease with the solution, but talked to each other carefully, lovingly, about the best thing sometimes being to just let something go. They complimented each other on their plans to be more responsible. As they moved, slightly restlessly, toward sleep, they were still fully unaware, aside from brief mention of his name in the newspaper stories, of the well-developed, habitually practiced tendency of Virgil Trucks Harris to write down, in one little book or another, most every single thing he saw or remembered from his precious little corner of the world.

SHOES

Back to the north and west from the crowded South Carolina coast, the land runs hot and flat and sandy, with small pines clustering here and there along the Pee Dee River as it snakes its way—inky and thick-looking—toward the ocean. It's the trees and the sandy soil that make the river look black, give it a feel of danger when you look down on it from a highway bridge. In the fields that roll away from the river, the flat land yields tobacco and cotton—crops from the last century, growing now in the same fields they grew in a hundred years ago, and waiting to be picked by smallish, scruffy people who look like they might be from the last century too.

The county roads, most of them paved now, lead back through the fields and out to low-built, bad houses. Most of the housing from that last century—built poorly and of wood and ever-threatened by fire—has returned to the land, and so the oldest houses you see are the flat-roofed shanties built in the twenties or so, many of them abandoned and falling down. The ones that are lived in, mostly by older people, tend to have no car beside them, or maybe a GM monster from twenty years ago sinking slowly into the sand. Then there are houses built not long before those cars were, square one-stories, some with brick facades and all with not much room in them.

The trailers came at about the same time, set down at any angle most anywhere back onto a field along the roads. The first generation of them—long and thin and white—must have seemed like salvation at the time. Here was cheap housing that looked like it had lots of room and all the conveniences till you moved in and things started falling off in your hands. Now most of those trailers, only a few decades old, are abandoned and decaying, their cheap siding tearing off in chunks and their doors hanging open like old men with missing teeth. Often not far from one of them is a newer trailer, maybe a doublewide, as if twice as much of bad materials set down on the hot sand will do better than the older trailers.

People who don't live here—who travel through this part of the South Carolina on their way to the beach—say you could put them on any one of these hot two-lanes and they'd have no idea at all where they were, because all the roads look the same. It's an endless reach of flat land, of low-growing crops begging for even more sun, of criss-crossed roadways leading past the bad housing set back against a sad little pine or two.

June Terry knows all these roads, and can tell you how each is different from the others. She knows them because for sixteen years she has driven them twice a day for the 180 or so days a year that the schools are open. Her own run-down house back along one of them—one of the newer ones, with a brick face on it—is different from all the others because except for the morning run and the evening run, it has a big, orange-yellow school bus sitting next to it. She parks it next to the dead red Camaro that broke down six years back, the same day that Eddie Terry decided he'd had enough of her. He walked away from the house one evening near dusk—away from his busted car and his angry wife, and never came back. He went to the ocean, she came to learn, and the most recent she's heard is that he has part ownership in one of the piers there along the Grand Strand, taking tackle and bait money from families on vacation so they can stand out on the pier for an hour or two before they realize that nobody catches anything.

What occurs to her as being a constant down here—more than the roads—are the kids who've gotten on her bus over the years. Whether they are white or black, they are always the same scraggly, undersized low-country kids every fall. The only things that change some are what they carry and how they dress. Brown paper sacks for lunches disappeared years ago, and then you had kiddie-movie characters on metal lunch boxes, and then space-movie characters on plastic lunch boxes. Now you see fewer boxes at all, what with the county lunch program. And the shirts. Used to be people just wore shirts—a blue shirt or a red shirt or a white shirt. Now every shirt has a message. A brand or a slogan or a big picture of a cartoon character. Still ratty and worn, the shirts, but all with something to say.

This is on an afternoon run a week and a half ago, with three weeks left in the school year. It is the junior high run, which comes after the elementary run. It is Friday, her last trip of the day, and she is looking forward to parking the big can and settling in. She has an invitation to go to the beach for the weekend with two of the girls from transportation in town, but hasn't decided if it'll be that or settling in with the offerings of her new dish—a little one that can get you a billion channels without the dish being so big that people ask you how long you've been growing the state flower out in your yard. It's a hot afternoon, as it is almost all the school year. Her run goes deep into the county, where the roads get even narrower and the houses even smaller and more run-down. She has the last kid—Kinnie is the name printed on his little backpack—a kid who only comes about half the time, and lives out in the worst excuse for a house of any kid she's ever delivered. It's concrete, like an old military bunker or something, perfectly square as far as she can tell, and about as big as one room in a regular house. No windows. It appears there never were any windows—just these up-and-down rectangular holes about as big as a folded up newspaper every few feet across the front.

About a mile down the two miles of road she has to drive to drop Kinnie off, she sees a young man at the side of the road ahead of her. Though she doesn't know how exactly, she recognizes almost immediately that it is Petie Carroll. Maybe it is the tilt of his head and the blondish, out-of-control hair that is the same as back in elementary school. She drove him all through elementary and into junior high until he quit, in the seventh grade, as well as she can remember. That was six or eight years ago, so as she heads toward him she calculates that he must be twenty by now. He's still smallish, still sort of hollow-eyed. He's waving her down. Kids over the years have tried from time to time to get a ride with her when it had nothing to do with school, and though it's against policy, there have been a half dozen times when she's done it. She doesn't know exactly why she lets him in, especially without telling him to wait till she's dropped Kinnie and is on her way back, but she does.

"Junie," he says to her, and grins.

"Peter," she says. She knows he hates being called Petie—the name he started school with—because it was such an easy tease. "Petie went peepee in the Pee Dee," or something like that was a favorite taunt. As he got older, he worked hard at getting people to call him Carroll, but then that sounded too girly and the last she knew him he had gone back to Peter.

"Just Pete," he corrects.

"Where you headed?"

"Back toward your area maybe," he says, and looks down. As he gets even with the seat where Kinnie is, he makes a fake punch at the little boy. Kinnie flinches and appears not to know whether to smile or not. Petie walks on to the back of the bus—the very last seat, where he always tried to sit.

"Haven't seen you," June says up into the mirror when he's seated.

"You either," he says.

She lets them bounce along a ways and then tries again. "Where you been?"

"Everywhere, nowhere," he says in a sing-songy way, like she's a parent. She wonders why she let him in. In all her days driving, he was one of the three or four who gave her the most trouble. He started tiny—first grade, she thinks it was, when he got off the bus and wrote a crude-printing SHIT in the dust on the side. It got worse from there. He once climbed out one of the little half-window spaces you have on school buses and ran across a field away from her for some reason while she was letting another kid out. You don't like to see any kid drop out of school, but she can't say as she missed him too much after he left. Which makes it all the harder for her to decide what she was thinking to pick him up.

"You were up in Columbia for a while, weren't you?" she tries. She's heard that he lived with an aunt for a time until maybe a year ago, although she's not sure she's seen him in the time since either.

"Might of been," he says, and looks up at the ceiling, working on being bored.

"You ride the bus just like you used to," she says.

"You drive it even slower," he says.

They are almost at Kinnie's house. "You know Kinnie?" she asks.

"Who?"

"Kinnie up here. The other passenger."

"Sure," he says, overdoing a sarcastic tone. "I know all the little weenie heads and river rats around here."

Kinnie almost smiles at June as he gets off. He can't bring himself to turn his head to look at you full face, or say anything, but sometimes he'll move his head half a turn that way, or maybe raise his hand up six inches as if to wave.

Kinnie gets off. He could be Petie ten or twelve years ago, except he's perhaps even smaller for his age. "See you Monday, Kinnie," she calls to him as he starts down the forlorn, grassed-over rock driveway toward the bunker. He moves his head again a little ways to one side.

"No, you won't," Petie says into her hair, and then there is something cold and metal being pushed into her neck. "It's loaded," he says. "It's not aimed at you, that's just the barrel across your neck so you know it's here, okay?"

She's not sure if she's supposed to answer. She feels herself halfway between laughing and crying. She doesn't answer.

"Okay?"

"Okay, okay," she tells him, with just a little impatience. "You want the bus, Pete, you can have it. Just let me out here and you'll be halfway out of the county before I could get to a phone."

He pulls the metal away from her neck. "Who'd want this piece of shit?" he says, looking around. He puts the metal back on her. "I think I'd rather have a chauffeur, you know?" As she wonders again if she's supposed to answer, she also has to overcome the temptation to taunt him that the reason he doesn't want the bus is that he doesn't know how to drive it. This is a kid she drove to school, who ran off the bus so he could pee in the bushes, who couldn't talk to a girl, who forgot his bookbag half the time. It's hard, despite the cold metal that she does believe to be a gun, to take him seriously. She asks him where they're going.

"No place," he says. "Who says we're going anywhere?"

She starts to ask him what he wants the bus for when her stomach sinks with the realization that maybe she's what he wants. She thinks to tell him she's twice as old as he is, but stops. What if that's *not* what he's thinking of?

"Not fucking Columbia," he says after a moment, and again pulls the metal away. She strains her eyes as far to the right as she can without turning her head to try to see what he has. She can't see it. She asks him why not Columbia.

"Who wants to know?" he says. He touches her quickly with the metal and pulls it away.

"Just wondering," she says, not venturing to remind him that he brought it up. They are still a mile from the closest thing to a main road in this part of the county, which is still a nothing two-lane where you see a car every five minutes.

They are quiet for a minute or so, the bus jostling like the old cans do. He sits in the seat immediately behind her. "Don't think it's not still right on you," he says.

"I don't," she tells him. While he's quiet, she tries to figure out how frightened she is. And then wonders why she is thinking about that instead of how to get this over with. She decides there's really nothing she can do right then and that she's not all that frightened because she doesn't think he'll shoot her. He's just a kid from the sand same as the rest of them, the same sand as she is. And maybe it's not a gun anyway.

At the intersection, they see their first cars. Two of them—one coming toward them to go down the road they've been and the other crossing in front of them in the direction she turns to go home. June pauses at the stop sign and watches them both go. She knows both drivers, and waves the same way she always does. She can't tell what Pete is doing, but there's nothing against her neck. When the cars are gone, she turns right same as always. Pete is quiet while she makes the turn.

"You wave like a candy-ass," he tells her.

"Practice," she says.

He snorts a small laugh at his nose.

"So you going on home?" he says. "Park the little bus beside the little house and eat some little dinner?"

She feels fear then. He does want her. "No," she tries, "the old can has to be serviced and they're waiting for me at transportation."

He snorts again. "That's good," he says. "That's good. On a Friday afternoon. I bet."

"Okay," she says, this time without thinking, "where *are* we going?"

"The beach!" he shouts, and laughs out loud.

"The beach? It's half an hour away."

"So?"

"Well, we'll have to get gas."

"So?"

"They'll know us."

"Big deal. Drive to where they don't and if they do, we'll say it's a field trip. You ever drive for field trips or are you too good for that?"

"One kid on a field trip?" she says. "One man?"

"Whatever," he says.

"The beach," she says after a quiet few moments.

"Damn straight," he says.

"When were you there last?" she asks.

"Who wants to know?"

The road is flat and open ahead of them, with the sun still high and the air hot. She is suddenly tired of this. Without thinking she slows the bus down.

"What are you doing?" he says. She feels the metal again.

"Take that away from my neck," she tells him.

He moves it a little, then puts it back. "I'm in charge here, remember?"

"I do remember, Pete, and I don't need the metal reminder, okay? Let's just do this," she says, now speaking faster than she should, "let's just find out what the hell it is you want and then we'll see if I can really help, and if I can, I will and you don't need the gun there or whatever, okay? And if I can't help, then I won't, no matter how much you do that. Okay? So what is it you want?"

"I told you," he says.

"Tell me again."

"The beach."

"You want to go to the beach."

"Right."

"Myrtle?"

"Yeah, like down in there."

"But where exactly?"

"I don't know, just down there," he says with a hint of anger.

"Just down there," she repeats. "Okay, Pete, let's do that then.

You take your big weapon away from my neck and go sit down in a seat, and if nobody stops us, I'll take you to the beach."

"The hell you will," he says. "It's a trick."

She puts the brake on and turns to him at the same time. His eyes pop open wide. There is a gun in his hand. "Look," she says, "it's not a trick—you don't hurt me and I'll take you where you want to go, okay?"

"Sure you will," he says. The gun is quiet in his lap.

She moves back to highway speed and they're on their way. He's quiet behind her. The air is hot but at least moving around. The bus bounces along, creaking louder than crickets, the way it does when it's empty. When they get near her house, he warns her not to make the turn.

"I told you I'll do what you want," she says impatiently. "But you never told me you're not going to hurt me."

"Probably I won't," he says. She can picture the little grin on his face, like the time he coated the steering wheel with motor oil.

"What about a car, Pete? We could take my car and be more comfortable."

"This is a damn bus trip," he says immediately and forcefully. "The field trip to the beach."

She wants to tell him it can still be a field trip in a car, but she doesn't. "Well, how about this then—how about you move out from right behind me and sit over there on the other side in the front seat. You could still fill me full of holes from there if you had to."

He gets up. "This isn't like a joke, Junie," he says.

"You don't have to tell me," she says.

The gas is no big deal. They are out on the highway by then, and nobody knows them and nobody pays any attention. It's too early in the season for the big crowds of cars that come down on the summer weekends, but there's a steady flow of plates from

North Carolina and Virginia mostly, and so a school bus—even with South Carolina plates—stopping in for gas is nothing to draw attention.

"Before long one of us is going to have to use the bathroom," June tells him when they're started again.

"Not me," he says, "I don't pee anymore at all."

As they move along the highway, he seems more and more interested in where they're going and less and less in her. "Where's that pottery place?" he asks. She tells him it's on a different highway. Then he asks if this is really the way to the beach or is she jerking him around again. She says it is the way and she never jerked him around in the first place.

"Yeah, right," he says. "You'd be the first." He has stayed in the seat she put him. He has spent most of the time at the window. They are up to nearly 55, and the bus is bouncing more than she's ever felt it. She realizes that when you go this fast in a school bus that there is basically no back end to it. It sits up high and overreacts to every bump in the road.

As they come up on the bridge over the river, Pete tells her to slow down. "I mean it," he says, his tone reverting to the start of their trip.

"Take it easy," she tells him. "We'll do it, we'll slow down."

"Can you stop on the bridge?" he says. They are climbing the long slow arch up and away from the level of the rest of the land.

She turns to look at him. "You don't have your driver's license, do you, Pete?" she says without thinking.

"Fuck you too," he says without turning toward her, without reaching for the gun.

She feels a push of shame at shaming him and foolhardiness for offending him. "We can stop at the far side of the bridge and walk back up," she offers.

"Don't even try to trick me," he says.

They ride in silence for a while. The air is getting thicker. You can smell the ocean. When they are nearly upon the coast, she asks him quietly if he's got a place picked out yet.

"Place for what?" he says.

"To go," she says.

"Paint ball," he says.

"What?"

"Paint ball." He looks at her hard, as if to judge if he's made a mistake, or she has.

"What's paint ball?"

"You lie, Juniejune, you lie."

"I don't," she says, "I don't."

"Where you go in and put on these helmets and get these guns and shoot paint at guys. You run and shoot."

"Where is it?"

"Like Myrtle."

When he can't tell her where, she talks him into letting them stop and ask, and for her to use the bathroom. In the stall, she thinks only briefly about escape or trying to turn him in. She finds out the place is right down in the middle of Myrtle, where she knows she'll have a hard time parking. She asks Pete what she's supposed to do while he goes in. He doesn't hesitate a second to tell her what she does is pay and then wait. They drive around for fifteen minutes and she finally finds a long enough spot—ten blocks from the paint ball place. They get out without incident, and there is no sign of the gun. He walks more slowly than she'd have thought, looking at everybody carefully. It is a Friday evening in early summer and the streets are full of beach-dressed people. They wear t-shirts that say things she doesn't even think, much less say, even less show off to the world. Baseball hats on everybody. Big shoes, big shorts, big people. Peter is dressed in a pair of torn khaki shorts that hang way too low and a plain white t-shirt that is worn thin. A pair of old-time tennis shoes with no socks and holes worn through where the little toes are. You can almost feel him envying the things other people have on. "Some bumpin' shoes," is the only thing he says to her while they walk. When he gets a step ahead of her at one point, she catches his face as he watches everyone. It's opened up in the eyes and the mouth, like a much younger kid seeing things for the first time. Then, as if he feels her eyes, he spins all of a sudden and tells her to stay even with him.

The paint ball place feels creepy to June. You go in on the ground floor and take a dirty elevator up to a dark hallway with red velvet walls. Then you come out to a sort of open area with windows out over the main street. There's loud rock music and a kid in a tie-dye shirt to take your money. It's eight dollars. Unbelievable. She hasn't thought about the money to finance this kidnapping. There's nearly fifty dollars in her wallet. She pays, and sits on a little platform kind of thing with other adults and kids waiting. Peter walks around in a hurry, as if he can't wait. The other people waiting are younger than he is, but he doesn't seem to notice. Then six or eight sweaty boys appear out of a curtain she hadn't seen.

They are grinning and pushing at each other, talking about *blasting* that guy and *toasting* somebody else.

By the time Peter comes out and begs to do it again, she is pretty well convinced that it has been a long, long time since he's been to the beach. His bravado is lost while he asks her to pay again, with a boyish desperation. "Just once more?" he says. "Please?"

After the second time, he is sweaty and breathing hard, and says he wants a Coke.

"How about one of those fancy snow cones?" she hears herself say, "with the shaved ice?"

"I want a Coke," he says.

She feeds quarters to the machine in the red hallway and they head out into the evening. There is more noise. More music, more color and more smells. More people. Cars move slowly down the street in the middle of it all, honking and waving. She has never been to New Orleans, but on TV she has seen the people on that one street there, and wonders if this is sort of the poor-man's New Orleans. Peter is more wide-eyed than ever.

"Let's get a foot-long," he tells her.

"Oh, we're including me too now?" she says, risking sarcasm.

"Aren't you hungry?"

In the end he gets his foot-long and she gets a cheese steak sub. Way too much money and way too many calories, but hey, they are on vacation, Peter and Junie, right? She was supposed to be at the beach with a couple of friends and wasn't going to do it, and now she's here sort of playing mom to what seems more and more to be a boy—a slightly deranged boy, but probably harmless. When the food is gone—they walked the whole time they ate—he wants to see the water.

"See the water?" she asks him. He has, she decides then, never been to the ocean. He has lived the twenty years of his life thirty or so miles inland, or in the inner city in Columbia, and has never been here. Half the nation, it seems, will get into its cars in the next few weeks, and drive down here to waste money at the arcade—maybe the reason Peter hasn't asked for that is that he doesn't know it's there—and at the paint ball and the race cars and the water park and the piers, and even play in the surf . . . and here is a boy who is a South Carolina native from just up the road and he's never been. He has missed the field trips. His family has likely never been cohesive enough to get here, and so now he has kidnapped the school bus driver to make the trip. She wants to ask him about all that, to comfort him, but cannot.

At the water, he peels off his shirt, and the ratty shoes just sort of come off as he runs to the water. The surf is relatively calm, and she guesses the water is not cold enough to shock him, because he stays in. He looks up and down the beach at those in the water around him, but doesn't go as far out as most of them. He does awkward dives at the little waves and tries to ride a few in, with no success. He walks back out with a grin, picks up his shoes and his shirt and then tells her he needs shoes.

"Shoes?" she says. "Yeah, you do need shoes, but this is your field trip, right? Not a shopping trip. I only have about thirty dollars left, Pete."

"So?"

"So shoes cost lots more than that."

"Oh," he says. "Time for the plastic then, huh, Junie baby?"

"Peter, you need to get your family to buy you shoes."

"Yeah, right," he says. "Like some more of these from the Salvation Army?" He holds up his shoes. "Besides," he says, "don't forget who's in charge here, right?"

"Yes, Peter, we know who's in charge, but now you're going to add robbery to the kidnapping charges."

"I can get you paid back," he says next. "The worker comes next week and you can tell her what you got me. She'll give it all back."

"Yeah, right," she says.

He looks at her with a quick smile, as if in recognition of her echo of his phrase.

On the way back to the bus to go to the mall, they see one of the shaved-ice places, and he agrees to try one. Once they're in the bus, and drive past the game arcade, he detours them there for an hour and for twenty-five dollars. It is nearly dark now, and June is tired. "So," she tells him, "once we do the shoes, then we're going home?"

"Could be," he says. "Could be."

At the shoe store, the sales people are dressed like referees. There are six or eight of them, probably all about Pete's age, but different looking. They have fuller faces and bodies, cleaner hair, a stronger look about them. They glance at Pete and June and move on to ask others if they can help them. The walls are filled with shoes. Pete's eyes are as wide as when they got to Myrtle Beach.

"What kind do you think I should get?" he says.

"Well," she says, "those there are women's, so let's move down to the men's."

"Oh," he says, without anger.

There are more shoes in more colors than she has ever seen. The kids who get on her bus have slowly moved toward these shoes, but are behind these models. The shoes on her passengers started out white and innocent-looking sixteen years ago—just little tennies so your feet didn't get sand on them while you were in the playground, or fried on the bottom when you walked out to the bus in the afternoon. Then maybe there was some blue color in there, or black. All leading up to what you see here—shoes that look like a cross between an army tank and an automatic weapon. Big shoots of color going in all directions. Pieces of shoe tongue and shoe side and shoe sole zooming up and out all over other parts of the shoes.

One of the sales girls gives Pete a pair of socks and he tries on a pair. When he stands up in them, his raggy wet shorts and his scrawny size make him seem anchored down by the shoes, sort of held to the floor by shoes that seem way too big and way too colorful for his little body and Salvation Army clothes. It's as if he's all Pee Dee from the top of his head to his ankles, and then something completely different at the feet. He struts around the store once they're on, grinning more openly than he has the whole trip. The sales people seem to have lost some of their wariness, as if they sense a boy about to walk away in something he's never had before.

And what she's never had before is a Visa charge receipt for a pair of shoes that cost more than three times what she's ever paid for shoes for herself. Pete tells the girl in the referee shirt she can throw the old shoes away. She makes a face at the thought of having to handle them, and then tells them thanks very much.

"These are great," Pete says when they're outside. As they walk to the bus she talks to him about heading back. He says she could leave him here. She tells him she doesn't think that's too good because then she could get into even more trouble than she already will be in.

"I'm twenty-one," he tells her. "I can do what I want."

"Right, but when I get back and they want to know why I stole a school bus to go to Myrtle Beach on a Friday night, then I'll have to tell them, and then they'll be after you. If we go on back and I can tell them you'd never been to the beach before, but agreed to come on back, then I think they'll be a lot easier on both of us."

He seems to be considering this as they get back on the bus. When they're started, he asks if they can go back the same way they came. "Across that bridge where we didn't stop," he says. She tells him they can.

"What about the gun?" she asks when they're back on the highway. "If you didn't have that and hadn't sort of threatened me with it, that might help, too."

"I might need it sometime," he says.

"What if they lock you up and you never get to need it?"

"Nobody's going to lock me up." There's an edge of temper in his voice.

She turns back toward him. "I hope not, Pete, I hope not."

"How far's the bridge?" he says.

"Just up here a little ways."

"So you'll stop and we'll walk up there and look down at the river?"

"If that's what you want." The bridge they are approaching is not particularly long, but it is one of those they build now where there's a long grade up to it and then it arches way above the waterway, as if to prepare for the possibility of the hugest flood ever.

In the dark, with cars whizzing by next to them as they walk, the bridge seems even higher up. She thought as they got out of the bus that Pete might take the gun up there and throw it in, but she can't see for sure if he has it or not. For a long distance as they walk up the bridge, there is nothing to see below but the black where the little trees are. Then, as they near the top, she can see the darker-black band of the water. It is water, it occurs to her, that has run from back where she and Pete are from, water that has carried the heat and sweat of the cotton and tobacco fields down here close to the ocean, water that the Pee Dee flowed into to help build this larger flow of water to the sea.

At the top of the bridge, Pete stands still, leaning on the railing and looking down for what seems like a long time, sometimes at his shoes and sometimes as if he's trying to see down into the dark water. "It's flat-out dark down there," he says, leaning out. June moves a step closer to him, as if to look at exactly the same spot he is. She can feel the slightest touch of her sleeve against his, up near the shoulder. "You jump here," he says, "and nobody would ever find you."

HOOKS

Nehemiah used to do this, used to sit on this wooden bench on a big pier like this one out into the ocean and push the hook through the worm as straight and smooth as a straw going into a milkshake. Or, I think sometimes in spite of myself, as painful to the worm as a catheter going into a penis must be to a man. It's a foolish and crude thing to think, I know, especially since I don't care about the pain I cause the fish I catch, but maybe it helps me think about the pain Nehemiah must feel all the time. He did all the fishing as a young man—he would come home with each rope-muscled arm hung with a big white bucket full of bluefish and crabs and marlin and all kinds of good fish. And after those years, we fished together for some years—maybe ten—out on the old blacks-only pier up the coast, every Wednesday and Saturday, and caught the fish to give us most of our main dishes for the week. That was for us and his daughter who lived in Conlee then, and two of my sisters and whoever they happened to have in their houses to feed at that time. That was the years Nehemiah worked construction and was so good at it that he'd take the Wednesday off to fish with me and still go back to a job on Thursday. Not that he just didn't show. He told them he'd be gone on Wednesday, and what they did was have him to do some of the security and site clean-up on Sundays to make up for it and still get a full pay check. He worked it out, told them he'd be fishing on Wednesday with Annie, and that's where he was. In those days he was both the best fisherman on the pier and the best stud man the company had. He could run up a skeleton of two-by-fours faster than anyone. Used a nail gun like it was a water pistol, I heard a man say once. Nehemiah didn't tell me he was the best, but you could tell it the way people talked about him, the way he got his Wednesdays with me. He helped build some of the first of the high rises along the ocean. His company had moved up from just the little two-story beach cottages.

And then he fell. He came home early one day and said he had landed hard on the sand and they had awakened him with sea water in his face. He said he wasn't hurt badly, and he went back to work the next day, and he fished that Wednesday, and he went back to work that Thursday, and I nearly forgot it for a week, until something was different. In bed it was first, where his breathing was different, where a man who had always reared up strong onto me every time we agreed to, suddenly turned unsure and unfull. Where a man who never used an alarm clock to get to a seven a.m. job site started to oversleep. He forgot things. He quit talking much. He shot a nail right through the top of his left thumb two weeks after he fell. He got sick, is what happened, and ended up in the hospital for almost a month, where they didn't figure out a thing because they said they couldn't see inside his brain. They did do a whole lot of things, including a catheter. I'll never know why and I'll never forget it.

Ah, Nehemiah. Enough for now. Enough to say that since then he's been at home in one of two places. On the couch or in the bed. And so I've been out here fishing by myself. His daughter—Caroline is her name, a professional woman working for the state and now living in a fancy apartment in downtown Columbia—said there was a grandfather of Nehemiah and an uncle of hers in New Jersey who did the same thing at about the same age, with or without the fall. Began to curl back away from life and strength and light. At *what* age, I asked her, and she shrugged. "Fifties, sixties," she said. I've been with Nehemiah twenty-four years and he's never told me how old he is. Maybe Caroline doesn't know herself. One day back at that time, Caroline took her daddy by the shoulders and shook him hard in the bed for what seemed like a full minute, and I let her do it even though it hurt me to see it, because I thought it might wake him up.

Sometimes he eats a little of the fish I bring, instead of just bread, and sometimes he'll turn his head a little up from the bowed-down way it hangs, and nearly smile over a bite of a blue I caught, and I think in a flash of a moment: *There's Nehemiah.* But then he's gone again. For a long time I told him about the fishing. About the pier and the people and the fish. I told him about what I was doing while he was hiding out at home. I told him about the tides, the rainstorms, anything I could think of. But then I quit because it seemed to make him angry, although who could tell for sure.

About a year after I stopped talking much to Nehemiah, I realized that at about the same time, I also stopped talking on the pier. Oh, I'll answer a question and lend a knife or a piece of bait, but I used to be a cut-up out there, razz the old farts about not catching anything, set my pole when it was slow and walk up and down and talk. They were mostly the only people I saw except for Nehemiah. There was one other thing that shut me up pretty good too, although it had nothing at all to do with Nehemiah, and happened only last Saturday. You know on a Saturday the pier is going to be crowded. The way I see what happened is that you look back ten thousand times, as automatically as you push open a door. You look back at the hang of the line and weights, at the bait, at who is back there behind you. You don't turn your head till after you start to roll your wrist to make the cast. I'm sure I've done it ten thousand times, but it was ten thousand and one that caught up with me. It was a small boy—three or four years old with these dark eyebrows that didn't go at all with his light skin. He jumped, I guess, from the other side of the pier—off a bench like the one I was on—and right onto my hooks. I felt the terrible weight of him hitting the line, and it made my body tremble before I knew what it was. The hooks—covered with big pretty bloodworms—came up the side of his leg and then tried to take hold well up on the thigh. By the time he hit the pier there was bright red blood and a terrible scream.

"Oh my God," the mother shrieked, and the whole pier came running. The mother was blondish, in white shorts and flip-flops, and a white Myrtle Beach T-shirt. She was burned red all over—the way so many of them are after the first day here. The sister was maybe seven, and she put her hands up to her mouth and screamed as loud as her mother, and then grabbed her mother's leg. She was just as burned, and dressed in the same clothes—white shorts and a beach t-shirt over a burnt little body. Dad too—white shorts and a pink golf shirt. He kneeled right away to work on the hooks. He grimaced hard when he did. He looked at the leg while the mother held the boy by the head and both mother and son shrieked. I turned and knelt too, on the other side of the boy, but when I did, the mother let go of the boy long enough to push me by the shoulder, back off my haunches and into the railings of the pier. The father stood up a second then, as if he was going to push the mother, and then he went back to the boy. The mother grabbed the boy's head again and wailed and glared at me through her tears, but she didn't say anything else. When the father had the hooks free, he picked up the boy and carried him back off the pier. He had wrapped his pink shirt around the leg and there were bright red spots coming through. The boy was sunburned badly. The mother turned especially to look at me before she led the little girl and followed the father.

"I'm so sorry," I said when I met her eyes. "I'm so sorry." I have no idea if she heard me. I went in off the pier then too. I put my fish in the trunk and I drove to Coastal Hospital where Nehemiah was after he fell. It's still the only hospital along the beach. I stopped and bought ice to keep the fish and I talked into the answering machine that Nehemiah's daughter put on our phone, so that he could hear I'd be late if he wanted to. I had never been to the emergency room, but had come close to living in that hospital for the weeks Nehemiah was in there. I went in in my dirty fishing clothes, and people looked at me and I asked about the boy with the fishhook cuts in his leg. They told me he wasn't out yet, and gestured back where he was. I edged down there toward the curtains and I could hear the mother talking. "The whole week, Bill," she said. "The whole week down the drain because of some crazy careless woman on the pier."

"He jumped," the father said.

"All that money on the condo and now we have to go home," I heard her say.

"I don't think we do," he said.

"But those cuts. They're so deep and ugly."

"Saltwater heals."

"It stings like hell," she said. "You know the doctor's not going to let him in the water with stitches."

"Take it easy, Shelley," he said. "It's all going to be okay."

"I don't believe this happened," the mother said, and started to cry again. "She could've been drunk for all we know. AIDS. Who knows what disease might have been on those hooks that Nelson might have now."

I decided I was a fool to wait—that she'd push me again or worse if she saw me. But I waited because it seemed proper, and I had to listen to her description of me to the doctor ("a fat old black woman with no business out there"), to Nelson crying, to the whole family about to come apart. When they did finally come out, she saw me first, and started right after me. Her husband saw it and stuck out his hand and pulled her back by the arm.

"I want you to know how sorry I am," I said. "I'd never hurt a child in my life. I've been fishing out here nearly thirty years and nothing like that has ever happened," I said. It sounded rehearsed, I thought. "The hooks were brand new and clean. There's no disease." I said that part faster and then hoped it didn't sound so fast to be mean even though she might have deserved it.

"Hooks are *dangerous*," she said at the same time the husband said, "It's okay. It's not your fault."

"You could've ripped his eyes out," the mother came back in.

"He'll be all right?" I said, even though I'd heard the doctor say just that.

They spoke at the same time again.

"Our beach trip is ruined."

"He's fine. The worst part was the tetanus shot, and that's done with."

They walked out first and I followed, far enough behind that he wouldn't feel obligated to talk any more and she wouldn't be as inclined to shout at me. It was breezy and hot on the lot, and there were a thousand bugs up in the street lights. The family got into a big red car and drove away. Their windows were up and I pictured them cool in there. Maybe even the mother cooling down. I still had the drive home to Nehemiah and nobody to tell what happened to me. I did end up telling him, but who would know what he heard?

On Wednesday I wanted to skip the pier, but we needed fish because I hadn't finished on Saturday. The visit weeks at the condos run Saturday to Saturday, so I knew there was a chance I'd see the mother and the family and Nelson. And I wanted to see him in a way, to tell *him* I was sorry. I drove in more slowly than usual. I also didn't even try to find my own worms. I stopped at the bait shop and bought bloodworms even though one reason I fish is that it's free except for the gas to and from the pier and the day fee. And while I drove, I looked around at things, looking for the boy and his family, yes, but also sort of looking at where I live, looking at the land. The land itself hasn't changed as far as I can tell or remember, in all the forty-eight years I've been alive on it. It's swampy, low-slung marsh country with mosquitoes the size of helicopters and waterbugs that live all year, and little stumpy trees you could about jump over. And enough humidity to keep mildew going strong into February. It goes cloudy most every afternoon in the warm months, and sea water can come through the water pipes just as brown as cider and salty as a pork chop any day of the week without warning. There isn't a storm drain I know of between here and Columbia. This is a poor swamp of a county and while I grew up it was full of poor swamp whites and poor swamp blacks in little separate clusters staying pretty much out of each other's way. And that part's still about the same.

What has changed a lot over a period as short as the last fifteen or twenty years has to do with the gift of God that's next to this county and which that county has claimed as its own. It is, as I said, a county made entirely out of sand and swamp and bugs, except for that one giant thing at its eastern edge—the great huge Atlantic Ocean. It has been here, if you take the Good Book's word, since the days of creation, and if you take what they teach in school and seems a lot more likely, then a lot longer than that. It has been sitting there as big as the moon and reaching all the way to Spain. And it didn't change a bit to cause the change I'm talking about in this county. You still have four tides a day and an easy-slope beach along this way, though it has gotten narrower. There are still sea nettles sometimes and the water gets like a bath in the summer months. It is the same giant salt pond it ever was, but what happened is that people discovered it. The pier I fish on—or some version of it—has been here since I was old enough to get carried out onto it in my mother's arms. The hurricanes come every few years and knock one down, but they build most of them back. Down farther toward Myrtle Beach proper they've tried to make them private—to let the condo renters out on them and keep the general county riffraff like me off. It's not so different from what they used to do with the white piers and the black piers. So far, city council has apparently said no to private piers, and what I've been hoping is that it'll hold until I'm too old to come out here to feed Nehemiah and me.

As far as I know, he grew up closer to the water than I did—in Atlantic Beach in the years when it was all black. All *colored*, I guess it was, and then all Negro and then all black. Now it is like a reverse firehouse dog—a few white spots. He used to tell about what a wonderful place it was—the Atlantic Hotel and the Boardwalk and the jazz bands. He knew the ocean when it was segregated. I grew up back up in Conway, where people seem to have gotten poorer and poorer over the years. The best I can figure, I am ten or twelve years younger than Nehemiah, though I was for a long time convinced we were about the same age. He loved the ocean in his own way. He never swam in it that I saw, but he knew the fish and the tides and the winds like nobody on these piers now. He'd see a school of blues before anybody else had a clue there might be any to see. He'd cast out so far that people would turn their heads to each other. He'd catch one on each hook, and *then* let the pier know there was a school. He was king of the pier.

What you have on the pier now is mostly the burned up condo renters with a few regulars mixed in—older men missing teeth who like to pretend they're just off the ship to stop by and show the condo renters what they know about fishing. "Oh yes," Charlie Branson will tell somebody every weekend. "If one of them crabs in your cooler there dies, then all of them will be poison to eat. Oh yes." And they believe it.

Or those little sharks you catch sometimes—the foolishness that gets told about them you wouldn't believe. They grow into Jaws. They will take your hand off. They are a rare species that mature into skate. And of course the condo crowd knows no better and goes along the pier spreading this kind of garbage to take back to Virginia and North Carolina and Maryland as the truth. On my slow drive in I seemed to get scared or something. I looked at the land enough that I got scared enough that when I was maybe half a mile from the pier I turned around and went back. I wasted the gas, the time, the effort to turn that old Plymouth around and go back for Nehemiah. This is foolish, I told myself. Eight years he's been sitting at home and you're going back to get him now?

"I need help," is what I told him when I got in the house. It felt dreamy and silly while I did it. "I need you at the pier because those people are angry at me. The boy I hooked—his mother is after me and I need your help, Nees." Maybe I hadn't called him that in years. Maybe I hadn't asked him for help in years. Maybe he remembered the pier. Maybe he didn't know what he was doing exactly, but he got up from the couch and started toward me. I jumped, scared again. He had on his robe, all tattered and swung open with old gray drawers underneath and so I stopped him and told him he needed a shirt and pants. I went past him back to the bedroom and got pants and a shirt and we put them on. And then he walked straight outside without so much as a hesitation. Slow, yes, but the first time in years. And he got in the car as pretty as you please. I had to run back in so as not to pee my pants with what I was seeing. When I got back to the car, I started out slowly to see what he'd do. He didn't look anywhere but ahead, and we were all of a sudden started out toward the pier together. I'll never know why I came back and I'll never know how he got in that car, but there we were. I continued to drive slowly—out onto Highway 17, which is completely different since he saw it. I don't know if he saw how it had changed, but just having him there made me see, I guess. What it is now is that every half mile you have a 7-Eleven, a Pizza Hut, a Dairy Queen, a Food Lion and a CVS, a McDonald's, a Burger King, a Kentucky Fried Chicken, a fireworks place, a seafood store and a beach towel store. That finishes the half mile and then you start over again: 7-Eleven, Hut, DQ, Food Lion/CVS, McDonald's, Burger King, KFC, fireworks, seafood, beach towels.

"Look," I say to Nehemiah. "You see what it is out here now?" He blinks. I laugh. "Maybe you've been right staying home all this time." I laugh again. When you turn off 17 in toward the ocean there's the whole row of real estate companies that rent the condos you can see down toward the water, rising up like a big seawall. Beach Realty, Ocean Realty, Dunes Realty, Goldcoast Realty, Shore Realty. All in a row like somebody passed a law that that was the only place in the world they could locate. On down past them, the condos go up ten or twelve stories each. I tell Nehemiah to look at them. "You helped build them, you son of a bitch," I say to him, and laugh. He blinks. He helped build them and I worked for three of them in the years soon after he fell. I cleaned the suites where people like Nelson and his family stay. *Units*, they call them at Ocean Realty or Beach Realty. What a unit is a cold little box of a place that has a little living room with sliding doors out onto a balcony as wide as a broom closet. Then a little dining room with a bar, and two little bedrooms that feel too cold to get comfortable in. All with long-pile carpet and ocean pictures screwed into the walls. I used to clean them on Saturdays after the condo families left. After they left crabs in the sink and suntan lotion squeezed all over the couches and beer bottles piled up everywhere, and the TV left on and you name it. Rooms full of trash, like they never heard of garbage cans or manners. The two-by-fours that Nehemiah nailed up were underneath all that carpet and tile and paint—long forgotten.

"Look," I tell Nehemiah again. "Look at that building at the edge of the ocean." I know I should be afraid to tell him all this because it's so close to where and how he fell, but I go ahead and tell him because what does he have to lose? Here he is farther into the world than he's been in years. Can he speak even less? Can he get any more lost than he is? I doubt it.

He looks. He does look. His head is up straight and he is looking hard out the window as we drive along the ocean road. He looks poorly colored out in the sun, but he looks strong in the neck and jaws—almost like himself. I drive slowly toward the pier. The ocean side is all condos next to each other with big parking lots out front and a dumpster off to the side of the lot. Nehemiah keeps looking at the high rises like maybe he's remembering something on this amazing day. When we park at the pier, I swear he makes a move to open the door for himself. Like he knew what to do but decided not to do it. I go around and pull his door open and he gets out and walks with me back to the trunk to get the poles. When I pick up his pole—it had been sitting there by the jack and the tools forever—it seems normal. We start slowly toward the pier, with me carrying everything—poles, buckets, bait, tackle, everything. People are looking at us left and right. A squat little woman in dirty painter pants and a faded pink sweatshirt carrying all this fishing gear next to a hunched but tallish man who's doing his best imitation of Tim Conway's slow-walking old man imitation. But Nehemiah keeps on moving—on through the tackle shop and past the game machines and the door to the restaurant and right out onto the pier. I feel like my heart should be pounding, but it isn't. Right then it feels as if I'm numbed to Nehemiah because I've not understood him for so many years, because he hasn't done anything for years. But here he is walking next to me out onto the pier. As we walk, I look around for the boy and his family and don't see them. Nehemiah and I get halfway out the pier, which is far enough for this tide, and I pick a bench and stop us. I nudge Nehemiah toward the bench.

"Sit down, Nees," I tell him. "Sit back on the bench and watch the water." He blinks.

I bait the old rusty hook on his pole, thinking of the milkshake and Nehemiah's catheter and the boy's leg. Then I pull the worm back off the hook and cut the hook off and pull on the line to see what strength it has left. I tie on one of my double-hook leader sets and put new bloodworms on both hooks and cast out in front of Nehemiah. After I cast I think: I didn't look. Maybe my heart *is* pounding. I was so caught up in Nehemiah being there and Nehemiah's pole getting into the water that I didn't look. Ten thousand times I looked and was safe. Ten thousand and one I looked and caught a boy's leg. Ten thousand and two I didn't look for the first time and I got Nehemiah's line in the water. I hold the pole out to him. He blinks. He takes the pole. I take the worm I had on his old hook and slide it onto my hook, bait my other hook, look back and throw my line out next to his. Right away I get two bluefish at once from a school I didn't even see. There's immediately a little crowd to see the two fish. I think to myself it must be new luck that Nehemiah has brought with us. The people behind us are all condo people, all cooked up pink under their white clothes and talking way too loud about two fish at once. I look over at Nehemiah and then I turn around and look at them. I search for the boy and don't find him. There are four or five versions of him, but not him. It's a new set of boys seeing the pier for the first time. Then I hear a new noise. I turn back toward Nehemiah before I know why. It's his reel, squealing with the rust. He's reeling in.

MOON BEACH

What Darrow likes to notice first is the way everybody—the maitre d', the wait staff, the busboys—the way they all crisp up a little when he comes in. It's clean and precise and predictable, like the feel of the vague match between the room's stiff, white linen tablecloths and his own off-white, beige-flecked suit. Darrow comes in in a hurry, like he's going to run back to the kitchen to check on a fire or something, and then, after they've all jumped their little jump, he slows down and greets the people he needs to. He scans the private tables—the ones back among the big rocks and the ficus trees, and stops a moment to check in with them on the drinks, the feel of the room, the sound level, the wine, the food. "The right kind of lighting and the right kind of attention are at *least* as important as the food," is what he tells people when they ask him how he does it—how on a small, dying resort beach where the front row of houses has already washed away and the new front row is beginning to look like houses at the edge of a big-city ghetto, he operates the whole area's best restaurant on the first floor of a high-rise motel where high tide sometimes sends pieces of wave splashing up into the pool, the way they are right now. He tells people he does it because it's *his* hotel—seventy percent anyway—and until the damn Corps of Engineers or the state of damn South Carolina or the county of damn Charleston does something about it, he is going to have to make at least as much off the restaurant as he does the twenty-four stories above it, which are a ghost town for eight months out of the year anyway, and are getting that way in the summer too as more and more people back inland start telling each other that Moon Beach is disappearing before their very goddamn eyes, is what he tells people.

Which is why when his maitre d'—the most solicitous, sweet-moving man Darrow has ever seen—tells him that the dining critic from the *Baltimore Sun* is "in town," Darrow comes as close as he ever has to grabbing Enrique by the neck and saying, listen to me you South American faggot, you either quit talking to me in riddles or I'll take your AIDS-attracting ass and float it out into the surf. That's what Darrow told his friend Bobby Fuller later that day that he wanted to say to Enrique.

But Darrow doesn't say that. He takes Enrique by the elbow and guides him up to the front of the room as if they're going to check on a reservation. Then Darrow narrows his eyes in a gesture that is usually a smile of them—a gesture that he knows to be the most valuable physical attribute he has—and says: "Enrique, could you point out to me please the party that includes the dining critic from the *Baltimore Sun*?"

"Oh, he's not here," Enrique says a little too loudly, as if he is secretly pleased to let his employer know this. "He's down at the Coastal House." Darrow smiles again with his eyes—too deeply, so that it turns into a strong wince. "The Coastal House," he repeats, and looks away a second. "The Coastal House." He looks down at the reservation book and then back at Enrique. "And how is it that I don't know he's in town until he's in the goddamn Coastal House, Enrique? And thereby missing the best meal on the coast of the Southeastern United States? Just how in the world can that be when the boy might catch ptomaine down there?"

Enrique smiles in a foolish, frightened way and Darrow walks back out of the dining room and into the lobby. Elaine has a phone up on the registration counter before he gets there, as if she knows from his gait that he needs one. "Bobby Fuller," he says to her before he gets to her, and by the time he does get there the phone is ready for him to hear two rings before a child answers. Darrow struggles for a second before he has the name. "Buddy," he says. "Buddy Fuller, *the* number-one elementary school shortstop in Coastal South Carolina," he says. "Maybe the whole daggone state." Buddy laughs and says, "Well, Mr. Darrow," and Darrow interrupts him to say it's no lie. "Where's Bobby?" "He's not here," Buddy says.

"Still at the paper?" Darrow says.

Buddy doesn't know.

Darrow tries the paper, and then Bobby's house again. "He was out back all the time," Buddy says this time, and then Bobby comes on the line. He doesn't know a thing. Darrow makes two more calls—one to a real estate friend up in Charleston and one to his brother—and learns nothing. He gives the phone back to Elaine, calling her darling. He goes back out of the front lobby and onto Second Street. Only now it is Beach Avenue. Even City Council finally got it through its mushy collective brain that people are going to get a hint when the name of the closest street you have to the water—and which gets wet four or five times a year—is Second Street. He looks down toward Coastal House. Its only lure, he's said a hundred times, is that it is old, and you know you have to eat your food before the tide gets it. Now, at high tide, the water is crashing around the pilings as the lights shine down from under the house—a liability turned into a show.

Coastal House is actually two houses—connected when they were made into a restaurant ten or so years ago—that were built in the 1920s on what at the time must have been ridiculously high pilings. The restaurant menu—a pansy-looking thing in beige and blue on paper, for Christ sake—tells you the houses used to have four dunes and a street between them and the ocean. Coast Street. Which was gone before Darrow was born. So now these giraffe-ass houses are sitting out in the tide over half the time. You walk up a ramp from the seawall to get to them. Darrow hates the restaurant because the food is lousy—or so his brother and Bobby tell him—and because they have the dumb luck of ambience built on some nut's seventy-years-ago paranoia about the ocean.

Darrow does not know, when he calls out to a boy on a bicycle—a tourist boy—and asks him to come over, exactly what it is he will do.

"Where you staying?" he says first.

"House down that way," the boy says, straddling the bicycle. He is perhaps fourteen, darkly tanned as he looks off into the dusk, appearing vaguely afraid of Darrow.

"Good house?"

"It's not on the beach," the boy says.

"You should've stayed here," Darrow says, gesturing behind him.

The boy looks down and doesn't say anything.

"Money, huh?" Darrow says, and does not wait for an answer. "We can take care of that, son," he says. "We can take care of that."

The boy looks away again.

"Really," Darrow says. "I think there's a problem down here and the only alarm is up there by the drug store." He points along the main street back into town.

"There's no fire," the boy says.

"Sea alarm," Darrow says as he reaches into his pocket to feel for several twenties. He hands the boy the money. "It's an alarm in case of night-time flooding." He pauses, looking down toward Coastal House. "They used to test it every day at noon. Now it goes for weeks just sitting there." He pauses again. "Listen," he says next, "you take this"—the boy has already taken the money— "and head on. We could use a test of that alarm, but if it's out of your way, that's okay." He smiles with his eyes at the boy. "You have a real good Moon Beach vacation, hear?"

Darrow turns and goes back into the hotel and down in the parking lot to get the car. It is a new white Continental with three sets of ocean coat protection on it. By the time he is pulling out of the lot, the alarm sounds. He pauses, as if looking for traffic, and then starts slowly down the street toward Coastal House. People are already coming down the plank. Darrow is not sure how it is he knows which man is the dining critic—in fact he does not think about how he will or won't know—but when the right person walks down the plank, Darrow is out of the car. He approaches the man with a careful smile and a hand.

"'Course we haven't got the crab cakes down this way that you all do up there," he says, "but then we do have a specialty or two of our own." He shakes the man's hand deeply and touches him firmly on the opposite shoulder. "Some tide, huh?" Darrow says, ushering the man toward the car, which idles silently and greenly lit inside, like a cool magic palace.

Christine Harris is Darrow's girl. She is twenty-nine—ten years younger than he is—and has just started her own business. A travel agency. Darrow calls it "a key move, and maybe more, in her life," and has been helping her with it. In the beginning, when she first brought up the idea, he got on the phone immediately and contacted three people. An ad agency owner to design the brochure, his own tax man, and his brother to see about good rental space up in Charleston.

"Impressed the holy hell out of her," is what Darrow told Bobby Fuller later, when they were talking about maybe a short piece in the business section of the paper. Darrow had known Christine for about two months when the business idea came up. She had seemed like such a kid—such a standard, but beautiful, beach girl. Until that idea. Now they have been together just over six months, and the business has been open for the last two. She has good contacts for the Caribbean cruise ships, and three good European packages. Plus an 800 number, a good web site and a good storefront right in the best section of town. She tells people she works sixteen hours a day and loves every minute. And that she wouldn't have had a prayer without the help of Bradley Darrow.

Right now they are walking along the beach. It is three o'clock in the afternoon—not the best time to walk on the beach, but you have to go when the tide leaves enough room instead of when you feel like it. At high tide the waves splash directly off the sea walls and the rip-rap. At low tide you can walk, but the sand is still wet-packed or squishy. Darrow doesn't care a thing for walking on the beach, but it's one of the things Christine said she really needed from him the last time they almost broke up. Their big fights are always over his hours or if he'll show up when he says he will, or how they can meet her needs too. "It's like she's a damn shrink," Darrow told Bobby after about three months. "You can send her flowers and it's fine—just like anybody else. But it doesn't stick with her. She's like analyzing the hell out of every damn thing every damn minute. Her inner needs, her love style, those personality letters—LPGA, ESPN or whatever it is."

Right now she is upset because he has been late four times in a row. The worst one was the dining critic night a little over two weeks ago, when he was due around nine and got there just after midnight. With the dining critic.

"I call, Darling," he says. "I always call. And that night was just something you need to understand. That little crabcake goes home and writes good stuff about us and that can make a real difference. It can make people decide to come down here and *see* us. Which means more money. I mean this is a for-profit deal, remember?"

"That's not the point, Bradley, and you know it," she says. Her nickname for him is Braddey, and the use of his real name is a signal of her anger. She has on a long white skirt made out of a sort of duck material, with no slip under it and a slit up onto her left thigh, and a loose beige blouse that flaps in the wind as they walk, sometimes pressing hard against her bare nipples, and then billowing out from them. "The point is that I'm about priority number six for you." Darrow looks out at the ocean and winces.

He has on a pair of white cotton slacks and a white shirt. The pants are rolled up and he has left his shoes in the car. He knows they are a handsome couple on the beach. "Why do you keep saying that?" he says.

"Because it's true. You have Bobby and your other buddies, your business, your brother and your father, and sports on TV, and fishing—all before me. If there's a slot in between all those that works out okay, then I get it. If not, tough penuche for Christine."

Darrow has heard all of this many times before—the last few times in the exact same form. He told himself last time that it would indeed be the last time. His view is that the dinners they share, the traveling they do, the gifts he provides, the help he gives her with the business and financial help are full proof of his feelings for her, and that she does not stop to think about how good she has it. It seems to him that she takes an almost juvenile approach to the relationship. That she has to check in every fifteen minutes to make sure he doesn't have somebody else's name on his notebook.

"Women do that, Brad," Bobby has told him again and again. "They can *look* like they came right out of Vogue, and they can even be worth a million, but it's almost inevitable that once you get underneath it all, they go back to being eight years old. And sort of proud of it. Either that, or they're just cold as shit." Darrow wipes the sweat from his neck as he thinks about Bobby saying that. He notices that Christine has widened the space between them as they walk. She is down nearer the wave line, where the water is foamy and cold-looking. He knows she'll go only so far, because she wouldn't want to get that skirt wet.

"It's my need, Braddey," she says, as if trying to soften them. "Whether you like it or not, it's my needs we're talking about. And if you can't meet them then I guess we're in trouble." She stoops to look at something in the sand, and after a few steps Darrow pauses to wait for her.

When she starts to walk again, he opens his mouth to tell her yes, they are in trouble, but then stops because he is aware that it would be emotion speaking. You let emotion talk in a business deal and you're dead. You let emotion speak with a woman and you're on her level—she has you talking on the plane she's picked. You're showing you believe in a lot of stuff that has no business being believed in. He feels certain that they might as well go ahead and part here, but he isn't quite ready. The last time they came this close was less than a month ago. They had gone through the same kind of sequence, and then Darrow told Bobby that Christine got on his nerves with all that crap, and that the only thing that kept him hanging on was that, as he put it to Bobby, "half the time when I get home, if she's not pissed as hell, then she's sitting there with a wide on for me like nobody's ever had before." Darrow said this in the newspaper office and thought nothing in the world of it. The only way it could have gotten back to Christine, he and Bobby figured out, was through the advertising secretary who was the only one around who could have heard it. Darrow asked Bobby to fire her, and when Bobby acted like Darrow was kidding, Darrow said he wasn't. Christine said she'd forgive him once and only once, because she knew he was kind of a boy who liked to brag—about a good deal, a good golf shot, and good pussy. That melted Darrow a little—bought her the month. But underneath that ability to touch him by talking about sex like that or by pegging his personality, she is still trying to change him, and he has no use for that.

"I guess you may be right," he says. "Maybe some of your needs really aren't getting met."

"Is this it then?" she says, and he knows what she'll say next: "Is that really what you want?"

He is suddenly soft and tender with her. As a younger man he went through the agony of hanging onto relationships—of people saying they're leaving just to say it, and then to see what happened next. But since his business success—since he started making serious money—he has quit that. If you know it's time to go, you go—same as you walk away from a deal you don't feel a hundred percent about. "I think it's more what we both *need*," he says. His attitude toward her is all of a sudden almost like the one he has with the women who work for him. He is polite, sincere, kind. But now, like the sucking-back of a wave, the emotion has been released from him. He is aware that if she cries, he will try sincerely to help her. He'll be caring but plainly honest: They just don't quite fit right any longer.

The whole outfield is way too deep. Darrow tries to wave them in, but they don't pay any attention. He does this every inning because they tend to stand in the positions where the grass is worn away instead of bothering to think about two things—that the hitters are middle-aged city officials who don't hit anything out of the infield except little hump-back liners, and that the sea breeze is so strong that it will take any fly ball—even one hit well—and knock it right down. It is a damp, warmish day. Your glove feels clammy, as if the breeze is carrying drops of the sea and depositing them onto it. It is a wind that nearly ruins a game that Darrow already can't really enjoy much. He plays in it—once a year in the middle of June—only because of the pitcher, who is his father. "Arch Darrow, sixty-seven-year-old president of Eastern Coast College, still has a good drop on his slow-pitch delivery," Darrow said in the first inning, as if doing play-by-play for the game. "Here in this, his thirty-fourth campaign, the six foot-three lefthander still works the corners, nibbles at the edges. What a dude, what a guy."

Arch Darrow plays only this one game a year now, and when he does he has no time for chatter. Especially chatter that has an edge of irony in it. Actually, he's the same on the golf course or the tennis court—intense, wary, attuned to the task as if he were a pro playing for first-place money. After a period of almost ten years when he and his younger son rarely spoke—during the time when Darrow made his best land deals and his father was testifying nearly every session in Columbia to try to get the state to protect the seashore by forbidding development—they now have a peace that is carried more by Darrow than his father.

"Daddy," Darrow said five Thanksgivings ago—it was the first time he had called his father daddy since his late teens—"Daddy, I think it's time we put this shoreline bullshit to rest. You see the beach the way you do and I see it another, and no matter what you tell the legislature or what I buy, it's still going to erode."

"It's not erosion," his father said immediately, ignoring the point. "These barrier islands *migrate*, Bradley, and have been since long before we started building on them. They don't erode. It's no more than our own myopic human perspective that makes us call it erosion. It's simply no such thing."

Darrow looked at his brother across the table and mouthed the word myopic, as if it were a question. The three of them were in a restaurant in Myrtle Beach eating brunch.

"Knock knock," Darrow said to them after a moment of silence, and looked toward his father, who pretended not to understand.

"Knock knock," Darrow said again.

Arch looked at him disdainfully. "Who's there, Bradley?" he said at last.

"Myopic," Darrow said.

"Myopic Who?" Arch said.

"My ol' picky poppa has no fucking sense of humor whatsoever," Darrow said, looking away from both of the other men, as if to let them laugh if they wanted to, and not laugh if they didn't want to. They both laughed genuinely. Darrow's brother—five years older and as sentimental as anyone in the world—cried briefly at the end of the meal over the progress toward reconciliation, all three shook hands, remembered Helen fondly and quickly, and went their separate ways.

Since then Darrow and his father have not discussed the coast much at all. Arch has been occupied with budget and enrollment problems at the college, and Darrow has been much quieter with everyone about his deals. General sentiment and general assembly legislation have made it plain that there's no sense bragging about your coast development projects.

In the third inning the city goes ahead by three runs when one of the college team's outfielders overruns a fly ball. Arch takes a moment to put his hands on his hips in a pitcher's pout—his body remains athletic and ready, but in that gesture Darrow sees a bow at the middle, the inevitable building of flesh at the midsection. A sixty-seven year-old man is due that flare, Darrow thinks, but it depresses him nonetheless.

The next batter—a balding left-handed hitter from the treasurer's office, takes Arch's first pitch for a strike, then swings too hard at the next one, and dribbles it down between first base and the pitcher's mound. Both Darrow and his father break for the ball immediately. Arch lunges quickly, reaches toward the ground with all his surviving athleticism, but the ball rolls under his glove. He pulls his glove back up and continues toward first without breaking stride. Behind him, Darrow comes in on the ball, scoops it up with his bare hand and floats it toward his father. The ball and the pitcher arrive at the same moment, and the soft noise of the ball into the glove and Arch's foot onto the base are simultaneous and ahead of the sound of the runner's foot by a comfortable margin. Darrow cringes for a moment as he envisions the runner crashing into Arch, but Arch continues across the base as he steps on it, carrying out the natural motions of the game a fraction of a second ahead of the batter. Darrow lets out an involuntary whoop. "Look at that," he says to those in the stands, again doing play-by-play. He drops his glove and begins applauding. "You all are way too young to remember Harry The Cat Brecheen," he tells the crowd, which immediately takes up the applause. He notices Christine in the crowd, applauding as he requested and smiling comfortably at him. He cannot tell if she is with the man next to her—he's at least fifty-five—or not. Darrow finds himself hoping that she is. "Or maybe even Jim Kaat," he goes on, "but my daddy at sixty-seven gets off the mound just like Harry the Cat did in the big leagues back in the thirties. And Kitty Kaat did in the sixties and seventies." He pauses, smiling toward his father, who is walking back to the mound.

"Standing O, Dad," he says to his father, and the turns again to the crowd. "Standing O," he says to the crowd, and they stand as they continue to applaud. Christine and the man next to her stand, laughing. "But look at Big Arch Darrow," Darrow goes on, speaking in his mock-radio voice. "Does he care? Not a bit, my friends, not a bit. He's already back at the mound, tugging at that cap and getting ready for the next hitter. Just look at him out there, everyone, the very epitome of the college president he is and has been for lo, these many years."

Two days ago Darrow was on the beach in Jamaica. Then he flew back to host his annual Moon Beach New Year's Eve Moon Watch and Beach Party, an event that actually began more than fifty years ago under a much tamer name, back when the town had a big arcade and a boardwalk, and the hundreds of guests at the Seagate Hotel looked out over three hundred feet of beach at high tide. But this year, the big storm that has already reshaped much of the coast all the way up to Kitty Hawk has also wiped out the party. Darrow didn't even bother to put anything on the radio or call anyone, simply because there is already enough bad news out there by itself—surge tides and beach-front flooding and high-wind warnings. He talked to Enrique on the phone and got as much as he could canceled. They had planned for food for about a thousand, but Darrow's contacts are good enough that he has been able to get out from under nearly all of it.

When Darrow drove into town—past the water-bloated swampland that separates the eastern edges of city and the increasingly isolated area of Moon Beach—he felt like he was heading into a ghost town. "It *is* a damn ghost town," he said aloud to himself in the car as he passed the long-neglected, half-finished condos back on the bay side, where fortunes were lost and the big concrete fronts stand gaunt and naked in the rain, like huge warning signs. He used to love the beach in the winter. It was cold, lonely, wind-swept and private. He could drive around and look, get out and inspect a piece of property as long and as carefully as he cared to, thinking about access and view, sun angles and drainage, traffic flow and parking. Today, at the bridge across the edge of the bay into Moon Beach—it seems more clearly an island today than it ever has—he had to move the two flashing traffic warning devices before he could drive into the water that the devices warned him against. Just over the bridge, he aimed the car carefully through half a foot of water. It was clear-looking, without foam or mud, and so it seemed even deeper as he drove into town. He saw no other cars and only two people on foot. As he approached the motel—the main street into town aims toward it as truly as a foul line does to a foul pole—the first thing he considered was whether or not it still stood straight. It did, and no water washed around it. He parked the car two blocks shy of the motel, in front of the community center building. There was no waterline on it or on the other little storefronts along the street. It occurred to him that there might not be any seawater in the motel.

Now, as he steps into the lobby, he feels the squishiness of the rug through his rubber boots, then stoops to feel and smell. The ocean is like a burglar. Once the alarm goes off you hope like hell that it's a mistake, a false alarm. And so is his hope here. There was simply no way the storm could miss the motel, and sure enough it didn't. There is no standing water, but the briney smell and the white splotches that prove salt are already present. He goes out to the big sliding doors that lead out to the pool, where the water is a mixture of beige-colored foam, fireworks debris, cans and other beach trash. As he is deciding whether or not to go out there, Darrow hears a noise behind him. He turns slowly, expecting to see the two men he has invited here, though it is a bit earlier than the time they'd agreed to. But it is his father, also wearing waders, and covered on top with a boyish-looking yellow slicker. Darrow is momentarily puzzled. It crosses his mind quickly that perhaps his father has been sent with news that the expected visitors have canceled.

"Bradley," his father says. "I'm sorry."

"What the hell," Darrow says. "People will just have to get drunk at home this year."

"I mean the hotel," his father says. "Not just the party."

"Thanks," Darrow says. "But what brings you out here?"

Arch looks up quickly. "Well," he says, "I came out to look at your property. I thought you might have heard the weather up here and just stayed in Jamaica, and I thought I'd check in."

Darrow considers the potential of having his father here—that showing the property on its worst day may be just the right thing to do or the worst thing to do—but having "a famed oceanographer, shoreline specialist and college president," as Darrow silently rehearses his introduction, can only help if it is played right and his father remains reasonable. "Well, I appreciate that, Daddy," Darrow says. "I really do. And you know what? I thought you were somebody else. There are two guys supposed to come look at this place this afternoon. To consider a purchase."

"Today?" Arch is wide-eyed, spreading his arms to indicate the water damage.

"Today," Darrow says. "Big guys from up on the Jersey coast who are looking for bargains down in the Carolinas. Guys who feel like you can overcome a few tides a lot easier than you can the crap that washes up on the beaches up where they are. They've been talking for years about property down here. Then I saw one of them on the plane yesterday morning and things just sort of started falling into place."

"To sell?"

"Maybe. And it occurred to me why not show it to them at what I can say is its very worst. They deal with floods up there too. So why not just bring them in today, is what I figured."

"But why are you selling?"

Darrow raises his arms and lets his hands fall onto his thighs. "Why not? It's hard to have to worry about it all the time, and these guys think they're magic marketers, so why not get out and let them have a shot?"

"And their approach to coastal management?" Arch has suddenly abandoned his fatherly role and become the conscience of the coast again.

"To keeping the water back, you mean?" Darrow says.

"Precisely." Arch pushes the hood of his rain slicker back, as if to emphasize his seriousness. "You know the kinds of things they've done along the coast in the northern states."

"No, not exactly."

"Panic, basically. Big walls, moronic replenishment programs that have caused more trouble—far more beach loss—than they've prevented."

Darrow motions his father back toward the dining room and asks if he'd like a drink. Arch narrows his eyes briefly, tells his son not to try to divert the conversation, and says yes, he'll have a Heineken.

"They'll build a new wall out there and shore it up for a few years and then get out," Arch says. "Up in Myrtle . . ."

"Daddy," Darrow interrupts. "I haven't even talked to these guys yet, much less sold the damn thing."

"What's it worth?" Arch says immediately.

Darrow opens two bottles and hands one to his father. "You going to make a counter-offer?" He laughs.

Arch looks out the windows toward the waning storm. "I wish to hell I could. I wish I could take the damn thing and knock it down and set the example for this town, for this whole state. What's it worth?"

Darrow laughs again at his father's persistence and doesn't say anything.

"Well then what percent of your total worth is it, if I may be so bold as to ask that."

"This motel?" Darrow says. "Oh, I'd say close to twenty percent."

"So if you got a little less than top-dollar, you'd still survive, still be able to afford your modest little vehicle out there and your little shack on the shore and the little junkets around the world and the little trinkets for the ladies?"

"Oh, I'm definitely going to get less than top-dollar," Darrow says. "A chunk less."

Darrow begins to sense what Arch is about to say just as Arch does indeed say it. "What would it be worth to you to know that your home state might find a use for this property. That maybe a college or university might be able to use it as is for a period of time and then perhaps find another use for the property—a more natural use. What if the legislature saw its way to . . ."

"Are you on assignment from the governor?" Darrow says. "Did somebody get wind that these guys were on the way down here and send you on a mission?"

"I'm serious," Arch says. "There might be possibilities."

Darrow steers his father back into the main dining room, and glances out front to look for the two men. Out the front door the rain is coming down a little harder than it was earlier. He wonders momentarily if the storm might run off the coast and then loop back in, the way they do once every few years. Then he looks on up the street for the Jersey buyers. He decides there's no need to commit to any offer made today. After all, a state legislature out to save its primary tourist attraction can afford to make a serious offer for a piece of prime coastal real estate.

THE FABULOUS GREENS

The first thing Cammy does whenever she takes over the driving is to jam her father's spittoon—an old one-pound coffee can—back up under the seat, where she tries to make sure it gets caught in the spring coils that stick out under there. Before she found him the can, he used to spit right out the window and leave a series of thin brown lines back along the side of the bus. He is all the way in the back now, lounging across the bed where the last four seats used to be, as Cammy aims the bus across the eastern part of West Virginia. She starts to yell something back to him about at least putting the lid on the can, and then decides the family doesn't need him getting mad and taking over the driving when she needs the money she gets for doing it.

Out in front of her, as she glances away from the inside rearview mirror and onto the road, is a long, gently curving reach of pine-lined black two-lane highway, wet with morning dew and rising softly up to her left where the sun—fat and orange—is just emerging from behind the trees. She takes in this scene, thinks about a phrase her mother uses in their shows—about *the Lord's majestic touch with pastoral beauty*—starts to mention the scene to the rest of the family, and then decides against that too.

She used to lecture her father—back when she was still married and before they traveled in the bus—about his tobacco. She would use the same moralistic, deep-voiced tone that he uses to preach.

"It's an ungodly habit, a dangerous and ungodly habit," she would say, using a male-depth voice, "and one that stains not only the teeth and the mouth but the very soul of the man who engages in it." Cammy—Camelia—is the oldest of the three daughters of Sonny and Dorothy Green. Sonny and Dottie will have been married forty years in the spring though neither of them is sixty yet. Though Sonny denies good-naturedly that it can be true, Cammy is thirty-seven years old—oldest and largest of the girls. She started performing in church—in her daddy's church back when he had one—when she was three years old. There are pictures on the walls of her parents' house of her in a short, billowing dress with matching bows in her hair—standing up at the altar with a prayer book in her hands. Cammy can't believe she is thirty-seven either. She looks at Dottie's big old arms and then at her own and wonders how she can be that big, that old, that heavy up toward the shoulders. She has gained a lot of weight since her divorce—from a wiry building contractor named Dennis Keenin—and since coming back on the road with the family. She and Dennis Keenin were married seven years, during which time Dennis got leaner and leaner, Cammy had two miscarriages, and her father seemed to like his son-in-law increasingly more than he did his daughter. Her mother tells Cammy that Sonny took such a liking to Dennis not just because of all the work he did on the house, but also because of what happened with Cammy's brother, who used to travel with them too. Ernie got sick of it when his father did miracles and healings on stage, and when Sonny didn't put all the money back into the church the way he said he would. Ernie worked hard on his father—got him to give up the idea of trying to get a regional TV show—and kept him home in the church for periods of time, a beautiful little church in the Virginia hills that now gets filled to overflowing every Sunday with people wanting to hear Earnest Green preach.

Dottie is not completely at peace with Cammy either. She sees her eldest daughter as a woman in need. One day when they were back from a trip and the women were having coffee, Dottie started in on Cammy being the kind of woman who just doesn't get along without a man around. Cammy stood up and looked at her mother in semi-horror and Dottie said no, it's just plain true—riding around in an old bus with your family isn't right if there's not at least a man back home. Cammy's sisters—Samantha is thirty-four and unhappily married to an insurance salesman and Pam is thirty-two and too single and too wild for her own good as far as the rest of the family is concerned—giggled at what Dottie said and then started talking to each other about the places Cammy could get some if she really needed it.

Cammy is driving southeast on a state route that will run them into Interstate 81 in an hour or so. Once they are on the interstate, the women will take turns pointing out signs for this place or that place for breakfast, and Sonny will put them off over and over again—talking about getting some miles in first—until he finally sees a Shoney's. Actually he has a complete mental list of all the Shoney'ses in the eastern part of the country, and they haven't had breakfast anywhere else for at least a year. He says they all like to pretend they don't like Shoney's, but once they get in there and start picking up plates, he doesn't see anybody not getting her money's worth and then some. Shoney's is one of the few things Cammy and her father agree on. They both start out with big stacks of those little French toast squares, plop some butter on top with the big butter scoop, and then spill three or four dippers of syrup over the whole thing. She quits thinking about food because it is making her hungry, and looks up into the inside rearview mirror. Dottie is sitting on the edge of the bed going through the receipts from the night before—they took in almost eight hundred dollars for two shows in a little country church pretty much in the middle of noplace—and her sisters are reading each other Trivial Pursuit cards without the board as they lie across one of the other beds. They are all surprised to have done as well as they did last night.

Sonny bought the bus four years ago when they were traveling in eastern Kentucky—back in the coalfield towns where it's so poor you get great turnouts but hardly any money. They were in a rental van when Sonny saw the bus, painted red on the bottom and white up along the top—making the small, rectangular windows look even smaller and more pinch-eyed—parked parallel to the road in front of a truck repair place. Up on the destination sign above the windshield it said STATESBORO SPECIAL, which Sonny told them later was the main thing that made him pull off for a look. And he's never changed that in all the time he's owned the bus. Dottie told him to put "The Greens" up there, and he said you mean "The Fabulous Greens," and she said whatever, but he never did it. He did have a Fabulous Greens logo designed for the sides, but up front it still says STATESBORO SPECIAL. The bus was built thirty-some years ago by General Motors, back when they still built good machines, according to Sonny. A year or so ago he got it painted a yellow and tan combination, with the logo in dark brown on the yellow, so it sort of looks like a giant banana. Nobody can understand why he didn't choose green, and nobody drives it except Sonny and Cammy. Dottie has moved it across a parking lot or two, Pam has driven it maybe two legs of a trip, and Samantha has never so much as put her fat bottom in the driver's seat. Samantha isn't really good for a whole lot when you think about it, except to fill a spot on the stage and deliver straight lines for Pam's imitations.

They are on the interstate maybe twenty miles before Dottie brings up breakfast. The responses come all in a row like they've been rehearsed, or at least like they've all been itching to talk about breakfast. Samantha says yeah, she's ready. Sonny says they ought to get a few more exits in first. Pam says whatever. Cammy says nothing and keeps on driving until she sees an exit that has a Shoney's.

"Hey, I know what," Samantha says with mock brightness when Cammy is halfway down the exit ramp, "maybe we could try a Shoney's for a change." Cammy parks the bus across about six spaces at the back edge of the lot, where it starts to blend in with a run-down old strip shopping center with a Kmart as the anchor. The Shoney's is a good-looking remodeled one with the glass room built onto the side.

They get a booth toward the back. The waitress is by in a hurry and Sonny and Cammy are first up at the buffet plates. They silently critique the French toast for softness, degree of overheating and richness of egg mixture. "Doesn't look too bad," Sonny says, pushing at Cammy's elbow and then pinching a stack to drop on his plate. Cammy takes almost as big a pile while Sonny moves on to the meats—two kinds of sausage plus bacon. Cammy leaves the meat alone. Then the rest of the family gets there. Samantha takes just a little bit of everything, as if that will help with her diet. She is not quite as heavy as Dottie and Cammy, but she is still a full-figure type girl. Dottie sticks with three things—eggs, grits and bacon—and Pam eats nothing but fruits.

"You need a little something to stick to those skinny ribs," Dottie says to Pam when they are all sitting down and having their first sips of coffee. Pam has a plate of strawberries, melon chunks and banana pieces. She looks up and says nothing. She is, Cammy has to admit, nothing short of beautiful—the one who got all the genes you can't even tell Sonny and Dottie have. She has big, fully curly hair and the same height and big chest as the rest of them, but with that little waist you can see her chest is actually there, instead of just part of a standard wide-body model. She's really a star that is stuck in the religion biz, is the way Cammy sees it.

"You don't do that self-puking stuff, do you?" Dottie says when nobody has said anything to her first comment to Pam.

"Mother," Samantha whines. "Is that the kind of garbage we have to hear at breakfast? And besides, you know she doesn't—just look at that creepy little shit she eats."

"Sammy," Sonny says sternly, and turns to his left as if to see if anyone has heard his daughter cussing in a Shoney's. Then he turns back to his French toast, which he and Cammy agree is a little dry.

"Under the heat lamp too long," Cammy says. She limits herself to two helpings while Sonny goes back three times.

They stand as a group when they're finished and Cammy catches a few glances from some of the waitresses. The Greens have had arguments in the bus over whether people look at them because they are the Fabulous Greens—who've been on TV in four different states, Sonny loves to say—or because they are a collection of pretty large people who make a major dent in any buffet they decide to go after.

Myrtle Beach is a lot like the other free-growing seaside cities up and down the East Coast. Atlantic City is the least controlled, but Ocean City, in Maryland—where the condos block out the sun on the beach by noon—is almost as bad, and Myrtle is catching up fast. The Greens have never worked in town before, though they've appeared in the flat little inland towns like Conway and Cheraw, and even out along Route 17 north of Myrtle Beach. This time they are booked into a big hall just off the Grand Strand. There are two big religious conventions in town for the week, and the Fabulous Greens are part of a five-act Christian entertainment package called God's Summer Blessings at the Beach. The last time Sonny talked to the promoter he said they weren't sure the hall, which holds about two thousand, was going to be big enough. They looked to pull a lot of mobile home traffic from the campgrounds along the coast and more families from the rental homes to the north and south of town, and then to get a lot of convention people looking for something to do at night.

"Maybe they've moved the show to the civic center," Sonny says while they're at a long light near the pottery complex, which stretches out for what seems like a mile in either direction. "If they have one." He has wanted for years to play a big-city size center, his main goal since back when all the TV ministers started getting in trouble and killed his TV show dream. With some help from Ernie.

The women are all up in the seats right behind Sonny, leaning forward and looking around outside like they are driving through the Grand Canyon or someplace. The traffic is heavy in both directions. Samantha has been talking about hitting the pottery place on the way back. She wants some new everyday dishes for home, she says. As if that's going to patch up a marriage that's way past the new-stuff-will-make-us-sweetie-pies-again stage. Pam has been talking about the car racing place in Myrtle Beach, where they have a vehicle and course for every age group, up by age and height until you have this Indy 500 thing full of teenage boys and middle-age men with beer guts. The last time they came this way Pam spent fifty dollars in one afternoon racing motorhead men around this little track like it was the best thing she'd ever found out about since she started getting pubic hair. And yet she won't even get near the driver's seat of the bus, is what gripes Cammy.

It's a hot, rumbly day in Myrtle Beach. The humidity feels like it's off the charts and even the breeze that comes and goes doesn't help much. Sonny finds a spot only about two blocks from the hall and they all walk down there to look at it. Dottie is nervous that there's no rehearsal and Sonny keeps telling her they've done this a thousand times and that he wrote out what they're going to do and sent it to the promoter, and so once they hit the stage they'll be fine. And when they get there, to Cammy's surprise, the promoter meets them almost at the door, takes them in and puts them up on the stage for a few minutes to go through the lights and sequences with the technical people. It is a big cold hall and the acoustics are real odd with no one in it.

Then the women decide to walk down toward the ocean while Sonny goes over the business end. By the time they've gone half a block Cammy feels like she's sweating through her clothes, and realizes that by the time they take a shower and dress, they really don't have that long—just enough time to grab something to eat.

The hall is one block inland from the main drag along the beach. It's a big, square-looking building from the outside—plain bricks with nothing much on the front, which makes the double-door entry way look real small. Almost directly across the street is another building about the same size but built entirely differently—with all these nooks and crannies and overhangs and compartments and doors all over the place. The sign out front says Welcome To Plymouth Rock, and the porta-sign with light bulbs flashing all around the outside says tonight is Old Car Night. Anybody in a car twenty-five years old or older gets in free. Right now the place is as dead looking as the hall where the Greens are going to play, but the sign—yellow background with black letters and red flashing light—makes it look like a lot is going to go on over there.

By the time they're dressed and ready, Sonny is so nervous he can hardly talk. Dottie goes over to him, puts a hand on his shoulder and asks him what's wrong. He looks at her funny and says, "Honey, it's a big show, you can just feel something in the air, can't you?" Dottie takes her hand away, looks around and says well, maybe so. The whole family is standing in the hallway outside the dressing room, and other acts are moving through and tuning instruments and warming up their singing voices. It feels a lot like showbiz to Cammy, and when she thinks that, she feels some kind of tension too. That's the thing that finally got her brother out of the show as much as the disagreements with his father. One time after they played a big church in Arkansas, Ernie got real quiet and depressed and wouldn't talk to anybody. Finally, back home, he talked to the women while Sonny was in town, and said he thought religion was getting real close to being treated like Chevrolets and breakfast cereal and rock groups. They all looked at him kind of funny even though he talked like that all the time, and he kept on going with that kind of stuff—about how God doesn't want His word put in big orange Tide boxes and sold in the corner store to do His cleansing, but wants it done small and real and one-to-one, in little country churches in the trees. It was less than a week after that that Ernie and Sonny blew up at each other.

All of a sudden Sonny says hey, he never got anything to eat, and starts looking around for something. Pam, filling up her mint dress like the original Grand Ole Opry queen, says she'll be glad to go get him something. At the very same moment that Sonny smiles and says how nice that is, Dottie frowns and says she'll go instead. Basically, she doesn't want Pam outside prancing around in that dress when she's doing a Christian show—especially out in front of that nightclub. In the end Pam goes, with the understanding that she'll come straight back—like she's fifteen or something.

About ten minutes after Pam leaves, Dottie starts talking about if she's ever coming back, and Sonny starts worrying about there being only about ten minutes until the first act goes on. Pam comes in just after he says that, carrying a grease-stained white paper bag and a little pennant that says "I Discovered Plymouth Rock." The pennant is on a little stick and Pam waves it around a couple of times while Dottie rolls her eyes. The bag has fish and chips in it.

"You need to watch yourself, young lady," Dottie says to Pam, again like she's about half as old as she is. Dottie's dress is darker than the girls'—about halfway between their color and the color of Sonny's suit.

"She's got plenty of other people to watch herself, Mom," Samantha says.

The first act is called the Gospel Honeycombs. It's a three-woman, two-man group—all in Sonny and Dottie's age range—singing up-beat a cappella stuff that is Lord-based and has a lot of well-timed, fairly intricate hand clapping and lots of position shifting tied to verses and who is singing lead at the time. The audience, which is slow to come in, seems to like them okay—a situation that makes Cammy optimistic because she knows the Greens can blow them away even on a bad night. But the problem is that every time the door opens and sometimes even when it's closed, you can hear horns and noise from outside across the street at Plymouth Rock. As the girls stand in the hallway by the dressing room and watch the Honeycombs, Samantha says it will probably get worse and worse, what with the nightclub over there. Pam says there must be a way to overcome it, and Cammy says she bets there isn't because it's probably been years since they used this building for a show.

"We could get some real noise from over there," Pam says. "There's a ton of people over there already, with the old car deal. You should have seen this old Packard I saw—you forget what monsters those cars were, like tanks..." She starts to go on, but Samantha is staring at her like she just said the end of the world was next on the program. "We go on in just a few minutes and you're talking about some old car?" Samantha says, like she can't believe it. "Maybe it had more to do with who was in it."

Pam mimics Samantha's accusing posture and then turns to Cammy and says yeah, maybe a little. "Kind of cute. Plays in a band that actually does some Christian numbers. Said he might stop over later."

It's Cammy's turn to be incredulous. "You beat all," she says. "You truly beat all."

Among the three of them, Pam is the only one who never went through what the family calls the Flying Nun Stage, where from about age eight until your early teens, you vow on the Bible you'll never kiss a boy or see a dirty movie or even sit on the toilet seats at school. Pam just went straight from little girl to star in a few weeks. Maybe it's because she's the youngest, but she has always kept a distance from what they do for a living.

The Honeycombs are singing "Rock Me"—doing each verse a little faster than the one before, which is one of the oldest tricks there is in Christian music. The hall is just over half full. When the door opens for someone to come in, Cammy gets a glimpse of what looks like a huge traffic jam out there, as if the street is frozen with cars. She wonders if it is this show or the nightclub or a combination. The Honeycombs come back for their encore—Sonny says that the promoter said nobody can have more than one or they'll run late—and then the emcee introduces Marion DuPree as the Spellbinding and Spine Tingling Voice of The Lord from The Gulf Coast. Marion DuPree comes running out onto the stage from the other side and the audience goes wild—loud enough to drown out the noise from the outside for once. He is a handsome man—well over six feet and thin at the waist but flaring at the shoulders in his dark suit. Cammy never saw him anywhere while they were dressing or waiting—he just sort of materialized from somewhere.

"Where I come from in Louisiana," he says immediately and loudly, pronouncing it "Loozana" and causing the cheers to go up again, "the weather *stays* hot like this *all* the time." His voice carries the rise-and-fall sing-songiness of most of the stage preachers, but with that odd accent. Dottie says it must be Cajun. You can still hear the cars and noise outside. And it seems to be getting louder and louder. It's hard to tell if the whoops and calls are from the audience or from the people outside.

"It's crazy out there," Dottie says, without indicating if she means the crowd inside or outside. Meanwhile, Marion DuPree has fallen to his knees and is bending forward on the stage as he completes his message that there is no part way with the Lord—nothing to do but to give yourself completely to Him because that's what He did for you. Finally he falls completely forward and lies on his stomach on the stage. The people in the back are going wild, just like you used to see at rock concerts. Then Marion DuPree suddenly leaps to his feet with agility of a gymnast and runs off the stage as suddenly as he appeared on it—off to the other side. You can see him over there taking deep breaths and looking up and flexing his shoulder muscles, waiting for his moment to run back on stage.

After Marion DuPree's quick encore, the emcee goes back out onto the stage, asks for another hand for the marvelous Marion DuPree, and then says he apologies for all the noise, and that they are doing all they can to control it. "The din of the secular and profane is ever at our door," he says. "And now," he goes on, "and now our next great Christian entertainers of this magical evening of God's Summer Blessings at the Beach, as sweet a family as you'll ever meet, coming to us from the Angels Gathering Church in the Virginia Hills, the Fabulous Greens!" The applause is okay but nothing great as Sonny strides out onto the stage by himself as he always does, gives a bright good evening and tells them how glad he is to be there. He delivers his first mini-sermon—on how good things come to those who wait. He is a good speaker—raising and lowering his voice effectively, using his hands well, marching back and forth across the stage to make his points. He quickly gets to where he says there's one real good thing they don't have to wait for any longer, and that is for him to introduce the pretty Greens that go with this one old and wrinkled Green. That is Dottie's cue. He receives her with a hug, presents her to the audience as his wife of forty years come next month, and they start to talk about how they met. The story they tell is that it was by a little brook near the edge of the mountains in Eastern Tennessee, when he was nine and she was seven and he was trying to float a toy boat while she was fishing with a plain piece of twine tied on the end of a stick. No hook, no bait, just a plain piece of twine. "Isn't it something the way the Lord gives us wonderful symbols of what's to come later in life?" Sonny says, beaming at Dottie. "Because some years later, I was caught not just by her, but at the same time by the Lord, and I would tell you today how blessed I've been for every day since. And the wonderful thing is that she didn't use bait for me either. Nor did the Lord for that matter. For His love is pure and unconditional. Yes, Dottie and I have been so very blessed over the years. So let me formally introduce to you the true light of my life, Dorothy Tanner Green."

The crowd responds well to Dottie, at least for a middle-aged, overweight woman when there is more noise outside than there is from the stage. Dottie raises her voice a little higher than usual to overcome the competition and to say good evening, and then to give her little talk about the blessings of her and Sonny's life together—the nearness to Jesus, the fine home in the mountains, the church, the good health and fortune that have blessed them. Then she moves back next to Sonny and he swings his arm back to the piano player and then they join hands. "But there's an even greater blessing for us than any of those," Dottie says while looking up into Sonny's face. "Yes," Sonny says, "yes, the Lord has visited us with the greatest gift His humble servants can know." And then they start singing "The Three Blessings"—a song that Sonny actually wrote, although originally as "The Four Blessings." As their parents start singing, the girls move out onto the darkened back edge of the stage. Cammy senses that the light from up front is leaking back onto them and that the drama of their introduction—if there can be any drama in all this noise—is going to be ruined. There's a verse in the song about each girl—about the birth and coming home and confirmation. Sonny and Dottie finish the song holding hands, and then step slowly away from each other, letting their hands touch as long as they can, and then part with just the tips of their fingers touching, and then the both reach back toward the girls as the lights come up.

"Ladies and gentlemen," Sonny says in the fullest voice he can muster as the piano player runs up and down the keys and the lights go from lime to yellow and back to lime, "Ladies and gentlemen," he repeats when there is a noise from the back, "I'd like you to meet our three little girls, the Green Sisters, Cammy, Sammy and Pammy." He and Dottie raise their arms heavenward as the spots intensify on each girl and the audience cheers and whistles. But through it all, as the girls step up to stand between their parents and they go through the family chat about who's oldest and if their names really are Cammy, Sammy and Pammy, the noise from the back is getting louder. There is an almost constant banging at the door now. Sonny is talking to Dottie about how the girls look extra lovely tonight, and Dottie says you know, you're right, honey, and then someone shouts, "Let them in," from the back of the room. Sonny looks out to the crowd and so does Pam. The rest of them look down and then they go back to the script. "Keep it locked," comes the next shout, just as Pam is about to talk about how the love from the parents is how a child gets it radiance. The last distinct call that Cammy hears is somebody asking about since when do we have to lock a house of the Lord. After that there is general shouting and noise at the back of the hall, and the banging gets louder and louder. The Greens try a few more lines and then Pam stops talking. She steps out of the group and closer to the front of the stage, as if to get out of the light and see what's going on back there. It occurs to Cammy with a little chill that if there is anybody who might be able to calm things down, it is probably Pam. At least she could divert some attention. "What's going on out there?" she calls out, using her microphone. People whistle and clap and shout. "What's back there?"

Then the house lights come on and you can see that a lot of people have moved back and crowded at the door, as if they're trying to block the way in. People are shouting at each other and at the doors. Then as the doors start to push open, the promoter comes out onto the stage and tells the Greens to get off. He takes the mike from Dottie and they do go off—except Pam. Then, as the double doors come open and a crowd of people comes bursting into the hall, the promoter hits the mike against the stage floor a few times. The noise is deep and booming. He tells everybody to just calm down. "We must have quiet or we'll have to clear the hall," he says. "We cannot have this." He looks over at the Greens, who are standing at the edge of the stage with people from several other acts. He puts the mike down between his legs and calls out to Sonny to call the police.

Now that the doors are open, the whole street seems to have spilled into the hall. Lots of the old cars across the street have their lights on—aimed into the hall, it seems—and people are all over the street and parking lot. And you can't tell who's on what side, or even if there are real sides. It occurs to Cammy from what people are shouting that maybe the people who were outside didn't want much more than to see what was going on inside, as if they were aware the building hadn't been used in a while. And when they found the doors locked, they got angry and tried to get in. Now the big double doors are slammed open against the inside walls of the hall, and you can see out across the street and down toward the ocean. There are people everywhere. The promoter tries to talk again and then stops and looks, as if he's trying to figure out what to do next. Pam is standing next to him, watching and still holding her microphone down along her leg. She is staring straight back into the crowd when a tall man in white pants and a white shirt comes bounding up onto the stage next to her. Cammy wonders if is the rock singer Pam met at Plymouth Rock. The promoter goes after him and knocks him to the stage floor. They wrestle on the floor, and Pam goes over to try to pull them apart. She pulls hard at the promoter's shoulder and finally he starts to get up off the younger man. But once the promoter is up, the man in the white clothes pushes him with both hands, as if in retaliation for being knocked down. Pam brings her mike to her face to speak, but then gets pushed out of the way as more people join the fight.

As she backs away, more and more people start onto the stage to get into the main fight. For the first time, Pam looks over at the rest of the Greens at the side of the stage. Dottie waves frantically and calls out for her to get off the stage, but Pam just looks at her as if she didn't hear, or didn't want to hear. The heat, which was bad when they started, is getting worse by the minute. Then Sonny finally comes back to say that the police are on the way. Dottie screams at Sonny to go get Pam off the stage before she gets crushed, but Sonny doesn't move. Dottie screams that they have to get to the bus so they can get out of there. Sonny shouts back that there's no way they could get through all the people outside. You can see what looks like thousands of people streaming across the street to the hall, and cars are stopping in the middle of the street. The lights of the Plymouth Rock sign are flashing like crazy as people run all over the lot. You can hear sirens now—the police must be on the way. Dottie is still screaming at Sonny to go get Pam, who is now completely surrounded by people fighting and shoving on the stage. She seems to be trying to find her opening to talk. Her hair is pushed to one side a little and one of her gown straps has fallen a little ways down onto her shoulder. As Pam backs up to get out of the way and steps into a greenish-colored spot of light, Cammy can't figure out if her little sister looks more like an over-the-hill nightclub singer waiting for her cue, a mint-green angel about to receive her savior, or a star about to be born.

GRAND STRAND

After Hub totaled the van just outside the Everglades in a sort of diagonal game of chicken with a loaded produce truck headed out of a field toward the road Hub was driving on, it took him just over fourteen months to pay off the vegetable and truck damage and save enough for his next van. The van was his fourth, and at $1,200, the most expensive he'd ever bought. He earned the money working for the company whose truck he had been completely convinced was trying to get in front of him, and had caused to turn over when he got to the spot where the truck would enter the road just as it did. The truck driver swerved, tipped up off of one side's wheels, and spilled hundreds of boxes of just-picked beans onto the edge of the field and into the ditch between the field and the road. Hub and Stella never made it to the Everglades, and Hub started working the next day, at first just to pay off the bill and then to avoid jail time. And by the time that was done, everybody's anger had calmed down enough that they let him stay on.

Not that he'd had a lot of other prospects lined up. It was the first job he'd had in his life where he had to be at a certain place at a fairly predictable time. And not that he wanted to stay in Florida anyway. He and Stella agreed that the Ever-lovin' Everglades Escapade—he was so proud that he thought to call it that—was a total fiasco. When he said that, Stella bit her tongue not to tell him that when you make your moving plans from watching cable

TV programs while smoking big fat marijuana cigarettes with your pothead brother, then this was a risk you ran. What she did instead was sit back, continue with her share of the fruit and vegetable harvesting, and wait for those kinds of things to dawn on Hub on their own. Sometimes they didn't, but telling him made absolutely sure they *never* did because then he would have to puff up and deny it all to holy hell.

She hadn't believed the Florida trip would even happen at all until they were into Missouri. Hub and Stella had lived their whole lives to that point—more than forty years each—in Phelps County, Nebraska, and Hub had spent his days since he was about sixteen gathering and selling hubcaps and earning a nickname when he was really Donald Leon Johnson. The downturn in the hubcap business in central Nebraska had been part of what got him to thinking about Florida. The clincher was what he saw on a vacation channel late at night—long after Stella was asleep and had left the two brothers to quantities of smoke and drink that would confuse Einstein. It was, as he explained it over and over again during the next two weeks, how close the Everglades and Miami and Key West and Disney World all were to each other, and what a hub cap heaven that must be.

So this time—headed out of Florida—Stella was more convinced that he would actually pack up and make another new start, a man now older than fifty trying to make up for squandering nearly all of his adult life setting up hub cap displays in the baking sun on abandoned strip mall lots in five central Nebraska counties and then trying to shift that lack of success to Florida. Plus without his brother around, Hub had a chance to make a decision without any more to muddle his head than his own peculiar ideas about things. What he talked about for weeks—to get them warmed up and ready to move again—was first what a fried-out, overrated hellhole the Sunburn State was. And second, that he had seen a fishing show on a TV—when he was sitting in the waiting room of a Ford dealership while they were looking for a part that they should have had ready and waiting for him—that talked about going out just off the South Carolina coast and catching marlin and tampon, he said it was, by the dozen. Big ones. Plus he told her he had always liked two-name states, with the exception of the Dakotas.

"You know what they call it up there?" he said to Stella.

"Call what?"

"Where we're going, dillweed."

"Myrtle Beach," she said right away. The first time he'd talked about it, she'd gotten out the big Rand McNally road book and looked at routes and distances and counted up how many more states that would give her.

"Woo woo woo, Miss Road Trip blows it again," Hub said, and then made a fist and pulled it back along his side while he said—full of triumph—"Wronnnggg."

Stella folded her arms at her chest and waited for him to finish.

"The Grand Strand," he said slowly, putting both arms up in the air. "Great fishing, good beaches, seafood, boardwalks, all that stuff that is the one hundred percent complete opposite of bake-ass Nebraska, and way better than fry-ass Florida."

Stella knew better than to say what she thought but went ahead anyway. "Seems like I heard the same kind of stuff from somebody or other about some sunny state or other not even two years ago."

Hub threw his arms down at his sides and spun halfway around. "Listen, I'll be perfectly willing—and able—to go all by myself if that's how it's got to be," he said—all puffed up and strong as if he could really do it. "I've been thinking I could really get into being on those fishing boats. Start out learning the baits and all, and work up to captain. So if you want to stay back here and get your ass taken off by either an alligator or a shark or a whacked truck driver, you go right the hell ahead."

Stella smiled and said the Grand Strand sounded good to her, and a week later they were on their way north and out of Florida forever. She felt just as amazed as she had when they left Nebraska. After they got on I-95 and were really underway and Hub was busy talking about all the crap that could happen along that road—fires, alligators, car-jackers, drive-by shooters, cigarette smugglers, gun-runners, you name it—Stella got herself turned just right in the seat so that she could look at him while he went on about stuff she had no idea how he knew. He was, even with his hair gone gray and his face cut with lines through the cheeks, and his three days of splotchy white beard, the same rooster of a boy she had first gone out with almost thirty years back. He had never gone to school for a day after somewhere in elementary school, and he could know he was absolutely right about things that he really had no idea about at all, but here he was heading out in a new van to a new place with a new idea once again. Stella thought about the two hundred and twenty dollar reserve she still had from when they left Nebraska and felt good sitting there in the van with him, headed up the interstate toward another brand new place.

The newspaper in Myrtle Beach was called *The Sun-News,* and had a goofy red and yellow sun-face all over the place, smiling at you like a nutcase. The paper was as skinny and funny-looking as the Grand Island paper, where Stella had tried running hub cap ads without ever telling Hub, and never even letting him know when he got three sales from one. On the front page of the first beach paper she bought was a picture of a patch of clouds over by Africa, with news that it could become a hurricane, and then a picture of a bunch of numbers and dots in the ocean to tell about hurricanes that had formed from patches of clouds in that very spot since like 1912, and that one of them had become a hurricane that hit the Grand Strand. Stella didn't even tell Hub about that. She read out some of the want ads to him, none of which had anything to do with fishing boats.

"I bet they've already got their crews for the summer," Stella said.

"I bet they already got their crews for the summer," he said back in his high voice. "What are you, like the queen of the fleet or something?"

Stella put down the paper to wait for him to calm down. He got testy when they had to work on learning a new town—even when they were stopping for the night—mostly because he hated it that he couldn't read the ads and other information himself, and still pretended with her—after all these years—that it had to do with his eyesight. It took only a minute or two of her reading anything out loud and he'd be yelling. Plus they were still looking for a place to stay and it was hot and they needed something to eat.

The next morning—they stayed in a little motel back up the highway toward Conway because it was so much cheaper—she told Hub the first thing they needed to do was go visit the beach, because she knew once they started looking for a place to stay and for jobs, they'd never get down there. To her surprise, he said okay, and they went just south of downtown, looking for a way to the water that wasn't private property of a giant motel. You could see between the buildings here and there, sometimes even a glimpse of the water. Finally Hub pulled off onto a side street back away from the beach, parked the van and asked Stella who the hell would know whether they were staying at the place or not. "We have to see the beach, we just *have* to see the beach," he said in his imitate-Stella voice.

They walked two more blocks south from town and then Hub led them through a parking lot between two not-so-tall motels. There was a set of wooden stairs at the edge of the parking lot, and when they were halfway up, they could see that the waves were rolling in over the bottom of the last two steps on the other side. Hub stopped at the top of the going-up steps, his mouth open as he looked one way down the beach and then the other.

"Go see *what* beach?" he said. Far down along the coast in the direction they'd come from was a spot of sand with some people on it, but in front of them and in the other direction there wasn't anybody on the beach because there was no beach to be on—it was all water.

"Must be high tide," Stella said.

"*No,*" Hub said, in full sarcasm. "She gets her first clue from where now?"

"How can they have a big town here and all these motels and nobody can even go out on the beach?" she said, not really asking him, but knowing he couldn't let anything just go by.

"Built them too damn close like they do everywhere," he said, all of a sudden an expert on coastlines. He stood at the top of the little steps, and Stella did too. She looked back along the coast at the high-rise motels. People were out on their balconies by the hundreds, and in the pools between the motels and the ocean, as if they were getting as close as they could to the beach.

"Come to the ocean and swim in the pool," she said.

"Look at that," Hub said, pointing at the sky. A small plane was flying along the beach with a long streamer behind it, with big red letters on the streamer. Hub squinted. "Are you supposed to be able to read it from this distance," he said, "or is it like a message for dolphins and sting rays and stuff out in the ocean?"

Stella put on her own squint and read slowly—one slow word at a time, as if she could barely see it: "Happy …Hour …3-6 …Ladies, uh …First Drink Free," she said. "And then there's an address and a phone number or something." She didn't want to give it to him because she knew he'd want to time out the day to get there right at three whether she had a drink or not. Because he'd work for twenty minutes to get the free drink for himself.

"Now there's a damn job," he said instead. "You realize that guy flies a plane all day? Just sits up there, watches the damn beach and the sharks and boats and all—just zooms along back and forth, waiting for people to look up at him?" He was leaning one arm on the railing of the steps, proud that he had understood the plane immediately. "I could live with that."

"I don't think it's exactly like driving a car, Hub," Stella said, and of course he gave her the sentence right back and then asked her if she thought the guy up there was like *born* flying that plane? He turned back away from the ocean, shaking his head at her from his waist up.

When they were back to the van and he was calmed down and they were talking about getting something to eat, he told her again how the plane just went up and down the beach all day and the guy got *paid* for it. "That's the Grand Strand *I'm* talking about," he said. "You ever see any of that down in Florida? Hell no."

They had been to only one beach, near dark and in the rain, in the whole time they were in Florida, was what Stella thought, but kept to herself.

The paper didn't have any ads for airplane flyers in it, and they spent that afternoon figuring out where the airport was so Hub could go in person and find out how to become a beach-message pilot. Once he found out about flying school, or at least lessons at a crillion dollars an hour and certain education requirements, and about no job openings for the rest of this summer anyway, he found some shade near a big drive-in gardens place along the main highway, drove the van across the shoulder and onto the grass and asked Stella if she was up for a nap too. He'd been questioned by cops four or five times since they'd left Nebraska for just kind of making his own parking places in the middle of nothing, but it was as if he didn't remember the last time each time he decided to do it again.

The next morning Stella put that day's want ads right next to the day before's to verify they were exactly the same, right down to the last one, and then Hub said they were going to have to leave the restaurants behind—even paying for one buffet and eating two—and hit the grocery store. They went into a giant BI-LO with a big picture of Maggie Simpson on the sign out front and got the peanut butter, bread and sodas they always bought when things were tight. Not that they really were yet, Hub told her, but what the hell, with the job prospects stuck right on zero, they might as well treat it that way. Then he said they should get on the road closest to the ocean and just keep on riding south for a ways, to see what happened to things down that way. "Up north of here, as of course Miss Roadmap knows, is North Carolina," he said, "and we came to the Grand Strand, not any damn Tarpaper State." He turned to her quickly then, as if to see if she was going to understand his joke or correct him.

"That's funny, Hub," she said, flat as she could. "Ha ha ha."

"I thought so," he said back, and they smiled at each other.

After some high rises and then a little gap with just sea grass, the road went by houses on both sides of the road. The ones on the ocean side were up on stilts and looked old and worn, and the ones on the other side of the road had grass out front with sprinklers running. When Hub had enough of that he cut back inland and asked Stella to look at the map to see how far south they were. She told him it looked like they were coming up on a place to cut back toward the ocean.

At the end of the little side road was a big chunk of the bay, with boats parked everywhere. Stella told him that map made it look like this was a big inlet from the ocean. Hub parked the van among a lot of fancy cars and they walked across the rest of the lot and out onto one of the docks into the water. It was the widest, sturdiest dock she had ever been on. Just as they got out toward the end, a little boat was coming slowly toward them, and cut its engine as they stopped walking. When the boat was still fifteen or twenty feet away, a man came running up behind them and stopped next to Hub. He was old and fat and tan, with thick gray hair curling around on his head. "What the hell are you doing in here now?" he shouted at the boat. "It's barely noon, for God's sake." The person in the boat looked to be no more than a boy. He was tall and thin and tan, with long brown hair onto his shoulders.

"I asked you a damn question," the man shouted. Hub and Stella edged back a ways as the boat came toward the dock. The boy—still silent—was holding a rope, getting ready to toss it to the man on the dock.

"I can't do it," the boy said at the same moment he threw the rope. "I just cannot do this crap one second longer."

"Two days!" the man shouted. "No, a day and a half. What the hell kind of deal is that after I train you and give you the damn job? You said you needed it." He pulled the rope and then began to wrap it around a metal thing on the dock that looked like an upside down anchor.

Once the boat was in front of them, Stella saw that it had a big sign-looking thing running above its whole length—maybe twelve or fourteen feet long and four feet high. It was all black, but had what appeared to be little light bulbs all over it. Hub was moving up and down on his feet, the way he did when he was just about to make a big cap sale. The man reached down and pulled the boy up out of the boat. Then he reached into his pocket and pulled out a wad of bills. He folded it open, flicked some of them, pulled a few out, handed them to the boy and told him to get the hell off the dock. The boy didn't look at the money and didn't say a word as he walked back off the dock.

"Little shits don't give a damn about anything," the man said to no one in particular, though Hub and Stella were the only people nearby.

"Ain't it the damn truth," Hub said.

"The fourth one already this summer," the man said. "Once I had a guy stayed for three years. Three years."

By the fourth day, Hub was to the point where he knew when to take the medicine and what to eat and not eat before they went out. Plus the ocean was the calmest it had been any of the days—just easy-moving little wakes that gave the boat only the gentlest rock as they headed out the inlet to turn north for the first pass of the day. Stella spread out the saltines and the ginger ale on the little counter just above the ice bucket and keyed in the messages to go up on the board for the day. Sievers had told them he had about half of the advertisers he usually had at this time of year, and for one reason only. "The lack of dependability we've shown this summer so far is all the hell it is. How the hell can you expect a guy to pay for advertising when he can't walk out on the beach and see it going by? Can't stand there and see people pointing to it, talking about it?"

Hub started to say something, but Sievers interrupted to say that that was the reason he hired them and that that was the only—the *only*—reason he was letting them go out together when he knew better, because the twice he'd tried it, the boat had turned into a party instead of a business. "But then you folks—no offense—you look at little old for that kind of crap."

Hub started to talk again, but Sievers kept on going. "It's like any other advertising in the world. You need a good clean message, you need it where people can see it and you need it in front of them over and over again to get it through their thick-ass heads."

Sievers had gone with them the first day and half of the second day, talking about looking out for fools in jet skis. "Plus low-slung assholes in sea kayaks," he said. "All kinds of nuts way too far out with way too little idea of what the hell they're doing. And of course if anything goes wrong, it's all our fault, every damn time." He showed Stella how to change the order of the ads, how to run verticals and horizontals, how to, as he put it, "make a simple, flat board really shout at people on the beach trying to decide what to do with their evening."

She could tell Hub wanted to love the boat. He sat with one leg cocked up and one hand on the wheel and looked out ahead of him like he was piloting an ocean liner, even when he was sick. He'd told Stella their first day out alone—between pukes and finally having given in to sunscreen—that this was the place for him. That it was fate that he'd made them walk out onto the dock at the very moment the boat was coming in. She didn't tell him how crazy that sounded coming from someone who was green and red at the same time.

"What could be easier?" he said. "Just sit here and ride up the beach, just sit here and ride back down. The grand dream job on the Grand damn Strand."

"What could be more boring?" she went ahead and said.

Hub came up out of his kicked back seating as quickly as he could without jostling his insides around too much. "Listen, I'll let you out the next time we're back near the dock." She decided to tell him she was kidding, and turned to watch some people going by in the sky—hanging under a big parachute-looking thing being pulled by a boat at the end of the longest rope ever.

Right after Hub gave Stella the wheel long enough to force down a few saltines and some ginger ale, she noticed that the sky had more of the tall white clouds in it than it had any of the first three days. Some had dark gray at their bases and were moving faster than she'd seen them on the other days. And just after that, Hub asked her if she felt that coolness in the breeze.

By the time they made their third turn of the day, the water wasn't so calm any more, and the breeze seemed stronger by the minute. Sievers had told them that there was nothing as sure at the beach as afternoon showers, and that if they brought the boat in every time they got fifteen minutes or a half hour of rain, they wouldn't last with him no matter how desperate he was. They'd had one shower so far—on the second day—and Stella liked it because you could sort of see it coming toward you over the water, and you could look in the other direction and see big chunks of blue waiting to fill the sky back up with better weather and people coming back onto the beach.

This one had lots more wind in it. In fact, it seemed to take only fifteen minutes from still fairly calm and a little breezy to sheets of rain and big whitecaps all over the place. They had just made the turn back to the south and had nearly an hour to get back to the inlet. Sievers had said that a few whitecaps were part of a pretty day at the beach, but if that if they saw as much white as blue for more than a half hour, then to think about heading in.

Worse than the sheets of rain, and even worse than the boat leaning way over to one side and then back to the other side, was Hub. Medicine or no, he was sick within ten minutes after the waves came up.

"I think we're headed out of it," Stella told him. "The ones we've seen so far have sort of come up from the south and then moved on, so I think we'll be okay soon."

Hub didn't seem to have the energy or feeling to make fun of her. The second time she told him that, he told her he hoped to hell she was right. He kneeled at the edge again to shoot some just-eaten saltines into the ocean, and just as he did, the boat lurched hard in that direction. Stella saw his knees come up off the floor almost to the level of the top of the side of the boat. Her stomach rose with him, and then he came back onto the floor with a loud thumping noise. He rolled back away from the side of the boat and then, when the boat lurched the other way, rolled over into one of the base poles that held the message board up. His hair was soaked to his head, and she could see white flecks around his mouth. He lay still on his back for a moment and then seemed to sense that he wasn't totally cleaned up, and pulled his sleeve across his mouth.

Stella held the wheel tightly and looked back and forth from Hub to the beach. She was sure the waves were washing her toward shore, and so she reminded herself to turn the wheel slightly away from the beach, to keep them on a straight track. Hub got back up on his knees and looked around, holding onto the pole he'd rolled into. "God," he said, "this is horrible. Do we just head in toward the beach, or stay out here and get turned over and drown?"

"Sievers told us no matter what happens, don't head in," she said. "We could chew up people with the propellers and wreck the boat in shallow water." Most of the time she could see the beach through the rain, except when a huge heavy sheet came along. She was holding the wheel as tight as she'd ever held anything as the boat rocked all over the place and pieces of wave splashed up onto Hub and onto her legs.

"I know what he said," Hub said from the boat floor, "but nobody's in the water and he never told us anything about a damn hurricane."

Stella felt the smallest smile at one side of her mouth, in spite of herself. All around her was nothing but pouring rain and wind and lightning, but she knew they were not in a hurricane, and that the storm would pass, and that if her arms didn't completely give out, they'd ride their way out of it. She was glad that Hub suddenly seemed to feel well enough to yell at her.

"The Titanic wasn't even in a storm and it was six billion times bigger than this crate and it went down," Hub said.

"It hit an iceberg, Hub," she said.

"So? Who knows what the hell we could hit out here rolling around like a toy." Hub sat next to the pole, with both arms wrapped around it to keep him from sliding around. "Or sharks." He looked up at her from the pole with an expression she wasn't sure was real or from the rain beating all the hair down into his face. He seemed to Stella to be acting in a way she had never seen before. The only time she'd ever seen him really frightened was the time his brother was driving in the snow on I-80 toward North Platte and the car had suddenly started spinning around right in the middle of the interstate, with other cars all over the place. Stella was in the back and she could see his face, completely opened up with just plain terror. And she had seen times when they were in real danger of some kind and he fought it off completely. She'd cried and wet her pants the time—back in the '70s—when they'd broken down out along the Platte River in the middle of noplace on the hottest day ever and been surrounded by a pack of wild dogs that slobbered all over the windows of the van and moved it around. Hub stayed right in the driver's seat with his hands on the wheel and rocked back and forth and just kept saying that everything would be okay.

Now he was somewhere in the middle. He seemed to realize that Stella was going to have to get them in and so there was no way he could bloat up and pretend nothing was wrong. And at the same time, he was not all the way panicked. She wondered if he was just so sick he couldn't quite care all the way, if there was some part of him that felt like if they sank he'd at least be out of his misery. She watched the beach for signs they were getting closer to the inlet. But all of the coastline, and all of the glimpses she got of houses looked the same. Ahead it was so white with rain and wind that she couldn't see whether the inlet was getting closer or not. At one point she wondered—for just a second—if she had somehow turned around and was heading away from the inlet.

"If we get back alive," Hub shouted into her thoughts, "then I'm quitting the second we get in. He can have this can."

Stella squinted into the rain, checked their distance from the shore and rolled with the waves. She felt like she was getting used to the way the boat moved, and the feeling that hit her stomach when it rolled was less severe. She thought about not being seasick, about moving the boat through the storm and getting the two of them back to the dock.

"I said I'm quitting," Hub said.

She had her mouth open to tell him—just to see what he'd say—that she'd run it by herself for awhile till he could see if he could get some sea legs—when she saw the line of rocks that marked where you turned into the inlet. "We're back, Hub," she called out. "There's the jetty." She was too far in toward shore and turned the wheel away to get them out far enough that they would make it around the end of the jetty. The whitecaps looked even stronger just out from the where the inlet met the ocean. She held the wheel hard and aimed the boat toward that water. Hub was back up on his knees—holding the pole and looking ahead into the rain. Then, the next time the waves rolled him over to the side, he stayed again, leaning over the edge with what she knew had to be dry heaves.

"Just around the rocks, Hub, and then I bet it calms down and we'll be in," she said. He continued to lean over the edge.

She left plenty of room between the end of the jetty and the boat as she moved them toward the inlet. And when she got to the water that seemed to be half inlet and half ocean, the boat began to move in different ways than it had as she was coming along the shore. First it seemed to want to pull her out into the middle of the channel, but sort of sideways, as if the side of the boat were the front. She turned the wheel back toward the jetty and suddenly she was pointed right at the rocks. She turned back the other way and felt the strange pull again, and so she pulled the boat back the other way again. The water was moving so differently that she felt she was losing control. She was still away from the rocks, but she wondered if there were some she couldn't see, just under the surface. She called out to Hub just as there was a noise that drowned out her call. The boat stopped moving for just a second as it slammed into a rock and Hub lurched all the way to the front pole. She called out to him again, and he turned and looked at her, still holding onto the pole.

"You're free," he said. "Just take it slowly on back away from the rocks." He was up on his knees. "Ease away from the jetty like you're doing. We bounced right the hell off, I think."

She could feel the deep ache in her fingers and arms and shoulders as she worked to do what he said. She looked down every few seconds—away from the rocks and at her feet—to see if water was coming into the boat and they really were going to drown. She couldn't see any, but there was another layer of floor under what she could see.

"You're good now," Hub said. "You're pulled away."

She looked ahead, squinting hard to see if she could see the dock yet. Then she realized there was no rain in her face for her to squint against. She turned to look at the rocks and saw rain hitting them. She looked ahead again and then to the other side of the inlet. No rain was hitting her and she couldn't see drops hitting the waves near her. "It stopped," she called out to Hub.

"Just stay straight ahead." He was moving away from the far pole back toward her, walking on his knees. "We're in now."

"Are we going to sink?" she said.

"It wasn't that hard a hit," he said. "If it can't take that, it doesn't deserve to float and we can probably swim to that close side from here." He sounded calm, not sick.

The wind was gone almost as suddenly as the rain, and before them the inlet looked much more the way it usually did—with current moving around but not much in the way of waves. They were maybe half a mile from the dock, and the weather had at last lifted away from them. But Stella was afraid to trust it all the way yet. She asked Hub to open the hatch and look down to see if they were taking on water. He slid over, pulled the hatch open and told her there was some water down there, but who knew if it came in from the waves or from hitting the rock.

"Come here, Hub," she told him. "You need to take over the wheel now and take it in, in case Sievers is there. He hired you to run it."

Hub opened the hatch and looked down again.

"Hell no, Stel," he said, talking into the hold. "You're the one that wrecked it—you take it in."

They had that slow half mile to go yet. Soon Hub stood up and walked around a little, getting almost his usual expression back on his face. Stella relaxed her arms. She knew it was just a matter of what he decided—whether he'd look more like a wimp if he hadn't had the wheel in the storm, or if he had to tell Sievers he'd put a gash in the side of his boat in some dinky little thunderstorm. She guessed it was fifty-fifty which way he'd go with it.